A PLUME

THE STORM

JENNA BLUM is the author of the *New York Times* bestselling novel *Those Who Save Us*. She lives in Boston, Massachusetts, and teaches creative writing at Grub Street Writers.

Praise for *The Stormchasers*

"The outer landscape of Tornado Alley and the inner terrain of sibling devotion are brought vividly to life in Jenna Blum's new novel, a powerful story that reminds us that love is always a pursuit—one that demands, over and over again, that we put ourselves in harm's way."
—Stephanie Kallos, author of *Broken for You* and *Sing Them Home*

"I could not put down Jenna Blum's tornado of a novel about the secrets we keep from even those we love the most. Her heroine, Karena, is a fearless and fascinating companion on one hell of a ride."
—Amanda Eyre Ward, author of
How to Be Lost and *Love Stories in This Town*

"[A] vivid novel about a set of twins with a dark history . . . Blum renders the stormy backdrop as richly as she does her nuanced characters."
—*Publishers Weekly*

"*The Stormchasers* is an emotional roller coaster of a story. . . . The parallels Jenna draws between tornadoes and the human condition is genius and makes for a must-read novel."
—Reed Timmer, star of the Discovery Channel's *Storm Chasers*

"An honest depiction of mental illness told with all the pain, humor, hubris, and guilt that the 'healthy' sibling bears." —*Library Journal*

"Moving."

"An emotional roller coaster ride of a story."
—*Fort Worth Star-Telegram*

"Fascinating." —*Philadelphia Examiner*

"Blum draws characters with a finely chiseled brush. . . . With an eye for detail and dedication to extensive research, this author brings authenticity and gripping suspense to a genuinely surprising tale of searching, secrets, and siblings. . . . Hang on; you're in for a wild ride."
—*New York Journal of Books*

Praise for *Those Who Save Us*

"*Those Who Save Us* is both vast and intimate in its reach . . . An absorbing tale." —*The Boston Globe*

"The book's power . . . lies . . . in examining the emotional and moral gray area between heroism and collaboration. . . . *Those Who Save Us* bursts with provocative questions about the ambiguous possibilities of culpability." —*San Francisco Chronicle*

"Blum's research illuminates this textured tale." —*Newsweek*

"A poised, hair-raising debut." —*Publishers Weekly*

"Impossible to put down . . . well-researched . . . compelling."
—*Milwaukee Journal Sentinel*

"The themes of love, sacrifice, and family secrets are at the core of Blum's powerful first novel . . . [a] fast-paced page-turner."
—*Jewish Book World*

ALSO BY JENNA BLUM

Those Who Save Us

THE
STORMCHASERS

a novel

JENNA BLUM

A PLUME BOOK

PLUME
Published by the Penguin Group
Penguin Group (USA) Inc., 375 Hudson Street, New York, New York 10014, U.S.A. •
Penguin Group (Canada), 90 Eglinton Avenue East, Suite 700, Toronto, Ontario,
Canada M4P 2Y3 (a division of Pearson Penguin Canada Inc.) • Penguin Books Ltd., 80 Strand,
London WC2R 0RL, England • Penguin Ireland, 25 St. Stephen's Green, Dublin 2, Ireland
(a division of Penguin Books Ltd.) • Penguin Group (Australia), 250 Camberwell Road,
Camberwell, Victoria 3124, Australia (a division of Pearson Australia Group Pty. Ltd.) •
Penguin Books India Pvt. Ltd., 11 Community Centre, Panchsheel Park, New Delhi – 110 017, India •
Penguin Group (NZ), 67 Apollo Drive, Rosedale, North Shore 0632, New Zealand
(a division of Pearson New Zealand Ltd.) • Penguin Books (South Africa) (Pty.) Ltd.,
24 Sturdee Avenue, Rosebank, Johannesburg 2196, South Africa

Penguin Books Ltd., Registered Offices: 80 Strand, London WC2R 0RL, England

Published by Plume, a member of Penguin Group (USA) Inc. Previously published in a Dutton edition.

First Plume Printing, May 2011
10   9   8   7   6   5   4   3

Ⓟ REGISTERED TRADEMARK—MARCA REGISTRADA

The Library of Congress has catalogued the Dutton edition as follows:

Blum, Jenna.
The stormchasers : a novel / by Jenna Blum.
    p.   cm.
ISBN 978-0-525-95155-1 (hc.)
ISBN 978-0-452-29713-5 (pbk.)
1. Twins—Fiction.   2. Brothers and sisters—Fiction.   3. Manic-depressive illness—Fiction.
4. Storm chasers—Fiction.   I. Title.
PS3602.L863S76   2010
813'.6—dc22   2010012471

Printed in the United States of America

PUBLISHER'S NOTE

This is a work of fiction. Names, characters, places, and incidents are either the product of the author's imagination or are used fictitiously, and any resemblance to actual persons, living or dead, business establishments, events, or locales is entirely coincidental.

For JRB

Wondrous and beloved always.

Human madness is oftentimes a cunning and most feline thing.

—Herman Melville, *Moby-Dick*

PART I

KARENA, JULY 2008

Karena Jorge's birthday starts as a quiet affair, but she doesn't mind. That's the way she likes it. She does have a couple of treats planned for later, an onscreen revival of *Gone with the Wind* tonight, dinner tomorrow with her best friend, Tiff. But generally Karena tries to keep this day under the radar, and it has gone mostly undetected for years, which is why on the afternoon of July fourteenth she is truly surprised to be called into her editor William's office on the pretext of discussing a story and finding most of the Minneapolis *Ledger* staff assembled there, along with a cake on William's desk so laden with flaming candles that Karena is fairly sure it's against fire code.

She laughs and sketches a little curtsy as they clap. "Thanks, everybody," she says. "Though I'm sorry to say someone made a mistake. There are way too many candles on that cake—I'm only twenty-nine."

"Again?" somebody calls.

"Really?" says Annaliese, the intern, looking anxious.

Karena's editor, William, a beautiful, haggard lion of a man, wiggles his eyebrows at her over his glasses. He knows very well Karena is thirty-eight.

"The question is, young lady," he says, "are you going to make a wish so we can eat the damned thing?"

"Most definitely," says Karena, and gathers her long hair back behind her ears with both hands. Then she pauses. She takes wishes

seriously and believes they are not to be made on the fly. Happy birthday, Charles, she thinks. I sure as hell wish I knew where you were.
Then she fills her lungs and blows.

All the candles go out except one, which threatens to remain stub-
bornly alight and then extinguishes itself at the last second—*poof!*
Everybody applauds.

"Whew," says Karena. "Thank goodness I gave up smoking."

Annaliese starts cutting slices, which the reporters fall on and bear
away to their desks, pausing, if they're not on a tight deadline, to give
Karena their good wishes. She chats with them all, smiling, meanwhile mounding her cake—yellow, vanilla frosting—to one side of her
plate with her fork.

"Sorry," says her friend Lisa when the room has mostly cleared.
She leans in as much as she is able—Lisa is a week from maternity
leave.

"I'll have you know none of this was my idea," she murmurs. "It
was that intern. You know how overzealous they get."

Karena smiles. "That's okay," she says. "This was really sweet, actually. Plus I've been working on that *Hot Dish!* piece all day and could
use the break."

Lisa gets what Karena thinks of as her reluctant-source look, head
tipped back, eyes half closed as if to say, Go on, tell me another.

"You miss your brother, don't you," she says.

Karena is startled by the prick of tears, though she's not sure
whether it's the reference itself or the fact that it's unexpected.

"I do," she admits. "Always, but today more than most days."

"Then it's time for your real present," Lisa says. "I think the coast
is clear."

They canvass the room. Everyone has filtered out except the intern,
who is stuffing paper plates into a garbage bag, and William, who is
hunched over his desk devouring an enormous slice of cake seemingly
without chewing it, like a dog.

Lisa leads Karena downstairs into the little-used ladies' bathroom
in the *Ledger* basement, where she presents her husband's plaid fishing

thermos. In it Karena finds a very dirty vodka martini, complete with three bobbing olives. She laughs.

"Thank you," she says. "You always know just what to get me."

"Cheers, birthday girl," Lisa says. She rubs her belly, which is at the stage of pregnancy that fascinates Karena, so enormous it seems like an optical illusion. "And don't forget you're drinking for me too."

She watches jealously as Karena takes a swallow. "What's your brother's name again?" she asks.

"Charles," says Karena.

"It must be so weird, being a twin."

"I don't know," says Karena. "I've never not been one, so I can't tell. It is strange not knowing where he is, though."

Lisa wrinkles her nose sympathetically. "What *is* that like? I've always meant to ask. If you don't mind talking about it, I mean."

"No, that's fine," says Karena. "It's kind of like . . . tinnitus. You're always off balance, but you learn to live with it."

She smiles down at her friend's stomach. "Can I say hi?" she asks.

"Go ahead," says Lisa, and Karena bends over Lisa's belly button.

"Greetings," she says. "This is your aunt Karena speaking."

A knob pokes at Lisa's stretched wine-red shirt, then streaks across it.

"Whoa," says Karena. She laughs. "I love that. It's so amazing. Elbow or knee?"

"Heel, I think," says Lisa. "He loves you. He's always super-active when you're around. You're going to be such a good mom."

Karena rolls her eyes. "I don't know about that."

"Well, I do," says Lisa. She winks and tips a finger at Karena like a politician. "All you need is a good baby daddy. Now drink up."

Back in the newsroom Karena swims pleasantly through the afternoon's primary task, which is interviewing a source for her *Hot Dish!* feature on Minnesota's regional foods. The source is sharing her recipe for lutefisk casserole, which combined with the vodka makes Karena's stomach churn. She is Norwegian through and through; she and Charles were fed floury rommegrod pudding and lefse bread in their high chairs, but this has only enhanced Karena's fear of the traditional rubbery cod boiled in lye. She smothers a martini belch with a hand and says, "Hey, here's something I've always wondered. What's the difference between a hot dish and a casserole?"

The source tells Karena that a casserole is covered and a hot dish is not. Karena thanks her and goes on to the next question on her list, commenting at appropriate times, writing the answers by rote. Meanwhile she keeps checking the Storm Prediction Center website, always open on her laptop, peering at the green computer-generated clouds as if she could see beneath them to where Charles is. And she finds herself thinking of a birthday back when she did eat cake, when she and Charles were—what, three, four? Young enough to still be in booster seats, anyway, bumped up to the table on their red plastic thrones side by side, in the dining area of their New Heidelburg house. Karena very clearly remembers seizing a fistful of cake, examining it, then reaching over to stuff it in her brother's ear, and Charles turning to boggle at her with comical surprise, then bursting into his deep baby chuckle and doing the same to her. Back and forth they went, mashing cake into each other's hair and eyes and mouths, laughing and laughing, until the adults quit snapping pictures and their mom, Siri, had to drag them apart, scolding, *You two never know when to stop.* The memory makes Karena smile, but as the afternoon wears on she feels herself descending into melancholy, a sadness at play in her like a wind. It is not like her. She is normally a very cheerful person. She blames it on the date and the alcohol.

2

After work, Karena decides to skip the movie and go for a drive. Being in the car has always soothed her—when she and Charles were fretful as infants, the only way they would sleep was loaded into their bassinet in the back of their parents' Dodge Dart, and as a teenager Karena liked to sing as she drove, harmonizing with her best friend Tiff, cruising up and down the empty farm roads. Now Karena listens to NPR as she navigates her Volvo out of the city, taking 494 toward the airport and cutting south over the Mendota Bridge. She doesn't have a plan, and it's not until she passes the single spire of the Lone Oak Church that she realizes she's leaving the exurbs behind: the new housing developments; the upscale strip malls with their shops for lattes and sushi and artisan bread.

Karena merges onto Highway 52 South, which would take her first to Tiff's in Rochester, then home to New Heidelburg if she'd let it. She passes the natural gas refinery with its thousands of twinkling lights—Nintendo City, she and Charles used to call it—and the truck stop whose sign just says FOOD. Finally, across from the House of Coates bar, Karena sees what she has been looking for all along without knowing it. She pulls over, parks with her hazards on, and gets out on the shoulder.

Standing by itself in the middle of a field is a limestone arch. It was the first sign Karena and Charles had as children that they were really nearing the Twin Cities, which they did four or five times a year to visit their Uncle Carroll. *There's the Arch to Nowhere!* whichever twin spotted it first would sing out, and in the front seat Frank, their dad, would clear his throat in a way that meant he might be laughing, and their mom, Siri, would turn to face them, her long nutmeg-colored hair swinging over the seat like a scarf. *Who can tell me what that arch used to be?* she'd ask, and Charles and Karena would say in unison, *A church!*

> *That's right, and who built that church?*
> *The pioneers!*
> *And who is related to the pioneers?*
> *We are!*

You bet, said Siri, *and don't you ever forget it. They were brave, strong, uncomplaining people, and we need to be just like them,* and then she'd face front again.

Karena tries to summon the awe she used to feel looking at the Arch to Nowhere, the sense of it being one of the few remaining signs of the past, a tangible relic of her family's history. She and Charles had long, whispered conversations about what might have happened to the church the arch was once attached to. Charles, of course, thought a tornado had taken it, and Karena still thinks this might have been true. Like most souvenirs of childhood, though, the arch no longer holds the magic it once did, and Karena now wonders how long it will be before it is knocked down for a subdivision or new mall. She thinks of the people who constructed it, carrying stones in their wagons and setting one atop the other, and of the disasters that likely befell them: illness, rattlesnake bite, the loss of children.

She sighs and puts her hands up to shield her face from her hair, which the wind from the west is whipping into tassels. The land is open here, and as flat as a game board, and the sunset over it is spectacular, a blaze of fluorescent orange and yellow. Popsicle colors streaked with purple clouds. Her brother is out there in the direction Karena is look-ing, somewhere in Tornado Alley. That's all Karena knows for sure. She doesn't know what Charles is doing for work—probably he's a prep cook or janitor, a transient job that pays him under the table, money for his expensive summer stormchasing habit. He isn't married, at least not legally, or Karena would have found those records. But is he alone? Is he lonely? Most importantly, is he hurt, is he curled in a ball in a motel room somewhere, is he all right? "Where are you, Charles?" Karena says. "I hope you're okay."

There is the hiss of truck brakes behind her, and when Karena turns she sees a man leaning across the cab of his eighteen-wheeler. "You all right, miss?" he asks.

Karena smiles and waves. "I am, thank you," she calls.

"Just admiring the sunset?"

"Yup, that's about the size of it."

"Well, it is a beauty," says the trucker. "You want some company to share it with maybe?"

Karena laughs. "No thanks. I was just about to head home, actually."

"All right," says the trucker. "Just checking. You have a good night now."

"You too," says Karena, and watches him pull off. He gives her a double blast on his air horn as he gets back on the road, and she walks back to her Volvo, feeling a little foolish. Well, what else did she expect to happen, standing on the side of the highway talking to herself. Of course somebody would think she needed help.

Still, it's nice to know she can stop trucks at thirty-eight. Karena twists the rearview to look at her reflection. Her long pale hair is wind-blown, her cheeks reddened. From the truck cab the guy wouldn't have seen the lines on her forehead, the circles under her slate-colored eyes. He would have just noticed a blonde—the Hallingdahl women don't go gray. "Not bad," says Karena, then crosses her eyes at herself and takes out her cell to call Tiff.

"I have officially become pathetic," she says when Tiff picks up. "I'm sitting on the shoulder of Highway 52 congratulating myself for being trucker bait."

"What?" Tiff says. There is a shriek behind her and she says,

"Mommy is on the PHONE." Tiff has five sons, ranging in age from fourteen to seven months.

"What'd you say?" she says. "Why are you on Highway 52? I thought we were going out tomorrow night, in your 'hood."

"We are," says Karena. One of Tiff's boys emits a vibrating scream and Karena holds the phone away from her ear, wincing. "Sorry," she says. "Bad time?"

"It's always a bad time at Testosterone House," says Tiff. "I cannot wait to come see you and drink about a hundred—do not hit him," she says. "Do NOT. Put your hand down, NOW."

"Okay," says Karena, "I'll let you go. Just checking in."

"Wait," says Tiff. "Hold on." There is a swishing sound as though she's in a washing machine, which probably means she's walking, and then she says, "Okay, I'm hiding in the pantry. How are you? Happy birthday, by the way."

"Thank you," says Karena. "I'm fine. Missing Charles a little, but—"

"Well, it's time you got over that bullshit," Tiff says pertly. There has never been any love lost between Tiff and Charles. Then she says, "No. NO. How many times do I have to tell you? That's it. Stand in the corner. GET IN THE CORNER—I've gotta go," she says to Karena.

"Good luck," Karena says and hangs up.

She is in a much better mood driving back to the Cities, and by the time she reaches her little house in Edina, she is humming. She enters through the back door and kicks her work heels into the corner of the kitchen with a flourish. The day has gone as well as can be expected, and now it is almost over. Karena has time for a short run before dinner, which she has decided will be wine and a take-out croque monsieur from Le P'tit Lapin. She changes into her jogging shorts and U of MN T-shirt, then scrubs up in the bathroom off the kitchen. Washing one's face, Karena believes, is one of the great joys of life, especially after a long day's work or being in the car. She plunges her face into water as cold as it will go and emerges sputtering like a horse, and it's then that her phone rings, her landline in the den.

"Crap," Karena says, dripping. She keeps forgetting to cancel that service. She likes the concept of retaining the landline for emergencies, but in reality it's a nuisance, since the only people who ever call on it are telemarketers and her dad's new wife, the Widow. It's probably the Widow now, in fact, since as soon as the phone stops ringing, it starts up again. Like many of her generation in New Heidelburg, the Widow hasn't quite caught on to the concept of voice mail, and she'll be wanting to fulfill her obligation of wishing Karena a happy birthday from her dad Frank, since Frank can no longer speak for himself.

Karena would dearly love to ignore the phone. But when it continues to ring, Karena says, "Oh, *fine*," and runs into her den to pick it up, whacking her shoulder on the door frame in her hurry.

"Ow," she mutters, rubbing it. "Hello?"

"Is this Miss Karena Jorge?"

It is a telemarketer. Karena narrows her eyes.

"Yes, this is she," she says, "but I'm just on my way out, so can you please call back another time?"

"Miss Jorge, my name is Gail Nelson, and I'm calling from the Wichita Medical Center Mental Health Clinic in Wichita, Kansas. Miss Jorge, do you have a brother Charles Hallingdahl?"

Karena's whole body flushes hot, then cold. She sits on the edge of her desk and looks around the little white room, as if somebody else is there to confirm that yes, this is it. The call. The call she's been expecting, rehearsing for, dreading for twenty years.

"Yes, I have a brother Charles," she says. "He's my twin. Is everything all right?"

Then she curses, because of course everything is not all right. If it were, this woman would not be calling her.

"I mean, what's wrong with him?" she asks. Suicide attempt, she is thinking. Or psychotic episode? Maybe both, but at least suicide attempt.

"I'm not really qualified to answer that, Miss Jorge," says the nurse. "I'm really only a patient liaison. It's best if you speak directly to the doctor about Charles's condition. I can tell you that he's here with us and he gave your name as his closest relative."

"That's right," says Karena, "I am." There's also their dad, Frank, but he doesn't count anymore, poor guy. Karena scrabbles on her desk for a steno pad and Sharpie. Her hands are shaking badly and she knocks a stapler to the carpet, but the familiar actions soothe her somewhat.

"Miss—Nelson, is it?" she says, writing. "Can you at least tell me if Charles is physically harmed in any way? And what his condition was when he came in? Was he agitated, manic? Was he hallucinating?"

"Again, I'm just a liaison, ma'am," says the nurse. "You'd have to talk to Dr. Brewster about specifics. I can page her and have her call you back."

"Yes, please do," says Karena, "and I appreciate your position, but please. Please. Any information you can give me would be helpful. Just so I know what I'm dealing with."

When the nurse speaks again, her voice is less formal. "I really shouldn't be saying this," she says, "and it's just a guess, mind you. But if Charles were physically injured, he'd be in a different part of our hospital. This is the psychiatric ward."

"All right," says Karena, "thank you so much. Now, can you please remind me, what's the doctor's name?"

She takes down this information, as well as the location of the hospital and the clinic's direct number, then repeats it back to the nurse along with her own cell number. Karena knows better than to trust herself at this point. Her thoughts have become very clear and cold and slow, as if she has gone into deep freeze, but she knows in this state she is perfectly capable of thinking herself just fine and then running out to the car without packing, finding her keys in the refrigerator. It's shock. Karena recognizes shock. She has been here before.

"Thank you," she says to the nurse when they are done. "Please have Dr. Brewster call me as soon as possible, okay? Anytime, day or night. I'll be waiting to hear from her."

When she hangs up Karena turns on her computer, then looks wonderingly around her den. She is surprised to find the little white room, which she sometimes likes to imagine as being the inside of a marshmallow, looking as serene as it did when she entered it. It occurs to Karena that she got what she wished for earlier: For the first time in twenty years, she knows where her twin is spending their birthday.

"Jesus, Charles," Karena says under her breath, in the way she has become accustomed to talking to Charles when she is alone. She opens a travel website. "Just hold on, brothah, I'll be there as soon as I can," and she starts scrolling through flights.

3

By eleven the following morning Karena is sitting in the reception area of the Wichita Medical Center Mental Health Clinic, awaiting Charles's doctor. Much has changed since the last time Karena visited her brother in a psychiatric ward. This one is sleek and beige, with comfortable couches and a pop machine, a far cry from the Black Wing Asylum's cracked green walls and barred windows. Here there is even a flat-screen TV. What hasn't changed, at least for Karena, is her feeling of almost painful alertness, as though she is trying to take in everything about this environment, a place about which she knows nothing but that contains all the secrets to helping her brother. She sits up very straight, her nostrils flaring at the scent of rubbing alcohol. Memory is a trapdoor.

Karena is trying to check her e-mail while she waits, but she can't stop glancing at the door to the ward. Any second now the doctor will come through it and take Karena to Charles, and then—what? What do you say to somebody after twenty years? Karena has tried and tried to envision it, but all she gets is a dark blank spot like the center of an eclipse. What does Charles even look like now? In their adolescence he was gorgeous, golden-haired, with big brown eyes and honey-colored skin—Rum Raisin and Vanilla, their uncle Carroll nicknamed them. *Some Sioux in that one,* Grandmother Hallingdahl always said darkly about Charles.

But twenty years is a long time. Charles's movie-star waves may have thinned, his waistline thickened. He may no longer have hair at all. He may have a handlebar mustache, tattoos, scars, a limp for all Karena knows. He could weigh three hundred pounds. Every few minutes Karena slides her one photo of Charles out of its plastic wallet sleeve. It is a snapshot taken on their front lawn in New Heidelburg the night of their senior prom, to which Charles brought Marie Hauser, the slowest girl in their class, because he knew nobody else would. The only dance Marie knew was the polka, and Karena retains a clear memory of her brother hopping solemnly around the gym floor with his date to that year's theme, Peter Cetera's "Glory of Love." In the photo Charles is standing next to their dad's Austin Healey, which he will wreck the following month. He is grinning sideways down at the grass—that big white smile one characteristic the twins do share—and wearing a baby blue tuxedo with ruffled shirtfront. His hair is short on the sides, long in back, teased so high in front that the sun shines through it in rays. At least he won't still have that mullet—Karena hopes.

She is smiling over this when the ward door opens and a small woman emerges—the doctor, Karena presumes, for she wears a white lab coat and carries a clipboard. She hurries across the waiting area with her hand out, sneakers squeaking.

"I'm Dr. Brewster," she says, "sorry to keep you waiting. You must be Charles Hallingdahl's sister. I can see the resemblance."

Karena hastily puts the photo away, claps her laptop shut, and stands up. "Karena Jorge," she says, shaking the doctor's hand. "I'm Charles's twin. You're good. Most people don't see it right away."

"The smile," says the doctor, "and something about the eyes." She is striking, with an auburn bob and a bright blue gaze, a pleasantly husky voice. Yet there is about her an air of professional watchfulness, a menthol-cool calm like a force field. Karena smiles at Dr. Brewster with the automatic respect she holds for any member of the medical profession, along with a more personal interest. The doctor is about Karena's age, and once upon a time, before Charles's illness and other factors dissuaded her, Karena considered becoming a doctor herself.

"Should we talk out here?" the doctor asks. "Or would you be more comfortable in my office?"

Karena looks again toward the ward door.

"I'm sorry," she says, "I'm confused. Aren't we going to see Charles first?"

"Didn't they tell you?" Dr. Brewster asks. She glances behind her at the RN on desk, then says, "Your brother was released earlier this morning."

"What?" Karena exclaims.

"Yes, at—" Dr. Brewster consults her clipboard. "Eight thirty A.M. I discharged him myself."

"Oh no," Karena says, "I can't believe it," and much to her embarrassment, she starts to cry.

Dr. Brewster hands her a squishy pack of tissues from the pocket of her lab coat and guides Karena to one of the couches. "I guess we'd better sit," she says.

She waits until Karena finishes daubing her eyes, blowing her nose as quietly as she can.

"I'm sorry," Karena says. "I didn't mean to make a scene."

Dr. Brewster raises her eyebrows, as if to say, We're in a psychiatric ward. "I've seen worse," she says, a little wryly.

"I'm just so disappointed," Karena says. "I've been looking for Charles for twenty years, and now this— So close and yet so far."

She checks her watch. How far can Charles have gotten in about three hours? Pretty far. Karena deflates with a sigh, then looks up.

"Please, can you tell me why he was released?" she asks. "I thought he was suicidal, or had at least had a psychotic break . . ."

Dr. Brewster doesn't move, but her gaze sharpens further.

"We don't usually hold people for panic attacks," she says. "What makes you say suicidal?"

"Panic attack?" says Karena.

"That's what we treated Charles for," says Dr. Brewster. "But it seems I'm missing something."

Karena shakes her head. "He didn't tell you," she says.

"Tell me what," the doctor says.

"My brother is bipolar," says Karena. She sighs and recites: "Bipolar One, but rapid cycling and with the occasional psychotic episode. A real mixed bag. He was diagnosed in 1984, by Dr. Amit Hazan at the Mayo Clinic. Later he was an inpatient at a longer-term facility called Black Wing Asylum, from 1988 until . . . sorry, I don't know exactly. There was a fire at Black Wing in the late nineties and they lost all their records. But the Mayo would still have them, I'm pretty sure."

Dr. Brewster is making rapid notations on her clipboard. Karena can hear the *pock* of her ballpoint pen.

"Why was Charles institutionalized?" she asks.

"That was the suicide attempt," says Karena.

"Any attempts after that?"

"Not that I'm aware of," says Karena. She shivers and rubs her goose-bumped arms. The air-conditioning is high in here. "I'd like to think I'd feel it if he were in that much distress, since we're twins, but . . . I just don't know."

The doctor looks up briefly. "You mentioned psychosis," she says. "Charles sees and hears things that aren't there?"

"Yes," says Karena. "Sometimes. He didn't mention anything like that when he came in, did he? A particular hallucination? Anything about stormchasing?"

The doctor peruses her notes, flipping back a page, and shakes her head. Karena sags against the couch, then makes herself sit up straight.

"What's the stormchasing connection?" the doctor asks.

"That's what Charles does," says Karena. "And he likes to chase when he's manic. At least, he did. As you can imagine, it's kind of an unholy combination."

"Interesting," the doctor says, almost under her breath. "Okay, one last question: Any reason you can think of that Charles didn't tell me any of this?"

"I'm fairly sure Charles doesn't think he is bipolar," says Karena. "He never accepted the diagnosis. He used to say he was just smarter than everyone else."

"Sure," Dr. Brewster says, "sounds like mania." She sets the clipboard on her lap.

"Well, Miss Jorge, here's where we are," she says. "Charles didn't disclose any of this to us. When he came to the ER, he thought he was having a stroke."

"Oh jeez," Karena murmurs. "Wait, can you hold on, please?"

She takes out her steno pad and Sharpie and smiles at the doctor. "Do you mind if I take notes?" she asks. "I can't remember a thing unless I write it down. Professional hazard."

"No, that's fine," says Dr. Brewster, though her glance at the notebook is a little wary. "They checked him out, ran the standard tests—blood work, tox screen, head CT, and when everything came back clean, they turned him over to us, figuring it was a panic attack. And Charles was presenting with shortness of breath, heart palpitations, dizziness, et cetera. Your brother's in fine physical shape, Miss Jorge," she adds, "but it took us a while to convince him a healthy young man wouldn't suffer a sudden cerebral accident. Charles was certain he was going to die—he was quite dramatic about it, actually."

"I'm sure he was," Karena says, thinking, Oh, Charles. "So what'd you do?"

"We had him breathe into a paper bag," the doctor says with a little smile. "And suggested he stay overnight for observation. By this morning, when I met with him again, he'd done a total about-face and was demanding to be released. This is when I'd decide whether to impose a seventy-two-hour hold, which happens if I feel the patient is at high risk for endangering himself or others. But there was absolutely nothing to make me think Charles belonged in this category—in fact, that he was anything other than a young man with mild panic disorder. I talked to him for a while about possible causes and how to manage it, then wrote him a 'scrip and let him go."

Karena's pen stops. "What did he say about the causes?" she asks.

"That he had felt unusually stressed lately," the doctor says, "and that he often feels this way around his birthday. Maybe because the two of you are separated?" she adds, smiling kindly.

"Maybe," Karena says. There are other, excellent reasons why Charles would be feeling anxious on their birthday, but she can't disclose them. She tucks her hair behind her ears and scans her notes, exhaling.

"Okay," she says. "Goodness. I don't suppose there's any way of tracking him? He didn't have to be released into somebody's care?"

"Not for an overnight," says Dr. Brewster. "Not for anxiety."

Karena rubs the third-eye spot on her forehead. "How about when he came in?" she asks. "Did he have to give an address to admitting?"

"You'd have to check with administrative," the doctor says, and Karena nods. She will, but she also knows what Charles will have told them: the location of a motel, or a P.O. box, or an entirely fictional house. NFA, as Karena's ex-husband used to say. No Forwarding Address.

"Miss Jorge," the doctor says gently, and Karena looks up. "I hate to put more pressure on you, but if there's any way you can, it's important that you do bring Charles back in as soon as possible. Or if not here, to another medical facility. Given what you've told me, he needs an entirely different set of evaluations. And although I'm probably preaching to the choir here, Charles needs to be on medication and monitored."

"I know," says Karena. "I'll try."

"Also," says Dr. Brewster, "since I didn't know about Charles's disorder, the prescription I wrote him was for Paxil. It's mild as antidepressants go, but if Charles is pre-manic, it could push him over the edge."

Great, Karena thinks, but she says, "I understand. Thank you for telling me."

Dr. Brewster is standing now, so Karena puts her pad away, gathers her belongings, and rises too.

"Thank you, Doctor," she says. "I appreciate your taking the time."

The doctor walks Karena toward the exit, soles creaking. At the door they exchange business cards, Dr. Brewster scribbling on hers first.

"My home number's on the back," she says. "Please call if you find him, day or night."

Karena knows what a concession this is. "Thank you," she repeats and means it.

"Hey," says Dr. Brewster as she opens the door for Karena, "is your brother really a stormchaser? He chases tornadoes? Like the guys on the Discovery Channel?"

"Yes," says Karena, because this is one thing, the only thing, she does know for sure about Charles. "That's what he does."

Dr. Brewster smiles and shakes her head. "Man," she says. "I can't even imagine it. I'm from Florida, and I thought we had storms there, but they're nothing like they are here. I'm a real baby about it too, I'll admit. The second that tornado siren goes off, I'm under the table."

"Me too," says Karena, quite truthfully. She thanks the doctor again and steps into the hall off the ward.

4

When Karena leaves the hospital it is noon, the sun sizzling down on Wichita. Karena drives her rental car a block over to a sandwich shop on the first floor of a skyscraper. She gets a veggie sub to ward off a hunger headache and shows Charles's mullet photo to the counter staff. They exclaim over the hairstyle and tux, but they haven't seen him. While she eats her sandwich Karena searches the Internet for all convenience stores, gas stations, and fast-food joints within a ten-mile radius. These are the places a stormchaser on the move would visit before heading out, and Karena spends the rest of the afternoon connecting the dots from one to the next. If only she could get some idea of Charles's trajectory! Although maybe he lives here, Karena thinks in despair, driving from Conoco to Exxon, McDonald's to Arby's. She expands her search to sit-down restaurants where Charles might work, then to the motels. Everywhere the mullet photo elicits admiring comments made with varying degrees of irony, but no recognition.

By the time Karena pulls into the lot of her own motel, The Sunflower Inn & Suites, out by the Wichita airport, her hair smells deep-fried and she is exhausted. The sun is descending over the service road; it's six forty-five P.M., prime time for the Dreads. Karena's mood is probably worse today because of the past twenty-four hours, but still, this low, scared feeling falls on her every evening between four and seven, no matter where she is, no matter whom she's with. Her ex-husband used to make light of the Dreads, to say they were why cocktail hour was invented. Karena's former therapist, Dr. B, said they were a circadian response in some people, a natural reaction to the withdrawal of the light. All Karena knows is that this is when she feels most alone, most unconnected and sad. As she checks in to The Sunflower Inn & Suites, Karena reflects as she often does on how strange it is that her twin's disorder is one of just this: moods, the shifting emotional weather healthy people take for granted.

She shares the elevator to the third floor with a family fresh from the pool, the husband's face pink and impassive beneath his feed cap, the children whacking each other with foam noodles around Karena's legs. "Stop that," the mother hisses and pincers them in the tender spot between shoulder and neck. Karena smiles down at the children, who turn instantly silent and sullen. With their limber little bodies and chlorine-stiff white hair, they remind Karena of herself and Charles.

In her room Karena does a quick sweep perfected over years of traveling on assignment. She yanks the sunflowered nylon coverlet onto the floor, whisks the sunflowered drapes aside, and karate-chops the yellow shower curtain, jumping away each time in case something unpleasant pops out. Nothing does. Good. Karena is not fussy, but she draws the line at live insects, hair that isn't hers, and suspicious stains. She once stayed in a B&B that had toenail clippings in the bed. Luckily, The Sunflower Inn & Suites, though a little kitschy, is spotlessly clean. Karena scrubs her face, orders a chicken sandwich from room service, puts on the Weather Channel with the sound muted. These routine tasks having been attended to, she settles on the bed with her cell phone. It's times like this she misses being married, having somebody who among other things would be obligated to help her during crises. But Karena has been divorced long enough, eight years, to know this kind of thinking is a trap, that she misses the idea of Michael more than she misses Michael. And it is her fear of exactly this crisis that eroded their marriage, though Michael didn't know it. Karena still can't imagine Michael and Charles in the same room, especially if Charles is manic. No way. It is far too risky.

Karena calls Tiff for the third time that day, saying, "Where *are* you?" when Tiff's cell phone goes straight to voice mail. "It's eight o'clock, do you know where your best friend is? Still in Wichita. Did you get my earlier messages?" She drops her voice for dramatic emphasis. "Charles . . . has . . . resurfaced," she says, then sighs. "Except now he's gone again. Call me when you have time. Sorry about missing the martinis."

Then, having put it off to the point when she no longer can, Karena dials her dad's wife—Karena can never think of the Widow as a stepmother. This is a very long shot, since Karena isn't sure whether Charles knows their dad married again, or what Frank's condition is, or even that their mom, Siri, died in 2000. He certainly didn't show up for Siri's funeral. Or Frank's wedding to the Widow. Nor has Karena ever encountered Charles at the New Heidelburg Good Samaritan Center, the nursing home where Frank is spinning out the rest of his days. It therefore seems unlikely that Charles would have tried to contact Frank now and been redirected to the Widow—but Karena suspects maybe, if her brother's hurting enough, he would have tried to go home, not knowing that home isn't there anymore. Besides, she has exhausted all other options.

The phone rings and rings in the Widow's restored Victorian, which Karena entertains herself by mentally revisiting as she waits. The army of stone creatures, squirrels and chipmunks mostly, peeking from the front bushes. The cardboard lady bent over in the garden, presenting her polka-dotted underpants to visitors. The boy and girl trolls kissing over the plastic wishing well in the yard. The sign on the porch announcing THE HALLINGDAHLS, FRANK~N~LOIS. As much as Karena wants to find her brother, she almost hopes Charles hasn't learned of Frank's remarriage and stroke, hasn't been to the Widow's house. It might just push him over the edge.

Karena is just about to give up and try again later—maybe the Widow is at bridge night—when the Widow answers.

"Helloooooo," she says, putting an extra-cozy spin on the *-o*.

"Lois? It's Karena."

"Oh!" the Widow says, and there's a muffled clatter as if she has just dropped an armload of cutlery in the sink and is stirring it around. "Oh, for Pete's sake," Karena hears her muttering.

"I'm sorry, who'd you say this is?" the Widow says. "You've caught me doing supper dishes."

"It's Karena."

"Oh," the Widow says. "Karena."

The line ticks. Karena waits for the Widow to continue, to say *Hi, how are you*, and tries to remember the woman isn't all bad. The Widow has plenty of reasons to be angry, none having anything to do with Karena. But Karena can't help picturing the Widow in her kitchen, in which everything matches: yellow gingham border entwined with vines, yellow gingham dish towels, yellow gingham vinyl on the chair seats. The Widow will be standing by the sink, round and poised as a doll, her little mouth smiling sweetly and poisonously at nobody.

"Well!" the Widow says finally. "This is a surprise. What can I do for you? It's a little late for a social call, isn't it?"

Karena looks out the window at the sunset, atomic peach striping the sky. The bedside clock says eight fifteen.

"I guess," she says. "Sorry, Lois. I didn't mean to disturb your evening. But I'm looking for my brother. Charles. You haven't heard from him by any chance, have you?"

There is a frosty pause.

"No," the Widow says.

"He hasn't been looking for my dad? Nobody's seen him around town?"

"No," the Widow repeats. "Although, you know, I'm not sure I'd even recognize him. It's been so many years since anyone here has seen him."

Karena closes her eyes and massages them.

"I know what you mean," she says. "But if anyone you think might be Charles does show up, any strange guy on your doorstep, would you let me know right away, please? It's urgent."

"Okay," the Widow says.

"Let me give you my cell number."

"Oh, goodness no," the Widow says brightly. "I couldn't possibly remember. Even if I write it down, I've got so many numbers floating around already, what with my kids and grandkids and all, it's a wonder my head's still screwed on straight! Say," she adds, "did you get the birthday card I sent you?"

Oh, crap, Karena thinks. She did indeed receive a card from the Widow, a week ago. It featured a cartoon teddy bear in a striped hat dusted with sparkles and a banner reading *For You Hunny Bear on Your Special Day!* The Widow had also enclosed a check made out for thirty-nine dollars, Karena's age plus a year to grow on. On the memo line in her former schoolteacher's round cursive she had written *Frank's daughter's birthday.* The card itself was unsigned.

"I did get it, Lois," Karena says, "it was a lovely card, thank you very much."

"Oh, good," says the Widow in her sweet little croaky voice. "I was worried you hadn't received it. The mail up there in the Cities can be so unreliable, especially when money's involved. . . . And when I hadn't heard from you, I just assumed . . . But now I know you got it, so I'll sleep better at night."

"That's good," says Karena.

"I brought it to the Center to show your dad before I sent it," the Widow continues. "I could tell he thought it was real nice."

Karena tries not to remember Frank as she last saw him a month ago, listing sideways in his wheelchair, his pink scalp visible through the cobwebs of his hair. Utterly unresponsive no matter how Karena pressed his hands and smiled and talked to him. One eye staring at the birds hopping and chirping in the nursing home's lobby aviary, the other fixed straight ahead.

"How's he doing this week?" Karena asks.

"Oh, the same," the Widow says. "Of course, if you'd come down, you could see for yourself. I know he'd appreciate a visit."

Karena makes a face at herself in the mirror across from the bed and pulls her hair.

"As soon as I can," she promises. "Listen, Lois, I've got to run, but please, you'll remember what I said about Charles?"

But the Widow says brightly, "Well, bye now!" and hangs up.

Karena takes the phone from her ear and looks at it, then tosses it aside on the bed. She stares at the TV. Well, Karena hasn't expected much from the Widow, and her expectations have been met. If the woman weren't so loathsome, Karena might feel sorry for her—maybe. The Widow had three husbands before Frank, the first purportedly beating her senseless night after night on their farm before suffering a fatal threshing accident. With each successive spouse the Widow has traded up financially and in community status, and she must have thought she'd struck gold with Frank Hallingdahl, Foss County's most successful attorney. Those twins were a negative, especially that crazy son, Charles. A threat. An embarrassment. But the Widow would have known Charles hadn't been heard from in years and Frank saw his daughter only for the occasional lunch. What the Widow could not have predicted was Frank's stroke two years into their marriage—an especially bad joke, considering Frank was a jogger and health nut long before it became fashionable. Now the Widow is in limbo, caring for her shell of a husband, unable to marry again.

Karena suddenly wants to see her dad so badly she can hardly stand it, not Frank as he is now but as he was when she and Charles were young—a skinny, tough little man gleefully rubbing his hands together and chortling over the facts of a particularly nasty lawsuit. Frank may have been an absentee dad, his motto being *Justice Waits for No Man*, but still, he's the only one Karena's got. Even more, though, Karena longs for her mom, Siri, with an intensity she hasn't felt since the days following Siri's death, when Karena felt she could spend the rest of her life wandering black-clothed through a desert, tearing her hair and howling, and it would still not express the dimension of her grief. If Siri were here, the two of them would drink white wine from the plastic bathroom cups, chilled with ice from the machine down the hall, and share a pack of Marlboros—although Karena quit years ago. They would laugh over the Widow's bile and uselessness. They would analyze the Charles situation and bitch about it and make a plan together. Karena lies back and closes her eyes.

5

That night Karena wakes suddenly, as fully alert as if she had never gone to sleep at all. She turns to the bedside clock: yes, four thirty A.M. on the dot. Just like at home. This happens to her almost every night, every unresolved thing in her life babbling away in her head at once. It's quite a party going on up there. An e-mail to a forgotten source. A response to a neglected wedding invitation. Heated arguments during which Karena says everything she wasn't brave enough to say during the day—*Why do you have to be so awful?* she asks the Widow, *I know your life's been hard but I didn't do anything to you. Can't you help me?* Then there are the usual suspects, such as, why is Karena alone in this motel room in the middle of the night? With no husband, no child? Thirty-eight years old and almost out of time, this is not how it was supposed to be. And, always, there is Charles. Charles, Charles, Charles, the fact of her absent twin like a radio signal that's sometimes stronger, sometimes fainter, but one Karena never stops hearing.

Tonight the signal is especially powerful because of her near miss. *Find him. Find him. Find him.* Karena gets up and goes into the bathroom for two aspirin and a dropper full of Bach Rescue Remedy, which is supposed to contain soothing flower essences but is, she's pretty sure, about 90 percent brandy. Sometimes this helps. Tonight it doesn't. Lying very still, Karena reminds herself she can't do anything about any of these situations tonight. She'll tend to them tomorrow. At five thirty, she turns on the light, throws back the sheet, and pads across the room to her laptop.

She looks first to see if Tiff is online, since sometimes Tiff likes to have a virtual chat while nursing her youngest, Matthew. But Tiff is nowhere to be seen. Karena opens her e-mail next, but of course there's nothing new since midnight when she last checked it because all the normal people are asleep. She dashes off the messages she was composing in her head, saving them in her draft file. Then she visits the weather websites, the Weather Channel and Storm Prediction Center and Wunderground, and finally Karena lands on Stormtrack.

Stormtrack is the stormchasers' forum, where the chasers have lively discussions of where severe weather will occur next and post accounts of chases they've just had. For a year Karena has been banned as a participant after one too many attempts to find Charles, the moderators letting her know in no uncertain terms that Stormtrack is for people looking for severe weather, not other people. *But I'm Charles Hallingdahl's sister,* Karena wrote, *and I'm trying to find him. I can't reach him any other way. Won't you please help me?* The reply was a week in coming, and then it was a terse *We have no way of verifying you are who you say you are, and our members' privacy must be protected.* Then, as an afterthought, *Sorry. Good luck.*

Karena goes to the Forecasts & Nowcasts page, hoping against hope that Charles will have contributed something, but she knows it's a long shot. It has been a dry summer for tornadoes, and there's no severe weather predicted anywhere in the country until the following week, in the Dakotas, so the message boards are quiet. Karena scrolls through the old posts anyway, in case she has missed one by C_HALLING-DAHL, but there's nothing. So she permits herself to do what she does on nights when missing Charles is particularly bad: She visits the Stormtrack archives. There are Charles's storm photos from earlier this summer, proof he is still chasing, until yesterday the only evidence Karena had that her brother was alive.

She clicks on each photo to enlarge it, although she has memorized them, their colors and composition, sometimes sees them floating on the backs of her eyelids as she tries to sleep.

The herd of white horses fleeing an oncoming storm: *rosebud county, montana, C_HALLINGDAHL*.

The Amish children gathered on a dirt road, their upturned faces fearful beneath their straw hats and bonnets, above them a triple fork of lightning: *near sioux city, iowa, C_HALLINGDAHL*.

A ghostly tornado in a rain shaft, backlit by lightning, white on gray: *cimarron county, kansas, C_HALLINGDAHL*.

That's it, for this year. And that's all Charles ever writes, the captions beneath his photos.

Karena looks at them until her head begins to ache, these images she would have guessed were her brother's even if he hadn't provided his name, because the wild and lonely and beautiful way the photographer frames the world is signature enough. She has tried so hard to find Charles. The private investigators she has hired—two of them, highly recommended, extremely expensive, and both useless—are just the tip of it. Karena has placed ads in all the Personals sections in every Tornado Alley newspaper, asking for information. She has done the same online. She has visited the weather websites, corresponded with a handful of stormchasers who say they have seen her brother here and there but he's pretty much a lone wolf, likes to keep to himself, happy hunting. She has used the *Ledger* databases, search engines that churn up every documented fact of a person's life, from birth to bankruptcy, felonies to divorces, weddings to addresses. Yet Karena has been unable to find anything on Charles. He has never owned property, never had an insured car, never paid taxes. He has lived entirely off the radar.

Karena puts her face in her hands and rubs, making a little whimpering sound. She wishes to God she had retained her childhood ability to always know where Charles was, so that whenever some grown-up asked, Karena could say of her more adventurous twin, *He's under the porch* or *He's up on the roof* or *He's over by the water tower*.

"Where are you, Charles?" she says.

The slice of window beneath the drapes is starting to glow gray. Karena clicks the refresh button to see if, by some miracle, C_HAL-LINGDAHL has posted something within the last ten minutes. The first part of the page to load is an advertisement, a brown tornado spinning across the top of Karena's screen, leaving WHIRLWIND TOURS: THE ADVENTURE OF A LIFETIME! in its wake. The debris settles to reveal a white van, its hazards blinking as it watches the tornado dwindle, wreaking havoc in the distance.

"Oh my God," says Karena. She shakes her head. How could she have been so stupid? How could she not have seen it before? This is how she'll find her brother. She clicks on the Whirlwind link.

6

Although she has excellent reason to be, Karena doesn't consider herself phobic about storms. Like every native Minnesotan, she has more than a nodding acquaintance with them. She's accustomed to lightning, thunder, hail. She knows how to recognize a wall cloud, the lowered part of a rotating storm from which a tornado might come. She's used to her summer evening programming being interrupted by the network meteorologists using Doppler radar to show her where the dangerous weather will be. If the sky turns green, if the sirens crank up, Karena goes to the basement.

That's it. No screaming meemies. No flashbacks, no hysterics. Karena simply takes precautions, as any prudent person would, to stay out of harm's way.

Which leads her to question, as she slips into the back of Conference Room B in Oklahoma City's Gateway Hotel: Who are these people?

The room is full of Whirlwind chasers and their clients, in the middle of orientation. As she takes the nearest seat, smiling an apology at the woman beside her, Karena looks at the guides with special curiosity. These three men, designated by their Whirlwind T-shirts as the tour's leaders and protectors for the next week, are some of the most respected chasers in the field. They might know Charles, might have had contact with him as recently as a few days ago. They are Charles's peers. But what makes them dedicate their lives to launching themselves into weather everyone else is running away from? Why would anyone do that, unless he was crazy? And speaking of which, the tourists. Karena looks at the pleasant-faced people sitting around the conference table, listening attentively to the tour director, Dan Mitchell. Karena counts seven guests, a mixed bag of men and women—which surprises her, as she'd expected mostly adolescent males would sign up for this kind of adrenaline ride. And some of them are middle-aged too. Why have they paid two thousand dollars a pop to get close to a muscular, roving column of air that could easily kill them? Don't you know this is real? Karena wants to ask them. Why don't you stay home where it's safe?

As unobtrusively as possible, she takes out her steno pad and sets her little recorder on the table. She is officially here on assignment, having persuaded her editor to let her write a feature on stormchase tours. And early this morning, on standby at the Wichita airport, Karena talked the Whirlwind president, Tim Tarrant, into letting her tag along on this one. *You know the van's all booked up, right?* Tim had said. *You'll have to follow along in your own vehicle. Can you do that? You have experience driving in bad weather?* Karena had hesitated for a second, then said yes. *Then go rent yourself a rugged vehicle with four-wheel drive and high clearance*, Tim told her. *And for the love of Pete, get full-coverage insurance.* Karena has accomplished all this in the past hour since landing in Oklahoma City, but still, she is late. Orientation is halfway over.

"All right," says Dan Mitchell, having dispensed with introductions and moved on to logistics. He is a huge, blond, snub-nosed guy with freckles, consummately ordinary in appearance, nobody Karena would turn to look at on the street. Same with the two guides flanking him: One is gray-bearded and wearing a floppy fishing hat; the other is a guy about Karena's age, short and stocky like a bouncer with a face as round as a pancake pan. Not what Karena would expect from some of the wizards of the chasing world, as they are regarded on Stormtrack.

"Let's talk about what you can expect from this next week on your big weather safari," Dan Mitchell says in a monotone, leafing through a three-ring binder. "How many of you have come on this tour expecting to see flying cows?"

Some chuckles from the tourists at this reference to the airborne livestock in the movie *Twister*. The heavy young man across from Karena raises his hand.

"How about a couple of tornadoes?" Dan asks.

More laughter, and now all hands go up, including, belatedly and reluctantly, Karena's.

"Good," says Dan. "And we're going to try to make that happen for you. But unlike what you might have seen in the movies and on TV, tornadoes don't usually fall from the sky one after the other. They're a lot harder to find. Most tornadoes last about thirty seconds and touch down over rural areas. And that can happen anywhere in Tornado Alley, from North Dakota to Texas. So guess what we're going to be spending a lot of our time doing?"

"A bloody lot of driving," mutters the young woman next to Karena in a British accent.

"A whole lot of driving," says Dan Mitchell. "Basically, we're going to be playing a game of chess with the atmosphere. Instead of chasing the storms, we want to put ourselves in position to catch them as they go up."

He leafs through the binder. "Some days the atmosphere may not cooperate," he says, sounding as though he's reading, "and we'll go see local attractions, like Carhenge, or the Corn Palace in Mitchell, South Dakota, or the World's Largest Ball of Twine. . . ."

"You know, I've been chasing nineteen years and I've never seen that damned thing," interjects the gray-haired guide. "What's it look like?"

The pancake-face guide leans past Dan. "Twiney," he says.

"Thanks, Kevin," says the gray-bearded guide.

"Don't mention it."

"Okay, since you guys are obviously in talkative moods," says Dan, "maybe you want to take it from here. Dennis?"

"Happy to," says the gray-bearded guide. He steps forward and flashes a peace sign. "Greetings," he says. "As your driver on this tour, not only do I have the privilege of transporting you hundreds of miles and getting you as close to storms as possible, I'll also be watching out for your personal safety—as will we all," he adds, looking at his fellow guides. "Who can tell me what the biggest danger is while chasing?"

"Uh, tornadoes?" says a maroon-haired woman in cat's-eye glasses.

"Wah," says Dennis, holding up his arms in an X. "Wrong."

"Lightning?"

"Second most dangerous. One more."

"Driving," says Karena despite herself.

Dennis points at her. "Bingo," he says. "Bad drivers. Like Dan said, most of the storms we'll see will be in the middle of nowhere, like in Farmer John's field, but we'll probably be sharing that field with a hundred other chasers. And believe it or not, not all chasers are responsible, traffic-law-abiding citizens like myself. Some of them get a *leetle* too excited when those tubes start to drop from the sky, and they're not watching what they're doing. So please, people, when we let you out of the van to take pictures, don't wander into the road. We like you the way you are, with your entrails on the inside."

"Entrails," says the husky teenager across from Karena, and hoots softly.

"Also there's wildlife," Dennis continues, counting on his fingers, "wasps and rattlesnakes. Don't wander into the high grass. And yes, lightning, if you're close enough to feel rain you're close enough to be struck, so don't hug any telephone poles or trees. Barbed wire, try not to run into any. And wind—if you're the last person out of the van, make sure you close the door. Otherwise it can slam shut and take somebody's arm off."

He turns to the pancake-face guide, Kevin. "What'd I miss?" he says.

"Hail," says Kevin. "As a rule we stay away from it, since some of those suckers can get up to softball size, and you don't want to see what that does to a windshield. But if we get in a situation where hail's unavoidable, wad up your jacket or fleece or whatever and put it between yourself and the window. You'll have to remember to do this on your own," he adds, "since once hail really gets going it'll be too loud in the van for you to hear us."

Karena shudders. She has forgotten about this until now. Kevin looks at her quizzically, and she shrugs and smiles.

"Thank you, Kevin," says Dan Mitchell, deadpan. "I think that about covers it—"

"Wait, hold up," says Kevin. He has a rich, pattery voice, like a big-city DJ's. "Liquid intake," he warns, "don't intake too much, because we try to make a pit stop every couple of hours, but if we're on a storm, that's not always possible."

Groans from the female guests. "That's when you make the Magic Stall," murmurs the woman next to Karena.

"What's the Magic Stall?" Karena asks from the side of her mouth.

"It's when you wait 'til everyone's across the road looking at the storm, then you pop 'round the other side of the van, open two doors, and cop a squat. Voilà, Magic Stall."

"Got it," Karena whispers.

"Ladies," says Kevin. He stops talking to fix them with a stern gaze. "Do we need to separate you?"

Karena's seatmate claps a hand over her mouth, while Karena sits up very straight and shakes her head and says, "No. No, sir. We're done."

"I think we're all done, actually," says Dan Mitchell. "Unless anyone has any questions . . ."

The tourists look around at one another and smile.

"Okay," says Dan, "then let's grab a quick lunch at the Panera next door and be back at the van in half an hour. Go."

As everyone stretches and stands and shuts off camcorders, Karena turns to the woman next to her. She is in her mid-twenties, Karena guesses, with hair dyed so sooty black it has a purple sheen and two piercings in her right eyebrow, but there is something winsome about her thin, foxy face.

"Karena Jorge," says Karena, "Minneapolis *Ledger*. I'll be following you on this tour."

"Yeah?" says the woman. "Cool. I'm Fern. Fern Michaels."

"Northern England?" Karena guesses.

"Yeah," says Fern, corkscrewing the word up at the end to indicate surprise. "How'd you guess? Most Yanks think I'm bloody Australian."

"I was married to a Brit," says Karena. "He was a Souf Londoner, though."

"Good on ya, mate," says Fern. "So you a virgin then?"

"Pardon?" says Karena.

Fern grins. "Is this your first tour?"

"Oh. Yes. Is it that obvious?"

"Yeah," says Fern. "No offense."

"None taken. I've got a lot to learn, that's for sure. Thanks for the Magic Stall tip."

"No problem," says Fern. "And that's nothing. Wait'll you meet your first shower pet."

"Shower pet," Karena repeats to herself as Fern stands up.

"Speaking of stalls," she says, "I'm off to the loo. See you at Panera then?" and she walks quickly across the conference room.

Karena gathers her things and catches up with Dan Mitchell outside the Gateway's revolving door, where he is overseeing the other two guides as they wrestle a mountain of luggage into a big white van. It is like watching a Tetris game, Karena thinks. The van bristles with antennas and has a longhorn skull wired to its grille.

She says, "Dan? Hi, I'm Karena Jorge, Minneapolis *Ledger*, your media escort on this tour. My editor threw me on this story last-minute—I hope Tim Tarrant had a chance to warn you I was coming?"

Dan nods. "Welcome aboard," he says, in exactly the same tone he might use to say, Walk the plank.

"I'm sorry I was late," Karena says. "It took a while to find the right rental at the airport."

"What're you driving?" Dan asks.

"The red Jeep," says Karena, pointing, "that Grand Cherokee Laredo."

"That's good," says Dan. "I don't suppose you have a ham in it."

"A what?"

"We communicate by ham radio," says Dan, "but lacking that, you'll have to rely on your cell phone, and in most areas we'll be in, the coverage is pretty poor. You'll have to stay right behind us if you can so we can keep an eye on you."

"Okay," says Karena, offering her brightest smile, "I can do that."

"You might want to pick up a scanner at a truck stop too," Dan says. "That way at least you'll be able to hear us."

"Scanner," says Karena, writing this down. Is Dan always this taciturn, or is he annoyed by the additional responsibility of having to watch out for a green reporter tailing his van? Karena doesn't want to burden the tour, but she is on assignment. Not to mention her ulterior motive.

"By the way," she begins, and is about to ask if by any chance Dan knows a chaser named Charles Hallingdahl when Dan overrides her.

"If you want lunch," he says, "you'd better go get it now. We've got a long drive ahead."

"Oh," says Karena, realizing she missed this part of orientation too. "Where are we going?"

"Kansas," says Dan, "to get in position for tomorrow."

Karena laughs, and Dan glances at her for the first time. "What's funny?" he asks.

"I just came from Kansas," says Karena. "I'll be totally retracing my steps."

"Welcome to stormchasing," Dan says. He nods at Karena and walks off across the lot.

7

At first, this is fun. After arriving late and spending the night in Hays, Kansas, the Whirlwind Tour continues north the next morning, toward Nebraska. During briefing Dan tells them he's optimistic about the severe weather potential that afternoon near Ogallala, which means Karena is hopeful about finding Charles there. Meanwhile, as the drive wears on, she allows herself to forget why she's on this trip at all. She feels as though she's playing hooky, a sense reinforced by the fact that she's not even wearing her regular clothes. She didn't pack enough for a week's trip when leaving Minneapolis, so this morning at the Hays Walmart, while the rest of the tour was at breakfast, Karena picked up a new wardrobe in addition to a scanner. Her pink madras shirt, a country cowgirl item Karena would never wear at home, exudes the sour smell of cheap new cotton. She drives along behind the van in a blissful dream, watching the colors of the land bleach as the sun climbs, listening to the guides' chatter on her scanner.

They cross into Nebraska and turn west on Interstate 80. There is nothing to look at out here but green corn, the faded highway, and the denim-blue sky. The sun shimmers off the van. The towns are an hour apart, trying their best to lure tourists with attractions like Harold G. Warp's Pioneer Village or the birthplace of Kool-Aid in Hastings. The Platte River sometimes runs alongside the Interstate, invisible behind a line of glistening cottonwoods.

Karena knows a lot of people who hate this part of the country, who get agoraphobic just thinking about all this nothingness beneath the immense sky. Karena loves it. She loves everything about it. She loves the ruler flatness of the land, which makes her want to gallop across it on a horse, singing at the top of her lungs. She loves that 80 percent of her vision is sky. She loves that she can see everything around her in every direction. This is probably a trait inherited from Karena's pioneering ancestors, who would have wanted to see whatever danger was coming at them, blizzard, prairie fire, locust cloud, tornado. When they pass the Great Platte River Road Archway Monument in Kearney, Karena cheers and honks her horn. She chants from memory the verse featured on a plaque in the museum, which she and Charles were made to memorize on their third-grade field trip here:

> *The cowards never left*
> *The weak died along the way*
> *Only the strong survived*
> *They were the pioneers!*

8

B y four o'clock, when they stop at the Sapp Bros travel plaza in Ogallala, some of the novelty has worn off. Karena is tired, rumpled, and cranky. Her face is oily from hours in the Jeep. Stumbling through the convenience store toward the ladies' room, she feels as though she hasn't blinked in hours. And this is only the first day. Karena wants to groan. Maybe it is the onset of the Dreads, but this whole trip suddenly feels ridiculous.

After washing her face and blotting it with a paper towel Karena feels a little better, and she walks back through the store to show Charles's mullet photo to the clerks. As usual, nobody has seen him, and Karena starts to wonder if this is a case of the hair wearing the person. Maybe the mullet is just too distracting. She strolls through the aisles, past the atlases and cans of refried beans, the snack food and automotive parts and Huskers memorabilia, comparing the photo with the men she sees. She'll start in here and work her way out. She rules out any guy under six feet, since Charles won't have shrunk, and the overweight, because Dr. Brewster said Charles is in good shape. Other than that, any male about Karena's age is fair game, and she stands by the ATM, the lottery ticket machine, even the men's room, subtracting a baseball cap and glasses from this guy, a beard and mustache from that. She has the strong sense that Charles is nearby—what Charles used to call their twindar. She just can't see him.

Once she's covered the convenience store, Karena buys a pair of awful white sunglasses from the spinning stand and wanders back outside. There she stops. The travel plaza has become a stormchasers' tailgate party. The parking lot is a maze of vehicles with radio and radar antennas, Skywarn stickers, orange bubble lights on their roofs. Chasers wander among them, drinking Big Gulps and eating microwave pizza. Karena often hears single women ask where all the men are. Now she knows the answer. She thinks she might propose a second article, this one for the *Ledger*'s "Lifestyle" section. Every unattached woman in Minneapolis will be taking stormchase tours.

Karena stands on tiptoe, scanning the lot for a slender six-footer with golden-blond hair. Charles is nowhere in sight, so Karena looks for her guides, figuring it's best to start close to home. But the Whirlwind team is busy. Dan is in the driver's seat of the White Whale, as Karena has nicknamed the van, watching the radar. Dennis is lecturing some of the tourists, gesturing animatedly to the sky. And Kevin is pacing the periphery, talking on a cell phone. Karena sighs, then plunges into the chasers, systematically working the lot from left to right. She doesn't bother with the photo this time, just asks if anyone knows a chaser named Charles Hallingdahl. Many say they do—they refer to him as Chuck—and look at her curiously or impassively from beneath baseball caps and behind sunglasses. But nobody has seen Chuck Hallingdahl, not this season, sorry. Good luck, though. The Stormtrack party line.

Eventually Karena retreats to the median, disheartened and sweaty, and sits in the shade beneath the giant red-and-white coffee can billboard. She fans herself with her steno pad. Are the chasers closing rank, or have they really not seen her brother? Charles, the lone wolf. Maybe he's really not here. Maybe he's in another state altogether. But Dan said the only real chance for severe weather today is right where they are. Karena slits her eyes and inspects the crowd. Come on, Charles, she thinks. Show yourself. I know you're here somewhere.

"Hiya," says Fern, the British girl. She ambles over, tapping a pack of cigarettes against her wrist. "D'you want company?"

"Please," says Karena. She might as well make a friend and get some material for her story.

"How you doing back there on your own?" asks Fern.

Karena smiles. "Fine," she says. "Though I do miss out a little on getting to know you guys. But I like driving."

"I'd go mad," says Fern. "You Yanks drive like nutters. No offense. Don't you get sleepy?"

"Sometimes," Karena admits.

"D'you smoke?" Fern says, offering her pack.

"Not anymore," Karena says.

"Shame," comments Fern, lighting a Marlboro. "That'd keep you awake. You could try sunflower seeds, though. That's how Dennis manages, since he can't smoke in the van."

She considerately exhales off to the side, the smoke forming a twisting parabola in the sunlight. You could die, you know, Karena wants to tell her. You're not immune. Cancer doesn't happen just to somebody else. She wants to tell Fern about her mom Siri, how at the end, after they took one of Siri's lungs and put her through chemo and radiation and steroids, there was nothing recognizable left of Siri except her voice. But Karena kept smoking three years after her mom died, stopping only when she began getting migraines from it. The habit is that hard to break. So she says nothing, and the two of them sit quietly for a minute like old farmers, Karena watching the chasers, Fern the sky.

"Nice Cu," Fern says.

"Sure is," says Karena absently. Then, "Wait, what's Cu?"

Fern laughs. "I keep forgetting you're a virgin," she says. She points with her cigarette to the white puffy clouds cruising over the truck stop.

"Cu," she says. "Short for cumulus, cumulus congestus. We've got a bit of a Cu field, actually, and they're agitated. See how they're blowing themselves up? Means we could get some action soon."

Karena laughs and takes out her little recorder.

"Agitated Cu," she says into it. "Cu field. That's great, Fern. The guides should give you a cut."

Fern looks aghast, as if Karena has committed some blasphemy.

"I'm shite compared to them," she says. "They're bloody geniuses."

"How many times have you been on tour, anyway? Do you mind if I record this for my piece?"

"No, that's all right," says Fern. "Six."

"Six!" says Karena.

Fern blows smoke into the sky. "Whirlwind's brilliant," she says.

"Apparently," says Karena. "How'd you hear about them? How'd you decide to do this in the first place?"

"I saw a documentary on Discovery Channel about chasing," says Fern, "and I knew I had to come. I've always been obsessed with tornadoes. I've loved them ever since I was a little girl."

"That's interesting," says Karena. "How come? It's not as though England has a lot of severe weather."

"Well, that's the point," says Fern. "English weather's shite. The most you ever get's some pathetic little thunderstorm, and everyone goes mad. It's bollocks. So I knew I had to come to the States. And that first tour changed my life."

"Interesting," Karena repeats, a little more alert now. There's a story here. "How so?"

Fern stubs her cigarette out on the sole of her boot, her grape-colored hair swinging forward.

"Fell in love, didn't I," she says.

"With the storms?" Karena asks.

"With a man," says Fern. "The best, smartest, sexiest man in the world—bloody bastard."

Karena makes a sympathetic face. "Ah," she says. "Should have known."

She waits while Fern lights another cigarette. Karena was right: This is turning out to be a much richer story than the one she had planned, as so often happens when the people get involved.

"So who is the sexy bastard?" she asks. "If you don't mind talking about it."

But before Fern can answer, somebody from the lot shouts:

"There it goes!"

Fern looks up and grins. She nudges Karena with an elbow.

"Look," she says, pointing.

Karena does. Her mouth opens, just a little. One of the big Cu has exploded like a Jiffy Pop container, and it is still growing, punching up and outward so fast that Karena can actually see it happening as if in fast-forward film. Its top is blinding white against the blue sky, and hard and knuckly, but its underside is dark gray, and as it expands its shadow eclipses the truck stop.

"Right," says Fern, "showtime."

She stamps out her cigarette, bends to pocket the extinguished stubs, then jogs toward the White Whale. Halfway there she turns.

"See you out there," she calls.

"Let's go, people," shouts Dan Mitchell.

The parking lot is a madhouse. The chasers are jumping into their vehicles and speeding toward the exit, which results in a nasty bottleneck. Horns blare, and some of the vehicles start plowing across the median rather than wait. One of them, a bizarre hybrid of tank and armadillo, gets mired in the grass, blocking the rest. Karena watches in awe.

"Hey, Laredo," yells Kevin, and it takes Karena a second to realize he's shouting at her, referring to her by the model of her Jeep. Of course: She hasn't introduced herself to him yet, so although she has been listening to him all day, he doesn't know her name.

"Saddle up, Laredo," he shouts and cranks his arm. "We've gotta move!" and then Karena is running too, sprinting like everyone else toward the vans.

9

They turn right out of the Sapp Bros and drive through Ogallala to pick up 61 North, Karena talking to herself in her Laredo. Come on, she tells herself. You can do this. It is not like last time. These guys are not Charles. They're professionals. They have radar. But Karena is shaking all over, so badly she can hardly hold on to the wheel. She can't help it. Every instinct in her screams to drive back to the Sapp Bros, where there is, if not a basement, at least a bathroom she can hide in, a windowless room in a cage of pipes. Instead she keeps following these total strangers into life-threatening danger.

She has snapped into hyper-alert mode again, her eyes ticking rapidly right and left in case some detail might be necessary later for survival. The warehouses and steakhouses of Ogallala. The bungalows on its outskirts. The Platte River again. The land becoming hilly as they head north, long, gentle swells beneath the grasses. A beautiful blue-green lake. A picnic table and pine trees like a 1950s postcard. The light is intense and jaundiced, choked off by the storm, as if Karena is wearing yellow-tinted sunglasses.

She starts thinking about what she could tell them: Her check engine light came on. She had a sudden attack of E. coli from her fast-food burger the night before. She got an emergency call from home. But then Karena would have to call her editor and confess she's aborting the assignment. Tell Tim Tarrant, the Whirlwind owner, the same thing—

after she assured him she could handle this. She imagines the tourists saying, *What happened to that reporter?* and Fern saying, *She did mention she was getting sleepy back there.* Dan would say nothing and probably be relieved. But what really bothers Karena, for some reason, is the you-all-right? look that guide Kevin gave her during orientation. She doesn't want to repay that small kindness by disappearing.

And there's Charles. She has come out here to find Charles. Karena straightens her arms, bracing them against the wheel, and keeps driving.

After a while, Karena starts to relax, hypnotized by following the van along the swooping highway—and here is a curious thing: The sun is out again, shining strong between the agitated Cu Fern pointed out, which sail like galleons over the Jeep. In the rearview the storm that exploded over the Sapp Bros is barely visible, looking like a scoop of melting vanilla ice cream. Karena hasn't seen any other chasers since leaving Ogallala, either. "What the hell?" Karena says. Why are the Whirlwind guys going in the wrong direction? There's a white line above the hills ahead, bulging upward in the middle like a contact lens, but that's not a storm. That's a front.

Suddenly her cell phone starts burring and moving itself around on the passenger's seat, startling Karena—she's forgotten about it. She grabs it. "Hello!" she says. "Karena Jorge."

". . . scanner," one of the guides says. She thinks it's Kevin. The phone beeps three times and goes dead.

"Damn it," Karena says and shakes it, as if this will help. The phone buzzes in her hand.

". . . scanner, Laredo," Kevin says faintly. "146.520."

"Oh!" says Karena as the phone dies again. She waves to the van, annoyed with herself. How could she have forgotten to put on the scanner? 146.520, she repeats, 146.520. This is the channel the scanner has to be on for her to hear them. She steers with her elbows while she programs the frequency in.

". . . with us, Laredo?" says Kevin on the scanner. "Flash your high beams twice if you can hear."

Karena does.

"Okay, copy. You doing okay back there?"

Flash. Flash.

"Copy that. Good. Just wanted to let you know there's a Wheel of Fortune on our storm now. We're looking to intercept in about twenty minutes."

"Wheel of Fortune," Karena repeats, bemused. She flicks her high beams rapidly, a blizzard of brights, and holds up her hand questioningly.

"Oh, sorry, Laredo," Kevin says. "A Wheel of Fortune's a little spinny thing, spinning icon, that pops up on our Threat Net when a storm starts to rotate. That's what we're looking for."

Karena flashes twice to show she has understood, and in response all the tourists stick their arms out the windows, then wave them up and down in unison so it looks as though the van is flying. Karena laughs and turns on her recorder. "Wheel of Fortune," she says. "Threat Net." Is this how Charles talks now too? Probably. Karena remembers him saying things like *punch the core* and *in the bear's cage*. He always did love the lingo.

Then she thinks, Wait, did Kevin say *our* storm?

She leans forward again and shakes her head. "Where?" she says. "I just don't see—" And then the van comes up out of the valley they've been traveling in and a moment behind it, Karena's Jeep, and she realizes that what she thought was a front is a storm, after all. It's just so big she didn't recognize it as such. She never would have imagined a storm could be this huge, a mothership filling the sky, taking up the whole horizon. It hangs there, the telltale anvil shape Karena recognizes from Stormtrack, the bottom flat and the top also, sheared off by upper-level winds. Any tornado, even as tall as a skyscraper, will look like a toothpick coming from that thing.

"Oh my God," Karena says.

Her scanner crackles. "Okay, Laredo," says Kevin, "in about two miles we should be coming to a farm road, and we're going to take it."

"Okay," says Karena. "Okay."

"Laredo? Copy?"

She has forgotten to flash her brights. She does, twice. Her hands are shaking again.

The tour continues toward the storm, the light fading as they drive under the anvil. The temperature drops. The prairie dims. They are in the shadowland beneath the base now, a place Karena remembers. The wind rushes toward the storm, and Karena can smell rain as well as see it, an opaque gray stem drifting from the storm's base. Lightning flickers within it. But there is no thunder.

"Here's our road, Laredo," Kevin says.

Karena flicks her brights and starts to cry as she follows them. They are driving *closer* to the storm. They are going *into* it. She knows this is the point, but she can't stop. She swipes her nose with her hand and tells herself Charles is probably parked right over there, taking pictures.

"Wall cloud, two o'clock," says Kevin, and Karena recognizes the lowering shelf from which the tornado might come. She makes a terrified noise and leans forward to look up. The base, a dirty brown, presses down on the Jeep, bulging with huge, hanging, breast-shaped lumps. Karena remembers these too, and she knows now they are called mammatus, and they indicate severe turbulence overhead. The light has been squeezed to a murky yellow stripe on the horizon.

"Okay," she tells herself, "you're okay, you can do this. All you have to do is follow the Whale," and she concentrates on this with all her might, not losing that boxy white van, because if she does, she's dead. Then Karena notices clouds the size of a house being sucked into the wall cloud and disappearing. Getting vacuumed up. Immediately to her right more clouds are rising off the prairie like smoke going up a chimney, that fast. And there's a little point coming from the wall cloud now too, trying to lengthen into a funnel.

"This is not safe," Karena says. "They are all fucking crazy. This is not safe at all!"

She takes her foot off the gas and falls way behind the van as it trundles toward the wall cloud, then wheels her Jeep around and speeds back in the opposite direction.

"Laredo?" Kevin is saying. "Laredo, we've lost visual. We can't see you, Laredo. Catch up, please."

Karena turns the scanner off and barrels along the dirt road toward the highway as fast as she can. Only something has happened, either the storm turned or she did somehow, because now the rain shaft is in front of her. The core. That's what Charles called it, anyway. *We've got to punch the core, K! No way out but through!*

But Karena also remembers all too well what happens in the core. And on the other side.

She looks behind her and sees the dark brown storm base rotating over the empty road. No sign of the van. She can't go back that way. What if they turned off somewhere? But she can't go forward, because the core—

Then it is too late because it sweeps over her, the rain immediately blotting out visibility, and the Jeep begins to rock. The wheels on Karena's side lift off the road, set back down, lift again. Karena grips the wheel, gasping. "Think," she says. "Think!" She knows the tornado will be on the other side of the core, in what her brother called the bear's cage. But what if she has edged into the bear's cage and this is the tornado, here, now? Hidden by the rain? She can't stay here. She'll get picked up and thrown.

She is struggling to put the Jeep in drive when someone pounds on her window. Kevin, his hand cupped over his brow so he can see in, his dark hair stuck to his forehead.

"Stop," he yells. "Put it in park!"

Karena does.

Kevin yanks open her door.

"Get out and go around," he shouts.

"What?" yells Karena.

"Or just slide over! Let me drive!"

"Okay!" Karena shouts.

She jumps out and is instantly soaked through her clothes. She runs around the back of the Jeep trailing one hand on it so she won't get lost. The rain is that blinding.

She climbs into the passenger's seat and slams the door. Kevin throws the Jeep into drive and accelerates. Every so often the Jeep tries to lift up again as the wind punches it broadside. Karena sees small branches scudding across the road. Then they are out on the other side and there is blue sky up ahead, the sun shining beyond the anvil.

The birds are singing in the fields. Karena remembers this now. The birds, how they sing after. How it is oddly peaceful. Her own breathing sounds very loud and harsh in her ears. She is sitting plastered against her seat, gripping the cushion.

"Where's," she says, and has to clear her throat. "Where's the van?"

"At our six," says Kevin and tips his head toward the backseat.

Karena turns and sure enough, now that they're not in the core she can see the White Whale's longhorn skull and grille in the rear window. They had to come back for her. She hasn't felt so ashamed in years.

"I am so sorry," she says.

Kevin cuts his eyes sideways at her.

"What happened back there?" he says. "You all right?"

"Yes," Karena says. "Just totally mortified. I feel like such a *girl*."

Kevin shrugs. "People panic sometimes," he says. "It happens."

He runs his hand down his face and shakes it, wicking droplets off his fingers.

"Bruh," he says. "Rain. I hate rain."

"But—you're a stormchaser," Karena ventures.

"Stormchasers hate to get wet, Laredo," Kevin says. "If you're in the precip, you're in the wrong place."

"Oh," says Karena, chastened.

Kevin keeps driving. He smells good, Karena thinks, like damp cotton and cologne, something safe and nostalgic sold at a drugstore. After a minute Karena has it: Old Spice. His brown hair is extremely short and cut in that style with the little flip in the front, and as it dries it lifts into porcupine quills above his round face.

"I'm Karena, by the way," Karena says. "I mean, I know you know that, but I don't think we ever got introduced."

Kevin looks startled. "You're right," he says. "I'm Kevin Wiebke."

Karena says, "Pleased to meet you," then laughs, given the circumstances. Kevin snorts.

"Seriously, thank you for helping me," she says. "I'm really sorry I made you get wet. But you were heroic to get out in the core."

Kevin gives her a quick glance. "The core?" he says. "What core?"

"All that rain we just drove through? Was that not the core?"

"Actually no," Kevin says. "It wasn't. It was just RFD."

"What's that?"

"The rear-flank downdraft. Just a little wind."

"Oh," says Karena in a small voice.

They drive on.

10

That night Karena is walking across the rear courtyard of the Pony Express Lodge behind the Sapp Bros, carrying a case of beer. She knows she's still a little shocky because she had a terrible time choosing the brand. She deliberated for half an hour in the travel plaza's beer cave, bemused and distracted by the alcoholic lemonade, the wine in a bag, the lime-flavored salt. Finally the clerk had to come assist her and, when they chose Budweiser, help Karena extract her ATM card from her wallet.

At the back of the Pony Express courtyard, almost hidden by the pines separating the hotel's property from the highway, is a hot tub. The pool next to it is covered as if in deference to the sign that says NO SWIMMING AFTER 10 P.M.! The hot tub is not, and the three guides are sitting in it. Or rather Dan Mitchell and Kevin Wiebke are, while Dennis is perched on the side, still wearing his floppy fishing hat. He's talking energetically about something as Karena approaches, but Kevin sees her. He tips his chin up, and Dennis turns.

"Greetings," he says. "You must be Our Lady of Budweiser."

"I am," says Karena, setting the case down near the edge of the hot tub and rubbing the insides of her elbows, where the sharp edges of the cardboard box have bitten into her skin. She's a little apprehensive about bothering them, but she theorizes that any group of men will be happy to see a woman with beer.

"It's the least I could do after that stunt I pulled today," she says. "Thanks again for coming back for me. I'm really sorry."

She looks at Dan Mitchell, trying to pretend he's not half naked, his beefy chest muscled and streaming with wet blond hair. He shrugs.

"It happens," he says, as Kevin did earlier.

"What, people routinely freak out on you?" Karena asks.

"I wouldn't say routinely," says Dan. "But sometimes. The storms are big, and they mean business. People get scared."

Dennis cracks a beer and hands it to Karena.

"Have a seat," he says.

"I don't want to intrude," says Karena. She has been planning to go back up to the room she is sharing with Fern and another tourist, Alicia, because the Pony Express is overbooked, and file notes for her story, and call all the area motels to see if Charles is at any of them.

"We insist," says Dennis, and Dan nods.

"All media in the hot tub," he says. "It's mandatory."

Karena laughs. "Somehow that sounds a little suspect to me, but . . . okay."

She toes off her new Walmart sneakers, lowers herself to the chlorine-smelling pavement, and eases her feet into the hot water. Dennis hands around beers. Karena sips hers. It's half warm and maybe the best beer she has ever tasted.

"Thanks," she says.

"De nada," says Dennis, and for a minute nobody says anything. The bubbling of the water seems very loud, and Karena feels supremely conscious of being the only woman in a hot tub with three men, even if two of them are wearing shirts. The jets keep pushing her feet across the pool toward Kevin's submerged lap.

"So," she says, "tell me it's not just the newbies like me. Or the guests. You guys must get scared sometimes, right?"

Dan Mitchell lets out a huff, and Dennis nods.

"Sure," he says. "If you're not scared, you should be worried. It means you're getting too cocky. Although—I wouldn't say scared, exactly. More like alert and respectful. You have to be willing to learn from the storms. They always teach you something."

Dan Mitchell stretches his arms across the back of the tub. "Or sometimes they're just plain scary," he says.

"That too," says Dennis. He swigs from his bottle and says, "HAH!"

"It must really take something to scare you guys, though," says Karena.

She pats her shorts pockets and wishes she had brought her recorder. But maybe these guys wouldn't talk to her candidly if she had.

"When's the last time you got yourself into a situation that scared you?" she asks, and holds up her empty hands. "Off the record."

"May twenty-second of this year," Dennis says promptly. "Before I joined up with Tour Four. Gove County. Central Kansas. Man, Mother Nature really let her dragons out to play that day."

He opens another beer. "I was supposed to be chasing with this goober"—he kicks water toward Kevin—"but he hadn't gotten his act together. Hadn't even left St. Paul yet. So I was tooling around on my own in the ol' purple PT Cruiser—"

"The Eggplant," says Dan.

"Yeah, the Eggplant," says Dennis. "And the SPC issued a high risk that morning—which actually I don't like to see because the storms can get messy," he tells Karena, "the situation can spin out of control real fast. Which is exactly what then happened."

He swigs his beer.

"So the cells were firing all around me," he continues. *"Boom! Boom! Boom!* All I had to do was get in position. It was that kind of day, when every cell that went up would be a monster, and they'd all produce. It wasn't even like you had to decide which one to chase. All you had to do was sit there and wait for them to come along, and when one was done the next would come spinning right up the dryline."

"Like shooting fish in a barrel," says Dan.

"Exactly," says Dennis, pointing at him. "It should have been. But it wasn't, because I got stupid. So there I was driving along this farm road, watching this cell at my eleven o'clock. It had already been warned, and it was rotating like crazy, and let me tell you, that thing was a beast. Something about the storms that day, it's not just that they were huge and moving fast. They seemed angry."

He pauses to take a swallow.

"So I'm watching this meso form right above me—you know what a meso is, Laredo? Sorry, what is your real name, anyway?"

"Karena," says Karena.

"Very pretty name," says Dennis. "Norwegian, I'm going to guess. But I'll stick with Laredo, since I'm used to it now, if you don't mind."

"I don't mind," says Karena, smiling. "So what happened?"

"So I'm watching this meso," Dennis repeats, "this tight little area of rotation the tornado's going to come from, what we call the area of interest. And the radar's showing this beautiful tight couplet and my scanner's going crazy, *wah, wah, wah*, tornado warnings all over the place. And I'm saying to myself, man, that thing's right on top of me, maybe I'd better drop southeast, when suddenly there's this *POP* and a light goes on on my dashboard."

He turns to Karena. "You believe that?" he says. *"POP!"* He laughs. "You know what that was?"

She shakes her head.

"My tire," says Dennis. "Rear left. Somehow I'd picked up a spike in it. Not a nail, a spike, with a washer on it the size of a quarter. I mean, that thing had *teeth*. So there I was sitting under this tornado-warned storm, and it was cranking, just going nuts, and my freakin' tire was gone."

"Wow," says Karena, frantically taking mental notes. Her pulse is rapid in her throat. "So what'd you do?"

"What do you think I did?" Dennis says. "I jumped out of the car and ran around the back and threw everything out to get the spare, except guess what?"

"Oh no," says Karena.

"Oh yes," says Dennis. "My brother'd borrowed the car the month before and had a blowout, and the nimrod never replaced the spare. So forget outrunning this thing. There was a farmhouse about a mile down on the left, and I was just about to drive my sorry ass—excuse me—down there on the rim and take cover when this guy came along." He nods at Dan. "With Tour Three. So we threw all my equipment in the back of the van and got the hell out of there."

"Storms were pretty violent that day," Dan says. "What'd that Gove County cell drop, an F-3?"

"Yup," says Dennis. "Right where I was. It's a pretty safe bet that farmhouse isn't there anymore."

He takes out a pack of cigarettes, offers it to Karena, lights one.

"So yes!" he says, spreading his arms. "Do I get scared? You bet I get scared! But that day taught me a valuable lesson. I never, never should have left the house without checking the spare. And ever since then, I carry this . . ."

He shifts to get at something in his back pocket and produces a Caribou Coffee notepad.

"The checklist," says Dennis, cigarette clenched between his teeth. He flips back the cover to show Karena the handwriting inside. "Every day I ask myself, how can I make this chase safer? How can I make it better for the guests? What have I overlooked?"

He puts the notebook back.

"You can't control everything," he says. "That's what makes chasing interesting. But the number one rule is, Be prepared."

"Actually, that's the Boy Scout motto," says Dan.

"Well, that too," says Dennis. "I'm the original Boy Scout."

Karena smiles and shakes herself.

"Whoa," she says. "That's quite a story. Thank you for telling it."

"My pleasure," says Dennis, bowing his head.

"So tomorrow," says Dan Mitchell, stretching, "I'm going to move one of you guys to her vehicle with the spare ham. Kevin?"

"No prob," says Kevin, punching down his Whirlwind T-shirt, which has bellied up from the force of the jets. Karena realizes although he's been listening the whole time, he hasn't—rather uncharacteristically, it seems—said a word.

"Oh, that's okay," she says. "I can't inconvenience you guys more than I already have."

"There's no alternative," Dan says. "We can't have you out of the loop. It endangers everyone. And media's not allowed to leave the tour. Tim would have a fit."

Karena laughs, although she's not sure if Dan is joking or not.

"In that case," she says.

She makes an apologetic grimace at Kevin. He raises his eyebrows.

"You're all being awfully nice," she says.

"We're all Boy Scouts," says Kevin. "At heart."

Karena gets to her feet, water sluicing off her legs.

"Gentlemen," she says. "I've caused enough trouble for one day. I'll leave you to your beer. Thanks for the war stories."

Dennis toasts her. "Thanks for the beer."

Karena hooks up her sneakers with two fingers. She is halfway across the courtyard when she turns back. She still must not be quite right if she's forgotten to ask them.

"Hey," she says, "any of you know a chaser named Charles Hallingdahl?"

The men are talking among themselves again, but at her question they all look up.

"You mean Chuck?" says Dennis.

"Yes, right, Chuck," says Karena, thinking, Chuck. Oh dear.

"Sure, we know Chuck," says Dennis. "Everyone knows Chuck. Why?"

Karena stammers for a moment.

"No reason," she says. "I mean—we grew up together. In the same hometown, and my editor thought it'd be cool if I could include him in the article. The personal-tie angle. He was always into chasing storms then too."

She smiles, although her face is burning. From across the hot tub Kevin is watching her with that squinty, quizzical expression.

"Haven't seen him this season," he says. He looks at the others. "Have you?"

"Not for years," says Dennis. "Man, Chuck H, that crazy mofo. Remember the time he—"

"We haven't seen him," says Kevin.

"Okay," says Karena. "If we do run into him, could you point him out to me?"

"You bet," says Kevin.

"Thanks," Karena says. "Good night."

She squishes off across the cement, swearing at herself. What was that all about? She feels bad for having lied to these men, especially after they've gone out of their way to help her. Saved her, in fact. She's not sure why she has. Probably because although they may be too polite to ask, the chasers would certainly wonder why Karena and Charles are estranged, why she can't find him any other way, and that's personal. Family business. *We don't talk about this*, Karena remembers Frank saying, as they drove back from the Mayo Clinic after Charles's first episode, the one at the Starlite. Also, lying gets to be a habit after a while. Secrecy too. Karena sighs and picks up her pace.

In the back corridor she is struggling with the pop machine, trying to mash a damp dollar into the slot, when the courtyard door opens and Kevin pads up the hall toward her. He stops very close, and Karena's stomach flips. Usually she doesn't like people being in her space, but Kevin doesn't feel like a stranger. He smells familiar somehow, of childhood maybe, water-heated skin and chlorine.

"Fear," he says. He plucks the dollar out of her hand and leans past her to feed it into the slot. "I just wanted to say one thing about fear."

"Which would be . . . ," Karena says, watching the machine eat the dollar with its *vssssht* noise.

Kevin turns to face her. His eyes are not brown, as Karena thought, but hazel. Bright slashes in his round face.

"Fear is good," he says.

"Do tell," says Karena.

"Most people think of fear the wrong way," says Kevin. "They fear fear. They get as paralyzed *by* fear as by *what* they fear."

"'The only thing we have to fear is fear itself'?" Karena quotes.

"That's right," says Kevin. "But you know what? Fear is your survival instinct kicking in. Fear is your body's primal way of saying I don't have enough information about this situation. How can I get more information? How can I learn more to keep myself safe?"

"I never thought of it that way," Karena says.

"Now, what'd you want?" says Kevin.

"What?" says Karena. "Oh. Diet pop, please."

Kevin presses a glowing button and a plastic bottle clunks into the trough.

"Remember," he says, "fear is good. Or can be."

He looks as though he wants to say something else, actually opens his mouth to do so, but then appears to reconsider.

"Is something wrong?" says Karena.

"Not a thing," says Kevin.

He hands Karena her pop.

"Sleep tight," he says, "don't let the bedbugs bite," and squishes off down the hall, leaving amoeba-shaped wet footprints on the carpet.

11

Karena has already shown the mullet photo to the clerk on duty at the front desk, ascertaining that although the hotel is full of chasers who have doubled back after today's storms, Charles is not among them. But she returns to the lobby anyway to ask for a local phone book. It's late, almost midnight, and her roommates will be sleeping. Karena doesn't want to wake them by rummaging around for her laptop. She sits with the Ogallala Yellow Pages on one of the leather couches, then on impulse gets up, goes up the staircase past the mural of stagecoach and horses, and exits the hotel again onto the rear balcony. For some reason she is drawn to look down at the hot tub. But the chasers aren't in it anymore, and the cover is pulled over it as though they had never been there. There is only the drone of eighteen-wheelers, invisible but powerful behind the cyclone fencing and trees, and a huge, fat orange moon.

Karena takes her cell phone from her back pocket, sees she has some signal here, and gets started, working her way through the motel listings. There is no Charles, Chuck, nor C Hallingdahl staying in any of them. Karena tries the campgrounds next, reaching mostly recordings, and then, in a last-ditch effort, the hospitals. Nobody has seen her brother. That doesn't necessarily mean anything, though. Charles could be using a fake name. More likely, Karena thinks, he is sleeping in his uninsured death trap of a car. Karena hangs on the railing, stretching her arms, and stares at the moon. The last time she saw it this big was when they were eight, and Karena told Charles a moon this size meant it was going to crash into the earth and kill everyone. Charles cried all night. Is he somewhere nearby, sleeping beneath it or looking at it too? Some instinct tells Karena he is.

Her cell phone buzzes in her hand and her breath catches—Charles?—but of course, it's not. It's Tiff. Karena flips the phone open.

"God, *finally*," Tiff says. "I've been trying to reach you all day. Where *are* you?"

"Kansas—no, Nebraska," says Karena. "Where are *you*? You sound like you're in a wind tunnel."

"I'm in the garage," Tiff says. The *FFfffff* sound comes again. "I'm smoking. I just can't take it anymore."

"That's not good," says Karena. "Put down the cigarettes and back away slowly. Why are you in the garage?"

"That kid," Tiff says, "I swear he has baby bat ears. Matthew, I mean. If I'm anywhere in the house, he'll hear me and wake up. And he's up like five times a night anyway. I've basically given up sleeping."

"Oh no, Tiff," says Karena. "I'm sorry. What about the pills?"

"Then I won't wake up when he needs me," Tiff says.

"But—what if he needs you while you're in the garage?" Karena asks.

"Baby monitor," says Tiff.

She exhales in a deafening blast of static. "So where are you again?"

"Ogallala, Nebraska," says Karena, "at the Pony Express Lodge!" She says this with a flourish, her tone implying, Ta da! but Tiff is unimpressed.

"Whyyyy?" she says.

"Because we were chasing a storm today and that's where we ended up, along with every other chaser in the universe. Except Charles."

"Uh-huh," says Tiff. "So you haven't seen him."

"Not yet."

"Shocker," Tiff says.

"Hey," says Karena.

"What?" says Tiff. "Has it not occurred to you that what you're doing is, how shall I put this, kind of . . . *insane?*"

"No," says Karena. "I'm on a story here, in case you forgot. This is my job."

"Pssh," Tiff says. "Whatever. We both know you'd never, ever be on this assignment except to find Thing Number Two."

Karena can't help snorting at Charles's old nickname. "Okay, maybe," she concedes. "But I *am* on assignment. And I have a good chance of finding Charles, statistically. Besides, what else would you want me to do?"

"Um, let it go?" says Tiff. "Get your butt home and get a life?"

"Nice," says Karena.

The phone crackles as Tiff chuffs out smoke. "Sweetie pie," she says, "I've known you longer than anyone, except maybe your useless dad, no offense, and I know how much you love Charles. I know you guys have this, like, *twin* thing nobody else can understand. But Charles is nothing but trouble, Kay, and frankly his problems are bigger than you can solve. What are you going to do if you do find him? Bring him home with you like a puppy?"

Karena, who has been pacing the balcony, stops and shakes her head. Because yes, actually, this is what she has envisioned. For years, all the while she's been looking for Charles, she's had this fantasy about him showing up on her doorstep one night. Footsore, exhausted, scarily thin. Maybe he has a patchy beard. He's clearly been living on the street, or worse—his donated clothes don't fit right, and he smells. But Karena asks no questions. She just takes him in, draws him a hot bath, fixes him a nourishing supper, and puts him to bed in her own room, with very clean, very cool new sheets. The next day, they go to the doctor together.

She is not so naïve as to mistake this vision for reality. She knows if she finds Charles—when—he may be balky. Resistant. Even, given how Karena left things with him, extremely nasty. But he has reached out for help, that call from Wichita the first signal in years he's ready to take it. Karena doesn't think this is so far-fetched.

"I could use a little support here, Tiff," she says.

"*Sweet pea,*" Tiff says. "Of course I support you. I'm just calling 'em as I see 'em, because if your friends won't do this for you, who will, right? And frankly I think if you had more in your life, like a husband and kids, you wouldn't be all tearing around the back of beyond, trying to find your brother."

Karena is silent. She holds the phone to her cheek, breathes, stares at the moon. Do not say anything, she tells herself, her face tight with anger. Do not say anything you'll regret. Tiff always gets this way when she's nursing. After having her third son two years ago, Tiff and Karena were at Girls' Night Out at Pepitos, and Karena was halfway through a description of a spectacularly bad date she'd just endured when Tiff smiled beatifically and interrupted, *You know what? Hearing this story is making me so happy to go back to my husband and babies.* Karena had felt as though Tiff had reached into her purse, taken out a small knife, zipped it up Karena's cheek, and put it back again. It turned out Tiff was postpartum and on all sorts of drugs, but if Karena has forgiven the comment, she has not quite forgotten it.

Now she waits until her throat has loosened, then says, "You know, I'm going to pretend you didn't say that."

"Oh my God," Tiff says. "Don't be that way. I'm just *saying*, is all. For your own good. You know I love you, Kay."

Karena sighs. "I know," she says, because she does. "Love you too."

When she hangs up she takes a last look at the moon, which is higher now and white and unremarkable, and then goes into her room. Fern and Alicia are both fast asleep, inert forms in the beds, the air thick with their exhaled breath. Karena holds out the glowing face of her cell phone as a flashlight until she finds her laptop on the round table near the window. She tiptoes into the bathroom with it, flicks on the light, and bursts into tears.

It's true, she thinks as she cries. Tiff is right. This is useless. What is Karena doing here in Nebraska, in the middle of nowhere, surrounded by sleeping strangers? They're on vacation. Karena is on a wild goose chase. She tries not to panic, reminds herself she's exhausted, starving, and headachy from the beer, and it has been an incredibly long and stressful day. A carousel of images advances behind her eyes: The chasers' tailgate at the truck stop. Fern smiling into the sun. The Jiffy Pop Cu exploding behind the Sapp Bros billboard. The giant white anvil. The storm base pressing down on the Jeep. The wind lifting her up. Kevin at the window with his wet face streaming, Kevin beside her in the hall with a towel knotted around his waist . . . The chasers, Fern . . .

Work. Work is the antidote to panic. Karena turns on her laptop and breathes deeply as it boots up. She resists the urge to check flights home from, say, Lincoln or Omaha and instead opens a new document. Then she realizes her little recorder is in the bedroom and creeps out to get it. Fern snores vigorously away, a mop of purple-black hair on a pillow, while in the other bed angel-faced Alicia, a Latina meteorology student from Dallas, sleeps as sweetly as a child, her hands tucked under her cheek. Karena smiles and wipes her face. She is feeling fond of both these women, who have been kind enough to take her in so she doesn't have to go look for another motel. But she'll sleep with Alicia, thank you very much.

Back in the bathroom, Karena listens to her recorder and files the events of the day. *Agitated Cu. Cu field. Wheel of Fortune.* When she is done, she e-mails the document to herself and her editor and rubs her eyes. As usual, the writing has had a soothing narcotic effect. It is very late, almost three, and Karena knows she probably has another long drive tomorrow. But she decides to check Stormtrack anyway, as a reward for having done a good night's work. And why not? She'd like to see where the other chasers ended up today, what they saw and reported.

Karena reads through the descriptions of the day's adventure. Most of the posts originate from Ogallala. No tornadoes sighted, but many chasers mention the nice structure of the storm that blew up behind the truck stop. Karena nods as she scrolls through the photos, recognizing vehicles she saw earlier, including the stuck tank.

On the final page she stops. The second-to-last post is a photo of the white Jiffy Pop cumulus as it burgeoned up behind the Sapp Bros billboard, except the handle of the red-and-white coffee pot is flipped, pointing south instead of north. The image was taken from the opposite direction, the other side of the truck stop from where Karena and Fern were standing. The caption reads: *exploding cumulonimbus, ogallala, nebraska, C_HALLINGDAHL*. Charles must have been behind Karena, a few hundred yards away, all along.

"You doing okay there, Laredo?" Kevin asks from the passenger's seat.

Karena blinks. "Sure," she says, "why?" Though she knows why he's asking. She wishes she were alone so she could slap herself across the face, but since she isn't, she settles for tickling the roof of her mouth with her tongue, a trick Tiff taught her years ago to stay awake in history class. It didn't work well then, and it doesn't now. Karena keeps graying into microsleeps. She'll think she's fine, and suddenly the scenery will have changed and the Jeep is drifting toward the shoulder. It's the three hours of sleep the night before, and the lack of caffeine. Not eager to use the Magic Stall, Karena hasn't risked her usual coffee intake.

And it is this place they're driving through, Cherry County, Nebraska, which Kevin has told her is the second-biggest county in the country but has only two major roads. They have been on one of them for ages, heading toward possible severe weather tomorrow in the Dakotas, meanwhile curving up and down and around an endless series of hills. Because that's all that's in Cherry County. Hills. Big green hills, hills like dinosaurs buried beneath the earth, hills humped in every direction as far as the eye can see. It is like Emerald City without the city, and it is hypnotizing.

"Whoa there, Laredo," Kevin says, grabbing the wheel to steer them back on the road. "You want me to drive for a while?"

"No, that's okay," Karena says. She sits up and bites the inside of her cheek. Yesterday, when Kevin drove, was different, an anomaly, an emergency. Karena likes being behind the wheel of her own car, and not just because Kevin isn't on her rental insurance. It's the only way Karena feels safe. She starts to blink out again, her head jerking, then remembers what Fern said about sunflower seeds. They don't have any of those in the Jeep, but . . .

"Could you pass me some of those corn nuts, please?" she asks Kevin.

"Sure," Kevin says. He rips open a bag and the old-sneaker smell of corn fills the Jeep. "Hold out your hand."

Karena does, and Kevin pours some fiery red nuggets into it. Karena sniffs them, then eats them. The corn nuts are teeth-rattlingly, deafeningly crunchy, but not bad. And Karena does feel more alert.

"Mmm," she says. "Barbecue."

"I can tell you're a woman of great taste and discerning palate, Laredo," says Kevin, tossing a fistful of nuggets into his own mouth. "More?"

Karena holds out her hand.

"Thank you," she says, crunching.

"Don't mention it," says Kevin. "So, Laredo, what's your story?"

Karena laughs and almost aspirates a corn nut. "Could you be a little more specific?" she asks when she's done coughing.

"Sure," says Kevin. "Let's see. How long have you been at the *Ledger*?"

"Nine years," says Karena and blinks, startled. "Wow."

"Kudos, Laredo," says Kevin, "it's a great paper. And how do you like it there?"

"I like it a lot. It's a great crew."

"Good, good," says Kevin. He is wearing aviator glasses that make him look like a cop. "That's what my friends in the biz say too."

"Ah, your friends in the biz," says Karena, grinning. "You have journalist friends, do you?"

"Sure," says Kevin, "went to school with a bunch of 'em. What'd you think, Laredo, that we scruffy chaser types have no intellectual life? That we just drive around all day, eating corn nuts and looking for storms?"

"Pretty much," says Karena, "and drinking Big Gulps and saying things like, Dude, you caught that tube down in Kansas, nice!"

She makes bull horns with her second and pinky fingers and stabs the air. Kevin pulls his shades down to give her a look.

"Tubes, huh," he says. "And yesterday you mentioned the core . . . Methinks our star reporter here is a secret storm groupie."

Karena shrugs. "I read Stormtrack," she says modestly.

"Uh-huh," says Kevin. "I see . . . So tell me, Laredo, what does your boyfriend think of this assignment? How does he feel about you tooling around the country with us scruffy chaser types?"

Karena gives the road a little Mona Lisa smile. Is Kevin flirting with her? Unless she's mistaken, she believes he is. The thing is, she doesn't mind. *Oh, please,* Karena can hear Tiff saying, *a stormchaser? Seriously? What's next, a sword swallower? Come on, Kay. Get real.* But around Kevin Karena feels something she hasn't felt around anyone she's dated in the past few years, maybe not even since the divorce. That includes William, her editor; the pilot who wined and dined her until one night he flew off and never came back; her neighbor the alcoholic, as gentle and dolorous as Eeyore. Well, everyone's got something, some secret fault line, and no doubt Kevin Wiebke does too. Karena certainly does. But for whatever reason she's attracted to this guy with his pie-round face and Old Spice cologne, and she feels safe and silly around him in a way she hasn't for a long time.

She decides to give him a run for his money.

"Boyfriend, huh," she says. "What makes you think I'm not married?"

"No ring, Laredo," says Kevin, holding up and waggling his own bare left fourth finger.

"Faulty reasoning, Mr. Wiebke," says Karena. "I could have dropped it down the sink. It could be at the jeweler's for resizing. Or—"

She looks sideways at him.

"—I could have had to take it off because my fingers are swollen from the pregnancy."

"Oh," says Kevin. "Whoopsie." He is wearing a brick-red University of Oklahoma polo today instead of his Whirlwind T-shirt, and the flush climbing out of his collar is the same color. "You're expecting? I wouldn't have guessed. Congratulations."

Karena laughs. She licks a finger and holds it up with a *tsss!* sound. "Score," she says. "I win. No, I'm not expecting, and I'm not married at the moment and I don't have a boyfriend. Thanks for playing, though."

Kevin shakes out another handful of corn nuts. "Laredo, Laredo," he says, crunching away, "I'm just trying to pass the time here. Playing twenty questions. Because in case you haven't noticed"—he sweeps his hand over the dashboard, palm up like a waiter carrying a platter—"we have nothing *but* time. This place is *made* of time."

"True," Karena acknowledges. In front of them the van, as tiny as a Matchbox vehicle against the giant hills, swoops up the side of one and disappears around a curve. Clouds are building in the northwest, filtering and concentrating the light until everything around them glows. The colors are surreal: the sky behind them periwinkle, the grass a bright lemony green, the formerly gray road red-purple.

"So my turn," says Karena.

"Turning the tables, are we, Laredo?"

"You bet," says Karena. "That's what reporters do. We like to *ask* the questions."

"Uh-oh," says Kevin.

"You started it," says Karena, smiling. "So, what do you do during the off-season?" There. This should pacify her inner Tiff.

"I'll give you three guesses," says Kevin.

"Wait, that's not fair, why do I have to guess?"

"You said it, Laredo. I started it. It's my game."

"All right," Karena sighs. She taps her fingers on the wheel. "You're a . . . bullfighter."

"Not since the accident. Try again."

"Male dancer?"

The blush climbs out of Kevin's shirt again.

"Stop, Laredo," he says. "My head's going to be too big to fit through the door. One last try."

"Hmmm," says Karena. She crunches a few more corn nuts, thinking about it. There's his obvious passion for weather, and the stern look he gave Karena and Fern during orientation . . .

"Science teacher," she says. "High school."

Kevin whips off his aviators and throws them on the dash.

"Holy moly," he says. "That is amazing! How did you do that?"

"I'm not just a reporter, I'm a psychic."

"And a damn good one," says Kevin. "I'm impressed. Except it's junior high. I teach at Fitzgerald over in St. Paul. Right across the river from you."

"Yikes," says Karena. "Now I'm impressed. Kids that age are brutes. You're a lot braver than I am."

"Oh, I don't know about that," says Kevin. "You did pretty well in that storm yesterday . . . Okay. My go. You said you're not married at the moment. Does that mean you used to be? Any kids?"

The Jeep swerves over the yellow line. "Jeez," says Karena, laughing, "good thing you're not subtle or anything!"

"That's me," says Kevin, "Mr. Savoir Faire," and the ham radio crackles into life.

"This is KE5 UIY," says Dennis. "KB1 SLM, you copy?"

Kevin detaches the handset. "This is SLM," he says.

"What's going on back there? Laredo drinking behind the wheel again?"

"Nothing, just having ourselves a little discussion, is all."

"Well, you're obviously having way too much fun," says Dennis. "Cut it out. KE5 UIY."

"KB1 SLM clear," says Kevin and puts the handset back. He turns to Karena. "You were saying," he says.

Karena smiles at the road. "I don't think I was, actually," she says.

But Kevin's questions have made her think about her marriage, and her ex-husband Michael, and the last time she saw him and the last fight they had. This was about a month after Siri died, when Karena's whole life felt so unfamiliar that her husband of eight years was the strange thing, the only recognizable object in an alien landscape. She and Michael had met at the U, when Karena was a junior and Michael was an exchange student, and gotten married right after graduation, and together had endured a number of hardscrabble years. At the time of the fateful conversation Michael was finally making good money as a realtor, and he and Karena were sitting on a bench by Lake of the Isles glumly watching the parade of strollers. *When d'ya think you'll be ready then?* Michael had asked. *Two years? Five? I don't want to be an old dad.* Karena had hunched her shoulders. *I don't know, Michael,* she'd said, *it's not a math problem,* and Michael persisted, *Don't you want to do it for your mum, though? Make up for what you lost?* and Karena had gotten up and walked away. She had been outraged by the equation, lose a mother, have a child, as though that made Siri's death all right. She had thought this was the reason she didn't want to be married to Michael anymore, to have to go through life with somebody who saw things that simplistically. But also she was thinking, What about Charles? I can't have a baby with somebody who doesn't know Charles. And the thought of Charles showing up, in their apartment, in a hospital room in a maternity ward, talking to Michael—it was literally unimaginable.

The divorce coincided with her thirtieth birthday, and Karena saw Michael only once after that. She was sitting at a stoplight in Uptown when she spotted Michael bopping along the street near his office at Apartment Search. His honey-colored hair was winging back in its Lady Di way, and his mouth was open and smiling, and he looked happy. Karena almost honked but didn't. She sat thinking how odd it was that nobody in the cars around them knew that the man on the sidewalk and the woman in the Escort had been married for eight years, made each other cheese toast at midnight, made love on the fishing dock at Lake Calhoun, made the bed on Sunday mornings after listening to church bells and laughing. Made each other happy. Then the light changed, and Karena moved on.

"I was married once," she tells Kevin now. "It just didn't work out."

"I'm sorry to hear that," says Kevin. "What happened?"

"You've obviously never been married," says Karena.

Kevin has put his aviators back on, and he pushes them down again to squint at her. "What makes you say that?"

"Because if you had been, you'd know there's no one answer to that question," Karena says. But she gives Kevin her standard line: "He was a great guy, but we got married way too young. No kids."

"Ah," says Kevin.

"So are my psychic powers still intact?" asks Karena. "Was I right?"

"About what?"

"About your never having walked down the aisle."

"Oh, I walked," says Kevin. He crosses his arms. "I walked that plank, all right."

"So I was wrong," says Karena.

"No, you were right," Kevin says grimly. "I just never took the plunge. She didn't show up."

"Oh," says Karena.

"Yes, oh," says Kevin. "Neither did my best man."

"Oh no," says Karena, wincing. She looks at Kevin, but he is staring straight ahead, the hills reflecting in his lenses.

"I'm so sorry, Kevin," she says.

Kevin shrugs. "Not your fault," he says. "You didn't know. And neither did I, obviously. You know what they say. The groom's always the last to find out."

Karena shakes her head. "That's horrible," she says.

"Yes," says Kevin. "It was. Big ouch. Very big ouch. It took me a while to get over it. I'd say trust issues was a major understatement."

"I can imagine," Karena says.

They are quiet for a while, watching the van surf up and down the big green hills. The clouds in the west are piling up over the sun, and the light dims a little, Karena's mood with it. So here's what he's got. Kevin's fault line is trust issues. How could he not, after what he's been through? And could there be anyone worse for him than Karena, with what she has to hide? There could not. So much for this one, she thinks.

Down, girl. Leave the poor man alone. But she is sad about it. She really doesn't want to.

"Yoo-hoo, KB1 SLM," says Dennis on the radio.

"Go," Kevin says into the handset.

"Since we don't have to be anywhere in a hurry, and since Dan's already booked us rooms in Valentine, the van is voting to swing by Carhenge," says Dennis. "How does the Laredo vote?"

In the background the tourists are chanting, "CAR-HENGE! CAR-HENGE!" Kevin looks at Karena, who shrugs and nods.

"Laredo votes as the van votes," says Kevin. "KB1 SLM, clear."

He puts the handset back and turns to Karena.

"Boy, do I know how to spoil a mood or what," he says. "I'm really sorry."

"No, not at all," says Karena.

"*Au contraire*, Laredo. A minute ago you were smiling to beat the band. Now suddenly you've gone all pensive on me."

"I'm just thinking," she says. "It happens."

"About what?" says Kevin. "Ah, there's the smile. You must be envisioning my alternate career as a male dancer."

Karena laughs. "That's it," she says. "Am I so transparent?"

"Not at all, Laredo," says Kevin, "in fact, quite the contrary. I find you a great mystery."

The sun comes out again, flooding the landscape with those brilliant Maxfield Parrish colors, so that Cherry County becomes a dream in which everything is wondrous, if not exactly comfortable.

"So okay," Kevin says, "here's my last question—you ready?"

"Do I have a choice?" says Karena.

"Nope. Here it is: What's your real relationship to Chuck Hallingdahl?"

Karena's smile winks out. She clutches the wheel.

"You tricked me," she says. "I don't like that. Why didn't you just come out and ask?"

"I'm sorry, Laredo," Kevin says. His voice is sheepish. "You're right. My bad. But I wanted to work up to it because it seems like a ticklish topic. You're good," he adds, "and I don't doubt you're here because you want to write a helluva story for your paper. But something about your face last night when you asked about Chuck made me think. . . . Plus it's just a feeling I had, something not adding up."

Karena looks stonily ahead. Her face is flaming now too, probably as red as Kevin's, as the corn nuts and the Jeep. She has the terrible feeling of being revealed in a lie—caught with her pants down, her dad would have said.

"So you're psychic too," she says.

"Maybe," says Kevin. "Anyway, I just wondered how you knew him. You don't have to tell me if it's too personal."

Karena sighs and relaxes her hands, then flexes them. There's no point in keeping this from Kevin anymore. It'll just be a bigger mystery if she doesn't tell him. Besides, for whatever reason and although she may be making a huge mistake, she trusts him. At least enough to want to give over this much.

"He's my brother," she says. "Charles is my brother."

"Your brother!" Kevin says. He whips off his shades again, and Karena can feel him studying her face.

"Now, that I would not have guessed," he says, more to himself than to her. "I thought maybe ex-husband or boyfriend, but—the name," he says, "you have different last names. I guess that threw me off."

"I kept my married name," says Karena. She restrains herself from touching her hot cheeks. Being beneath Kevin's scrutiny is like sitting under a sunlamp.

"So you must be the twin sister Chuck talked about," he says.

"I am," says Karena. She glances at him and sees his hazel eyes, intense and curious, scanning her face. And there's something else there—pity? respect?

"You sound like you know him pretty well," Karena says.

"I did," says Kevin absently. "As well as anybody did, I guess. We used to chase together quite a bit . . . Wow," he says, running his hands over his hair and exhaling. "Okay. Now I totally see it—it's like one of those trick pictures, you know? Find the twenty things in this drawing.

Your smile's the same as his, and the way you talk, and the shape of your face. . . ."

"Thank you," says Karena. "But when was the last time you saw him?"

"Oh," says Kevin. "That would've been back in . . . '02? '01? The year of the Guymon storm, so '01, it must have been. Yeah. You?"

"Not for a long time," says Karena.

"How long?" says Kevin, then adds, "Sorry, sorry."

"That's all right," Karena says. She has the feeling of having pushed off down a hill and now traveling faster and faster, unable to stop. "I'd prefer this didn't leave this Jeep, okay? But—twenty. Twenty years."

Kevin lets out a low whistle.

"But I'm trying to find him now," Karena says quickly. "And it's really important that I do, so do you think . . . could you please help me?"

"Sure," says Kevin. "Of course. But Karena, do you mind if I ask why—"

"KE5 UIY," says Dennis over the radio.

Kevin swears and grabs the handset. "Go, God damn it!"

"Jeez, SLM," says Dennis, "what's got your undies in a bunch? I was just going to tell you about this purty rainbow we're going to stop and take pictures of, but if you're going to be all like that about it, I won't."

Kevin leans forward and looks up through the windshield. "Rainbow, photo op, copy," he says shortly. "SLM, over and out."

He hangs up and turns to Karena, who is gliding the Jeep to a stop on the shoulder behind the White Whale.

"To be continued, okay?" he says.

"Okay," she says. She suddenly feels very tired.

Kevin pats her forearm and gets out. Karena watches him slide his shades back on and hitch his shirt down as he walks over to the van, from which the tourists are stiffly climbing. They move in the dazed, zombielike way of people who have been sitting a long time, stretching their necks and legs, and Karena tests herself to see if she knows their names. In addition to Fern and Alicia, there's Marla of the cat's-eye glasses and her husband, Pete, Iowans on this trip to celebrate Marla's fiftieth. The teenage boy is Alistair, also British, a mild autistic who has seen *Twister* 1,408 times and who's accompanied by his aunt Melody. The woman with the halo of curly blond hair is Scout, a Californian, who told Karena she's on this tour because she likes riding in vans with strangers. And of course Dan Mitchell, and Dennis, who steps out of the Whale and lights a cigarette. Kevin goes over to him and Dennis claps him on the shoulder.

Then Alistair hoots and starts waving upward, and everyone *oohs* and *ahhs* and takes pictures. Karena gets out of the Jeep to see too. A spectacular double rainbow is arcing between two hills behind them, its spectrum vibrant and shimmering against the purplish sky. Karena admires it, then glances over at Kevin. She can't help it. She shouldn't like him, but she does. She feels happy suddenly, standing at the bottom of this huge inland sea, as if in comparison to the hills her problems are as tiny as she is and maybe, just maybe, solvable. She turns back to the Jeep for her camera and notices as she does the spot on her arm where Kevin touched her, leaving a powdery barbecue imprint.

The tour stops that night at the Sandhills Lodge & Suites in Valentine, Nebraska. Fern and Alicia ask Karena to triple up with them again and Karena happily agrees, but she begs off going for a sit-down dinner with the group. She has to file notes for her story, and she wants to make the usual round of calls to local motels about Charles. As much as she likes Fern and Alicia, she would rather do this without them in the room. Karena is feeling nervous enough about having let even Kevin in on her ulterior motive for this trip, as though she has invited a jinx.

She sits at the ubiquitous round table to work, under a scratchy gold-shaded hanging lamp. The Sandhills, like many of the motels Karena has seen out here, seems to be a refugee from the fifties, enhancing her impression that the farther they travel into the country's interior, the places that can be reached only by driving, the more they go back in time. Karena is sitting on an orange vinyl chair; the walls are paneled in knotty pine like an old station wagon, and the TV has rabbit ears. She is charmed by this. She describes it for her story, along with the Sandhills' billboard being the shape of an artist's palette and the playground with its old-fashioned wooden swings, then closes her piece and opens up Stormtrack. Charles has not posted anything since the Sapp Bros photo. But Karena's twindar is still pinging her, gently and insistently.

She sits staring at the screen without seeing it, twisting a lock of hair the way she always does when puzzling something out. She is thinking of the noncommittal responses she got from the chasers at the Ogallala travel plaza, of Dennis referring to Charles as a crazy mofo, of Kevin's expression in the Jeep today when he discovered Charles is Karena's brother. Karena thinks she has parsed Kevin's look now: one part pity and two parts wary respect, as if he had discovered she had a lifelong job handling nitroglycerine. Given what Karena knows of Charles's behavior, this isn't surprising. What she wonders is how much Kevin and the other chasers know about Charles's disorder. Karena hasn't said anything about it because, unfairly or not, bipolarity still carries a stigma. She hasn't wanted to out Charles if he isn't open about it. Besides, she has been raised to protect him, to keep it quiet. *We don't talk about this,* Frank said grimly while they were driving back from the Mayo after Charles's first major episode. *This is family business.*

This happened when the twins were fourteen, during the Father's Day dinner at the Starlite supper club—though everyone had always known Charles was different. Karena had heard him called so many things: wild, a handful, the evil twin, a live wire. *That one's trouble,* Grandmother Hallingdahl always said. *Charles marches to his own drummer,* was Siri's explanation. When the twins were ten, Siri took them up to the Cities to have their IQs tested, and Charles scored off the charts. He was a genius, which generally excused his behavior. But in the days leading up to the Starlite incident he had been acting even stranger than usual. His moods turned on a dime: He was chattering and laughing one minute, talking a hundred miles an hour about things nobody could understand, then screaming the next because there was no root beer in the house. He stopped eating. He didn't sleep. At night Karena could hear him pacing in his lair downstairs like a caged animal.

So that afternoon at the Starlite she wasn't surprised when Charles lost it. She could feel it coming. The air around Charles was charged with it, a kind of dark energy. He was sitting across from Karena, at the round center table her family was sharing with the Budges, Frank's partner Don Budge and his wife Ann, and their pale, quiet daughter Amelia, and the whole table was shaking with Charles's leg beneath it. He was slouched in his chair, arms folded, looking at all of them with a disbelieving half-smile as though he just could not believe the idiocy of the people he was surrounded by, and when the light faded and the TV over the bar went *beep beep beep* and a thunderstorm warning started crawling across the bottom of the screen, Charles said, *See, what'd I tell you! I told you, I told you before, but you were all too dumb to believe me*, and he leaped up, overturning his chair.

Frank, sitting next to Charles, cleared his throat. *Charles, sit down*, he said.

No way, Pops, said Charles, although he knew Frank hated to be called Pops. *You stay there if you want, but you'll be sorry. Because it's coming, I can feel it, and it's going to be a big one too, an F3 or F4*, and he bolted for the door.

Charles Oskar, you come back here, Siri called, as people looked up from their dinners to watch Charles with surprise. *This kid's going to be the death of me, Frank*, she said, standing. *Don't just sit there, do something!*

Frank put his fork down.

Oh dear, said Mrs. Budge, *that poor boy*, and Amelia wrinkled her nose and said, *What's he even talking about?*

Tornadoes, Karena said to her chicken dinner. She was glaring at her plate, totally mortified. *He's talking about tornadoes*, and by then they could hear Charles yelling to somebody outside, *It's coming! Tornado— yeah, big one! You'd better get in there and take cover!*

Karena, said Frank, and Karena looked up.

Let's go, Frank said, and Karena threw her napkin down and grabbed her purse, and she and Frank walked through the dining room to the bar. Which was mostly empty, because if the diners hadn't wanted to interrupt the chicken drummie dinners they'd paid good money for, the drinkers wanted to see the action.

Outside Charles was already at the end of the lot climbing into

Frank's Mercedes—he must have hooked the keys right out of their dad's pocket, Karena thought, how oblivious could Frank be?—and Charles was right about one thing, there was a gust front moving in, driving dust and corn chaff through the air. In the southwest, just over the border in Iowa, a cloud bank towered, the sun glaring through a keyhole in it. The wind was preventing any would-be heroes from going after Charles into the lot. They stood on the Starlite's steps or just below them, screwing their faces up against the grit.

Charles, Siri called. This was before she had cut her hair, and it blew straight out to the side. She cupped her hands around her mouth to be heard. *Charles Oskar Hallingdahl, you come back here right now. I mean it!*

In answer Charles gunned the engine of Frank's Mercedes. He didn't have much experience in stealing cars yet and he banged a dent in the door of Mrs. Russert's Buick as he backed out of the space.

Oh, crap, laughed two of the guys watching, and one of them yelled, *Floor it! Floor it, Charles!*

Siri turned on them. *You shut your mouths,* she said, *you ought to be ashamed,* and then she looked up at Frank and Karena on the top step.

Frank, she said, and Frank put his hand on Karena's shoulder.

Go get him, Karena, he said. *You're the only one who can.*

And Karena knew this to be true, from the nights she was the only one who could sing Charles to sleep, the only one who could coax him off the roof, keep him from climbing the water tower, make him stop chanting that song, stop bouncing that ball, stop kicking that door. She ran out into the lot, tasting the dirt in the air, positioning herself between the rows of cars where Charles would either have to stop or run her down on his way out.

Charles, she shouted, trying in vain to tuck her hair behind her ears—it was whipping all over the place. She held out one hand like a crossing guard. *Charles, stop!*

Luckily, he remembered which was the brake and which was the accelerator, and the Mercedes lurched to a halt with its bumper six inches from Karena's knees.

Wait for me, Karena yelled, and ran around to the passenger's side. Charles popped the lock up.

Hey, sistah, he said, as if they were just hanging out in their yard. *Want a ride?*

Sure, said Karena, climbing in. *Except let's not go very far, okay? Let's just drive to the end of the lot and you can show me the storm.*

Okay, said Charles, somehow piloting the big car around the others without dinging too many bumpers and plunging onto the grass bordering the lot, where he threw on the brakes. Karena caught herself on the dashboard.

Okay, said Charles, *okay, okay, see, K? There it is. There's the anvil, and there's the overshooting top, and there's the wall cloud, see it? See? And holy shit,* he yelled, grabbing his hair, *there it is, dropping right in front of us, oh my God, I don't believe it! Check it out, K! Check out that funnel!*

Karena looked at the cloud bank, then back at her brother, and goose bumps popped out on her arms. He believed it. He really thought it was there.

Charles, she said. *There's no funnel, Charles. It's just a storm.*

Charles looked at her and smiled, his face full of love and pity.

Oh, K, he said, *don't you see it?* and then he opened the door and took off running. He sprinted down to the highway first, causing a sedan to honk and swerve, then hooked right into the Elmers' feed corn and disappeared. In the end, it took Sheriff Cushing and two deputies five hours to find him, all the way out on the Swenson farm having tea and coffee cake with that scary old German lady, Mrs. Swenson, and bring him back.

Now Karena sits up and rubs her eyes. She is thinking how amazing it is that as mythic as the story quickly grew—*Did you hear what that crazy Hallingdahl kid did? Tried to steal his own dad's car! Ran almost all the way to Iowa!*—nobody ever figured out that Charles was manic-depressive, as the diagnosis was called then. They just thought he was a joker, a cutup, a wild card. They were distracted, when Charles came home, by his dislocated shoulder—the Hallingdahls never did learn how he'd done that—and his numerous infected scratches from barbed wire. And Frank and Siri and Karena worked very hard to keep the diagnosis a secret. *We don't talk about this,* Frank said, as they drove home from the Mayo, leaving Charles behind in a little room, sedated. And, as a rule, Karena rarely has.

She hears a scuffle at the door that means one of her roommates is inserting the key, and by the time Fern and Alicia tumble in, laughing, Karena has mustered a smile.

"Hey," she says. "How was dinner?"

"Brilliant," says Fern. She holds up a Styrofoam box. "We brought you back some chicken-fried steak, in case you'd want food before the party."

"What party?"

"Marla's fiftieth birthday," says Alicia. "She specially requested we bring you."

"Oh, I don't know," says Karena. "It sounds great, but I really should . . ."

"Come on," says Fern. "All work and no play makes a dull chaser chick."

"I wouldn't mind an early night either," Alicia says diplomatically. "I'll go over with you just to say hi, if you want."

Karena stands up. She's tired of sitting around feeling bad. And the calls can wait a little while. If Charles has settled into the vicinity for the night, what difference will an hour make? And if he hasn't, there's nothing she can do about it but try again tomorrow.

"Okay," she says. "You twisted my arm. One drink."

They cross the parking lot under a high, soft purple sky, bats dive-bombing the Sandhills' pines. Fern knocks on the door to Room 117 and it flies open.

"Welcome!" Marla says. "So glad you could make it." In addition to her cat's-eye glasses, she is wearing sequined red sneakers, a T-shirt that says "Don't MAKE me get the Flying Monkeys!" and a black trucker cap with flames on it.

"Wow," says Karena. "That's some headgear."

"Thank you," Marla says modestly. "I just thought it said fifty better than anything else."

The three women file in, wishing Marla a happy birthday. Pete, her husband, turns from the impromptu bar on the dresser. "Ladies," he says. "Drink? We've got this"—he holds out a bottle of Jägermeister—"or Chuck Norris."

"What's Chuck Norris?" Karena asks.

"Vodka and Red Bull," says Pete, swirling a handle of vicious red liquid. "Smooth by night, but it kicks your ass in the morning."

"Oh my," says Alicia, who is, Karena remembers, a fairly devout Christian.

"Yes please," says Fern.

"Karena?"

"Sure," says Karena. "It's research."

She accepts a keg cup full of Chuck Norris, thanks Pete, and looks around. Everyone who's anyone is here—almost. Dennis is holding court in the corner, fishing hat bobbing animatedly, telling war stories. ". . . so I jumped out and scooped some of 'em up," he is saying, "put 'em in the cooler, and that night we had hail cubes in our drinks. HAH!" Alistair is intently watching *Twister* on a mini DVD, Scout sitting beside him. Dan Mitchell stops by to wish Marla an unsmiling happy birthday from the doorway. But where is Kevin? Karena has expected to see him here, freshly showered and smelling of Old Spice, mingling like a good guide should. She's a little annoyed by how disappointed she is that he's not. She bumps cups with Alicia, who sips her Chuck Norris and hastily sets it on the floor. Karena grins and takes a swallow of her own. The drink tastes like children's cherry cough syrup and goes down with alarming ease.

Scout nudges Karena with a foot. "Hey, Mystery Lady," she says. "Come sit by me," and she pats the bedspread next to her.

"Okay," says Karena, settling in. "Why am I the Mystery Lady?"

"Because we don't know anything about you," says Scout. "You're always behind us in the caboose." She smiles. "How's it going back there, anyway?"

"Very well, thank you," says Karena, "especially now that I've stopped freaking out and driving away."

"Well, you've got a good guide now," says Scout. She winks. "I'd say a smitten one too."

"Oh, I don't know about that," Karena says. "He has to be nice to me. That's his job. . . . And how about you?" she asks. "Are you still liking the tour now that nobody's a stranger anymore? Or is the honeymoon over?"

"Yup," Scout says, "let me off, I'm done." She laughs. With her crinkly blond bob and white smile, she reminds Karena a little of her mom, Siri. Scout has that slightly leathery look too, though hers is from being outdoors instead of marinating in smoke. Back in California, Scout is a professional equestrienne.

"Just kidding. Actually, I'm loving it," she says. She swirls her drink, which since it's clear is either water or straight vodka, and takes a thoughtful sip. "When I came out here I thought it was just this year's flavor. Every year I try something I haven't done before, like fly-fishing or dude ranching. But you know, this might be it for me. I think I might be hooked."

"Wow, really?" says Karena. "Already? On what?"

"Oh, I like the rhythm of chasing," Scout says. "Waking up every morning not knowing where you're going to land that night or what's going to happen. Going places you can't see any other way—places that don't even exist anywhere else, like this," she says, and toasts the room. "And the people are so great, and then there're the storms, of course. I know we haven't seen a really big one yet, but that one yesterday by Ogallala—that was amazing, wasn't it?"

"It was," says Karena.

"I'm not religious," says Scout, "but that storm made me think I could be. It was like . . . communion, to be that small in comparison to something but still a part of it, something so much bigger than yourself."

"Now that is a great quote," says Karena. "Do you mind if I use it?" She has forgotten her recorder—she has to do better—but she uses the Sandhills' scratch pad from the nightstand. Even as Scout repeats the quote, though, Karena is thinking she's heard or read something like it before. Where . . . And then she remembers. Charles, Charles saying, *It's so beautiful, K, I swear it's almost enough to make you believe in God.*

"Okay, everybody," Marla calls, and the music stops. She beckons them over to the round table. "Come here—you've got to see this. Birthday girl's orders."

"What is it?" Alicia asks, craning.

"Only the funniest video ever taken," says Marla, "of the very best birthday, by the very best husband," and she grabs Pete's cheeks and gives him such a long, passionate kiss that his bald spot glows bright pink.

"Okay, Marl," he says when she releases him, "maybe go a little easier on the firewater."

"Whatever," she says and twirls her hands, reeling her guests in. "Everyone ready? Hit play, honey."

Pete does, and the screen, which shows a frozen Marla standing next to a convenience store display of hats, comes to life. Karena recognizes the place as the Chevron station they gassed up in earlier, in Chadron, after Carhenge. Marla winks at the camera. *Hi,* she announces, *I'm Marla Johannssen, and I'm on a mission to find just the right hat for my birthday.* She turns, puts on a pink cowgirl hat, shoots her fingers at the camera and says, *Peew! Peew!* Shakes her head sadly and puts it back. Chooses a mesh and foam feed cap, about which she pronounces in a Barry White voice, *Sexy.* Then spies the hat with the flames, which she pounces on and holds up and says, *Oh, this is it.* She crams it on and adjusts the brim.

What are you, honey? prompts Pete, off camera.

The new face of fifty! Marla says and throws her head back for a wolf howl.

Then the rack starts to tremble, and a man pops out from behind the hats. He makes a face of astonishment, throws out his hand, and shakes it at the lens as if to say No no no no no to the paparazzi, then shrinks from view. A few seconds later, he glides into the other side of the frame with a rose between his teeth. He presents it to Marla, says *Happy Birthday!*, kisses her cheek, and leans forward to grin into the camera. Then he moonwalks smoothly backward until he is off-screen.

Everyone is in stitches.

"That is hilarious," says Alicia. "Where did he come from?"

"I don't know," says Marla, "but don't you just love him?" She turns to her husband. "Are you sure you didn't pay him?"

Pete shakes his head. "I think he came straight from the meth lab, honey."

"No way," says Scout. "He's too cute for that. Did you save the rose?"

"No," says Marla, looking sheepish. "It was chocolate. I ate it."

"He's a bit of all right, isn't he," says Fern. "I wouldn't kick him out of bed for eating biscuits. Could we watch it again?"

"Sure," says Marla.

Alicia leans over to tap Karena, her long dark hair brushing Karena's arm.

"Hey," she says. "Are you all right?"

Because Karena is staring at the laptop with her hands clamped to her cheeks.

"Karena," says Alicia. "Do you want to go? Do you need some air?"

Karena looks around.

"What?" she says. "Oh. Sure. That's a good idea. I am feeling a little woozy."

She smiles at Alicia and waves away her offer to help, then gets up to leave. But in the doorway she looks back at the laptop, on which the man is again popping out from behind the hat rack. He is tall, slender, with dark blond hair and skin darker than that. As Karena has imagined, he has a scruff of black beard. Other than that, though, he isn't much as she's envisioned him, exhausted and skinny and ragged.

On the contrary, he appears to be glowing with good health. He leans into the camera, that grin like a slice of white watermelon in his tanned face filling the screen, then starts gliding backward. Charles always did do a good moonwalk, Karena thinks. She bursts from the room, startling Dennis who has stepped out for a smoke, and strides out across the lot.

14

For a few minutes she runs around like a chicken with its head cut off—Karena has had the unpleasant privilege of witnessing this on her grandparents' farm, and now she imagines she knows how it feels. She jogs to the entrance of the lot and looks up and down Highway 20, as if Charles might actually have been at the party and just driven away. Then she turns and scans the Sandhills' grounds. She is so mad, at Charles and at herself. How could she have missed him at the gas station? Where was she, the ladies' room, showing Charles's picture to the checkout girl? And how could Charles have missed her? Karena has always thought, given the childhood accuracy of the twindar, that if she got that close to Charles, she would just know. Apparently not. Either she has had really, really bad luck or Charles is playing some sort of game.

Karena has checked with the Sandhills receptionist earlier, and Charles isn't here. But she hasn't called the rest of the motels yet, nor hospitals or campgrounds, so she hurries back toward her room. Then she sees the lamp on and stops. Alicia has come back early after all and is sitting with her head bent over a thick book, one of her meteorology texts or maybe the Bible she carries in her backpack. Karena reverses direction and heads for the lobby. It's empty, and as she dings the bell and waits for the receptionist, she watches the TV over the couch. It is showing the Weather Channel, as most televisions seem to be out here.

The graphics show a big red blob sliding down from Canada to eclipse Montana, Wyoming, and the Dakotas. Tomorrow's severe weather.

"Help you?" says the receptionist, coming out to the desk. She is wearing a shirt that might be a hospital johnny, thin blue material imprinted with teddy bears.

"Do you have a local phone book?" Karena asks.

"Yellow Pages in the corner," the receptionist says. She gazes at the TV for a moment, then wishes Karena a good night and disappears back behind her curtain.

Karena sits on the couch and makes her calls from a phone with a curly cord on it. Her brother is not registered anywhere. At the campgrounds, she gets mostly recordings. At the hospitals, weary or indifferent voices confirm no Charles, Chuck, or C. Hallingdahl has been checked or brought in. Not that this is a total surprise to Karena. He looked amazing on Marla's video. But sometimes that antic good humor was a signifier of his mania, of bad things to come, and what if he is nearly full blown? Or already there? Or is careening around doing something awful, then tomorrow will start his descent? Into the Black, he used to call it. Karena puts her head back and shuts her eyes against tears of frustration and fear.

She must sleep, the vodka and empty stomach and long hours of the road hitting her all at once, because when she wakes the TV is off and the sunburst clock on the opposite wall reads four thirty A.M. Of course, Karena thinks. She gets up, a little dazed, replaces the Yellow Pages, and walks outside. Everyone has gone to bed, and the night is so still Karena can hear the soft patter of moths hitting the lobby, a bright and empty box. Karena knows she should sneak back into her room, since they have another long drive to the Dakotas tomorrow. The more sleep she gets, the better. But now she is wide awake. She wanders to the swing set and sits, pushing herself back and forth with one foot. Karena has always loved swings, but not as much as Charles, who for several summers was obsessed with the double-boat swing in their backyard. *Come onnnnn, K*, he would whine and wheedle and plead, until Karena agreed to go on it with him, and then he'd make her stay there for hours, jackknifing his body to see how high he could make them go and singing, *Ninety-nine bottles of BEER on the wall, ninety-nine bottles of BEER!*

"Hiya," says somebody behind Karena—it's Fern, wobbling a bit in her high-heeled cowboy boots and hoodie.

"Hey, Fern," says Karena, her hand over her galloping heart. "Jeez. You scared me. What're you doing?"

Fern holds up the vodka handle, which now has only about an inch of Chuck Norris swirling around in the bottom.

"Drinking," she says. "You?"

"Swinging," says Karena.

"Mind if I join you?"

"No, please, that'd be nice," says Karena, and Fern comes around the swing set. She hands the vodka bottle to Karena, lowers herself cautiously onto the swing, then takes it back.

"Cheers," she says.

They swing for a couple of minutes, the chains creaking gently.

"Can't you sleep?" Fern asks.

"Not tonight," says Karena. "Or most nights, actually. I've got pretty bad insomnia."

"Me too," says Fern. "All I do is lie awake thinking about *him*."

"Who—," Karena begins, then remembers. "Oh, the sexy bastard guy. You mentioned him back at the truck stop, in Ogallala."

Fern squints for a second, then says, "Right, right." She takes a drink and adds, "That's him, all right. Bloody bastard. It's bad enough at home, when we're half a world apart. It's so much worse when he's right here."

Karena has a sudden unwelcome thought. "Is it—it's not Kevin, is it?"

Fern gives her a sly smile. "No," she says, bumping Karena's swing with hers. "No worries. He's still free."

"I'm not worried, I'm just trying to figure out . . ." Dennis? Karena thinks. Maybe a little old for Fern, but— Then, suddenly, she knows.

"Dan?" she says. "It's Dan?"

Fern nods gloomily. "Told you," she says. "The best, sexiest, smartest man in the whole world, and he don't fancy me. I could just die."

She starts to cry, a tear trickling down her nose, then another. Karena looks away in case Fern doesn't want to be watched, but when Fern keeps snuffling Karena plants her feet in the dirt to move her swing closer.

"Hey," she says, rubbing Fern's back. "It's okay. It'll be okay." Dan? Karena is thinking. He's so scary. He's like one of those old-school cowboys who talks without hardly moving his mouth. But maybe Fern likes the stern, silent type, and who is Karena to comment on the vagaries of love.

Fern wipes her eyes with the sleeve of her hoodie. "I love him so much," she says, her voice wobbly. "I have done ever since I set eyes on him. I'd do anything for him, move to the States, have his children. I'd bloody dip myself in a deep-fat fryer if only he'd have me. But he won't."

"How do you know?" Karena says practically. "Did you tell him? Does he know how you feel?"

"Oh, he knows," Fern says savagely. "I made a move on him, didn't I. Tour Three, 2004, we met up early and chased together a few days before meeting the rest of the gang, and it was pure heaven. But then like an idiot I had to spoil everything by making a play in a Super 8, and he told me no in no uncertain terms."

"What'd he say?" says Karena. "Maybe you misunderstood."

Fern swipes at her face. "Hardly," she says. "He said he thought I was a great girl but he just didn't have those feelings for me, and he liked his life the way it was. Said he was a happy bachelor and likely to remain so, and I should go find somebody my own age who'd treat me right."

"Oh," says Karena. "I'm sorry, Fern. That's rotten. I know how you feel."

"Do you," says Fern, glancing sideways.

"I do," says Karena. "Somebody said almost exactly the same thing to me once," and she tells Fern about William, her editor, her first lover after the divorce and in some ways harder to get over. "It was partly my own fault," she says, wrapping up. "I just couldn't let him go. I tried, but I couldn't."

Fern lights a cigarette. Her hands are trembling a little, but she seems calmer. "How'd you get over him?" she asks.

"Slowly," says Karena, "then suddenly. It was like having a terrible fever. For so long he was all I could think about, last thing before I went to sleep, first thing in the morning, and then one day, *poof!* I woke up and it was gone."

Fern nods. "Yeah," she says. "*Poof.* That's what I'm waiting for. Where's my *poof*, I'd like to know"

"Probably on its way," says Karena. "Any minute now."

"I bloody hope so," says Fern. She starts swinging again.

"Thanks for putting up with me being so pathetic," she says.

"I don't think you're pathetic at all," Karena says. "Love can be hard."

"Too right," Fern sighs, then bumps Karena's swing.

"What about Kevin then?" she says.

"What?" says Karena. She laughs, taken off guard. "What about him?"

"You and him," says Fern. "Go on, don't tell me you haven't noticed he's got a thing for you. He's utterly smitten. We've got a pool going in the van."

"You do not!" Karena says.

"S'truth," says Fern and holds up her hand. "I swear."

Karena shakes her head, smiling. "Boy," she says, "we've got to find you people some storms soon, because you're clearly hard up for entertainment."

"True," Fern admits. "But still. Have you got a boyfriend?"

"No," Karena says.

"And you're not married."

"Not anymore."

"And don't you fancy Kevin even a little?"

Karena laughs. "He's very nice," she says.

"He's *quite* nice," says Fern, with an entirely different intonation.

She puts out her cigarette. "If I weren't so hopelessly, desperately, pathetically in love with Dan, the bloody unavailable bastard, I might have a go at him myself. Why don't you go for it?"

Karena pushes her swing back and forth. She doesn't want Kevin to be her focus right now, doesn't want to think about how much she likes him and all the reasons—one in particular—she should leave him alone.

"I do think Kevin's great," she says, "but I've got other stuff on my plate."

"Such as," Fern persists.

"Well, I'm on assignment, for one. And . . ."

"Go on," Fern prompts.

Karena digs her toe in the sand, pausing her swing.

"You know that guy on the tape tonight?" she says slowly, her throat dry. "That's my brother."

Then she winces, waiting for the sky to fall. She can't believe she has told Fern this. But revealing it to Kevin was such a relief, and Karena could use the extra lookout. She hasn't been doing so well on her own.

"The tape," Fern repeats, sounding puzzled. "Oh, the video-bomber?"

"Exactly," says Karena. "That's my brother, Charles. I'm looking for him."

"Right," says Fern. She swings a bit, then says, "I'm utterly lost."

Karena laughs ruefully. "Sorry," she says, "my fault. I'm not used to talking about this. . . . Charles is a chaser, and he's—not well, so I need to find him and help him. I haven't told anyone because it's kind of a family thing. And I didn't want Dan to think I was on his tour under false pretenses."

"Riiiiiiiight," Fern says and lights another cigarette. "I won't say a thing. Mum's the word. But d'you think he's somewhere nearby then?"

"I'd imagine so," says Karena. "I missed him by inches today. So

I'd like to keep it quiet, but I'd also love your help. If you see anyone who looks like Charles . . ."

"Definitely," says Fern. "On both counts. Definitely."

"Thank you, Fern," says Karena.

"It's nothing. No worries. We'll find him."

Karena feels the sudden pinch of tears behind her own eyes then, surprising her. She sniffs them back.

"Boy, it's been an intense couple of days," she says.

"Hasn't it though," says Fern.

She hands the bottle to Karena, who takes a swig and passes it back. Then they swing idly for a while, finishing the Chuck Norris and watching the sun come up. It appears first as a gray patch in the east, then shoots white rays over the buildings across the highway. Finally, when it casts a fine gold net over the Sandhills lawn, they get up to go back to their room. Karena is stiff from sitting, and chilled and damp with dew. But while they are crossing the grass their movement startles a flock of birds in the vacant lot next to the motel, and she stops to watch them rise as one and circle into the sky. It seems an omen of something. Karena just doesn't know what.

15

That morning when they leave the Sandhills, Karena asks Kevin to drive, since although it still makes her uneasy to have somebody else behind the wheel, Karena doesn't trust herself. She's used to surviving on not very much sleep, but not this little. It's like having a hangover. Karena's stomach rolls, her eyes are grainy and tender, her reflexes off. Everything looks too bright, is moving too fast. Karena figures she'll nap for an hour, maybe two, then take over again. By the time they finish gassing up the vehicles, she's out.

When she wakes she has no idea where she is, only that she's very hot. The Jeep is stationary, and the windshield concentrates the sun into a laser beamed directly on Karena in her seat. She sits up, her body running with sweat, feeling like a bug under a magnifying glass.

The dashboard clock says six fifteen P.M. Kevin is in the driver's seat, his door open, tapping on a laptop.

"Good morning, Laredo," he says.

"Morning," says Karena. She wipes her mouth and looks at her hand with disgust.

"Where are we?" she asks.

"Badlands," says Kevin.

"The Badlands!" Karena repeats. "Goodness. I have been sleeping a long time."

She steps out of the Jeep, and a hot wind like the blast from a hair dryer evaporates her perspiration instantly. A yard from where she is standing, the road drops off and a canyon begins, stretching to the horizon and filled with rock spires. The shapes are fantastic, turrets and spikes, and the colors amazing: red, rust, purple, gold. But at Karena's back, there's an entirely different ecosystem, grassland punctuated by mesas. Prairie dogs poke from invisible holes to regard Karena with their bright, somber preacher's eyes, then vanish to pop up again somewhere else. Like a Whack-a-Mole game, Karena thinks.

She surveys the canyon, feeling a little sad. They were meant to come here once on a road trip, her family. To find the place in South Dakota where the pioneer Hallingdahls had their homestead, then drive through the Badlands to Mount Rushmore. But before they even made it over the state line Charles got wild in an A&W, pitching a fit when he didn't get a second root beer float and running round and round the tables with Siri chasing him, and they had to turn back and go home. The twins were ten then.

On the shoulder in front of the Jeep the White Whale is empty. "Where is everyone?" Karena asks.

"Down there somewhere. Sunset photo hike."

Karena shades her eyes. It will be a beautiful evening. The sky is a clear, ringing blue.

"So what happened to our storms?" she says, walking back to the Jeep and leaning against Kevin's door.

"Busted," says Kevin, without looking up from the laptop. "No soup for us. This is what we call a blue-sky bust, Laredo. The cap was too strong. It didn't break."

"Wait, hold on," says Karena and takes her recorder from her pocket. "Blue-sky bust," she says into it, "soupcap," and then she asks Kevin, "Do you mind going on the record?"

"Not at all," says Kevin. He bends toward the recorder and says, "Kevin Wiebke here, stormchaser and underwear model. What did you want to know?"

Karena snorts. She can't help it. "So, Mr. Wiebke, our storms today have not cooperated. What about tomorrow?"

"Well, funny you should ask, Laredo," says Kevin, turning the laptop toward Karena, "because tomorrow looks very good. I'm very optimistic. See this area here, over north-central South Dakota?"

Karena leans in farther to look at the area Kevin is describing. The Storm Prediction Center is showing a fried-egg shape over the Dakotas, the white outlined in green, the yolk in red. In the center of the yolk is the abbreviation MDT.

"That means moderate risk of severe weather," says Kevin. "Doesn't sound like much, does it? But it's unusual for them to issue a moderate the day before. It means they're pretty sure something's going to go up. And look at this," he continues, clicking on the tornado link. "Forty-five percent probability is impressive, usually means significant, long-lived tornadoes. I wouldn't be surprised if we got upgraded to a high risk by morning."

"That's good, right?" Karena says. "I mean, depending who you ask."

"Indeed, Laredo. It means we could have an outbreak on our hands. But remember Dennis's story," Kevin says, "the one about the tire. That happened on a high-risk day. Things can get ugly fast. We'll have to watch our timing."

"Wow," says Karena. "That's scary." But a high risk also means a higher possibility of finding Charles, she thinks. He won't be able to resist that setup.

"Not scary," says Kevin. "A learning experience. Remember what I said about fear too. You just need to know what you're doing."

He lifts his arm and curls his bicep into a muscle, then points to himself. "Like me," he says in a meathead voice. "I'll learn ya."

"Oh boy," says Karena. "Now you're just showing off."

"True," says Kevin. "But any more lip from you, young lady, and I'll make you stay after school."

He clicks the laptop shut. "Want to walk, Laredo?"

"Sure," says Karena and pockets her recorder.

They lock up the Jeep and set off into the canyon. Karena feels more overheated than ever, picturing being in Kevin's classroom after hours. She fans herself with the neck of her T-shirt, another recent purchase that says "Save a Horse, Ride a Cowboy." The road winds down in hairpin curves, the scenery changing every hundred yards. The spires tower over them, growing ever more improbable. A boulder balanced on a bottleneck. Two spines fused together, forming a key-hole. As they near the canyon floor the road curves into shadow, although the walls above them, still in sun, are lurid red as if aflame.

"Check out those striations, Laredo," says Kevin. "Pretty neat, huh?"

He comes up beside Karena and puts his hand on her shoulder, turning her.

"Like those," he says, pointing. "Know what they are? Sediment. This whole area used to be underwater, and what we're walking through now was the ocean floor. Amazing, isn't it?"

Karena nods, trying not to look sideways at his hand. Her stomach is melting.

"Oh God," says Kevin and takes his hand away. "I'm geeking out again, aren't I. Sorry, Laredo. I think I have lecture Tourette's. Occupational hazard."

Karena grins. "That's all right, Mr. Wizard," she says. "I kinda like it."

They resume walking, their sneakers gritting on white sand.

"So anyway," Karena says casually, and her stomach tilts as if she's tumbling down a hill; she's still not used to talking about this. "I saw Charles last night."

Kevin stops.

"You *saw* him?" he repeats. "Where? At the motel?"

"Not exactly," says Karena, and she tells Kevin about Charles's guest appearance on Marla's video. "It's driving me crazy," she says, "to be so close and yet so far. It's like he's playing some game with me. And I'm worried . . ."

Kevin nods. He is running a hand over his chin as if to check for five o'clock shadow, and he looks at her thoughtfully.

"You're worried he's manic," he says.

Karena stares at him. She once fell off a makeshift trapeze in

Tiff's yard and landed square on her back. She feels much the same way now.

"You knew," she says. "You knew and you didn't say anything."

She starts walking again. "This is the second time you've done this to me," she says. "How did you know? Does everyone know?"

"Hold on, wait," says Kevin, jogging up beside her. His face is flushed. "I'm sorry. I just didn't know if you knew— Well, I know you knew, but I didn't know how much you knew— Oh Jesus," he says, "I sound like a fucking sit-com."

He touches her elbow. "Please," he says. "Can we just sit? Let's sit and talk for a minute."

Karena pauses, blows out a ball of air, and nods. They have been passing nature stations along the road, wooden platforms bordered by informational placards, and she lets Kevin lead her to one a few yards away.

"Oh yeah, like this is a good idea," says Karena, looking at the signs. In addition to describing the dinosaurs that once roamed here, and giant jackrabbits and wild ponies the size of dogs, there is a large, sun-faded photo of a Western diamondback and a warning to stay on designated paths. Karena has never been fond of rattlers since coming eye to eye with a coiled ten-footer sunning itself in the New Heidelburg quarry.

"Don't bother the snakes, Laredo," says Kevin, "and they won't bother you." He sits and pats the metal bench and it makes a hollow bonging sound.

"Okay," says Karena, sitting beside him. She puts her arms around herself and shivers. Without the sun, the wind is cool down here. "So, you knew Charles is bipolar. Why didn't you say anything?"

When Kevin doesn't answer right away, Karena looks at him. He is squinting at the cliff face opposite them, at a hologram of sunshine halfway up.

"Karena," he says, "did you think I was going to make a move on you?"

Karena gives her head a brisk shake of surprise.

"Yes," she admits.

"And did you want me to?"

Now Karena looks away, at the bleached-board path leading into the desert on their right.

"Yes," she says.

"Good," says Kevin. "Because I was. Am. Am considering it. Very seriously. But there's something you need to know first. About your brother and me."

He touches her hand on the bench, and Karena turns back. Her stomach flips. Kevin is scrutinizing her, his bright hazel eyes so intent on her face she wants to look away again.

"And there's something I need to know too," Kevin continues. "This may be inappropriate, a little accelerated—after all, I hardly know you. But I do feel like there's something between us we could maybe test-drive, and if you feel the same way, I have to know going forward that you believe in honesty. Because after what happened with my ex, I believe in truth. Not half-truth, not sort-of truth, the whole truth. As in everything out on the table. Do you agree?"

Now Karena does look away, at the patch of light Kevin was peering at. It shimmers on the rock like a living thing. She takes a breath. Makes a decision. Turns back to him.

"Of course," she says.

"Good," says Kevin. "Glad we got that out of the way. So now I guess I have to tell you what happened with me and Chuck. Although maybe you won't want to go for that test drive with me after you hear it. But that's a risk I have to take."

"God," says Karena. She laughs nervously and rubs her palms on her shorts. "What is it? Am I sure I want to hear this? You weren't secret lovers or something, were you?"

"No," says Kevin. "Chuck's cute, but he's not my type." He takes her hand again. "Seriously, I don't have to tell you. I just figured, well, if it were my brother, I'd want to know. I mean, obviously you know he's bipolar. You know him exponentially better than I do. But when you said you hadn't seen him in twenty years, I just thought . . . maybe you don't know what he's capable of now."

"That's true," says Karena. "I don't." She puts her free hand to her throat. Her heart is knocking there, her mouth dry.

"Please," she says. "Just tell me. Before I have a freaking heart attack."

"Okay," says Kevin. "If you're sure."

"I'm not, actually. But I need to know. Information trumps fear, right?"

"Right," says Kevin. "Atta girl." He gives her hand a quick squeeze and begins.

16

"So this was in Oklahoma," Kevin says, "in 2001—remember I was trying to think what year I last saw him? It was in '01, and the reason it was the last time I saw him is what happened on this chase.

"I think I mentioned we used to chase together pretty regularly, Chuck and I—Charles, I mean. Whatever. Your brother. I met him at OU when I was getting my masters and he was a lunatic even then, but everyone loved him. They called him a crazy motherfucker—'scuse my French—a real wild card, but in a weird way that only added to his credibility. Because some of the best chasers are like that—I guess it's that way in any field, you've got the straight-and-narrow successful types, and then you've got the savants. Chuck was one of the savants, though definitely not of the idiot variety. He was the exception that proved the rule. The rest of us diligent meteorologists would spend our mornings, noons, and nights analyzing the data, for like *weeks* before a chase, and then two days beforehand Chuck would swoop in from whatever odd job he was doing at the time, look over our shoulders at the models, go, 'Mmmmm, nope, actually I'd play over here,' and take off. And you know what? He was always right. I'll be fu—freaked if I know how, but we'd all end up chasing our tails for at best decent shots, and Chuck would go off into the wilderness and come back with insane footage, like close-ups of touchdowns a hundred yards away. Every single freaking time.

"Of course that was because he took incredible risks, like core-punching high-precip superbeasts and getting right up in the bear's cage, and you knew you were taking your life in your hands when you chased with Chuck, but during my last year I started doing it anyway. I respected his instincts—I was always trying to learn from him—and to me he was good company. He had his off days, as you surely know, but most of the time he was upbeat and high energy and absolutely fucking hilarious. I guess too because I was about to move up to the Twin Cities with The Ex and I had this sneaking suspicion my life as a man was almost over, I was in the mood for something wild. But most of all, again, what it came down to was when it came to predicting where a storm would be, or which one to go after, or what it was going to do when you got there, Chuck was almost always right.

"So this particular day, June tenth, 2001—a little late in the season for Oklahoma Panhandle Magic but that's the thing about that area, you never know. It's my favorite place to chase, actually, No Man's Land. They call it that because it's this little strip between Texas, Kansas, and Colorado, and at first nobody wanted to claim it, and they probably had the right idea because in the thirties it got eaten alive in the Dust Bowl. The people there are tough as boots. But anyway, if I had to choose a dead center of Tornado Alley it'd be Highway 412 in No Man's Land, which bisects the Panhandle horizontally straight as a string. It's so flat there the locals say you can stand anywhere and see fifty miles, and if you stand on a tuna can, you can see a hundred, which makes it prime atmospheric playground. The fronts collide and get cranking and the storms just bowl right down 412. So that day even though the models said we'd be better off in Amarillo, I was perfectly happy to hang out with Chuck in Boise City.

"And that's what we were doing. Hangin' on the hood of Chuck's station wagon—he had an old beater in those days, God knows where he got it, but one of those seventies rockers with the wood-paneled siding like the walls of somebody's rec room. He called it the Whirl-mobile, but we all called it the Chuckwagon. It was a total piece of shit, but man, could that thing go. Anyway, there we were at this Conoco, eating burritos and watching the radar and shooting the bull with the locals, telling them, yeah, they should watch the skies, there might be some action later. And just waiting for the Cu to go up. Good times, you know. Those are my good times.

"The Cu did go up too. Nice agitated Cu like you saw the other day in Ogallala, except these were really taking off. And one of them just exploded, again like you saw but this one didn't bust. Nosiree, it went up like an H-bomb and took off down 412, and we jumped in the Chuckwagon and went after it. I was pretty freaking psyched too, I don't mind telling you, because this storm was phenomenal. Within an hour, it grew into this beautiful laminar supercell—which means it had rings, Laredo, sculpted bands wrapped around it like the rings of Saturn from its rapid rotation. And it was this deep blue-green from hail, a real icemaker, a gorgeous mothership sitting on the north side of the highway. I was out of my mind. I said to Chuck, 'You've hit it out of the park again, man. Let's reconfirm our escape options and then just sit here and wait. I think this thing's going to produce real soon.'

"But your brother said no. He wanted to keep moving, he was really agitated that day—yeah, somehow I forgot to mention that, although it's really the fact most pertinent to the story. Freudian slip, maybe. Anyway, I was wound up too, we all get that way, you have to kick it up a notch when you're chasing, to be your best and sharpest self. And that's part of the fun. But I knew Chuck could go over the top with the edgy thing, I'd seen him do it before, like three-day trips when I'd chased with him and he didn't sleep a wink, or times I'd hang out at this dive he was living in off Meridian and he would've been up for a week straight, editing video. He had this weird—dark energy about him at those times, and to myself I called it cookin' with gas. I got that from ol' Dave S. on the Weather Channel, remember him? He was one of the original anchors, and whenever there was a severe warning out he'd get all gleeful about it even though on-air you're not supposed to.

Ol' Dave just could not contain himself, though, and the moment a red box was issued for, say, Nebraska, he'd be like, 'Mmm mmm mmm, North Platte, you're cookin' with gas.'

"But that day Chuck was not only cookin' with gas, there was something different about him, something more. I didn't notice it while we were driving up there or at the Conoco, I was too distracted by checking out what was going on in the sky, but once we were out on 412, I could totally see it. It was like—well, I know this is going to sound melodramatic, but it was like he was possessed. I swear I could almost see somebody else beneath his skin. I don't know any better way to— what's wrong, Karena? Are you all right?"

Because Karena is gripping Kevin's hand. The djinn, she is thinking. He saw the djinn. The Stranger. She nods and detaches her nails from Kevin's palm.

"Sorry," she says. "I'm sorry. Go on."

"You sure?"

"Uh-huh. That last part just sounded familiar . . . now please, tell me the rest."

"Okay, if you're sure . . . Okay. So where was I. Oh yeah, the guy under Chuck's face. It was like that and not like that, if you know what I mean, it was just that he had this barely contained energy in him, like something was about to burst out, and his expression had changed and gotten all dark. He was restless and fidgety, bouncing his foot and talking nonstop about the storm, and the other storms, and maybe we'd chosen the wrong one, and he had a bad feeling we were in the wrong place, he was just sure something bad was going to happen, stuff like that. And I don't mind saying it worried me a little. Not that I thought he was going to do anything—not then. I didn't even attribute my nerves to him. I just thought, you know, his instincts were so good, maybe he sensed the storm we were looking at was going to drop some horrific wedge or something.

"So I said to him, 'Chuck, man, it's your car so it's your call, and we can move if you want to, but I think our chances of seeing something are virtually guaranteed if we stay right here.'

"And he gave me this look like I was yanking his chain—but not only that, like I was suddenly against him, like I was somebody he'd known and had trusted who suddenly wanted to do him harm. He wiped his mouth, like totally spooked, and he said, 'Are you kidding, Wiebke? You're kidding, right? We can't stay here, don't you know that? You're just fucking with me, right? We have to move, Wieb, and we have to move fast. Because otherwise he'll see us.'

"It was such a weird thing to say, coming out of the blue like that, that at first I didn't understand. Although I did get goose bumps, actually, and all the hair on my arms stood up like it does when I've gotten a little too close to a CG field—sorry, Laredo, that's cloud-to-ground, cloud-to-ground lightning. So I guess my body knew before I did, but at the time I just didn't get it. I looked all over the place, and I said, 'Who're you talking about, Hallingdahl? There's nobody out here!'

"And that was true, although we had seen some spotters back near Boise City. But out here there was nothing, literally nothing but yucca, for a hundred miles in either direction. And the storm, of course. Just sitting there and turning and growing sweet as you please.

"But Chuck got that wild-eyed look horses get near snakes, and he said, 'You are. You are fucking with me, Wieb. You're not seriously telling me you haven't seen him.'

"Then my head caught up with the rest of me and I realized he wasn't joking and I thought, Uh-oh, we're in trouble here. Still, I didn't know what it was. I had the idea that maybe Chuck was dealing, like crank or coke or meth or something, and that's why he was so wired—and no offense, Karena, but it wasn't the first time I'd wondered that. And unbeknownst to me his supplier was coming after him and had just caught up with us and that's who he was worried about.

"So I said, 'No, Hallingdahl, I guess I must be pretty dense because if somebody's tailing you I've totally missed it.'

"And he gave me that walleyed look again and said, 'You really don't see him, Wieb. You're really telling me you haven't seen him.'

"And I said, 'No, man, I haven't.' And maybe I made a mistake then, but I was so weirded out I laughed. I said, 'Who're you talking about, anyway, Hallingdahl? The Stay Puft Marshmallow Man? Jesus, man, if somebody's giving you trouble, just tell me.'

"And he nodded then, like he was relieved, and he said, 'I am. I am in trouble, Wieb. Because he's after me, and I think he's almost got me. I think he knows exactly where I am.'

"And I said, 'Who?'

"And he said, 'Motorcycle Guy.'

"And I said, 'Who?' but then he looked in the rearview, he was looking all around him all the time, and he screamed, 'HOLY SHIT, there he is!' and he gunned it so suddenly I'm lucky I didn't break my fucking neck. I did have some serious whiplash that day, I can tell you.

"But still, when I looked behind us there was nobody there. The highway was the definition of empty. So I started yelling 'Slow down, Chuck, Jesus Christ, slow down before you kill us,' and Chuck was yelling, 'Shut up, shut the fuck up, Wieb, don't fucking distract me or he'll catch us and kill me!' and I kept saying, 'Who, man, you're out of your fucking mind, there's nobody there! Just slow down! Just pull over and let me drive!' We went on like this for maybe ten miles, both of us screaming our heads off, and then Chuck must have thought he saw this mythic badass Motorcycle Guy gaining on him, because suddenly he cranked the wheel and drove us off the highway into the yucca. So basically we were off-roading in a 1977 Dodge station wagon, doing eighty, ninety miles an hour even though you'd think the tires would've gotten mired, but no such luck. Chuck was practically standing on the fucking gas, and he was still yelling and I was still yelling, and he was heading us straight into that tornadic storm. And there was a nice big gray anteater-snout funnel coming from it by then too.

"But we did get lucky, in a manner of speaking, because he flipped us before we got there. We must have hit a gully or a big rock or something because the next thing I knew the sky and ground were switching places, a couple of times in fact, and I felt like I was in a washing machine. My head got banged up pretty nicely and I broke my left wrist, though I was so hopped up on adrenaline I didn't feel it at the time. And then we came to a stop, luckily again right side up, and Chuck had knocked himself out. Which was also a good thing, because it gave me time to get out of the car and run back to the highway and flag down some help, which came along about ten minutes later in the form of this really rockin' EMT chick named Sylvia Ramirez. I've never forgotten her. She was out spotting for the Guymon Fire Department, and she got us both back to Guymon before the tornado did anything too majorly bad. Although it did put down an F2 tornado, that's what the NWS said the next day, so despite everything, Chuck had been right. He'd been right about that at least."

Kevin pauses, for breath, Karena assumes. She is staring straight ahead, concentrating on her own breathing. Forcing shallow sips of air, in, out, in, out, because ever since Kevin mentioned Charles seeing the man who wasn't there, Karena has feared she might pass out. She just about has the dizziness under control now, though. She looks down the baked-board path into the desert between the rock walls and says, "Please, continue."

"So," Kevin says. It seems to take him a few seconds to warm up again, but then he gets his stride back. "So. So, they stitched us up in Guymon, because Chuck needed stitches on his forehead and had some broken ribs, and I had my wrist, and while the ER doc was setting that I said . . . well, I said, 'I think my friend's not right. In the head.'

"And he said, 'Are you sure? What makes you think so? Do you think he's a danger to himself or others?' and I hesitated, because I knew if I was right and if it wasn't drugs causing this, they could maybe lock Chuck up for a while. But I was scared, for him and for myself and for other people too, because what if I just said, 'Nah, you know what, it's probably nothing, just some bad trip or something,' and the next day he went out and did it again? And maybe broke his fool neck this time or killed somebody else.

"So I did. I did say, 'Yes, that's right. I do think he's dangerous. And he was talking to a man who wasn't there.'

"So what happened was, they let me go but they kept Chuck overnight, and when I came back the next morning they'd carted him off to a psych ward in Oklahoma City because they didn't have those kinds of facilities on the Panhandle, and by the time I got back down there, they had him on some pretty heavy-duty drugs. Antipsychotics, I gather. Thorazine. Some bad shit. And at that point I kind of went ballistic, because, well—let's just say Chuck was not himself. I had never seen anybody in that condition, and it was pretty horrifying. He—"

Then Kevin maybe remembers who he's talking to, because he stops.

"Sorry," he says. "You get the general idea. Anyway, I asked the psychiatrist in charge was it really necessary to keep him doped up like that, couldn't they find anything a little mellower? Like Thorazine Lite, maybe? And the doctor gave me a real dressing-down. He was probably tired or used to being yelled at or had a hundred other patients to deal with or whatever, but he got this look and he said, 'Mr. Wiebke, your friend Mr. Hallingdahl is bipolar. At the time he injured himself and you, he was in the grips of a severe manic episode. He was also having a psychotic break. He has continued to exhibit psychosis, and he is terrorized by the visions in his own mind. We need to stabilize him before we can determine what else we can do for him. So yes, Mr. Wiebke, the antipsychotics are necessary.'

"Well, that took the wind out of me, and I left. The next day I had to go up to the Twin Cities for a while, because The Ex was setting up house in St. Paul and I had to go be domesticated. By the time I got back to OKC, about a week later, Chuck was gone. They'd released him. I couldn't believe it. I pitched another fit, I'm afraid. I was definitely not that doctor's favorite person. But I just could not understand how somebody who'd been in Chuck's condition could be let go. He was, though. According to his doctors he was somehow ready. I tried as hard as I could to find him after that. I went to his apartment, asked around all the places he'd worked. But he was gone. Just gone. And that was the last time I saw him."

Kevin stops. He pinches the bridge of his nose. Wind drives sand along the road, the platform, the desert floor. After a minute Kevin touches Karena's hand. His eyes are red.

"I'm sorry," he says.

Karena nods and looks away. She bites down on her lips, trying not to cry.

"Basically, it's my fault you can't find him, Karena," Kevin says. "I drove him underground when I ratted him out. I think he was too embarrassed to face anyone after that. That's why I didn't know if you'd even want to talk to me again when I told you this. But I had to tell you. And I had to turn him in. I just didn't know what else to do."

Karena nods again to show she understands—oh, she understands. She tips her head back. The sky overhead is the clear blue of a gas flame, arcing to navy in the east. The moon is up now, riding alongside a spire, and there is a single bright star.

"And, Karena," Kevin says. "I will help you find him. I'll do everything I can to make that happen. I just didn't know if you knew what you were getting into, if you have a plan in mind for when you do. Do you?"

Karena shakes her head.

"No," she says, her voice hoarse. She clears her throat and sniffles. "Not really. My friend Tiff asked if I was just going to bring him home like a puppy, and that's about as far as I've gotten. But I've just always wanted to, you know?" she cries, turning to Kevin. Her eyes fill again, her chin trembling. "I know it's stupid. I know it probably won't work. But I just want to help him. I just want to stabilize him, get him to a doctor. I just want to get him home."

"That's not stupid," Kevin says. "It's totally understandable. And it's doable. It is. It'll just take some planning, that's all."

Karena shakes her head. She glares sideways at the road and wipes her eyes on her forearm.

"It's going to be all right, Laredo," says Kevin. "Come here," and when he folds Karena into his arms she leans her head against his chest. She closes her eyes and listens to his heart lollop sturdily along, *lub-dub, lub-dub*, and when he does finally kiss her, slowly, exploring, Karena hears what could be her own blood rising to meet his or maybe the mysterious rush of wind in her ears.

17

They stay in the bottom of the Badlands until they are summoned back up, which isn't very long. Their conversation has taken a while, and shortly thereafter Kevin's cell phone rings. "We were wondering," says Dan, "whether you're planning to rejoin us or start your own nature hike company." Karena and Kevin hurry up the road holding hands, which they drop when they get within sight of the Whale. Scout winks at them, and Fern mouths, *Good on ya*, and Karena's cheeks feel scrubbed with embarrassment and sunburn, wind and Kevin's stubble.

But they don't have a chance to do anything else until an hour later, once everyone has finished checking in to the J&J El Rancho Fergusson Inn & Suites in Kadoka. Karena slings her bags into the room she's sharing with Fern and Alicia and goes back out to secure the Jeep, which is parked in the very last space in the full lot, beneath some old pines. Kevin is in the driver's seat, unhooking his laptop and the ham from their power cords to be carried safely in for the night.

"Hello," says Karena.

"Laredo," Kevin says.

Then, although she doesn't know who starts it, they are suddenly going at each other in a session the likes of which Karena hasn't experienced since high school, when she and Tiff called it mashing. That first kiss down on the wildlife platform in the Badlands was amazing, delicious and slippery and investigative in the way only first kisses can be—and this one was a doozy. Now shirts are pushed up, Karena's hair comes down, her bra snaps undone with a deft flick of Kevin's wrist. "Left-handed," she murmurs. "Nice."

"I'm ambidextrous in that category, Laredo," Kevin says against her neck. "I am a man of many skills." They kiss and grapple with each other until their mouths are swollen and their skin flushed and the windows are completely steamed, and Karena is sliding her hand up the nearest leg of Kevin's shorts and he is looking a question at her— *shall we move to the backseat?*—when suddenly Kevin pulls away. He holds up a finger.

"Excuse me a moment," he says.

Then he opens his door and steps out of the Jeep.

"AUGH!" he yells at the sky. "AUUUUGGGHHHHHHH!"

Karena laughs, though she is bewildered. She pats her hair and combs her fingers through it—it's in what her mom would have called a rat's nest. The air from Kevin's open door is pine-scented, damp and chilly, raising goose bumps on Karena's bare skin and painting her flushed cheeks. She refastens her bra and pulls her shirt back down.

Kevin has been stomping around the parking lot, circling his arms and talking to himself. Now he returns and opens Karena's door. "Ma'am," he says, ushering her out. "Welcome to the Coitus Interruptus Tour, 2008."

"Thank you," says Karena. "What's going on?"

Kevin pulls her in tight and they stand stomach to stomach, swaying a little. Karena can feel the evidence that Kevin's circuit around the lot hasn't done him much good. She sympathizes. She feels somewhat deranged.

"Laredo," Kevin says, his breath stirring her hair, "I'd rather poke myself in the eye than say what I'm about to say, and I'm sure every red-blooded male in America is screaming in protest—but frankly, this kind of . . . activity . . . makes me a little nervous. For one thing, I'm on the clock here. I have this awful work ethic that makes me respect professional boundaries, and you're a guest on my tour."

"Actually, I'm media," Karena reminds him.

Kevin draws back to give her a look. "All the more reason," he says. "I don't want you to give me bad press." He pushes her hair aside. "Besides," he says in her ear, "I've had it with this gearshift in the gut thing, haven't you? I'd rather do this right, Laredo. I'd like to be horizontal with you."

Karena's stomach jumps in happy agreement, and her thinking self is relieved. She is on assignment too, and she needs to keep her head clear for Charles. "I concur on all points," she says.

"You do?" Kevin says, and sighs. "I was afraid you'd say that. I was kinda hoping you'd talk me out of it. Oh well. We'll figure something out."

He takes her face in his hands and they kiss awhile longer until Kevin steps back with a grimace, adjusting his shorts.

"Okay, now I'm really done," he says, "unless you want me to do something illegal. Say good night, Laredo."

"Good night, Laredo," Karena says.

"Smartass," says Kevin, giving her a whack on the corresponding body part. Karena lets out a startled squeak. "See," Kevin says, turning and walking away backward, "that's what I'm talking about, that little noise right there. I want some more of that." He tips a finger at her. "Good night, Laredo," he says, "sweet dreams."

Then he drags himself across the parking lot in an exaggerated Quasimodo lurch. Karena laughs. She knows how he feels, though she hasn't felt it since—high school? College? Sometime back in the beginning, when everything was brand-new. She watches Kevin until he's gone into the room he's sharing with Dennis, then turns away, shaking her head and smiling. "Whoo," she says, and locks the Jeep for the night.

18

The next morning Karena wakes up grinning. She lies gazing at the ceiling, listening to the air conditioner and Fern's snoring, replaying the events of the previous day. Then she rolls her head to the side and looks at the clock. Eight fifteen. They are right on the cusp of Central and Mountain Time, so Karena's not sure whether they're supposed to be at briefing in forty-five minutes or if they have an extra hour. But she decides not to take any chances. She gets out of bed and cracks the curtains, peering out. The light from the lot dazzles her.

"Good morning," Alicia says, pushing herself up on one elbow, her hair a dark skein across her face.

"Good morning," Karena says. She loves how everyone on tour starts the day with this simple civility. It should be commonplace back in the Cities too, but with traffic and weather and the rush through daily obstacles, it's often not.

"Bloody hell," says Fern from beneath her pillows. "What bloody time is it?"

"After eight," says Karena. "Rise and shine."

She twitches the curtains back farther to see the J&J El Rancho Fergusson Inn & Suites billboard. Such a long name for such a modest motel. Karena loves it. She loves that there's a café attached to it. She loves the fact that heat is already simmering off the vehicles in the lot, meaning there's plenty of energy for storms later and she might find her brother. She loves everything about this morning.

Alicia pads over in her Cowboys T-shirt and boxers, her pretty face screwed up against the glare. "What's it like out?" she asks.

"Sunny," says Karena. "Steamy. Perfect."

Alicia smiles and bumps her hip against Karena's.

"Somebody sure is in a good mood this morning," she says. "Could it be because of a sunset walk she took with somebody else?"

"Sunset walk, my arse," says the lump that is Fern. "She got a jolly good rogering is more like it."

"Fern!" says Karena. "Good Lord."

"Oh my," says Alicia, then, "What's a rogering? Do I want to know?"

"No," says Karena, "you don't," and she throws a pillow at Fern.

Fern rises majestically up out of her nest of blankets, her eyes slitted and her purple hair every which way.

"'Course you do," she says grumpily. "Everyone should have a good rogering once in her life, even you. It's the kind of quick and dirty shag that bangs your head against the wall and blows your bloody socks off," and she tosses the pillows aside and stomps toward the bathroom. Halfway there she pauses and looks back at Karena, putting up a hand to shield her eyes.

"Just as I thought," she says. "Afterglow. Bloody blinding."

"It is not," says Karena. "Because nothing like that happened, Fern!"

The bathroom door slams.

Alicia peers at Karena with interest. "You *do* seem to have a glow about you."

"I do *not*," says Karena. "If anything, it's sunburn."

She goes into the alcove to wash her face. She is sunburned, Karena sees, as she applies makeup in the cramped space crowded with bulging toiletry bags and hair dryers and cell and camera chargers. She should look like hell. She hasn't exercised in days, she's running on sleep fumes, she's been subsisting on a convenience store diet of pretzels and

V8. Her brows are like something from a nature special and her fingers bristle with hangnails from washings with gas station soap. But the red cheeks and feverish eyes and even the few extra pounds suit Karena, making her look less like an anemic, exhausted thirtysomething reporter and more like the girls in her grandmother Hallingdahl's samplers. Actually, she has never looked better.

Fern comes out of the bathroom in a turban and towel.

"Glowing," she says as she passes.

"Zip it," says Karena.

She packs up, deciding to forgo a shower in exchange for a decent breakfast, and carries her bags out to the Jeep. It is already hot and humid. The sun glitters off mica in the lot. Karena pauses to snap photos of the J&J El Rancho Fergusson Inn & Suites billboard.

"Good morning," she says to Dan Mitchell, who is wresting his breakfast, a Mountain Dew, from the vending machine near the motel office.

"Good morning," says Dan, unsmiling as a pirate.

Dennis is smoking outside the café, and when he sees Karena he hastens to open the door for her. "Hilloo!" he says, in an Inspector Clouseau accent that reminds Karena of Charles. "Good morning! Fancy meeting you here!"

"Good morning," Karena says, grinning.

Inside, the café has an attached gift shop, gray-and-red linoleum, red vinyl booths, and Formica tables. Locals in plaid and overalls turn to eye Karena with faded interest as she enters the dining room. The wall chalkboard offers bottomless coffee for ninety-nine cents, daily specials for under five dollars. Karena decides Kadoka is one of her favorite places. She spots Kevin in a corner booth with Pete and Marla, his hair seal slick from his shower, and her stomach leaps. She nods professionally. Kevin nods professionally back. Karena takes a seat at a center table with Dennis, Melody, Scout, and Alistair.

"Good morning," she says.

"Morning," says Scout, smiling at Karena. "Did you have a good night?"

"I did," says Karena, and Scout quickly touches her hand, then gives Karena a menu.

Karena orders the coffee and the Eighteen-Wheeler Omelet, which contains bacon, ham, sausage, tomatoes, peppers, onions, mushrooms, and hash browns and comes drenched in cheese sauce. She eats the whole thing and two slices of rye toast besides, for a while happily conscious only of filling her empty stomach, the sun slanting through the blinds, and Kevin's presence warm at her back. When she is done she gets out her recorder as Dennis explains the day's setup. He draws diagrams on a place mat with such enthusiasm that his pen rips the thin paper.

"So this," he says, circling a dot several times, "this is the target. If it were me, I might go a little more north, toward the Cheyenne Grasslands Area. But Dan's set on playing this region right here, between Pierre and Oweeo. And Dan's the man."

"Dan's the man," repeats Alistair. He is focused on a handheld video game, rocking slightly, thumbs working.

"You're the man," says Dennis to Alistair, who smiles but keeps playing. "How'd you like to see a tornado today?"

"Brilliant," says Alistair. "Eight thousand four hundred fifty-five."

"That's the number of tornadoes he's seen," explains Melody. "From *Twister*."

"Seen the film one thousand four hundred nine times," says Alistair to his game, "six tornadoes in the film, eight thousand four hundred fifty-four."

"Right!" says Dennis. "Gotcha."

"That's amazing," says Scout, smiling. A stripe of sun tangles in her blond hair for a second, turning it into a nimbus. "You're an amazing guy, Alistair, you know that?"

"Brilliant," says Alistair.

"Today could very well be eight thousand four hundred fifty-five, my friend," says Dennis. "Yup. Mother Nature could very well let her dragons out to play today."

"Dragons," says Alistair and hoots softly.

Kevin's party heads through the restaurant, and Karena's table too gets up to leave. Karena lingers to eat the remaining toast crusts, then uses the ladies' room—always a priority before hitting the road. By the time she gets back out to the gift shop to pay, she is last in a line of locals, so while she waits she browses the books on South Dakota history, the polished rocks and pine soaps and sketches of Mount Rushmore. Trinkets, Karena thinks. Beneath the counter is a display of silver-and-turquoise rings.

"Are those Sioux?" Karena asks the woman at the register.

"You bet," the woman says, "Lakota. Fella brings 'em in from Pine Ridge Reservation, guy by the name of Black Cloud."

"They're beautiful," Karena says. She wishes she could buy one, but she doesn't have time to try them on.

"Are you all tornada chasers?" the woman asks. She has a severe overbite and cropped brown hair like Carol Burnett, a similar toothy warm smile.

"Some of these guys are," says Karena. "The rest of us are just along for the ride."

"Well, I hope you brought a basement with you," says the woman. "Remember the '97 tornada, Bob?" she says to an old rancher standing behind Karena with his check in hand.

"Sure do," he says. "Spencer. Destroyed the town. Peeled the paving right off the road."

The woman hands Karena her change, and Karena sets the mullet photo on the counter.

"You haven't seen this guy, have you?" she asks.

The lady slides on glasses hanging on a string of flowered beadwork from her neck.

"You know," she says, "I believe I have. Only without the fancy hairdo. Is this the fella who had the ring that looked like Howie?"

She passes the photo to the rancher, who holds it at arms' length.

"Who's Howie?" Karena asks.

"Howie's this guy right here," the woman says and taps her finger on the display case, indicating a ring with a stern sterling-and-turquoise face, along with a headdress and feather earrings of inlaid onyx. "Never thought we'd see anyone else with a ring like Howie, did we, Bob?"

"Nope," says the old rancher. "But this fella had one, all right."

He flaps the photo, pinching it in an old man's long yellowing nails.

"He still got this poofy hair?" he asks, squinting one eye at Karena.

"I hope not," says Karena.

"'Cause if you're talkin' a guy with much shorter hair than this, and a little darker and about twenty years older, I think you got your man."

"Excellent," says Karena, beaming, "thank you so much! When was he here?"

The woman turns to Bob for confirmation. "I'm going to say . . . yesterday? For dinner?"

"Yep," says Bob. "Alls he had was the soup. He coulda used more, I remember thinking. High wind'd blow him away." He hands the photo back to Karena. "He got some Lakota in him?"

"Not that I know of," says Karena. "Why?"

"Just had that look," says the rancher. "And we figured why else would he have that big ring? Welp, don't let the tornada boogeyman getcha."

"I'll try not to," Karena says as she leaves.

The Whale is already idling at the entrance to the lot, the Jeep behind it with Kevin in the driver's seat. Karena has missed briefing.

"Sorry," she says breathlessly as she swings in. "But we had a Charles sighting."

"Hold on," says Kevin, and into the handset he says, "We got her. Proceed."

"Copy that, SLM," says Dennis. "KE5 UIY, mobile," and the Whale turns left out of the lot.

"So guess what," Karena says as Kevin follows suit. "Charles was here yesterday."

Kevin nods. "Good," he says. "Not surprised. He's probably chasing the same setup we are—along with everyone else. It's going to be a zoo out there."

His tone is matter-of-fact, his face impassive as a cop's behind his aviators. Clouds play across the lenses as they drive across the overpass. Karena looks at him, startled and a little hurt. Why is he still being all business when they're alone? Did she do something wrong? Is Kevin going to pretend last night, yesterday, didn't happen? But then he reaches over and curls his hand around the nape of her neck.

"How did you sleep?" he asks.

"Like a baby," says Karena, and is amazed to realize this is true. For the first time in ages, she didn't wake at four thirty A.M. "You?" she asks.

"Terrible," says Kevin. "I was up all night in agony, thanks to you, Laredo."

Karena laughs.

"Now you mock my pain," says Kevin. "Nice. Very nice."

They merge onto I-90 East behind the Whale. Karena toes off her sneakers and props her feet on the dashboard, watching the land fly past. Silver roll clouds float across the highway like submarines, the sun shining through them. Standing sentinel atop a ridge is a lonely water tower, blue and lollipop-shaped in the dissolving mist.

"This could be a very big day," Kevin says. "I think today's the day, Laredo."

"I know," Karena says. The water tower is just like the one in New Heidelburg, the one Charles loved to climb. She turns to watch until it is out of sight.

Kevin laughs. "Somehow I suspect we're talking about different things."

"I know," Karena says again. She pats his knee and looks out the window, smiling.

19

All morning they travel east on I-90, the mist burning off as they go but a thick cloud blanket developing. "Stratus deck," says Kevin, squinting up through the windshield. "That's not good." He and Dan and Dennis discuss strategy on the ham while Karena listens and watches the land blur past outside the window. She has never seen anything like it, territory so untouched it looks prehistoric. Just grasslands rolling to the end of the world. Karena knows there are people here, that although the towns grow sparser and the distances between them greater, there are rich and complex and damaging lives being played out just beyond her vision. Still, she is entranced. She half expects to come upon a brontosaurus lifting its head from one of the small ponds that nestle among the swells, vegetation dripping in its jaws as it watches the Whirlwind convoy pass.

"I love it here," Karena says suddenly. "I'd love to live here someday."

"You would?" says Kevin, hooking the handset back in its cradle. "Now that surprises me, Laredo. Here I'd pegged you for an urban girl, never without her latte. You are a woman of great complexity."

"Well, of course I'd have an espresso machine," Karena says. "Still."

She resumes her contemplation of the land flowing by, the horizontal layers of blue sky, green grass, clouds. How to explain why it makes

her heart leap, her throat hurt with wistfulness and longing, just looking at it?

"I guess it's hereditary," she says. "Our great-greats had a homestead out here, we don't know where exactly. Somewhere near Martin,
we think. They had a soddie at first, then an actual house. But they
must have suffered some kind of loss, locusts or blizzard or something,
because they had to retreat to Minnesota where there was already family set up. My great-great grandmother, Libby—Lisbet—she never got
over it. She pined for the empty space."

"Wow," says Kevin. "That's fascinating, Laredo. You know this
how?"

"Letters," says Karena. "Letters Libby wrote to her cousins in New
Heidelburg, where she ended up. My dad has them. Or maybe the Foss
County Historical Society."

"I'm jealous, Laredo," says Kevin. "My family's just a bunch of
little Polish sausage makers from Chicago."

"Well, that's nice too," Karena says diplomatically. Then she sighs.
"I do romanticize it," she says. "I know it was a harder life than I can
possibly imagine. Just to get water you had to walk miles sometimes, or
you could die from something we wouldn't think twice about now, like
childbirth or appendicitis. . . . But sometimes I wish I could be transported back there, just to see what it was like. No TV, no phone, no
Internet, just people sitting around and talking in the evenings. Listening to the wind."

"You don't think you'd get bored?"

"Maybe," Karena says. "But I think I'd find it . . . peaceful."

Kevin nods.

"That's nice, Laredo," he says. "I think peace is underrated."

A few miles later they exit onto 83 North at Murdo and stop at the
travel plaza off the highway to hurry up and wait. The tourists pinball
lazily around the area. Alistair wanders the railroad tracks behind it,
taking pictures of the rails. Melody stands to one side to watch him
while chatting with Pete. The other women form the usual line at the

ladies' room, so Karena stays outside to eavesdrop on the guides. They have gathered by the driver's door of the Whale, conferring. The cloud cover is a problem, suppressing the heat necessary for the storms to form, and the debate is whether to drive out from beneath it or wait for it to erode. "I keep thinking we should be farther north and west," says Dennis, leaning in to tap Dan's laptop. "There's already clearing there, and we could catch the cells as they go up."

But Dan shakes his head. "Then you're getting into the Cheyenne River Reservation, and there's no road network," he says. "We could get spanked. Here we'll have our choice of escape options, and given how fast this stuff's going to move if and when it gets going . . ."

Dennis massages his beard. "True," he says. "Still. I just have a feeling—"

They bring up screen after screen of data, and Karena wanders off. She uses the now-unoccupied ladies' room, shows the mullet photo to the convenience store clerks, canvasses the chasers. There are a good amount of them, including a vanload of meteorology undergrads eating Bomb Pops and playing Frisbee. But it's nothing like the tailgate party at the Ogallala Sapp Bros, and as more and more chasers depart, Karena starts to fret. What if Charles is playing a different area too? Karena makes herself a root beer float, Charles's favorite drink, and carries it outside to where Fern and Alicia and Marla and Scout are sitting on the wall of ice-melt bags piled against the convenience store.

The women fan themselves and eat candy Marla passes out, Mallo Cups and Nut Goodies and Cherry Mash. They stare at the tall grasses across the highway. Fern smokes and gazes gloomily at Dan. Everyone seems listless and scratchy. The air is sullen beneath the thick gray clouds, so humid that they're all dripping with sweat.

"I sure hope we see something today," Scout says.

Marla examines the sky from beneath the brim of her flame hat. "Doesn't look promising, does it?" She leans past Karena to Alicia. "Maybe you could pray us up some, Allie," she suggests.

"Oh, I have been trying," says Alicia, "believe me."

She smiles at Karena.

"I've been praying we find your brother too," she says.

Karena's mouth drops open. She turns to Fern, sitting beside her, with a glare of hurt and reproach: *Thanks a lot.*

"Bloody hell, Alicia," Fern says, grimacing and chuffing out smoke, and Alicia looks mortified.

"Oh no, I'm sorry," she says. "I forgot I wasn't supposed to know."

Flushing miserably, Fern starts to apologize, but Marla grabs her arm and gives her a shake. "Don't blame Fern," she tells Karena. "It's not her fault. We ganged up on her."

"We did," Scout agrees. "We bullied her mercilessly. After you ran out of the party the other night, Karena. We could tell something was going on."

Karena shakes her head. "Never mind," she says. "It's fine."

"It's not," says Fern. "I shouldn't have said anything. I never betray a trust, as a rule." She grinds out her cigarette viciously. "I just thought, we've so little time, and five sets of eyes are better than two—"

"We want to help," says Scout.

"And we didn't tell the guys," says Marla. "Honest. We're very discreet."

Karena can't help but laugh.

"I know," she says. "It's all right. Really. Thank you. Fern?" Fern hunches her shoulders. "It's okay," Karena says. She maintains eye contact and nods until Fern manages a smile.

Karena stands and slaps off the seat of her shorts, looking at the Whale. She'd better go over there right now and tell Dan what she's been up to, since it's only a matter of time until he finds out. What did Karena expect? This is what happens. Information leaks, people play telephone, situations mushroom out of control. Karena doesn't blame Fern. It's Karena's own fault for having opened her mouth in the first place. And while it's not necessarily bad the ladies know about Charles—in fact, Fern is right, from a logistical standpoint the more lookouts the better—what's dangerous is the erosion. Karena just cannot afford her new habit of confession, of blabbing things that need to be kept private. Because what if this too spirals out of control? What if Karena blurts something out or starts talking in her sleep? Karena sighs and sets off toward the Whale, but before she can reach it Kevin and Dennis turn, reeling them all in, yelling that it's time to go.

20

Kevin drives again, and despite the sugar from Karena's float, or maybe because of the crash following it, she falls asleep, for when she wakes up they're at yet another gas station. This one is in a city, though, a small two-pump operation instead of the travel plazas she's gotten used to, and Karena is a little discombobulated by the busy intersection alongside it, the series of streetlights marching into the distance and the pickups and muscle cars zooming past. As Karena sits up two beaters cut across the corner of the lot and plunge back into traffic to make the light, rap thumping from their windows. Toto, I guess we're not in Kadoka anymore, Karena thinks. She feels sticky all over, her mouth from her float, her hair tickling her face in spiderweb strands, attaching itself in the humidity. It must have just rained here, for steam is rising from the pavement.

And Karena realizes something else: The sun is out. Oil rainbows dance on the tar. But the sky ahead is that dark blue like a bruise, and everything around her glows that saturated Technicolor that happens when a storm is forcing light into one quadrant of the sky.

Uh-oh, Karena thinks.

She opens the door and gets out, planning to ask Kevin where they are. But she doesn't see him. The gas pump is sticking in the tank, and Karena pulls it out, screws on the cap, collects the receipt. She has been covering all her own expenses because the *Ledger* will reimburse her; now she makes a note to repay Kevin. He comes out of the store toward her, chugging a canned espresso drink.

"Bruh," he says and shudders. "I don't know how you can drink this stuff."

"Well, I don't drink *that*," Karena says, peering at the little can with its rattlesnake pattern. "Are we in Pierre?"

"We are," says Kevin, "and we're gassing up one last time before we head into it."

He motions Karena into the Jeep and swivels his laptop toward her—back in Valentine he somehow mounted it onto a stand. Karena hooks her hair behind her ears and stares in at the radar. A huge green-and-red pinwheel is eclipsing most of the county just north and west of Pierre.

"Zoiks," she says. "That looks like a huge one."

"It's healthy all right," Kevin says. He pulls her back out of the Jeep and points toward the blackening sky. "That's what we're seeing over there. And check out the flags. What do you notice?"

Karena looks at the pennants on the adjoining car dealership, the American flag over a Subway. They are all standing out stiff, flying toward the storm.

"They're pointing northwest, right?" Kevin says. "That means the wind is from the southeast, what we call a backed wind. That's what we like to see, Laredo. That wind's carrying moisture all the way up from the Gulf to feed our hungry storm. And this thing is ravenous," he adds, checking the radar again. "In fact I'd guess it's a beast."

Karena shivers despite the heat and rubs her sticky arms. Now that she's more alert she sees lightning flare on the horizon, hears the corresponding static on somebody's radio, then the *wah-wah-wah* of the emergency broadcast signal. Karena's blood freezes at the sound. Still the traffic flows past, the truck emitting the signal moving through the light. Karena can't believe these people are just going about their business as if it's a regular day.

Dan calls from the parked Whale, "Let's go, people!" Dennis and Fern, who are smoking out on the sidewalk, quickly snuff their cigarettes and jog over.

"You ready, Laredo?" Kevin asks.

"As ready as I'll ever be, I guess," Karena says, climbing into the Jeep.

"Then buckle up," says Kevin. "Seriously. This is the real deal."

They wind through the steep, stepladdered streets of Pierre, careful to stay behind the Whale despite the heavy traffic. Karena has the sense of reaching a new elevation, climbing ever higher. She opens the glove compartment and wipes her face with a wet-nap, ties her hair back, readies her recorder and camera. She is not terrified this time, not with Kevin, but she does have that preternatural feeling of alertness, her skin crawling, her eyes ticking from side to side as if to store up information. As they leave the city Karena's hair stirs on her arms and tries to stand up, and she wonders if it's adrenaline, or if she's reacting to a drop in barometric pressure as animals are said to do before a bad storm, or if the air, which tastes metallic, is electrified.

They proceed through the suburbs, and Karena looks at the little houses on their neat lawns beneath the now-hissing trees and hopes they will be there later. Amazingly, a woman is out mowing her grass. She waves at the Whirlwind vehicles and shouts something. Karena shakes her head. Then Pierre is behind them, and they are in the grasslands as abruptly as if the capital had never existed. These plains feel different to Karena from the ones outside Kadoka, more desolate, wilder, and again she has the sense of climbing, that they are driving along the roof of the world. Her ears pop. The sky is closer. It's darker too, shading to black on the horizon. The storm looms before them, the grasses bending toward it, and Karena thinks of Dennis saying, *Something about the storms that day. . . . they seemed angry.*

It is almost familiar by now: Karena's awe at the storm, her wonder and dread; her tiny helplessness in the face of it, the Whirlwind vehicles like ants approaching a carousel. They start to see chasers parked in the turnarounds, setting up tripods and video cameras. Karena waves. The chasers wave back. None of them is Charles. She also notices something new—and her stomach drops—law enforcement. Sheriffs' prowlers and statie SUVs parked on the shoulder, flashers lit, pointing toward the storm. They must expect it to be bad.

"How big is it now?" she asks, leaning over to see the laptop, which Kevin has facing him, and she hears her younger self saying, *How close is that?* and Charles replying cheerfully, *Oh, not so far . . . I'd say about five miles.*

Kevin glances at the laptop. "Don't know," he says briefly. "No signal. I wish to God we had Threat Net in here," he mutters, more to himself than to Karena, and she looks at the Whale with its signal-boosting antenna.

Kevin unhooks the ham handset. "KB1 SLM calling KE5 UIY," he says.

"This is UIY," says Dennis. His voice is smooth and crisp, all jocularity gone.

"I have no signal, UIY," says Kevin. "What is Threat Net showing? Do we have a Wheel of Fortune on this storm?"

"Stand by," says Dennis. Then he says, "SLM, we have three. One shear marker of a hundred twenty knots. Threat Net's showing upward of five-inch hail."

"Copy that," says Kevin. "Is there a hook echo? Has the storm been warned?"

"Affirmative, SLM. There is a classic hook echo, and this storm is tornado warned."

"Copy, UIY. Thank you. What's our ETA?"

"We're looking to intercept in about fifteen," says Dennis. "Dan thinks this storm might be a right-mover, so we're keeping an eye on our south option. Better to turn tail and face some RFD than try to punch the core of this thing. We'll keep you posted. Stand by."

"KB1 SLM, standing by," says Kevin and replaces the handset.

Karena has been scribbling notes on her steno as a backup to her recorder, and now she runs over them. Some of what she's heard she knows, for instance that a hook echo is a tornadic signature on radar, the little curl showing where the tornado will form beneath the storm. Other facts she's less clear on.

"Five-inch hail, is that softball size?" she asks.

"A little bigger than softballs," says Kevin.

"And a right-mover, what does that mean?"

"It's when a storm takes a sudden dive east," says Kevin distractedly. He is leaning forward, hugging the wheel, to peer through the windshield. "When that happens the storm usually encounters warmer air, and it turns into a superbeast."

"Oh," says Karena. "Okay."

She writes this information down, then closes her steno pad and sits back. The road has curved slightly and the wind is rushing into the storm from their eight o'clock now, buffeting the Jeep and making the overhead wires shriek like a teakettle coming to boil. The base rounds into view as they approach. This is always a surprise to Karena, how something so huge can have structure as opposed to just encompassing the whole sky. This storm's base, however, is nearly touching the ground. Karena tries to swallow. Her throat clicks.

"Kevin," she says, pointing, "is that a wall cloud? At our eleven o'clock?"

"If it is," Kevin says slowly, "it's the biggest one I've ever seen. It must be three miles across, but . . . yup, I think it is. Good eye, Laredo."

He unhooks the handset and is transmitting this information to the Whale when they pass a Volvo station wagon parked on the shoulder. It is just like Karena's at home except it is bright canary-yellow, vibratingly aglow against the storm-blackened sky. A man is standing next to it, beneath a sign that says OWEEO, 10 MI. He is wearing shorts and sandals and a T-shirt, and his clothes and hair ripple in the wind. His dark blond hair. His skin darker beneath it. He has a beard, and as the Whirlwind convoy passes he waves cheerfully, his grin a startling white in his tanned face.

"Kevin," Karena cries. She grabs his arm, making him drop the handset. "It's Charles! That's Charles back there! Stop the car, go back!"

The Jeep swerves, and Kevin swears. He guides it back onto the road, then bends to grope for the handset, which bobs on the end of its curly cord near his feet.

"Excuse me," he says, "but do not ever ever ever do that again. It's dangerous under any circumstances but especially right now, and you must never interrupt a ham radio operator when he's transmitting, okay?"

"Okay," says Karena, "but we just passed Charles, Kevin, that was him, I'm sure of it. We have to stop and go back!"

"SLM, what's going on?" says Dennis. "Is there a problem?"

"No, sorry, UIY, we just had a moment here," Kevin says.

"Did you copy my last transmission?"

"Negative. Say again, please."

"Dan thinks a funnel is developing at our eleven thirty," says Dennis. "Stand by."

"Copy," says Kevin.

"Please," Karena says. "Please, Kevin." She doesn't dare touch him again, but she implores him with her eyes. She holds her hand up level with the dash to show him how it's shaking. "Just for a second," she says. "Just let me say hello and find out where he's going, then we can catch up with them."

Kevin glances at her, his expression flat and tight. Then he swivels to look at the wall cloud, from which a black nub is protruding.

"Please," says Karena. "It's been twenty years!"

"Fuck," Kevin says.

Without slowing significantly, he wheels the Jeep around. The tires squeal and smoke and there is the smell of burnt rubber. Then they're speeding back toward Pierre, in the direction they've come.

"Oh, thank you," says Karena, "thank you so much—"

"I could lose my job for this," says Kevin. "Not to mention compromising everyone's safety. You never leave the tour! Never ever ever! So a little silence will be much appreciated."

"Okay," Karena says humbly.

"One minute, Karena," says Kevin. "That's it. If we get back there and don't see him . . ."

Karena leans forward in her seat as if to urge the Jeep on faster. The sky is a light gray ahead, black in her wing mirror. The Jeep rocks on its frame. The grasses bend toward them on the diagonal, nearly flattened.

"SLM, where are you?" says Dennis. "We've lost visual. If you're behind us we can't see you. Keep up, please."

"UIY, we'll catch up with you," says Kevin, his face grim.

"What's the problem, SLM?"

"We'll catch you, UIY," says Kevin again.

"This is not good, SLM," says Dennis. "We've got a massive right-mover here with tornado on the ground. Repeat, cone tornado on the ground. We need you to catch up immediately—"

"Copy that, UIY," says Kevin and sets the transmitter down.

"Okay, Karena," he says, casting quick glances in his rearview and side mirrors, then looking back at the road. "Where the fuck is he?"

Because they have reached the OWEEO, 10 MI sign and the shoulder is empty. The road is empty. There is no sign of the yellow wagon. There is nobody there.

"Oh no," Karena moans. "Oh my God."

She whips around to look in every direction.

"But he was right there," she insists. "He was!"

She shakes her head. "Maybe he dropped back a little," she says, "toward Pierre. Maybe if we just keep going a tiny bit in this direction—"

"Maybe nothing!" Kevin says. "Maybe he's not there at all!"

He smacks the dash and Karena flinches.

"God DAMN it!" he says.

"I did see him, Kevin," Karena says. "I swear."

"That is NOT the point," Kevin roars. "The point is that even if he was there, he's not there now, and meanwhile we've lost the van and we are MILES behind them and there's at least one tornado on the ground between us and them—God DAMN!" He brings the Jeep to a stop.

"Hang on," he says and cranks the wheel back around.

"I'm sorry, Kevin," Karena says. "What can I do? Can I do anything to help?"

Kevin is accelerating out of a hasty three-point turn, but suddenly he slows, then brakes.

"Ho-ly Christ," he says.

"What IS that?" Karena asks and puts a hand over her mouth.

For the highway ahead of them has disappeared into the storm. It is not a tornado, at least not like any tornado Karena has ever seen. It is more that the storm has simply come down onto the ground. The road now runs straight into a churning brown-black mass, a mile-high wall that has swallowed the prairie in front of them.

"What is it?" Karena whispers. "Is it . . . a dust storm maybe?" She is thinking of the famous Dust Bowl photograph of a black cloud like a tidal wave bearing down on a tiny farmhouse.

Kevin is still staring at the giant brown-black wall, but at the sound of Karena's voice he comes back to himself.

"No," he says. "Holy fuck, no. That's no dust storm. That's a wedge. It's the biggest fucking wedge tornado I've ever seen. It must be two miles wide—"

He scrabbles for the transmitter.

"KB1 SLM calling KE5 UIY," he says. "UIY, do you copy?"

The radio doesn't respond. Kevin fumbles for the volume knob and screws it all the way up. His fingers are shaking.

"This is KB1 SLM. UIY, come back, please."

. . .

"KB1 SLM for UIY. UIY, do you read me?"

. . .

"UIY, this is SLM. Copy?"

. . .

Kevin looks at Karena, who stares back at him. Kevin shakes his head.

"We've lost the van," he says hoarsely.

21

They pull off the road, hazards flashing, to let the wedge pass. Kevin calls the local National Weather Service office on his cell to report what they're seeing, their position, and what course the storm seems to be on. Straight east now, a right-mover as Dan predicted, tracking toward Oweeo. When he hangs up they sit on the shoulder, their faces flashing yellow, every so often saying, "Oh my God," but otherwise not conversing. They just wait. Karena has always heard tornado survivors say the sound of the tornado is like a train, and she thinks it is something like that but not entirely accurate. People must say this because a train is a noise that can be felt with one's feet, in the stomach, as it rumbles closer. This giant wedge is vibrating the Jeep, shaking dirt down into the drainage ditch, but the sound it is making is much lower, almost below human auditory range. It is as though the earth itself is growling.

When the rippling black-brown wall exits stage right, when they start to see a strip of light beneath the storm's base and Kevin determines the worst of the danger has passed, he puts the Jeep in drive and they head back north toward Oweeo. Several times he pulls over to let emergency vehicles pass, fire engines and ambulances and the sheriffs' prowlers and SUVs they saw earlier. Karena is sitting with her behind a few inches off her seat, craning in every direction for the yellow Volvo. Kevin never stops working the radio.

"KE5 UIY, this is KB1 SLM, copy?" he says, over and over. "KB1 SLM calling UIY, come in please."

About three miles outside Oweeo rain is falling, gently, and something else: pink material wafting out of the sky.

"What is that?" Karena whispers. Her throat is hoarse. "It looks like cotton candy."

"It's asbestos," says Kevin. "Insulation."

Karena glances at him, his strained face, then goes back to scanning the scoured landscape for her brother's car.

"UIY, this is SLM," she hears Kevin saying. "Come in, please."

They crawl along, starting to see damage. It looks familiar to Karena from the Weather Channel, the evening news, footage the whole world has seen of tornado-strewn destruction. Except, of course, the perspective is different. Everything is bigger. Closer. They are right up next to it. And it's not just two-by-fours piled on the ground, some sentimental cameraman focusing on a teddy bear or family photo in the wreckage. There are animals. Cows. They lie at unnatural angles, some twisted, some impaled. Some still lowing, with a sound that raises Karena's guard hairs and reminds her of her brother crying. One cow has been torn in half. She sees a horse too, on its side, kicking and nickering. Raising its head, trying in vain to get up. There is a pole driven neatly between its ribs. Its eye rolls as the Jeep passes, and Karena can hear it screaming.

"KE5 UIY, this is SLM. Do you copy? KE5 . . ."

And the smell. Nobody has ever told Karena about the smell. It is a thick, green, wet musk of stripped vegetation. As they near what used to be Oweeo, they start to see trees too, or what remains of them, stripped branches sheared off at shoulder height. They have been whittled to points, their white inner meat showing. It is as though a giant lawnmower has come through here and chewed off everything above five and a half feet. Then they start to smell natural gas from pumps ripped out of the ground, the rich fruity smell of it choking through the Jeep's closed windows. Kevin shuts the air vents.

"KE5 UIY, this is SLM. Come in, please . . ."

Karena touches his hand and pulls her T-shirt over her nose, breathing through the thin material. She repeats her roadkill prayer under her breath: *God bless souls of animals, God bless souls of animals, God bless souls of animals.* She adds, *God bless the people of this town.* And: *God bless my brother, please bless my brother. Please let me find him. Please let him be all right.*

Suddenly something thunks on the Jeep's hood, and Karena jumps, then turns to watch it roll away: a can of Campbell's tomato soup.

"KE5 UIY, come in . . ."

Kevin guides the Jeep onto the bare dirt to go around a door lying in the road, an inner door with a child's sparkling stickers on it, spelling out CAROLEE. The backside of the storm bulks to their right, white on top and black on the bottom, bulging with breast-shaped mammatus. Another is moving in from the west. It is like being caught between two atomic mushroom clouds—the storms are that immense. The light is strained, choked. Insulation drifts pinkly down.

"Where are you, Charles?" Karena mumbles into her T-shirt. "Where the fuck are you?" She closes her eyes to pray.

"KE5 UIY, this is KB1 SLM. Do you copy?"

"SLM, this is UIY," Dennis's voice crackles faintly. "We're all okay here. You?"

Karena sits up and drops the T-shirt. "Oh, thank God," she cries, and Kevin starts nodding.

"Yup," he says, "yup, yup. Yes, we are," and he quickly blots his eyes with the back of his wrist.

"Give your position please," says Dennis, as Karena says, "Please, ask if they've seen a yellow Volvo station wagon."

"One minute, UIY," says Kevin.

He glides the Jeep to a stop and peers around.

"We're somewhere in the damage path," he says. "As you're probably aware, there are no road markers because there's no road. I can see what looks like a two-story brick wall about a half mile to my right, at my one o'clock."

"We're about a quarter mile ahead of you, then, SLM. Keep coming."

"Copy that," says Kevin. "Also, we need to know, has anyone seen a yellow Volvo station wagon?"

"Stand by," says Dennis, and Karena twists the hem of her T-shirt, rips off a hangnail.

"Please God," she says. "Please God please—"

"Negative, SLM," says Dennis. "Nobody in our vehicle has seen a yellow wagon."

"Oh no," Karena moans and starts to cry.

"Copy," says Kevin. "We're coming to find you, UIY. We may be a little while, with the debris."

"Copy, SLM," says Dennis. "But as quickly as you can, please. Dan wants to drop south. We've still got debris falling and another cell to our ten o'clock. It's not safe."

"I see that, UIY," says Kevin. "Over and out."

He puts the receiver back in place and reaches for Karena's hand. She clutches his, looking through her window and weeping.

"Okay, Karena?" Kevin says. "Hang in. We'll find him."

About ten minutes later they come upon the van with its hazards on, canted on what used to be the road. Dennis is standing by the driver's door, his hands on his hat, staring around. Dan is on the phone. The tourists are huddled near the side door, looking stunned, and although Dennis has said they're all right, Karena does a quick head count: Fern Alicia Melody Alistair Scout Marla Pete oh thank God. Melody is bent over, her fluffy yellow head hanging between her knees, Marla rubbing her back. Fern and Pete are talking, Fern holding a cigarette that because of the gas she can't light. Scout is looking transfixed at one of the whittled trees. It's Alistair who spots the Jeep first, and he barrels toward it, yelling.

"Eight thousand four hundred fifty-five," he says, batting at his head. "Eight thousand four hundred fifty-five, eight thousand four hundred fifty-five, eight thousand four hundred fifty-five!"

"What, buddy?" Kevin says, catching him, but Alistair beats Kevin's arms away and screeches.

"The tornado count," Karena says, "the number of tornadoes he's seen," and then, because Alistair's aunt is still hyperventilating, Fern comes rushing over to help.

"Right, Allie," she says, "Eight thousand four hundred fifty-five, brilliant." She pushes back her sweatshirt hood to give Karena and Kevin a kiss each, then draws Alistair away.

Dennis walks toward them, and they meet in the middle, picking their way through boards studded with nails, skirting downed wires. The light is peculiar, lemon bright, making Dennis's lined face look malarial.

"What's up, brother," he says to Kevin, and they hug, slapping backs. Dennis hugs Karena too. He smells acridly of smoke and sweat.

"Man," he says, when he lets go. "This is bad. This is worse than anything I've ever seen. And we're not even within town limits. God help these people."

He takes off his fishing hat for the first time in Karena's acquaintance and holds it to his chest, his gray hair flattened in a ring beneath it. "Man!" he says again. "Man, that was bad. I think I screamed like a girl when I saw that thing change course and come at us. I never, ever want to see anything like that again."

"You're not alone, believe me," says Kevin. "Where'd you guys go to get away?"

"East," says Dennis, "then south. Luckily Dan found a little ranch-to-market option that wasn't too bad. At least it was gravel. If it hadn't been for that . . ."

He shakes his head.

"But you made it," says Kevin.

"We did," says Dennis. "We had to run in front of that wedge for about five minutes, though, and man, I'm telling you, those were the longest five minutes of my life. I thought this was it this time. That's all I could think. This is it."

He shakes out a cigarette, considers it, and sticks it behind his ear.

"Where'd you two ride it out?" he asks.

"South also," says Kevin. "But back more toward Pierre, about ten miles out of town."

Dennis nods. "That's right," he says, "you totally dropped out of sight, I almost forgot. What's up with that?"

"We had an emergency," Kevin says, nodding at Karena. "She thought she saw her brother."

Karena winces, then looks straight at Dennis. It's time for the truth now. Charles will be best served by it.

"Your brother?" Dennis repeats. "That doesn't make sense. Why would your brother be all the way out here? Is he a chaser?"

"Yes," says Karena. "He's Charles Hallingdahl. Chuck, I mean. He's driving the yellow wagon I asked about."

Dennis stares at her for a minute, then says, "HAH!"

Karena glances at Kevin, who shrugs. Dennis stalks a few feet off with loose-jointed, bobble-headed grace, kicking boards and talking to himself. "This is just blowing my mind, man," he is saying. "Blows my frigging mind. First the world's biggest wedge tornado almost kills my sorry ass, and now . . ."

He circles back and bends down to peer in Karena's face.

"Sure," he says, "I see it now. Christ on a pony. Chuck Hallingdahl's sister. Why didn't you say anything?"

"It's a long story," says Karena.

"I bet it is," says Dennis grimly. He shakes his head. "I just bet it is," and although this isn't her top concern right now, Karena can see she's lost Dennis's trust, and she feels bad.

Then a state police SUV comes toward them, lights whirling, tires crunching over the debris. The statie's window lowers, and he leans across his seat in his Smokey Bear hat. He's so young, Karena thinks, bright-cheeked and open-faced, he looks like he's nineteen years old.

"Excuse me, folks," he says, "but I'm going to have to ask you to return to your vehicles and vacate the area. We need to secure it for safety purposes."

Dan Mitchell steps out of the Whale, papers in hand.

"We're aware of that, officer," he says. "We're a licensed stormchasing company, and we got separated from one of our vehicles during the storm. I was just waiting for them to catch up and now they have, and as soon as we plot a safe course out of here, we're on our way."

"I appreciate that," says the statie.

"Officer," Karena says, "have you seen a yellow Volvo station wagon?"

"No, ma'am," he says, "sorry, I haven't. Now please return to your vehicle."

He looks at Dan. "More storms on their way," he says. "Think we're in for a long night?"

"Unfortunately, yes," Dan says. "It's a very active system, and they're going to keep training over this area."

The statie sits up and looks through his windshield, chewing gum.

"That's what I was afraid of," he says. "Well, you folks move along now, and be safe."

"Thank you, officer," says Dan. "Same to you."

"Wait," Karena says. She taps on the statie's window as it rolls back up, and it stops in its track.

"Please," she says. "I'm searching for my brother. I saw him earlier in the Volvo and I'm afraid he was caught in the storm. Isn't there any way I can accompany you into town? Just to look?"

The statie shakes his head. "Sorry, ma'am," he says. "Emergency personnel only. If we find him and he's in need of medical attention, we'll bring him to one of the three area hospitals, St. Mary's, the Gettysburg Med Center in Pierre, or the Holy Infant."

"Hold on," says Karena, taking out her scratch pad, "could you please repeat that?" and that's when Marla comes up beside her.

"Officer," she says, "I'm Marla Johannssen from Iowa, and I'm an RN. I'd like to help any way I can."

The statie looks dubious, and Marla snatches off her flame cap with a curse.

"You have ID, ma'am?" he asks, and Marla opens her wallet and hands it in. The statie considers it, then passes it back.

"All right, Mrs. Johannssen," he says. "Hop in."

"Thank you, officer," says Marla. "Just one more thing. This is my partner, and I don't go unless she does," and she picks up Karena's wrist and waves it. "She'll help us get the word out about whatever support we need. She's with the Minneapolis *Ledger*, you know. She's press."

22

They rejoin the Whirlwind tour that night at the Taco Hut in Pierre, where Dan Mitchell is calling around, trying to find lodging in a city choked with chasers, media, and emergency management. The tourists sit pushing cardboard boats of fast food around plastic trays. They are subdued, saying little. Karena, after hugging everyone hello, sets up shop in a corner with her laptop and her cell phone, calling the hospitals about Charles and filing a story about the destruction of Oweeo for the *Ledger*:

> *. . . As of 10:30 CST the tally is 14 known dead, 47 wounded, 11 critically. But it could have been far worse, said Oweeo's town manager, Chris Sides. "The town is totally destroyed," he said. "There's nothing left. But the sirens did go off, the NWS issued a warning. We had 17 minutes of lead time. Without that, casualties would have been unimaginable."*
>
> *But as the National Guard was called in and sealed off what remained of Oweeo except for emergency crews, another supercell thunderstorm moved in, jeopardizing ongoing rescue efforts. "I can't even stand to watch," said Marla Johannssen, 50, an RN from Iowa who was in the vicinity with Whirlwind Tours, a professional stormchase company. "The way the trees*

were snapped off," said Johannssen, "the tornado sharpened them like pencils. And to see them reaching up toward another storm, in that green light like they were underwater—it's just something most people never see, a unique version of hell."

Contributions to help the tornado's victims can made through the Red Cross.

Karena reads her piece over, combs out two hundred words, and sends it in as an attachment. Instantly her phone rings, the *Ledger* copy desk verifying facts. When she is done going through the story with them, she again calls St. Mary's, the Gettysburg Medical Center, the Holy Infant. Nobody matching Charles's description is at the hospitals. Nor in their morgues. This is good, Karena tells herself—right? Empirically, it's good. Charles isn't dead. He isn't critically wounded. But that could mean he is still out there somewhere, injured. He could be trapped in his yellow wagon, pinned beneath an eighteen-wheeler or a refrigerator. He could be lying on the ground, bleeding in the rain, more storms moving in.

Karena rubs her eyes and checks her phone again. Already four new messages from the copy desk. Then there is a hand on her shoulder, and Karena looks up. Kevin.

"Hi," she says. Kevin looks tired, delicate purple patches beneath his eyes.

"Hi," he says. "How's it going?"

Karena nods, then shakes her head, then shrugs. "It's going."

"No news?"

"Not of Charles."

"Good," Kevin says. "I'm sure he's fine. We'll find him."

He puts a hand on the adjoining chair and Karena waits for him to sit, but he remains standing. "Listen," he says, "I don't mean to bug you, but do you have a second to talk about something?"

"Sure," Karena says. "One sec," and she rapidly texts a correction to the copy editor. Then she looks up at Kevin inquiringly.

"Karena," he says, and now he does sit. "The tour's leaving."

"Okay," Karena says. "Where're they going? We can catch up."

"No," says Kevin. "You don't understand. I'm sorry to have to tell you this, especially right now, but they're leaving-leaving."

Karena shakes her head, not in negation but because this information does not compute. She can't process it. Her brain won't take it in.

"Leaving Pierre?" she says.

"Yes," says Kevin, "leaving Pierre, but also the area. Going way south. Dan couldn't find rooms for this big a group, they're all booked up, but we would have had to do some driving tonight anyway."

"What?" Karena says. "Why?" She stares at Kevin, stumped. "What do you mean? To get away from the storms?"

"To get back toward Oklahoma City," says Kevin. "Look, the tour's only a week long. And the guests have to be in OKC day after tomorrow to catch their flights home. So tomorrow would have been a drive day anyway, but now we're way, way north. Much farther than we should be. So Dan's decided to get a head start."

"Okkkaaayyyy," says Karena. "So—where are they going?"

"Back to Nebraska," says Kevin. "Dan's booked rooms all the way down in North Platte, which I personally think is insane, but there you go."

Karena just sits there, trying to comprehend all this. It doesn't quite work. She is tired, so tired she can't think. The bad food, the late nights, the giant wedge, the injured of Oweeo, Charles. She is trembling slightly, a rocket shaking itself apart as it enters the last stages of the atmosphere.

"Laredo?" says Kevin. "You still with me?"

"Sure," says Karena. "So . . . what happens now? I guess we could switch off driving, if we have a lot of coffee . . ." She looks at her laptop, her phone. "Except no, what am I talking about, I can't go. The story's almost put to bed, but I need to be here in case there's follow-up. And Charles—"

"I know," says Kevin. "You need to stay to try and find him. Of course you do."

He puts his elbows on his knees and leans forward.

"Karena," he says, "I'll stay with you, if you want."

"Oh," says Karena. "Really?"

She looks at him. He is blushing slightly. "Kevin, that's sweet, but I can't let you do that."

"It's not sweet at all, it's self-interest. I'm a helluva lot closer to home here than I am in Oklahoma City. I'm from St. Paul, remember? Why would I want to go all the way down there just to yo-yo back up? Besides," Kevin adds, "no offense, Laredo, but you look beat. I think you could use the help."

Karena scoops her hair back and sighs. "That's true," she admits. "I probably could." She can feel her body shutting down, as if somebody's going around inside and turning off all the unnecessary systems to conserve the main power source.

"You would really do that?" she asks.

"I would really do that," says Kevin.

"Okay then," Karena says. "Please do. Stay. With me." She looks down at her lap, suddenly shy. "Thanks," she says. "Thank you."

"My pleasure," says Kevin and stands. Dan Mitchell is beckoning him over.

"Up and at 'em, Laredo," says Kevin. "Let's go say good-bye."

He holds out a hand to Karena to help her out of the chair, and she lets him pull her up, then glances at her laptop. But it'll be safe here. There's nobody else in the Taco Hut. Karena pockets her cell phone and follows Kevin outside.

The night is humid, the air drenched. Lightning flashes, illuminating towering Cu in the distance. Thunder mutters. The tourists are already gathered by the passenger's door of the Whale in slickers and sweatshirts. They shuffle, none wanting to be the first to say good-bye. Then Melody leans from inside the van, where she is sitting with Alistair.

"I guess this is it, then," she says. "Lovely meeting you. Be safe."

"You too," says Karena, and waves to Alistair, who is intent on his handheld computer game.

"Bye, Alistair," she says, and Alistair bobs his head. Then Scout steps forward.

"I'll go," she says, and pulls Karena in for a bone-crushing embrace.

"Be good, kiddo," she murmurs. "Hold on to your guide. He's a keeper."

She steps back, smiling, and Pete comes over next. He gives Karena a quick squeeze, then waves to his wife.

"Come on, Marl," he says.

Marla shakes her head. Beneath her flame cap her face is red and swollen with all the tears she didn't shed back in Oweeo, when she was attaching IV lines, arranging mangled and bleeding people on stretchers. She steps forward, enfolds Karena in a damp hug, starts to say something, chokes, and flees to the van. Pete gives Karena a last apologetic wave and climbs in beside his wife. In the Whale's dim interior light Karena can see him talking to Marla, Marla's head bowed.

Alicia is next. She kisses Kevin, then Karena. "God bless you," she says to Karena. "Your brother too. I'll be praying for both of you."

"Thank you, sweetheart," says Karena, "we could use that," and Alicia gets in the van. And then there's only one tourist left.

"C'mere," says Karena and holds out her arms to Fern, who looks very small and pointy-headed in her enormous hoodie. Fern crushes out her cigarette and walks slowly over. As they embrace Karena can smell smoke and tacos in Fern's purple-black hair.

"I think I'm going to miss you most of all," she says in Fern's ear, and they both laugh, sniffling a little. "Good luck with that fever breaking."

"Bless," says Fern. "And you get some good rogering. Be in touch, yeah?"

"I will," Karena says and means it.

Fern detaches and shuffles away. A hand reaches out to pull her into the Whale, and the passenger's door slams behind her. Dennis leans over to buss Karena's cheek, more a scratch of beard than anything, though he won't quite meet her eyes. He squeezes Kevin's shoulder and climbs in the driver's seat, and Dan Mitchell, opening his own door, shows a crack of teeth that might, Karena thinks, actually be a smile.

"Nice to have you with us," he says. "I hope you find your brother."

Karena puts a hand on her throat. She can't speak.

Then Dan gets in too, and Dennis puts the Whale in reverse. The big van backs up, cruises behind the Taco Hut in the drive-through lane, reemerges on the other side. As Karena and Kevin watch, the Whale turns left onto the quiet, rain-slick street. Karena catches a glimpse of Dennis in profile, saying something, Dan leaning toward the glow of a screen. The radar. The Whale glides past, and although Karena can't see the tourists behind the tinted passenger windows, she waves. Kevin does too. They stand side by side as the Whale accelerates down the street, pauses at a blinking yellow stoplight, speeds up again. Then it vanishes, with one last wink of taillights, beneath the apocalyptic dark sky.

23

The Taco Hut manager asks them to leave at midnight, regretfully explaining he's already stayed open an hour past his usual closing time. Kevin and Karena apologize and drive down, down through Pierre to the motel Kevin has found for them, the Hi-Plains Inn & Suites. Karena stays in the Jeep while he checks in, staring through the windshield. She has progressed to the stage of exhaustion beyond thought or movement—only her right eyelid twitches, a periodic little flutter.

Kevin returns, jogging past the Jeep's headlights in the rain, which is coming down hard now. He drives them to the very end of the lot, next to the chain-link fencing, the territory of flatbeds and truck cabs. This looks ominous, Karena thinks, gazing at the encaged lightbulbs in the stairwells, the gray doors dented as though people have tried to kick them in. She has heard the tourists' horror stories about occasional nightmare rooms, default options when everything else for miles around is booked up. Holes in the walls. Bugs in the beds. Floors that vibrate for no reason. Karena has had good lodging luck on this tour, but maybe it has just run out.

Kevin frowns through the water-runneled window. "Sorry, Laredo," he says. "It was the best I could do."

"It's fine," Karena says. "I appreciate your finding it. Thank you."

Kevin hands her a plastic key card advertising a car wash. He appears a bit abashed.

"I got two rooms," he says, running a hand over his wet hair. "I didn't know whether—I mean, given the circumstances—well, it's been a really long day, and I wasn't sure if . . ."

". . . if I had enough energy to satisfy your perverse animal lusts?" Karena says, a flicker of life returning.

"Exactly," says Kevin, looking relieved. "You're gonna need to eat your Wheaties to do that. Meanwhile, I figured we could both use some sleep."

"That was very thoughtful."

"However, Laredo, the rooms are adjoining. Separated by just a door. And judging from the looks of this place, it's probably a very thin and flimsy door. So if you get scared in the night . . ."

"I'll come a-knockin'," Karena says and turns to retrieve her laptop and bag from the backseat.

"Or if you get cold," suggests Kevin, "or if you want to play cribbage—I'm a mean cribbage player, Laredo. Or if *you* start to experience base animal desires . . ."

"Got it," says Karena.

"Because, you know, the rooms are *adjoining*," says Kevin in his meathead voice. He flexes a bicep and points between himself and Karena. "That means they're, like, right next to each other. They're *together*."

Karena leans over to give him a kiss.

"Good night, Mr. Wizard," she says.

"Good night, Laredo," he says. "Don't let the bedbugs bite. Literally."

Karena makes a face at him, then runs through the rain to her room. Once inside she flips on a light and stands against the door. It's not that bad, really. It couldn't be more bare-bones: forest-green coverlet, carpet, and curtains, two prints of exactly the same painting, an Indian drum, hanging askew over both beds. But it seems clean enough, except for a cloying sweet smell. On her way to the bathroom Karena

notices a couple of belly-up beetles. That explains the odor. It's fumi-
gation.

She washes her face, pinches the coverlet onto the floor—she
doesn't even want to think about what's living in the fabric—and settles onto the sheets to make her calls. Her story has been filed, but she
needs to check the hospitals again. No Charles. Then the motels. No
Charles anywhere. Without undressing, just kicking off her sneakers,
Karena shuts off the light and lies down.

Instantly the room seems to surge forward as if she's still in the
Jeep. Whenever she closes her eyes this happens. Worse, Karena becomes convinced there's a person in the next bed. She knows this can't
be true, but she's sure if she looks over, she'll see the guy there, a gray-
faced dead man. She rolls on her side, her back crawling, and stares at
the window, which lights up every few seconds like an X-ray plate with
lightning. Another storm moving in. Karena counts: one-Mississippi,
two—and the giant crump of thunder shakes the motel, setting off car
alarms in the lot.

"Great," Karena says. She gets up, shoves her feet in her sneakers,
and pads to the window, pulling the curtain aside. Lightning and thunder explode simultaneously, like a bomb, making the room phone go
ting! The rain gusts sideways, the trees beyond the fence lashing back
and forth like undersea creatures in a strong current. Then there is
a strange sound: *rrrrOOOWWWwww! RRRRooooowWWWW!* At first
Karena thinks it's a cat caught out in the storm. It takes her a minute
to realize it's a tornado siren, rotating on its pole.

rrrRRROOOOOwwwww! RRROOOwwwwww! "Okay, that's it,"
says Karena, and knocks on the door between the rooms.

"Kevin," she calls. "Are you up?"

The door opens.

"I am now, Laredo," says Kevin. He is in his boxers, which, Karena
is bemused to see, have fortune cookies on them. "You change your
mind about a little Wiebke sugar? Come to Papa."

"That sound," says Karena, ignoring him, "it's the tornado siren,
right? Should we get in the bathroom? Or is it safer to drive away?"

Kevin reaches out and takes her arm.

"Come on in here," he says. "It's nothing to worry about, just a sheriffnado or something. False alarm."

"Are you sure?" Karena says dubiously.

"Sure. I'll show you."

Kevin guides her over to the dresser, where his laptop glows like a night-light. The radar shows a thick green line sweeping across both of the Dakotas and northern Nebraska. There are red patches embedded in it, and lots of blinking white lightning strikes, but no Wheels of Fortune.

"See," says Kevin, "little to no rotation. It's gone straight-line now, a big linear mess."

"Is that bad?"

Kevin shrugs. "Bad, good, depends on your definition. It means the storms aren't tornadic."

"Okay," says Karena, and then the wind, which has cranked up to a steady keen, utters a bifurcated shriek that makes it sound like the motel itself is trying to take off. The laptop winks out and Kevin's cell phone beeps as they lose power. The lights die in the lot.

"Jeez," Karena says, wrapping her arms around herself.

"Why don't you let me do that, Laredo?" Kevin suggests. "Come lie down."

They adjourn to the bed, where Karena faces the window and Kevin fits himself in behind her. The sheer animal comfort of his body against her back is amazing. His skin smells of warm rich bread now since he's been sleeping, and warmth kindles in Karena's stomach. But with the wind still screaming and the siren rotating—*rrrOOOWWWWW! WWRrrroooooowwwWW!*—desire seems far away.

"Why do you do it?" Karena asks.

"Hmmm?" Kevin says. He is easing his hand up beneath the back of Karena's T-shirt. "What's that?"

"Chase," she says. "Why do you chase?"

Kevin's hand pauses, a starfish of heat on Karena's skin.

"I chase because I love storms, Laredo," he says. "Simple as that."

Karena sighs, and Kevin seems to take this as a challenge, because he adds, "I was born this way. I've always loved storms. My first memory is of dragging my mom outside to show her a T-Cu—that's a thunderhead to you, Laredo. I didn't know what I was looking at, I just knew I loved it. I must have been three, four years old."

Karena shakes her head.

"You and Charles," she says. "He was the same way. He used to crawl toward lightning. Sleep on the doormat during thunderstorms. Our mom would find him in the morning when she went for the paper. I guess—I just don't get why, exactly."

"Why what?"

"Why you can't admire them from a distance. Why you have to put yourselves in harm's way. I do understand to some degree. The storms are beautiful. And weird and awe-inspiring. But they're so destructive too."

Kevin slides his hand out from under Karena's shirt and rests it on her waist.

"First off," he says, "you know better than that by now. We don't put ourselves in harm's way. We stay out of its path—exceptions like today notwithstanding. Who was better off, us or those poor people stuck in Oweeo?"

"Yes, but—"

"Hold up, Laredo, I'm not finished. Plus, if it weren't for us, a lot more people could have died. You said it yourself, in your article: The NWS issued a tornado warning *seventeen minutes* before that thing hit the town. Who do you think called that in? Spotters. Chasers. Dennis and Dan. We do a public service, you know."

"I can see that, but—"

"Wait, Laredo. Sorry, but you've hit a nerve here, because these are misapprehensions so many people have, and it just really turns my crank. So finally, the destructive potential of storms—yes, it can be horrific. As we saw today. But today was an *anomaly*. Do you know how many mile-wide tornadoes there've been in the last century? Like, fifty. Over a hundred years. I've been chasing twenty years, and I've seen

only three: Greensburg," Kevin says, tapping fingers on Karena's hip
as he counts, "and Moore. And today's. And do you know how many
tornadoes are categorized as violent?"

"No," says Karena, "but I suspect you're going to tell me."

"Damn straight," says Kevin. "Less than two percent."

He gives her hair a gentle tug.

"Severe weather," he says, "it's really just Nature's way of correct-
ing an imbalance. It's wind and moisture rushing from one place to
another, and when the imbalances between them get serious enough,
there's a storm. The more extreme the imbalance, the more severe the
weather. But the storm corrects the imbalance, Laredo, and afterward
the atmosphere is stable again."

"Okay, Mr. Wizard," says Karena. "Thank you."

Kevin is quiet for a minute. Then he tents his fingers on her
tailbone.

"You sound unconvinced," he says.

"Not necessarily," says Karena, "I'm just thinking," and she is.
She's thinking about imbalances. She's thinking Nature is majestic,
yes, but vicious too. She's thinking that whatever Kevin says, Nature is
something to be wary of, because of its two-faced system. Because
storms are necessary to scour the atmosphere. Because chaos is re-
quired before order. Because a human brain can be so scrambled—
naturally, scientifically, just chemicals and synapses—that a few hours'
peace, let alone euphoria, must inevitably be followed by a descent into
hell. Nature may be beautiful, but it is cruel in its extremes.

"Charles used to think there was a connection between his instability and atmospheric instability," Karena says. "That that's why he
was so good at finding storms. Because in essence he was one."

"Did he?" says Kevin. "He never told me that. Interesting theory."

The siren starts up again, swinging round and round on its pole.
RrrrowwwWWWW! WwrrOOOOOwwww! Karena bolts up.

"God, that sound freaks me out," she says. "It used to terrify me.
Not Charles, though. It was his favorite. *Siren* was his first word."

"Not yours, I take it."

Karena shivers. "Hardly," she says. Her first word, come to think of it, was *Charles*.

Kevin sits up too and puts an arm around her.

"Are you scared now?" he says, his breath warm in her ear.

"A little," Karena admits.

"Don't be," says Kevin. He pushes her hair to one side and kisses her neck. "Trust me, I'm a professional. I'm here to protect you with my superior skill and knowledge."

"Oh boy," Karena says, rolling her eyes. "We're toast."

"Now, that is just not very nice, Laredo," says Kevin, hooking his fingers into the waistband of Karena's shorts and sliding them around to the button. "After everything we've been through," he adds, undoing it, "you haven't placed complete and utter faith in me yet?"

"No way," says Karena, as her zipper clicks down inch by inch.

"Wise girl," says Kevin, and pulls Karena back onto the bed.

24

When Kevin makes love to Karena, she goes places. This astonishes her. She has had younger lovers and taller ones and fitter ones, and she would never have believed that this short, stocky stormchaser with his sun-reddened arms could drive her mad. But he does. Kevin is clever and inventive and extremely energetic, and there's something about his body that feels like home to Karena. She loves everything about it: his calves blocky from soccer, the sweet spot on his neck, the heat of his mouth. Maybe it's pheromones, the way he smells, good ol' chemistry at work, but everything about him fits Karena just right.

And then there are the places. During their first lovemaking session, while the siren is still going off, Karena finds herself transported to her backyard in New Heidelburg, the air smelling of pine, the grass spiky beneath her feet. The second time, before dawn, it's the house on the Hallingdahl farm, with its glorious white snowball bushes. The third time, when they wake at first light to find each other naked and together, it's the New Heidelburg town pool, where Karena sunbathes slick and sizzling, her skin fragrant with baby oil.

"Wow," says Kevin, when Karena tells him about this. He is lying on his back with one arm around Karena, blinking thoughtfully at the ceiling. "I make you go places, Laredo? Nobody's ever said that to me before."

"Nobody's ever taken me anywhere before," says Karena, sliding her hand down Kevin's stomach to pluck at what she and Tiff used to call the goody trail. Karena loves Kevin's stomach most of all, although it is admittedly more beer belly than six-pack. The solid curve of it reminds her of the drawings of bread in the Richard Scarry picture books she and Charles loved as children. In those illustrations the loaves always had wavy lines of heat coming from them.

"Watch it there, Laredo," says Kevin, "unless you want to be starting something."

"Again?" says Karena. "Aren't you done yet?"

"Woman," he says, "I am just getting warmed up." He kisses Karena's temple, then asks, "So, these places I take you, are they good places?"

"They are," says Karena. "They're my favorite places."

"Then I'll take that as a compliment," says Kevin.

Suddenly he rolls over and parts Karena's knees with one of his own in a single, fluid movement.

"Patented Kevin Wiebke Knee Sweep," he says. "You like? Now, tell me where you want to go, and as your trusty guide, I will be happy to take you there."

An hour later, when the sun is spoking through the parking lot's chain-link fence, they stagger into the shower. "Good grief," says Kevin. "Okay, my legs are weak. I have to say, Laredo, you may look sweet, but you're an animal."

"Me!" says Karena. "Who literally pushed me off the bed? You're the animal."

"I'm an animal, I'm an astrotravel machine, make up your mind," Kevin says, uncapping the tiny bottle of shampoo. "So what's our plan for today?"

Karena stands with her head down as Kevin massages the gel into her scalp. She feels like a bird with salt on its tail, hypnotized. She loves anything to do with her hair.

"Well," she says, "I'd like to stay another day at least. To keep checking the hospitals and emergency centers until the search-and-rescue's done. How long do you think that'll take?"

"I don't know," says Kevin. "Probably a day or two. It depends on the extent of the damage."

He turns Karena to face him. She is shivering despite the hot needling spray.

"Look," Kevin says, "if Chuck's here, we'll find him, but frankly I don't think he is. We saw him as we were going *toward* the wedge, right? And then we turned around and came back, and he wasn't there. For him to get anywhere near that tornado, we would have passed him. He probably dropped back when he saw how dangerous the situation was, and now he's miles from here, safe and sound."

"Well, safe, anyway," says Karena. "I hope."

She thinks he probably is—not so much because of Kevin's theory, although its logic is comforting, but because Karena believes if Charles were dead, she would know. And not because of the twindar, which has proven fairly ineffective. Karena would just know in the same way she knew Siri died an hour before Karena actually confirmed it. At the time Karena was driving home from Norwegian Ridge, the town one over from New Heidelburg, with some of the rommegrod the old ladies made there—thinking if Siri could be persuaded to eat anything, it might be this pudding. But as Karena passed Siri's favorite field, the one with contour-farmed pillowy rectangles of corn between rows of grass, Karena had started to cry steadily. There had been no call from the neighbor sitting with Siri. There had been no pinch. Karena had just known.

So Charles is probably alive now. Karena just needs to stay and make sure. And, of course, to find him.

She tells Kevin this, adding, "Can you do this? What's your schedule?"

"I'm officially a free man until August fifteenth, when soccer starts," Kevin says. "Turn around, I'll do your back," and he soaps it briskly.

"I was thinking," Karena says, "in addition to the hospitals, we could drive around to the fast-food places and gas stations to look for Charles's car."

"That's a good idea," says Kevin. "What was it again, a yellow wagon?"

"Volvo," says Karena.

"Okay, let's download an image of one to photocopy and hand out," says Kevin. "With a photo of Chuck too, if you have one."

"Oh, do I," says Karena. If Charles really is unharmed, please God, it'll serve him right to have his mullet photo plastered all over Pierre.

"You're brilliant, Mr. Wizard," she tells Kevin.

"Pshaw, it's nothing, Laredo," says Kevin. "Oh dear, look at that, I dropped the soap. It's right by your foot—could you pick it up, please?"

"Nice try," Karena says. "I'm not falling for that one. . . . Oh my, in the shower, Mr. Wiebke? I thought stormchasers didn't like to get wet."

"Extenuating circumstances, Laredo."

"I can feel that," says Karena. "Very extenuating."

"My, you're mouthy," says Kevin. "Let's put that mouth to better use, shall we?" He kisses her, hands busy. "We've got a long day, Laredo, so let's hurry and see if we can make you go somewhere you can behave."

25

They leave on Wednesday afternoon after another day and night of fruitless searching, leaving Charles's mulleted and tuxedoed image and Karena's cell number all over Pierre. Again they head east on I-90, Karena driving, then Kevin. As they near the Minnesota state line, Karena watches the topography change. The high plains give way to farms, first one, then a handful, then more and more until finally that's all there is. Dark green fields of soy and corn—*knee-high by the Fourth of July means a good harvest*. Red barns with white piping. Clusters of silos. Cows. These are prosperous family spreads with big houses and numerous vehicles, proud and clean beneath a blue sky dreamy with Cu, the late-summer sun flowing golden over the land like syrup. It's as perfect as the picture on the back of a cereal box, and it fills Karena with dread.

She tries to parse the source of it: Is it because she's exhausted, traumatized, because this strange adventure is over, because she doesn't have that much to go back to? Because of her uncertainty about what will happen with Kevin? Because of her uncertainty about what has happened to Charles? All of the above. Nothing seems stable. Karena thinks of the grasslands outside Kadoka, and then of Fern and Alicia and Marla and Scout, and then her grandmother Hallingdahl, her uncle Carroll, her mom, Siri. For all intents and purposes, Frank. And Charles. Karena turns to the side window to hide the tears. Why even bother, when all you love will be taken away?

"What's up, Laredo?" Kevin says. He gives her knee a gentle shake.

"Nothing," Karena says, but it comes out in a tiny squeak.

"Nothing," repeats Kevin in a Minnie Mouse voice, "nothing? Doesn't sound like nothing to me."

"Well, it is and it isn't," says Karena. "I'm just having a mean attack of the Dreads."

"The Dreads, what's that?"

Karena explains the wall of fear and bad feeling that sweeps toward her every evening.

"I know the Dreads," Kevin says.

Karena gapes at him. "You do?"

"I do. I don't get them every day, but I do get them situationally. Ex Dreads, for instance. That whole best-man-eloping-with-my-fiancée thing—that kinda messed me up for a while. I was afraid to leave the house. I kept feeling like something was going to fall on me."

"*Yes,*" says Karena. "Like you'll be walking down the street and an air conditioner or piano or anvil will smash you from a clear blue sky. What *is* that?"

"Anxiety," says Kevin, "something you haven't coped with usually."

Karena sighs. "Yes," she says again. "I'm sure you're right." This is something her former therapist, Dr. B, used to say quite often.

"So, Laredo," says Kevin, "what do you think these Dreads of yours are about?"

"The tour, partly," Karena says. "I miss everyone. But Charles mostly. I failed, Kevin. I came out here to find him, and I failed."

"You haven't failed," Kevin says. "You just haven't achieved your objective yet. But I don't think you need to worry about it right at this moment."

"Oh, I don't? Why not?"

"Because you're exhausted and you've been through serious trauma and you probably have scurvy. You need to go home and take a long hot shower and get a good night's sleep and eat as many green vegetables as possible. Recharge. Then we'll find Chuck."

Karena raises her eyebrows. "We will?" she says.

"Yes, we will," says Kevin, perhaps not hearing Karena's slight emphasis on the pronoun. "I'll start making inquiries in the chasing community, send up some flares. No offense, Laredo, you're a superlative reporter, but nobody knows you. And the media has done so many slam pieces on chasers that make them look like screaming yahoos—of which, regrettably, there are many—that the good ones are often wary of talking to the press. You've probably found you haven't gotten very far asking about Chuck, right? But I will. At least, I'll try."

"Thank you, Kevin," Karena says. "That's a lot of trouble to go through."

Kevin reaches for her hand.

"(A) it's no trouble," he says, "and (B) it's a bribe. I'd like to keep seeing you, Laredo. When we get back to the Cities. Under less—adrenal circumstances."

He is blushing wildly. Karena bites her lips to hide a smile.

"You would?" she says.

"Yes. I would."

"Good," says Karena. "Because I'd like that too."

"You would?"

"Yes. I would."

"Fantastic," says Kevin. "Then that's what we'll do."

He kisses her hand and pats it back into her lap.

"Meanwhile, if you could keep your paws off me for a while, I'd appreciate it. You'll have to wait 'til the next rest stop to satisfy your rapacious animal desires. I'm trying to drive here."

Karena folds her hands.

"I'll do my best," she says primly.

She is smiling out the side window, feeling dozy, when Kevin says suddenly, "Pukwana Wiebke."

"Goodness," Karena says. "Bless you."

"Ha, very funny, Laredo. No, it's this game I play sometimes to keep myself awake on the road. I always thought, wouldn't it be great to name a kid after the place it was conceived? And out here that'd make for some unique names. Hence: Pukwana Wiebke."

"Oh," says Karena. "I get it."

She finds Kevin's atlas in the backseat.

"Liiiike—Pedro," she says. "Pedro Wiebke."

Kevin nods. "Good for a girl."

"Or Blunt," Karena says. "Blunt Wiebke? Somehow that seems redundant."

"Hey," says Kevin.

"Eureka!" says Karena. "Eureka Wiebke, don't be lookin' at me like that! I'll slap you upside the head!"

"Very nice," says Kevin. "I can tell you have a gentle touch with the wee ones, Laredo. Speaking of which," he adds, "something I should perhaps have—ahem!—ascertained before, but are we protected against an influx of little Wiebkes?"

"Yes," says Karena, "at the moment."

"Good. I mean, I'm not *opposed* to offspring or anything," says Kevin, and when Karena glances over she sees he is flushing again. "I actually intend to procreate quite profusely. It's just, you know, all in good time, my little pretty."

"Good to know," says Karena, smiling down at the map. "Mmkay, how abouuuutttt . . . Badger Wiebke?"

"Meh. A little too school-mascot."

"Ideal Wiebke? Oh, here, Winner Wiebke."

"Better," Kevin agrees. "Alliterative."

"Winnebago Wiebke. Wilder Wiebke."

"Uh-huh," says Kevin. "Sounds like we'll be doing a lot of traveling."

"Athol Wiebke," says Karena and snickers. "Poor kid."

"Okay, Laredo, I think it's time to put the map away."

But Karena can't stop now. She starts to chuckle, then snort, and then she is laughing so hard she's crying. "Tennis Wiebke," she chokes. It's not even that funny, which makes it all the funnier.

"Wakonda Wiebke," she howls, "Okobojo Wiebke, Spink Wiebke, Holabird!"

She laughs and laughs, clutching her stomach, wiping tears from her eyes. "Oh, oh," she gasps. "Holabird!" Kevin twitches the atlas off her thighs and throws it in the backseat, which makes her laugh even harder. Finally she tapers off to hitches and giggles.

"You okay, Laredo?" Kevin asks. He hands her a napkin. "You done?"

"I think so," Karena says. She wipes her eyes.

"Holabird," she repeats softly, and snorts.

Kevin shakes his head. "Holabird," he repeats. "You're a holabird." But he takes her hand again, and he is smiling.

26

They stop in Austin, MN, for the night, which on the one hand is silly because they are only a few hours from home and on the other is necessary because they are both so punchy. Besides, Kevin points out, Austin is home to the Spam Museum, which, wonder of wonders, both Karena and Kevin have managed to live their whole lives without managing to see. It would be a crime of nature, Kevin insists, to pass that up. They check into a Best Western, which seems like an incredible luxury, and walk—walk!—to an adjoining Applebee's. Sitting across from Kevin in a booth, Karena can't get over all the people, the faux memorabilia on the walls, the number of TVs all tuned to cable sports channels. In her grubby sneakers and limp, days-old clothes, Karena feels as though she has flies around her head.

"I can't figure out why I'm so unsettled," she tells Kevin. "It's good we're getting back to civilization, right? I can't wait to have strong coffee. And shower with non-generic soap. But I feel like my friends who've been war correspondents—they're so thrilled to get home, after being in these remote places, and then they see fresh fruit and they freak out."

"Well, that's an apt analogy, Laredo," says Kevin. "We have been through a pretty hair-raising situation. Far above and beyond the norm. And it's always a little jolting coming back from chasing anyway. Have you ever been diving?"

Karena tilts her head at the non sequitur. "Once, on my honeymoon in Mexico. Why?"

"Because then you know about the bends," says Kevin. "When you've been down sixty, seventy feet, you need to come up in stages. That's really why I wanted to stay here tonight. The reentry can be rough otherwise."

He orders Karena prime rib to go with her salad because of the chasers' custom of getting steak when they've seen a tornado. "And we missed our chance in Pierre," Kevin says. "Ideally, though, we should be at the Big Texan in Amarillo, where they have the infamous seventy-two-ounce sirloin. A fitting counterpoint to that horrific wedge—"

He breaks off and takes Karena's hand across the table, and they are both quiet for a while.

The next morning they wake early and turn to each other. "Austin Wiebke," Kevin murmurs as he moves inside Karena, and "Faith Wiebke," she whispers back. They have morning skin, sweet and musky and slightly sticky. Outside the window the day dawns fine and fair.

Afterward they go down to the lobby for breakfast. It's only seven thirty on a Sunday, but there are a fair amount of people in the dining area, still in sweats or combed and washed and smelling of aftershave, moving among the food stations in a sleepy travel ballet. Again Karena is struck by fear and wonder at how populated it is here, the babble of world news from the big flat screen—goodness, she has a lot to catch up on—and the sheer volume of traffic flowing past the window, beyond the Best Western's manicured grounds. The TV shows a thirty-second segment on the cleanup efforts in Oweeo, and Karena stops, arrested by the sight of so much remaining debris, those whittled trees in bright sunshine.

She gets coffee—better, but still the first thing she's going to do when they near the Twin Cities is hit Caribou—and carries it to the table where Kevin is checking e-mail on his laptop.

"Dan says hi," he says as she sits.

"Oh," Karena exclaims, "how is he? How is everybody?"

Kevin turns the laptop toward her, and Karena swivels it a few more inches still to move the screen out of the sun. Dan has written two lines:

Made it back to OKC despite active embedded cells on the night of the 22nd, gave us a good light show. Guests all departed on time, currently I'm en route home. DM.

Karena smiles. "Bless," she says in a British accent, imitating Fern. "When you write back, will you please say hi from me?"

"Will do," Kevin says.

Karena starts to ask if he thinks Dennis will be receptive to her writing to make amends when her cell phone starts buzzing madly in her pocket. Apparently it has just discovered it can get a signal and is downloading all her messages. Karena scrolls them: several from the *Ledger*, though nothing urgent, since Karena's Oweeo story has earned her a few days' rest. Reader comments, mostly. There's also a photo from Lisa in the newsroom of a squashed-looking infant—she's had a boy! And a text from Tiff: *Where the F ARE YOU? That tornado article was CRAZY. Get the F HOME!!!!!!* Karena smirks and saves this. She has stories to tell Tiff, all right.

But there is nothing from Charles or anyone who might have seen him.

"Kevin, do you mind if I check Stormtrack when you're done?" Karena asks.

"Not at all. But as of ten minutes ago there was nothing new from Chuck."

Karena nods, then picks up Kevin's hand and presses it over her heart. Kevin blinks at her, surprised. He looks this morning much as he did the first few times Karena saw him, hair wet from the shower now, clean Whirlwind T-shirt. His eyes are very bright.

"Thank you, Laredo," he says, kissing her hand. "Okay, if you want breakfast you'd better hustle. I want to hit the Spam Museum before the lines get too long."

"Yeah, because that'll happen," says Karena, standing.

Kevin smacks her on the behind. "Get movin', mouthy," he says.

Karena floats over to the breakfast stations and browses them, plate in hand. She can't handle anything too heavy after the steak last night, her stomach is already groaning, but she takes a few wilted slices of microwave bacon because they're there. And two pieces of whole wheat toast, but what she really wants is an egg. She is starved for protein after all those banana-and-pretzel breakfasts on the road. And they do have eggs here, or at least they have a single hard-boiled one left, rolled into the corner of its steam tray. Karena transfers her plate to the other hand to reach for it, smiling as she remembers her mom saying Karena and Charles were the easiest kids in the world to cook for, because all Siri had to do was boil an egg and Karena would eat the white, Charles the yolk.

But somebody else reaches for the egg at the same time. Karena knows as soon as she sees his hand, large and square and brown, even before she sees the ring. The silver-and-turquoise Lakota ring with its stern and ornate face.

She looks up.

"Hi, Charles," Karena says.

Her brother grins.

"Hi, sistah," he says.

PART II

KARENA AND CHARLES, 1988

27

The Hallingdahl house is a little ranch, sitting in a modest yard near the intersection of Lincoln and Main. Across from the B&M gas station, two doors down from Ellingson's Used Cars. Pretty small house for a lawyer, people say. They wonder why Hallingdahl didn't buy one of the Sprague houses, the stone edifices the banker erected for his daughters at the turn of the century. Or the old Alma mansion on St. Paul Street, set high on the crest of its sloping lawn. They don't know that when Frank Hallingdahl was a boy on the farm he watched his mother get worn down by the caretaking of just such a big three-story house, rubbed away bit by bit, and he vowed that his own family would have a modern home, as lightweight and easy to care for as possible.

Inside, the Hallingdahl house is carpeted throughout in beige and smells like the interior of a lady's handbag, dusty, sweet, a little mysterious. If people tend to decorate at a time in their lives when they're full of energy and optimism and let it slide thereafter, then the lawyer's wife, Siri Hallingdahl, hit her peak era in the late nineteen-sixties, early seventies. There is a sunburst clock on the wall in the kitchen. The table is Formica, the chairs aluminum and red vinyl. The bathroom wallpaper is a psychedelic field of green, orange, and pink poppies. Everywhere there are afghans, ashtrays, newspapers, glasses, and plates, because Siri is an indifferent housekeeper at best. She likes to visit with her friends, to play bridge, to sit in the sunken sunporch off the kitchen and smoke and watch television. Her prize possession is the desk she bought in La Crosse as a young bride, a heavy piece of walnut furniture with a glass top under which photos can be slid. The family is preserved there in snapshots. Newlyweds Siri and Frank honeymooning in the Wisconsin Dells; Frank squinting in front of his newly opened practice; the twins as infants; the twins in a wading pool, their bowl-cut white hair and plaid sunsuits identical although they themselves, of course, are not—there was some talk about dressing a boy and girl alike, but Siri has always been considered progressive. There's Siri's brother Carroll, who lives up in the Twin Cities, mustached and paranoid behind huge sunglasses. There are plump pink-faced cousins, gray-haired elders, children whose shy school smiles bristle with braces. In spots liquid has gotten under the glass and stuck the photos to it, erasing the faces to milky blurs.

28

When Karena lets herself into the house, creeping in from the garage, she hopes her mom will be asleep, but no such luck. Karena smells smoke, hears the laugh track from the TV. She tiptoes past the sunroom, whose louvered pocket door is closed. Smoke curls out from beneath it as from a genie's lamp. Karena tries to make it across the kitchen linoleum without hitting the creaky spot, but it doesn't work: The sunroom door accordions open with a smash and Siri, revealed there, says, "I wasn't born yesterday, you know."

Karena freezes. "No kidding," she says.

"Where have you been?" Siri retreats to the scratchy green couch, but Karena knows Siri can move quickly if she wants to, could be in the kitchen in an instant to take a smack at Karena or flick a dish towel at her head.

"Nowhere," says Karena. "Around."

She opens the refrigerator to buy time. Besides, she's thirsty. The cigarettes and beer have dried her mouth out. But Siri has drunk all Karena's Diet Pepsi. There's only one half-open can left, and it will be flat. Otherwise the fridge is littered with mystery dishes, Bakelite bowls containing two carrots, a handful of canned string beans, Jell-O. A moldy stack of olive loaf. Karena slams the door.

"Jeez," she says, "doesn't anyone ever go shopping around here?"

"You could go," Siri suggests. "Nothing wrong with your legs." She fires up a Marlboro, her lighter clicking and hissing. "Come over here so I can see you. I bet you're drunk."

Karena makes a *psht* noise. "You're right, Ma. I am soooooo drunk. How'd you guess? By the way I staggered in here? By the way I can hardly stand up?"

"Get over here. Now."

Karena minces with exaggerated care to the sunroom.

"There," she says. "Happy now?"

Coolly, Siri surveys Karena from top to bottom, squinting extra-hard at Karena's neck to check for hickeys.

"You look like a slut," she says, turning back to the Golden Girls cavorting in the big old TV.

"I do not," says Karena, stung. Of course, she does, and moreover, this is just the effect she was trying so carefully to achieve before she left the house. Not to be slutty exactly, but her acid-washed mini and matching jacket, her pink tank top with its glittering sequined heart, her hair permed and sprayed to twice the size of her head—all of this is meant to telegraph availability to a certain someone. But her mom is hardly the person Karena was aiming for.

"You know what that outfit says?" Siri continues. "It tells everyone your brains are between your legs. I suppose you were out necking with that Mike Schwartz again."

Karena flushes.

"God, no, he's a troglodyte," she says. "And you're so out of it, Mom. Necking," she scoffs. "Please."

Siri ashes in the waist-high ashtray. "Whatever you want to call it, Karena Lien, I know what you were doing. And let me tell you one thing: If you get pregnant, forget about college. Forget coming to me for help. In fact, don't bother coming home."

Karena's mouth hangs open a little at the irony of this accusation. There's no way she could get pregnant—she's still a stupid virgin! She wasn't even with Mike Schwartz tonight. She would have loved to have been. They did hook up over the weekend, in the backseat of Mike's Bronco, doing what Karena and Tiff call Everything But. However, despite her best efforts Karena must not be very good at Everything But, because has Mike Schwartz called her since then? Has he talked to her even once? No, all he does is stand with his friends and laugh whenever Karena's nearby, that mean, goatish boy laughter whose only intent is to hurt, and tonight Karena has been driving around with Tiff in Tiff's dad's truck, smoking and drinking beer from Tiff's dad's fishing cooler and trying to act as if she doesn't care, as if she were just practicing on Mike Schwartz; trying not to ask Tiff what she did wrong and pounding warm Old Milwaukee as if her stomach were not one big cramping ball of misery.

"Don't worry," she tells Siri. "If I got pregnant I'd never come to you. I'd go to Dad."

Siri laughs through her nose, exhaling.

"Really?" she says. "Great. Good luck." And Karena has to concede the point. She hasn't seen Frank for more than breakfast for months. Some big corporate case in Des Moines has been keeping him away. *Justice waits for no man.* And admittedly Frank is pretty useless when it comes to practical matters outside the law, like pregnancy. Karena imagines her papery little dad, with his glasses and iron-gray hair, confronted with this news. Clearing his throat and rubbing his hands together. Well, he would say. Well.

"All righty then, good night," Karena says. "Thanks for the mother–daughter chat. I feel ever so much closer now."

"Oh, don't be so thin-skinned," says Siri in one of her classic about-faces. "C'mere."

She pats the cushion next to her. Karena stands in the doorway a moment more, then walks in and sits on the very edge of the couch. Is it a trap? What kind of mood is Siri really in? Covertly, Karena examines Siri while Siri watches TV. She is sitting cross-legged, a paperback novel tented on her thigh for the commercials. Next to her is a jar of cold cream, tweezers for pulling what Siri calls her witch hairs out of her chin, a couple of hair combs, and a soft pack of Marlboro Reds. This is all standard—Siri's nests, Charles calls them. Siri makes them wherever she goes. But there is also a box of Kleenex, and when Karena tips forward she sees the ashtray bowl is full. Okay, what has happened with Charles?

Karena waits until the commercial comes on, then asks casually, "So, where's Thing Number Two?"

Siri glances at her, and Karena is struck by the purple-brown half moons beneath her mom's eyes.

"I was about to ask you the same thing," she says, and Karena thinks, Uh-oh. She tries to remember when she last saw Charles—this morning, at breakfast. Eating Lucky Charms straight from the box, scattering purple hearts and blue moons and pink diamonds all over the linoleum. Karena relaxes a little. That's not so bad. Charles can't have gotten into that much trouble in twelve hours. Then she remembers something else.

"Oh my God," she says. "He took the Healey, didn't he."

Siri nods. "It was gone by the time I came back from Sandy's," she says. "He must have found Frank's spare keys."

"Holy crap," says Karena, with some awe. The Healey, unlike the other cars Charles has wrecked, is her dad's favorite, his pet. He drives it only on special occasions, in the summer, with the top down. He shines it with a chamois cloth.

"Dad's going to go ballistic," Karena says.

"Good," Siri says with sudden viciousness. "Maybe when Frank runs out of cars, he'll get his head out of his . . ." Then she shakes herself and takes a deep drag of her cigarette. "Don't listen to me, honey," she says. "I'm so tired, I don't know what I'm saying."

"You do, though, Ma," Karena insists. "And it's okay. You have a right to say we need Dad's help with Charles." Although Karena can't imagine anything Frank would do that would make the situation anything but worse. What could he do, bribe some judge buddy of his to lock Charles up? Which reminds Karena.

"Did you call the sheriff?" she asks, scissoring her second and third fingers together toward her mom's cigarette.

Siri pushes the pack of Marlboros across the couch cushion. "Light your own," she says, and Karena does. Siri exhales, staring at the silent

TV. "No," she says, "not this time. What's the point? All he can do is bring Charles back and give him a slap on the wrist, and meanwhile there's more public humiliation. I'm through with that. I'm so sick of people talking. Just for once I'd like to walk into the IGA without everyone pretending they don't feel sorry for us."

"Amen," says Karena, because this is one part of the conversation she heartily agrees with. She too is so tired of the half-hidden grins when she enters a room, watching people labor to come up with some New Heidelburgian witticism about Charles's chases.

Siri grinds her cigarette in the ashtray and immediately lights another. The first continues to smolder, so Karena reaches past Siri and puts it out. "I mean it, though," Siri says. "I literally don't know what to do anymore. What can we do with him? More drugs? Different ones? Should we . . . put him away somewhere? I can't even stand to think about it." She drags deeply, the ember lighting up and emphasizing the clown lines running from her nose to the corners of her mouth. She shouldn't have permed her hair, Karena thinks with pity. Sure, it's the style, but Siri looked so much better when her hair was a long, shiny sheet, or pinned up with combs. Now it is a pyramid of light brown frizz.

"What did I do?" Siri is asking. "Where did I go wrong? How did I make him turn out this way?"

Karena rolls her eyes, she hates these questions so much. "*Nothing*, Ma," she says, exhaling an exasperated cloud of smoke. "You know that. Dr. H said it. Everyone says it, all the books. It's a chemical thing, remember? It's like—having a recipe not turn out right or something when you've made it a hundred times."

Siri smiles wanly and reaches out to tuck Karena's hair behind her ear, pulling her hand back when Karena ducks her head away.

"You're sweet," she says. "Thank you for trying to make me feel better. And I know you're right, logically. But in here"—she thumps her chest and sips her Diet Pepsi—"you just feel so guilty," she says, "when you're the mother. You'll never be able to stop feeling responsible for your child. You'll see."

Karena puts out her cigarette and stands up. If she doesn't go to bed now Siri will start listing all the genetic predecessors, both on her side and Frank's. The uncle who drowned in his boat on the Mississippi. The great-aunt who jumped down a well. Siri's brother Carroll, who's gay and God knows what else.

"It's not your fault, Ma," Karena says again. "Besides, you're not coping with it alone. There's me, remember?"

Siri squeezes Karena's hand. Karena sits back down. "You are such a help to me," Siri says. "You're my good girl." She shakes her head, her eyes reddening. "And Charles is good too," she insists. "He is. Underneath it all he really is. What is going to become of him? Poor baby. What *can* become of him? What is he going to *do* in this world? How is he going to survive?"

"Don't worry about it, Ma," says Karena. "I'll take care of him."

"That's not your job," Siri says. But she is smiling again.

"Of course it is," Karena insists. "He's my twin."

"Oh well," Siri says, opening a new pack of Marlboros and adding the cellophane to her nest. "Maybe we're just borrowing trouble. Maybe he'll bring the car back tonight safe and sound and he'll stay on his medications and get into college or get a job, and all of this worry will be for nothing. Right?"

"Right," says Karena, though she seriously doubts it. She suddenly feels very heavy, as if her blood has solidified, weighting her to the couch. "Right, Ma."

"So," says Siri. "How was Tiff tonight?"

Karena lights another cigarette and tells her, and the two of them talk until the conversation winds down. Then they just sit together for a while, smoking in companionable silence, watching the news.

29

After Karena kisses Siri on the cheek, leaning into her mom's smell of night cream and smoke, she goes to the bathroom to lather up her own face with soap and wipe it down with toner, then retires to her room. There she switches off the lamp and hooks the ashtray containing her cigarettes out from under her bed. It's her parents' old party ashtray back from the days when Frank still smoked, bright red and about the size of a hubcap. Karena remembers sneaking into the hallway with Charles to watch the grown-ups shriek and laugh, the ashtray brimming the next morning. She sets it on the floor between the twin bed nearest the window and the wall, then wedges herself in there, on the blue-and-green shag rug. Siri has never said anything more about Karena's smoking than *Don't let the cigarette* hang *from your mouth like a farmhand, use your fingers.* And Frank, who is the worst kind of nonsmoker, a former two-pack-a-day man, isn't home enough to catch Karena and give her one of his interminable lectures. Ditto Charles, who has recently become Smoking Police, Jr. Still, caution is a habit, and Karena exhales through the window, dousing the room with Obsession body spray every few drags.

She curls her knees to her chest and props her chin on them, feeling terrible. She lied to Siri tonight—more than usual. A serious lie, a lie of omission. Karena should have spoken up when Siri mentioned Charles's medication, because Karena knows Charles isn't taking it, in fact has been hiding his lithium, and all the other pills Dr. H prescribed, in the very places Charles used to stash his Flintstones vitamins when they were kids. In the holes in the kitchen radiator. Dug into the dirt of the Norwegian pine by the front door. Beneath the davenport cover in the living room, worked into the couch's seams. It was a full month ago Karena caught him stashing a prescription bottle into a Seagram's liquor bag, which he stuffed under the cot in his lair the second he saw her. *Please don't tell, K,* he said. *Please. You know how they make me get. I just get so sick. Please.* And Karena, who had watched aghast at the side effects the drugs had produced over the last couple of years, who had sorrowed in secret over her brother's blackheads and rotten stomach and stutter and shaky hands, had said, *I promise.*

And she hasn't told, but maybe she should have. Because what if Charles is lying in a ditch somewhere? Worse, what if he is curled in the front seat of the Healey, knees pulled up, crying in that very specific way—low and drawn out, almost too quiet to hear? What if he is deliberately aiming the little car toward the cement stanchion of an overpass or off a bridge? Karena thinks of Dr. H saying, *Ironically, it is when Charles is coming out of a depressive period that he must be watched most closely, for then he is capable of more than suicidal ideation. Then he has energy enough to carry out the act.* But Charles hasn't seemed too down the past few days—has he? He hasn't been lying in his lair with the lights off. Karena hasn't needed to station herself down there. Maybe Charles is just off raising hell, as their grandmother Hallingdahl would have said.

Karena rubs out her cigarette, shoves the ashtray under the bed, then climbs on top of it. This is Charles's old bed, which for some reason was never removed when the twins turned ten and were decreed too old to sleep in the same room, and Charles lobbied for and received his lair in the basement. Karena presses her face into the flowered coverlet and inhales. It doesn't smell like her brother anymore, of course, but of dust and must and faintly of mildew. A comforting smell. She lies breathing it in and thinking that at least she did tell one truth tonight: Karena has no idea where Charles is. The thought causes her actual physical pain, a needle in her throat. Where are you, Charles? Karena thinks. Do you hear me? Answer. She tries to send out the twindar, imagines herself rising above the room and the house and the yard and the town, traveling across the dark land, peering down to zero in on where Charles is. But the twindar doesn't work anymore. It seemed to evaporate about the same time as the belief in Santa Claus. All Karena knows is that her brother is out there somewhere without her.

She turns on her side, hugging herself. Eventually she hears Siri's going-to-bed noises: flush of cigarettes down the toilet, running of water in the sink to rinse Siri's ashtray, creak of refrigerator to get the last half-open Diet Pepsi. Siri's door closes, her light clicks, and Karena is left in a silence so profound she seems suspended in it, as if in a hammock. She stares at the wall, the leaf patterns shifting in the orange light from the street. The boughs of the pine scratch at the window screen.

Eventually Karena gives in and allows herself to replay her favorite memory, which she does only on nights when missing Charles is too bad for sleep. The recollection is of an afternoon when Karena and Charles were four, when Siri had put them down for a nap and Charles was sleeping but Karena wasn't. This was unusual, since normally the situation was reversed: Karena spent naptime lying with her arms straight at her sides, pretending to sleep, while Charles banged his head against the wall and sang, *Say, say, my playmate / come out and play with me / and bring your dollies three / climb up my apple tree / slide down my rain barrel / into my cellar door / and we'll be jolly friends / forevermore. . . .* He did this so frequently the plaster behind his bed was cracked in a bowl shape. But on this particular day Charles was sprawled on his stomach, his face mashed into the pillow and his lips pooched out, probably because he'd been up the last four nights in a row, bouncing off the walls and screaming whenever Siri tried to calm him down.

So Karena alone was awake in the hot flat heat, listening to the *ticka-ticka-ticka* of the air pump from the gas station across the street—a sound that contained all the mystery of the sleepy midafternoon and would continue to signify all things adult and secret even after she was grown. And she alone saw the sun squares dim on the shade, saw the canvas puff out and suck back in, heard the wind come up and hiss through the trees. The room darkened and there was shouting outside, and when Karena went to the window she saw people running. *Charles,* Karena said, *Charles, wake up.* She shook him. His body was damp, his hair curling in wet white-blond commas on his forehead. He clucked when she pinched him. But he didn't wake. Neither did Siri: In her parents' bedroom, where Karena pushed and pulled at Siri and begged, Siri just kept snoring. Later Karena would understand about the prescription bottle on her mom's bedside table, the sleeping pills Siri sometimes used to buy herself and Charles some much-needed rest. But meanwhile the window screens clattered in their frames and the jewelry and Kleenex boxes slid across the dresser as if pushed by invisible hands, and Siri slept on.

Since the Hallingdahls are farm people on both sides of the family, Karena had known since toddlerhood what a green sky and sirens meant: Go to the cellar. But she didn't want to sit down there on the braided rag rug while her brother and mom slept on upstairs; what if they died? While she was left alive? She pushed herself instead under the davenport in the living room, and from there she watched the hail fall, closing her eyes when it shattered Mrs. Zimmerman's windshield next door, opened them again just in time to see the twister silhouetted perfectly in the picture window. It moved lazily from left to right, the bottom of its tail twitching, a black and sinuous rope. Then it pulled up, like the finger of a glove turning inside out, and was gone. Later that evening, when the sun was shining again as though nothing had happened, Karena heard her dad saying the Ryans' hog operation just west of town was gone too.

This is the part of her memory Charles debates, how Karena could have seen the tornado from beneath the couch, how at age four she could remember so accurately the direction in which it moved. He argues that its path would have made it almost impossible to see from their house, the town's rooftops being in the way. He has presented

Karena with several photocopies of the New Heidelburg *Eagle* from that day, eyewitness accounts claiming that the '74 Tornado was not an elephant trunk but an inverted triangle, like an ice cream cone. Karena doesn't care. Let Charles have his say. She knows he needs to dismiss what she saw because one of the greatest disappointments of his life is that he slept through it. And it's not the tornado part of this memory Karena treasures anyway, no matter what Charles believes. It's the part beforehand, the peaceful time before anything started to happen. Just Karena and Charles in their room together on a hot, quiet afternoon, their shade breathing in and out, its thread-wrapped ring ticking gently, intermittently, against the sill.

30

C harles doesn't come home for three more days, and although she
has been waiting and hoping and praying for his return, Karena
is unprepared when it happens. She has just gotten back herself, coming
off her shift at the Chat 'n' Chew, and is in the bathroom changing into
her bikini so she can catch an hour's rays at the town pool with Tiff
before supper. Karena is hanging her head upside down and applying
an extra layer of Aqua Net, just to be sure, when the door flies open to
reveal her brother's sneakered feet and hairy calves.

"Aha," Charles says in his Inspector Clouseau voice. "I knew there
was somebody in this rheum."

"Jesus, Charles," Karena says, flipping upright and putting a
palm on her breastbone, her heart galloping beneath it. "Ever hear of
knocking?"

Charles flaps his hand in front of his face. "Ever hear of the ozone
layer? It's like solid hairspray in here."

"Well, nobody asked you to come in," Karena says. But secretly
she's so happy he has. She puts on more eyeliner so she can inspect him
covertly in the mirror: He has no new scratches, no bumps or bruises
or black eyes, thank goodness. Instead Charles is deeply tanned, his
hair bleached from the sun and curling over his shirt collar in the back,
his eyes clear and deep brown. As always when she sees her brother

after an absence Karena is struck by how different they look for twins, and she wonders whether maybe it's true, what Grandmother Hallingdahl says about Charles having gotten some Sioux blood. The great-great-Hallingdahls did have a soddie in South Dakota, prime Lakota country, and maybe one day great-great-grandmother Lisbet did turn from the creek, adjusting the water bucket yoke on her shoulders, when BOOM! she spotted a handsome brave on the bank. Whether this is true or not, Karena looks like the quintessential pale Norwegian, whereas Charles appears dipped in honey. It is hardly fair. But what's most important is he looks healthy and whole. And like himself. There is no sign of the Stranger—that dark brooding expression, the condescending amusement, that energy like a basket of snakes beneath his skin. At the moment, anyway.

"What're you looking at me like that for?" Charles says.

"I'm not looking at you like anything. Could you be more vain?"

"Hey, I'm not the one plastering on the war paint," Charles says. "Who're you after, anyway? Schwartz? Wisneski?"

Karena flushes. "Nobody. Just going to freshen up the tan."

"Uh-huh," says Charles. He leans against the counter, arms crossed. "That a new bikini?"

"Yes," says Karena, looking around for her T-shirt. "Why?"

"It's nice. Makes you look like you actually have a rack."

Karena swats at him, but he ducks away. "You are a filthy pig," she says.

"I try," Charles says modestly. He digs in the pocket of his Jams. "Think fast!"

He tosses something at Karena, a clear plastic bubble. She fumbles it with her right hand, catches it with her left. Both twins are ambidextrous.

"What is it?" she says suspiciously. It looks like the prize from a gumball machine.

Charles shrugs. "Open it and find out."

Karena starts to pry off the lid. "It's not something that's going to jump out and hit me in the eye, is it?"

"Jesus, K," says Charles, "paranoid much?" He beckons for the bubble and Karena hands it over.

"Ow," he says, recoiling as he opens it, "my eye! . . . Just kidding. Look, it's a necklace."

He dangles it before her and Karena sees it's a lightning bolt on a black lanyard. "That's nice, Charles," she says, a little puzzled. It doesn't look like something she'd normally wear—her taste runs more to rhinestones—whereas Charles is usually very good with presents, giving people exactly what they didn't even know they wanted.

"Thanks," she says, pretending enthusiasm. "It's really neat. Where'd you get it?"

"Little mom-and-pop grocery store," Charles says, "on the Nebraska Panhandle. I had to feed about a hundred quarters in the machine to get it too. Want me to put it on you?"

"Sure."

Karena turns and lifts her crunchy hair off her neck so Charles can fasten the clasp. She can feel his body heat radiating at her back, his breath on her nape. He smells like he always does, of Irish Spring and fast food. Karena's heart convulses, seems to swell up into her throat. She has never said this to anyone, not even Tiff, for fear of being ridiculed or told she's wrong, but Karena has a very clear and treasured memory of herself and Charles in the womb. It was like being peas in a pod, lying at a forty-five-degree angle with her feet uptilted, resting on Charles, the pea behind her. Watching light flicker through a red membrane, almost like what Karena sees when she closes her eyes in the sun. When they saw slides in health class of babies in utero, including twins, Tiff had leaned to Karena and whispered, *Look, it's you and Thing Number Two,* and Karena had nodded, thinking, Yup, that's just how it was. Now Charles is a head taller than Karena. How did this happen?

"There you go, sistah," says Charles and steps back. Karena lets her hair fall and glances down.

"Oh my God," she says in delight, "it's turning colors!"

For the lightning bolt is green, then cobalt, then bright aqua.

"I know," says Charles. "Just like that ring you loved so much and lost—when we were kids, remember? The mood ring."

"Of course I do," says Karena. She throws her arms around him and hugs him. "Oh, thank you so much! I love it, Charles."

"I know," says Charles. He reaches into his shirt and brings out his own bolt, which, like Karena's, is glowing turquoise. "I got one for myself too, see? I figured it'd be really cool when you're up at the U to call you and see if we're in the same mood at the same time."

"Totally," says Karena, "we have to do that," and then she takes her time pulling her shirt on so Charles can't see her face. Her stomach plummets whenever he mentions college—which is stupid, because it's not as though she's not going. She sure as hell is. She's worked hard for her scholarship, and she can't wait to get out of New Hellishburg, as Charles calls it. And it's not her fault Charles isn't going—he should have spent more time in school and less on his stormchase trips. But what is going to happen to Charles once Karena leaves? She can't stand to think about it.

"What're you doing now?" Charles says when she's dressed.

"What does it look like? Going to the pool."

"To meet Shamu?" Charles asks.

"Don't call her that, Charles. Tiff's not fat."

"Sure she isn't," says Charles. "She's just calorically dense."

"And you're an asshole."

"Sorry, sorry," says Charles, grinning. "Oh, look what I got for our madre," and he whips a lighter out of his pocket. GO HUSKERS, it says on it in big red letters, and when Charles depresses the button a foot-high flame leaps forth. Karena jumps back.

"Jesus, Charles," she says, "not in here! The hairspray? Hello?"

"I know," says Charles. He grins more widely, and Karena knows he's thinking of the time he turned Tiff's lighter all the way up at Jeff W's house party so that when Tiff tried to light her cigarette, the flame shot up through her carefully sprayed bangs and incinerated them.

Everyone had fled the room, saying things like *Phew, it totally reeks in here!* while poor Tiff screamed and grabbed her suddenly bald forehead.

"That was the antithesis of funny, Charles," Karena says.

"Actually it was extremely funny," says Charles. "But anyway. You're not going to the pool."

"Oh, really?"

"Nuh-uh. Come downstairs with me—I want to show you what I've been doing."

"But Charles—"

"Oh, don't worry about Shamu," says Charles, tugging Karena from the bathroom by the wrist. "She'll forgive you. She'll probably be thrilled when you don't show up. It'll give her a chance to stoop for the troops in the pool locker room."

"Charles, you are foul beyond redemption," Karena says as she lets herself be pulled through the kitchen and dining area toward the stairs that lead to the basement. Karena does glance at the kitchen wall phone as they pass, but Charles is right about one thing: Tiff won't mind so much if Karena doesn't show. She's got her eye on Tim McDermott, the lifeguard who always carries a copy of *Catcher in the Rye* and who Tiff says will clearly be a good lover because he's sensitive. Karena will call her later to find out what happened and to say Siri came home and made Karena start supper. Karena certainly won't tell Tiff the real reason Karena's standing her up, which is that it's so rare to see Charles these days, and especially in this kind of mood, and Karena has so little time with him left.

The temperature drops ten degrees as they descend into the basement. The smell of old linoleum, musty and sweet, never fails to remind Karena of all the nights she and Siri and Charles spent down here, when the tornado siren went off and Siri burst into their room and grabbed a twin under each arm and ran them to the cellar. And how they sat on the oval braided rug at the foot of the steps and Siri smoked her Marlboros while Karena and Charles puffed candy cigarettes and they watched the storms rocket past the picture window upstairs with the speed and ferocity of freight trains. There was a poster of Laurel and Hardy down here too, and Karena has always been scared of the two comedians because when the lightning strobed it animated their faces and made them look alive.

Now the poster is long gone, probably water-damaged or sold at some house sale, and the storm memories are overlaid with other, more recent ones: all the time Karena has spent down here on the same rug, except stationed instead at the door of her brother's lair. Sitting and doing her homework or reading or just listening while Charles cried within—or lowed, actually, like a cow, because he didn't have enough energy to really cry. These are the times Charles can't eat, can't sleep, can't respond, doesn't do anything but lie curled in a ball. They are the times the Hallingdahls most fear, that Karena dreads more than anything, those periods when she sits and prays her brother will keep crying because of what it will mean if he stops.

But Karena rarely goes in Charles's lair itself, not even when Charles is on the road. And not because Charles has forbidden it, although he has. Karena is frightened of the lair because it is the evidence box of her twin's disordered mind. Yet when Charles ushers her inside now and pulls the string on the lightbulb and ceremoniously seats Karena on the cot, she looks around and notices that actually the lair is highly organized, in patterns. The walls are hidden beneath layers and layers of paper: magazine and newspaper clippings and photos. They are chronologically arranged, and everywhere the image of the tornado repeats in them, rope tornadoes, cone-shaped ones, the squat and fearsome wedge. The shelving that once contained Mason jars is full of Charles's equipment, thermometers and barometers and radios and things Karena can't even begin to name. And on the bookcase beneath the high arrow-slit window are Charles's lightning lamps, orbs and disks in which branches of electricity crawl as if alive and seeking a way out.

"Okay, K," Charles says. He has been busy digging through an old leather satchel and now apparently he's found what he's been looking for, because he comes to sit next to her on the cot. "You ready?"

"For what?"

He puts a photograph in her hands, still exuding its chemical-bath smell. It shows a white strip sandwiched between two black ones.

"Cool," Karena says dutifully.

Charles snorts. "You have no idea what you're looking at, do you."

"No," Karena admits.

"It's a supercell," says Charles. "A tornadic thunderstorm. See?" and he traces the stripes of light and dark with his forefinger. His hand looks like a man's hand, Karena notices, big and tan and square. It is not shaking. If Charles were taking his lithium, it would be.

"This is the ground," says Charles, "and this is the base. See how close they are together? The storm was super-intense. It was awesome. A real juicy monster of a cell."

"Cool," Karena says again, though she means anything but. "Isn't that so dangerous, though?"

"Please," Charles scoffs. "Don't be such a girl. Okay, look at this," and he shuffles the photos and exhibits one of a large white lump. "Hail, tennis-ball-size, produced by the same storm. But this, this is my prize," and he brings out a snapshot of a dark shape against a murky background. "Check it out, K! Isn't it amazing? I was about a hundred yards away when I got this. I had to throw myself in the ditch like three seconds after."

"What is it?" Karena says.

Charles taps her on the forehead. "Oh my God, you airhead! How can we even be related? It's a tornado, K, it's a classic, beautiful stovepipe!"

"Oh," says Karena—and now she does see the funnel. "God, Charles! You were that close?"

"Yup," says Charles modestly. He pulls his shirt away from his neck and shows Karena a puffy bruise bisecting his collarbone.

"Debris," he says solemnly. "It was too dark to know what hit me, but there was shit flying around all over the place. At those wind speeds it could have been anything, like a sock or a drinking straw, and still leave that kind of mark."

Karena lifts her hand to touch the bruise, but Charles shies away.

"Don't show me stuff like that, Charles. It's terrifying! Why do you *do* this?"

Charles calmly slides the photos back into an envelope marked *kearney, neb 9 july 1988*. "Research."

"Well, I know that, Charles, but do you have to get so close?"

"Because it compromises the data otherwise," says Charles. "I have to get right under the updraft to observe the cycling."

He tucks the envelope into a black-and-white marbled composition book—his storm ledger—along with a newspaper clipping from the *Kearney Hub* that says, "Twisters Take Aim at Arthur County." Karena eyes the ledger with mistrust but also with respect—and a sneaky, treacherous hope. Everyone in New Heidelburg makes fun of Charles's scientific aspirations. But maybe they've been selling him short, Karena included. So Charles has stopped going to school. So he's flunking out. So what? Isn't there a reason they call scientists mad? Charles might never go to college or follow the typical career path. But if he really is getting this close to his tornadoes, might he not make some contribution after all to . . . what's the weather -ology? Meteorology.

"Charles," says Karena, "what are you going to do with all this data, anyway?"

Charles grins and pats Karena's hair, and she twitches her head back.

"Don't!" she says.

"Don't!" Charles mimics. "Sorry, K, I couldn't help it. You're just so adorable in your ignorance. I'm going to submit it, of course. I'm going to correlate it and write it up into an abstract and send it to the *Journal of Meteorology* and *Stormtrack* and *Popular Science* and I'm going to change the face of meteorology forever. I'm going to win the Nobel Prize for this, wait and see."

"But Charles," Karena begins, and she's about to ask him what the article is, exactly, when the door from the garage scrapes open overhead.

"Yoohoo," Siri calls. "Karena? Charles? I know you're down there."

Both twins freeze, and then Charles pokes Karena in the ribs and she pushes him back. Their faces work silently as they bat at each other, neither wanting to be the first to laugh. Karena doesn't dare look at Charles. But then she does and he mouths, as she knew he would, *Yoohoo!* and she can't help it, she snorts. The pig noise sets Charles off, and then it's all over—the two of them rock back and forth, howling, shoving each other, weeping with laughter.

"Exactly what is so funny," Siri calls. "There's nothing funny up here, I can tell you that. Charles? Charles Oskar, I'm talking to you!"

"Yoohoo," says Charles to Karena. Then he calls, "Yes, Mother."

"What happened to the car?" Siri calls.

Karena stops laughing and wipes her eyes. Why did Siri have to come home now, of all times, when things were going so nicely? And why does she have to start? Why can't she just leave well enough alone? Karena draws away just a little so she can watch Charles more carefully. He looks irritated, he's combing his hands through his hair, but there's no sign of the Stranger—yet.

"Don't you play games with me, mister," Siri says, and Karena hears the *click* of her lighter. Smoke drifts down into the lair, and Charles gets up to crack the window. "You know what I'm talking about. What happened to your dad's car?"

"Nothing," Charles calls.

"Nothing?" Siri repeats. "It sure doesn't look like nothing to me. I doubt it's going to look like nothing to your dad."

"Well, I can't help that," Charles says.

"What?"

"That's your problem," Charles shouts. "I can't be responsible for your and Dad's warped perceptions. The car still runs okay—I got home safely, didn't I? So why don't you just drop it."

There's a pause, and then Siri says, "Where have you been?"

"Around," says Charles.

"What?"

"He said AROUND," Karena calls, and Charles yells, "Nebraska."

"Why? Doing what?"

"Collecting data. For my abstract."

"Your what?"

"My abstract, MADRE," Charles shouts. "It's a scientific article. Forget it. I don't expect you to understand."

"I assume this means you didn't get your application in," Siri says. She's referring to the possibility of Charles going to Mankato State next spring—or maybe to his being the assistant manager of the IGA market.

Charles rolls his eyes. "Like that's going to happen," he mutters, then calls, "I'm working on it, Madre. Okay? So why don't you go watch your very important little programs on TV now. I've got stuff to do. And don't worry about the car. I'll deal with Dad when and if he ever comes home."

There is a silence, and then Siri's footsteps creak away across the floor. Karena lets out her breath. She can tell from where Siri is walking that she's going to the kitchen liquor cabinet for a scotch, which she'll take into the sunroom to drink while she watches the evening news and talks to herself, or to the anchors, saying, *What is going to become of this kid?* and *I gave up my life for this?* and *What did I do to make him turn out this way?*

Karena feels bad, she really does, but mostly she is relieved. It could have been so much worse. Charles didn't charge up the stairs, didn't back Siri against a wall, didn't scream in her face. And Karena can't help thinking maybe Siri is bringing this on herself a little. If only Siri didn't push Charles all the time. If only she'd leave him alone—maybe he could actually do some good.

"I'm going up," Karena tells Charles. "You here for supper?"

"Sure," says Charles. "I've got some work to do, but I'll be up in a bit. See if you can get Madre calmed down. Tell her to take a chill pill or something."

"I'll try," Karena says.

She is halfway up the stairs when it occurs to her to wonder,

What did happen to the car? On the landing she opens the door to the garage.

"Holy crap," she says.

Her dad's Austin Healey must run, because as Charles said he got it here, but how is an utter miracle. Its grille is indented, its hood sticking up so it's almost blocking the windshield. Karena can't imagine how anyone can still drive it.

"Hey Charles," she calls.

"Hey what?"

"C'mere."

Charles appears at the foot of the steps.

"The car's practically totaled!"

"Oh yeah," says Charles, "that." He is grinning sideways at the floor, as he always does when caught doing something bad.

"Oh yeah," says Karena. "That. What the hell happened? Was it the tornado?"

"Not exactly," says Charles.

"What then?"

"It wasn't my fault, K. Sincerely."

"Whose fault was it then?"

"The cow's."

"What cow?"

"The cow that got in the way of the car."

"Oh," says Karena. "That cow."

"Yes," says Charles somberly. "It was a suicide cow, or maybe homicidal. He jumped right on the hood. Tried to kill me."

"Officer, he went that-a-way!"

"Officer, put out an APB on a black-and-white Holstein!"

Karena starts to laugh. She bites her lips and puts her hands over her mouth and does everything she can to try to stop it, but she can't. She hears Siri turning up the volume on the TV and feels Siri's injured silence leaking from the sunroom like smoke, and Karena knows she'll pay for this later, that this minute of laughter will cost hours, maybe many evenings of assuring Siri she's sorry, she didn't mean to encourage

Charles, and no, she didn't mean to gang up with Charles against Siri and yes, she knows how important it is that she and Siri present a united front and of course Karena will talk to him about his college and job applications. But at the moment none of this matters except that Karena and Charles are both laughing so hard Charles is slapping the wall and Karena has to sit down on the basement steps, clinging to the railing, and here he is. Maybe things will turn out all right, maybe Charles has been through a rough time but will be okay now, with his data and his project? Maybe they've all been wrong, overreacting, because when Charles is like this, when he's himself, there's no safer and more delicious place for Karena to be than with her brother.

B ut then, two days later: July fourteenth, the twins' eighteenth birthday, and Karena is in the kitchen, cubing cheese for pea salad. Normally the Hallingdahls go to the Wagon Wheel in Creston for birthdays and special occasions. Since Charles's incident at the Starlite it's too embarrassing to go there. But Karena has begged for one last dinner at the house, anyway. It's only a little over a month until Siri drives her up to Minneapolis and the U, and who knows when her next supper with her family will be? Siri has agreed, and Frank has sworn to close his practice early and be here, and Karena is making all of her and Charles's favorite foods. Hamburgers for the grill. Grandmother Hallingdahl's potato salad. And the pea salad, a goopy concoction of canned peas, onions, mayonnaise, and cheddar cubes that only the twins will eat. Even Siri can't stand it, although the pea salad is as much a part of the Hallingdahl gastronomic tradition as lefse and lutefisk and summer tomatoes sliced and piled high with sugar.

Karena rubs the dirty sole of one bare foot against the other and sings along with the radio as she cuts. Late midsummer is a dreamy, peculiar, dangerous time of year, a feeling in the thick air that all bets are off. Just this morning Karena gave her notice at the Chat 'n' Chew, and this afternoon she and Siri went to La Crosse to shop for Karena's college wardrobe. Of course, Karena will buy her own clothes when she gets to the Cities, but she didn't want to hurt her mom's feelings. So she acquiesced to the sweaters and cardigans and new parka, and now as she looks out the window over the kitchen sink at the lawn and the old boat swing set and the enormous pine bush Frank keeps promising to trim but doesn't, Karena is imagining her transformation. She will wear all black and high-heeled boots. She will have gold bangles and hoop earrings. She will smoke those little skinny cigarettes that look like joints—Capris. And although Karena's English score on the SAT is the highest ever in New Heidelburg, she might go premed. Or maybe not, but it would be nice to have an office full of grateful patients, whom Karena will know how to help because of her early experience with Charles. And Charles himself will have long passed the danger point and be a prize-winning scientist, and they'll meet for lunch and congratulate each other in a sunny restaurant with classical music and ferns. Maybe Charles will have a beard.

It is because Karena is dreaming, being impractical and unwary, that she doesn't hear Charles come up the stairs. It's because she is counting her chickens and singing that she doesn't register him yelling at Siri. Karena is being stupid, pretending that once she's gone, everything will just magically be normal. So it's not until the radio goes to commercial and she turns it down that she hears Charles shouting at their mom.

". . . just *give* them to me," he is saying. "God! Why do you have to make everything so difficult all the time?"

"Me?" Siri says. "That's a laugh. Forget it, kiddo. You're not taking my car."

"Why not?" Charles says. "Give me a reason. Come on. Just one good reason."

"I don't have to explain myself to you," says Siri. "No means no."

"I knew it," Charles says. "I knew you couldn't think of a reason. No surprise there. Your whole little life is governed by illogic. But just because you don't do anything with it doesn't mean you should stop someone who's trying to make a difference."

Karena snaps off the radio, wiping her hands on her shorts. "What's going on?"

Charles looks at her over his shoulder.

"Mind your own fucking business," he snarls, and Karena sees she should have left well enough alone, because Charles is gone, and the Stranger is here. The djinn, Dr. Hazan calls it. The wicked genie of her brother's disorder, a being who comes into Charles when he's manic, slips in behind his face and changes his expression so that it's scornful, a sly, malicious intelligence that babbles a hundred miles an hour and whose sole job it is to figure out what's most hurtful to say, where to stick the knife in. *It's like demonic possession,* is how Karena described it to Dr. H at the Mayo, and Dr. H had nodded. *Yes, family members often say this,* he said. *Try to remember, it is not Charles saying these things. It is the djinn, his disorder, the synapses misfiring in his brain. What he says may be very hurtful, but it is not Charles saying them. The chemicals are in control. The djinn is driving the car.*

The djinn, Karena reminds herself, the Stranger. Not Charles.

"Where are you going?" she asks, since the only thing to do when the djinn is here is try to play along.

"To chase," says Charles, "duh."

Karena looks outside. It is a beautiful afternoon, clouds floating in a sunny blue sky. "But there aren't any storms," she says.

"'But there aren't any storms,'" Charles mimics. "What the fuck do you know? As it happens there are plenty of storms, firing all along the dryline down in Iowa, but would you know about that? Do you listen to the spotters' network? No. I didn't think so. So why don't you stay the fuck out of it."

He turns back to Siri, wiping his lips where white spit has gathered at the corners. "Give me the keys," he says to Siri. "Keys keys keys keys keys."

"No way," says Siri.

"Oh my God," says Charles, his voice rising with indignation. "I cannot believe you are so determined to prevent me from gathering my data—although now that I think about it, Madre, actually I can. Why would you want me to contribute? Why would you want me to succeed? Why would you want anybody to be better than you, some stupid housewife just sitting around watching TV and leeching off everybody? Of course you don't want me to collect my data. You can't stand the thought I might succeed because you're nothing but a fucking parasite."

"Hey," says Karena. "Don't you talk to her that way."

"Oh, and you," says Charles. "Here we go, more comments from the Idiot Brigade. I suppose you think you're all special now you're going to the U, like, Ooooooo, big whup, you can take gut courses and pledge some sorority and there'll be a whole new crop of guys for you to blow. I'd tell you again to shut your mouth, but I know that's hard for you, little Miss Blow-job Queen."

Instinctively Karena's hand flies up to cover her mouth. The djinn, she reminds herself, the fucking djinn, although she would dearly love to say to Charles, *That's enough! What is* wrong *with you? They should lock you up and throw away the key.* But this is one of the worst things about her brother's illness. He can say anything he wants to Karena or Siri or anyone, and in fact not just awful things but the worst possible things he can think of, the things everyone else thinks but nobody would ever say. And they are not allowed to respond, to defend themselves, because they wouldn't be fighting him, they'd be fighting an illness. It is such an unfair, slippery thing.

But now it's Siri who says, "Stop right there, mister. Don't talk to her like that."

"Why not?" Charles asks, eyes glittering. "Don't you want to hear the truth? That K and that fat friend of hers are sucking off everyone in Foss County? Why don't you ask her? Go ahead, ask! Everyone knows they're the town sluts, trying so hard to be popular, what a joke. Don't you know they all laugh at you, K? Don't you know what they say? That you should get monogrammed kneepads for Christmas!"

Karena shakes her head. "That—is—not—true," she says, her voice wobbling.

Charles laughs. "Sure it is, and you want to know what else—"

"Charles," says Siri.

"What!"

"Did you take your medication today?"

Karena sucks in her breath as the room goes still. It is the one question Siri has every right to ask and the one that will most surely bring disaster.

Charles shakes his head as if he has water in his ear. "What?" he says.

"I said, did you—"

"I *heard* you," says Charles. "I just can't believe the idiocy of the question. For your information, the answer is no. I didn't. Why? Do you really think they make a difference? Because I'll tell you something, they don't. They're just tranqs, Madre, they don't do any fucking thing except make me sick. They're that bearded quack's way of thinking he can control me. That's all."

"Okay then," says Siri. She sounds calm, but as she lights another cigarette the flame trembles. "You know the deal. No medication, no car."

Charles smacks his forehead and throws out his hands.

"Oh. My. Goodness," he says. "That is about the stupidest thing I've ever heard. I mean, I've come to expect that from you, Madre, but this just takes the cake. First of all, there's no deal. The word deal implies consent between two parties, and have I consented to anything like this? Would I ever? Of course not. This is some weird rule you've made up and expect me to abide by. But okay, let's try—try, Madre—to look at it logically. Here's your equation: medication equals car. But even you must be able to see how ridiculous that is. Why would I need lithium to drive the car? Do *you* take lithium? Does *Dad* take lithium?"

"Don't bully me," says Siri. "No car. Case closed."

"Sure, of course, disengage," Charles says. "I knew you'd do that. You can't deal with logic, so you pull back in like a little kid going *lalalalalalala* I can't hear you because I don't want to hear you, but I know you can hear me, Madre, so let's keep going. Do *all* drivers in the state of Minnesota have to take lithium? Is it a requirement that responsible drivers take lithium before they get their licenses? *She* doesn't have to take lithium," he says, whirling and pointing at Karena, "blow-job queen over there."

"Hey!" says Karena.

"Oh, right right right right riiiight," says Charles, holding up his hands. "When you're in a car you're in the backseat, not driving, so it's a moot point."

He walks closer to Siri and stands over her, arms crossed.

"For the last time," he says, "give me the keys."

Siri stares grimly ahead as if Charles weren't there.

"No," she says.

"All right," says Charles. "You've forced me into it. I didn't want to have to do this, but I'll have to take them from you."

Siri scoffs.

"Just try it," she says. "I'm not afraid of you—" and then Charles reaches past her for her purse. Siri smacks his hand aside and jumps up, and for a few seconds they stare at each other. Then Siri slaps Charles neatly across the face and he pushes her shoulder, and the next thing Karena knows they're tussling as Charles tries to get past Siri and she stands her ground.

"No!" says Karena and suddenly she's in the sunroom. She doesn't remember how she got there, doesn't feel her feet touch the floor. All she knows is that she's jumping on Charles from behind, throwing her arms around him. It's like trying to hold a bag of snakes. Charles's muscles flex and clench, incredibly strong. But Karena is banking on the fact that he won't hurt her, of all people, and she's right. He doesn't. He just shakes her off, and she falls and lands on her tailbone.

"Ow," she says, more in anger than in pain.

"Oh, honey, did he hurt you?" Siri says. She pushes past Charles to make sure Karena's all right, then turns on him.

"You listen to me, you little bastard," she says. She pokes her cigarette at Charles with every word, and Karena can't help flinching each time the lit ember nears her twin's skin. "You ever touch her again and I'm calling the sheriff. I'll have you locked up, don't think I won't. I'll have you taken away. In fact," she says, "I think I'll call him anyway. You are out . . . of . . . control."

"Okay," says Charles, pushing Siri aside and grabbing her purse from the davenport. "Wow, that's a good idea, Madre. Did you think of that all by yourself? Go for it. Call him. Tell ol' Deputy Dawg I borrowed your Jeep for a little while to conduct some perfectly legit scientific research on my perfectly legal license and I'll bring it back whenever I'm done, maybe tomorrow, maybe by tonight even. I'm sure he'll love that, I'm sure he'll thank you for wasting his time, not to mention the taxpayers' money, but if you really feel you must, Madre, you gotta do what you gotta do. Meanwhile"—and he jingles Siri's keys triumphantly in the air—"thanks a lot for the ride, catch you on the flip side, see you in the funny pages, bye!"

Then the door to the garage slams behind him and he's gone.

The air quivers in his wake. Both Siri and Karena are stunned. Siri goes to the phone in the kitchen but stands staring at the dial. "Oh God," she says. "What am I going to do? What can I do?"

Karena is still sitting with her legs splayed out before her like her old Raggedy Ann doll. She's ashamed to look at Siri after what Charles said. Instead she stares at her mom's belongings scattered in the rug. Hair combs. A pack of Marlboros. Several lighters. A nicotine-flecked hand mirror and some lip gloss. Was it just this morning Karena was serving breakfast at the Chat 'n' Chew? Was it just earlier this afternoon she and Siri were in La Crosse, buying things for Karena's dorm room?

Then the garage door rumbles up and Karena springs to her feet.

"Be right back," she says.

"What?" says Siri. Now she is on the phone, calling the sheriff or maybe Frank. She's on hold. "No, sweetie," she says, cupping her hand over the mouthpiece. "Don't go out there. He's dangerous."

"Which is exactly why he shouldn't be driving," Karena says as she jogs up into the kitchen and snatches her bag from the back of a chair. She doesn't have time to stand around arguing about this. Of course she has to go. Isn't Karena the only one who can control Charles?

Hasn't she proved it time and time again? Did she not talk him down when he climbed the water tower last year? Did she not stop him at the Starlite? True, Karena wasn't able to save him from the dislocated shoulder, but that wasn't her fault, and if Charles had succeeded in taking Frank's car then, things could have been so much worse. It's common knowledge that Karena is the only one Charles listens to, the only one who can calm him down. She might not like it, but she doesn't have to. She just has to do her job. "Don't worry," Karena calls to Siri, "I'll go get him and bring him back," and feeling weary but resolute, she marches toward the door.

They drive southwest on Highway 44, which carries them through towns whose order Karena knows as well as a childhood prayer: Norwegian Ridge, Luverne, Clinton, Accord, Creston. Norwegian Ridge is where her great-grandparents met, courted, and married. Luverne is Charles's favorite because a tornado tore up the golf course in 1967, three years before the twins were born. Right after Clinton there's a t-junction marked by the abandoned State Line Motel, in whose weedy parking lot the Amish sell quilts and pies. Karena considers asking Charles to stop and let her look at the wares, anything that'll get him out of the Jeep and onto solid ground. But Charles calls the Amish wagon the Ptomaine Stand, and he's in a hurry anyway. He swings south onto Highway 52, and within a minute the sign flashes past: WELCOME TO IOWA.

Karena doesn't know the towns here as well, but she recognizes them a little, because many's the afternoon Siri dragged her along on antiquing expeditions with her friend Sandy, the two women poking endlessly through bins of junk in cold limestone buildings and holding up a lefse pan or carpet beater and saying, *Remember these? My mom had one just like it!* A lot of these towns have dried up now, their storefronts closed and streets deserted, their hopes having dead-ended when the railroad passed them by. The next big town is Decorah, where

Karena plans to request a pit stop so she can call Dr. H from a pay phone. Because it has occurred to her—why didn't she or Siri think of this before?—that the Mayo is where Charles should be, and maybe Dr. H or his nurses can give Karena pointers how to best lure Charles in.

Then Charles swings off Highway 52 onto a smaller road, and everything starts to look unfamiliar. The land here is different from around New Heidelburg, more hilly and wooded. The road whips left, then right, then sharply left again. Karena sees a sign for Stillville and breathes a sigh of relief. But to her horror, when the two-lane curves right, Charles sails straight off onto an unpaved road. Gravel ticks and pops and punks under the Jeep. The land grows stranger and stranger. A farm with rotted outbuildings. A creek bed with dense undergrowth, dead twisted trees mixed in with live ones. Karena feels like Gretel without the bread crumbs. She tries desperately to memorize their route while Charles drives and turns and turns and talks. But most of the roads aren't marked, and when they are the names all sound the same: Amity and Valley and County, 290th Street, 190th Street. The light fades, and everything around them becomes dark and gray, and before Karena knows it, she is lost.

Charles, however, is not lost. Charles is operating by his own set of markers, all having to do with what he sees in the sky. Ever since they got in the car he has been carrying on an enthusiastic monologue, talking and talking and talking and talking and talking. Pressured speech, Dr. H called it, a symptom of mania—in Charles's case, a rant about this storm and that storm and his data and how Siri is always trying to stand in his way. Suddenly there's a crack of thunder and a cold gust of wind buffets the Jeep, and Karena receives a nasty volt of fear: The sky, which has gotten more and more overcast the farther they've driven into Iowa, has congealed in horizontal layers. Some are gray and some are white and beneath them all is a wall of dark blue like a bruise. Periwinkle, Karena remembers from her box of Crayola 64s. That's what that color is called. It also means they're driving into a pretty nasty storm.

"How close is that?" she asks. She doesn't like to risk invoking the wrath of the djinn by interrupting Charles, but that storm appears to be speeding at them faster than horses can run.

Charles cranes his head to peer beneath the windshield's tinted strip.

"Not so far now," he says cheerfully. "Yup, I'd say about five miles or so."

He rubs his mouth where the dry white spit has gathered at the corners and starts in again.

"Really it's tragic when you think about it," he says, "though understandable, I guess. Yeah, yeah, sure it is, if you put yourself in her position. Think about it, K. Your life's basically over. You're all dried up. You've gotten married and you've had your kids and they're flying the coop and your husband doesn't notice whether you're alive or not, like he ever did, so what are you going to do? Go to bake sales and play bridge and sit around bitching with the menopause club about how your kids ruined your life. It's awful, yep, it's heinous, but that's the way it is, K. Our madre can't stand for anyone, even her kids, to succeed. She's so unhappy it's subverting the natural order, her maternal instincts. She can't accept her life is over and it's our turn. I'm sorry to say it, K, but our madre is really a very sick woman."

"Uh-huh," says Karena. She doesn't agree, of course—she thinks Siri is pretty content with her life, or would be, if not for Charles. Ironically. But that's the thing about Charles's disorder, it shackles Karena, makes her agree with all sorts of absurd statements because the consequences otherwise are so awful, and does any of this really matter right now? It does not. Karena scans the land around them, looking for shelter. She sees an abandoned chicken farm, its roof rusted out. That's it. The grass, corn, and trees are bowing toward the storm, which now looks like a blue-black tidal wave about to break.

"But WE are getting out," says Charles. "I'm so proud of us! Look at you, going to the U, even though it's kind of basic and there're a lot of idiots there, but I suppose that's true anywhere, you'll just have to be careful not to fall into cookie-cutter thinking. Maybe I can help you," he says, talking and driving faster and faster, "maybe when I'm not collecting data I can come stay with you, yeah! During the off-season, won't that be great? We can stay together, K, I can live in your dorm room, I can work on my project there, it'll be awesome!"

"Sure," says Karena, clinging to her seat as the speedometer creeps past sixty, then seventy. "Any time, Charles. But do you think you could slow down a little?"

Charles either doesn't or can't hear her. The red needle climbs past eighty and the Jeep slaloms along the rutted road. Lightning prongs in a double fork a mile away.

"And you can help me, K. OH MY GOD! Of course! I don't know why I didn't think of it before. You can be my assistant. I'll even put your name on the abstract, though below mine because it's my study. But I'm telling you, K, this study is going to be groundbreaking. Earth-shaking. It's going to blow all the preconceived ideas right off the map, and all those poor little eggheads down in Norman with their radar and dinky little theories are going to be smacking themselves and saying, HOLY CRAP! Why didn't we see this before? That Hallingdahl kid's a fucking genius!"

"I'm sure they will, Charles," says Karena. She's staring up through the side window, and what she can see looks very bad. The clouds directly above them are molded into large, hanging lumps like the underside of an egg carton. About a mile away the road disappears into a curtain of white. "But Charles, I think we should turn around—"

"What? Why? Are you scared? No. Don't be silly. Trust me, K. I know about storms. Look look look look look, you're thinking about it the wrong way. You see storms as some big outside destructive force, separate from us, independent of us. But that's so not right, K. Storms are organic. They ARE us. They eat warm air and they dump cold—they eat and excrete, get it? And they're mostly water. What are we? Our bodies are eighty percent water! And lightning—what do you think our brains are run by, K? Electricity! And check this out, this is the very coolest thing of all. You ready? You ready for my hypothesis, K? Ready? Ready?"

"I'm ready, Charles," says Karena. She clings to the side of her seat as the Jeep hurtles along. It is like being on a game show in a nightmare. If she says everything right, they might get out of this. If she answers wrong—

"Okay!" says Charles. "What do storms have to do in order to produce tornadoes? They cycle, right? HELLO! Sound familiar? Not like I have a *disorder* or anything, that's just what that bearded idiot Hazan says. BUT I'm going to prove there's a link between storms that rapid-cycle and ones that produce tornadoes *because I'm a rapid cycler myself*. In fact I'm the closest thing a human being can be *to* a storm, and in case you think it's far-fetched consider the overall pattern, the grand design, the webbing that holds the universe together: Everything is like everything else. Look look look. I'll help you see it. The veins in a leaf are like capillaries, which are like lightning. See? Or the cochlea of your ear is like a shell is like a spiral staircase is like a corkscrew is like a whirlpool is like a tornado. Get it? Once you see it you can't stop seeing it, I can't turn it off, and I'm so grateful for that, because it's so beautiful, K, it's so fucking beautiful I swear it's almost enough to make you believe in God."

Something large and white smacks off the hood of Siri's Jeep, and Karena jumps. She has been pinned against her door by the police-hose force of Charles's rant—the saddest thing about which is, it almost makes sense. Between cyclothymia, Charles's type of bipolar disorder, and cyclone, which is what their grandmother Hallingdahl called tornadoes—*Run to the cyclone cellar!*—there does seem to be a logical link, and Karena feels if she just tipped her head the right way, she might figure it out. Charles is, after all, a genius, and Karena knows from the psych texts she's borrowed from the La Crosse public library that many manic-depressive people are. Schumann, Melville, Woolf, Van Gogh, Edgar Allan Poe—all brilliant. All bipolar. Maybe Charles too could give something amazing to the world.

But trying to make sense of what he's saying now is like hearing a piece of music with one wrong note played over and over, and the hail plowing up divots on the road and shredding the corn around them reminds Karena even if Charles is a genius, she is also trapped in this Jeep with her manic brother and he's intent on driving them into the storm.

"Charles," she hollers over the hail. "Charles, we have to go back!"

"It's all right, K," Charles yells, cranking the wheel as the Jeep fishtails on the ice. "Trust me. I know what this storm's going to do."

Abruptly the hail stops. Karena's ears feel stuffed in the sudden silence. The storm is rotating overhead, turning slowly, letting in only a strip of weak, dirty yellow on the horizon. Charles smiles at Karena.

"See?" he says.

Then there is a *CHUNK*, and another *CHUNK*, and *CHUNK CHUNK CHUNK*, and the windshield in front of Karena's face cracks in a thick web. She screams. She can't help it. Hailstones the size of softballs accumulate in the ditches.

"Excellent," Charles shouts. "I forgot I heard a spotter say that once—when the small stuff stops and it gets really quiet, that's when the big ones start. Okay, hold on, K! We're gonna punch the core!"

"Charles, no—"

"We have to," he yells. "Can't go back now, nope, no way, no way out but through. Besides, if there's a tornado, that's where it'll be! In the bear's cage! It—"

But they are into that white curtain across the road, which turns out to be rain and more hail, and Karena can see Charles's mouth moving—barely, the light is so scant—but she can't hear him. She is yelling at the top of her lungs and can't hear herself. The sound is deafening, a fusillade, like nothing she ever imagined. And she can't see anything in front of them. The road has disappeared, the cracked windshield is a watery blank. It is like driving into a movie screen.

So Karena feels what they hit more than she hears it. It's a frame-shaking shock, a *thud* that comes from Charles's side of the Jeep and travels up through her feet to her stomach. The Jeep swerves right and Charles struggles to keep it on the road, a tough call anyway in dirt that's turned to mud, is as slippery as lard. Karena yells as the Jeep tips.

She catches a glimpse of her brother's face in the weird, snowy half-light, blank with conversation as he spins the wheel in the direction of the skid. Then they slide to a stop, diagonally, but still on the road.

And just like that, the hail stops again. They must have passed through what Charles called the core. Karena's ears pulse and ring. She looks around at the land, soaked and icy and dripping beneath the storm that still turns above it. But the gap on the horizon is bigger, letting in more lemon-colored light. Somewhere a bird is singing.

Karena and Charles stare at each other.

"What was that?" they say at the same time.

"That bump," says Charles. "You felt it too?"

"I felt it."

He scrapes back his hair, which is plastered in wet golden curls to his forehead. His chest is heaving, his eyes showing the whites all around the pupils. He is terrified, Karena knows, as she is. But she can also see, like water filling the pitcher, the sanity flowing back into his face.

"Maybe a deer," he says. "Or a cow. Do you think . . . ?"

"Had to be," says Karena.

She waves around at the fields, meaning, There's nothing out here.

"Yeah," says Charles. "Totally. That's all it was."

But they keep staring at each other, as if afraid to look anywhere else.

"Charles," Karena says. "Charles, we have to go back."

Charles's face works as if he's trying to swallow something.

"I don't know if the Jeep will make it," he says. "The road—"

Karena nods.

"We have to," she says.

"I can't," says Charles.

Suddenly he throws the Jeep in reverse and, looking over his shoulder, rockets backward down the empty road. The tires whine a little; the strange, strained lemon-ice light glints off the lightning bolt at his throat.

"Be careful," Karena says. "Slow down!"

But they don't have to go far before they see the motorcycle. It is lying half on and half off the road. There's something trapped beneath it. There's only one thing it can be. It's not as though the motorcycle just happened to be out here and fell sideways on a deer or a mattress. Still, until Karena cautiously gets out of the Jeep on legs that feel like gelatin and approaches the cycle, she can't believe it's a man. It's as if her mind can't make sense of what her eyes are seeing.

But she walks a little closer, stopping near the driver's headlight of the Jeep. The man is wedged beneath the motorcycle—Karena doesn't know anything about choppers, but she thinks it's a Harley. It's a big one, anyway. Lots of chrome. The man is in his forties or fifties maybe—grizzled, thickset, long yellow-white hair. Gathered in a ponytail that's askew on the road. He wears no helmet—at least none Karena can see. Maybe the hail knocked it off.

What is he doing out here? What was he thinking, riding into this storm? Maybe Karena's own mind is playing tricks on her. Maybe he doesn't really even exist.

A shower of raindrops patters down from somewhere. The air smells like April, fresh ice and wet dirt. Close by, the bird sings.

Karena approaches the man. He is lying awfully still. His face is in profile, the one blue eye she can see is open. He's pink-skinned with white lashes and mustache, like an albino, like one of her own cousins. He looks surprised.

"Hey," Karena says.

Holding her breath, she edges closer and nudges the man's boot with the toe of her sneaker. It's solid. It scrapes on the road. He exists, all right.

"Hey, mister! Are you conscious? Can you hear me?"

Nothing. Just the Jeep's engine idling. The bird trills again: *whit-whitwhitwhit—whit-too!*

"Hey, mister," Karena says, more loudly this time. "Can you hear me? Say something if you can hear me!"

She circles a few feet to the right. The shaking has traveled up her legs to her arms now. She puts a hand over her mouth and it's ice cold.

When she's directly in front of the man she can see that half of his scalp has been ripped off. The bike must have dragged him a little after it fell, because the side of his face against the road looks like ground beef. A puddle of blood is spreading from the top of his head, shockingly fast. That is what amazes Karena: how fast it is. There is also something that looks like instant oatmeal.

"Oh my God," she moans. "Oh my God."

And her brain, maybe unable to sustain what she's looking at, makes a sudden, weird cross-connection: a bird embryo she once found that had fallen out of a nest. In their backyard. From the big pine bush. She had picked up the blue egg, delighted and wanting to take it inside with her, and the embryo slipped out. Covered in mucus. She had gagged then as she is gagging now, unable to stop, staring at it in pity and revulsion.

She backs away from the motorcycle man. About two feet away, the Jeep's wing mirror. What hit him.

"What did you do, Charles?" Karena screams. Her brother is standing by the Jeep, staring in horror, rubbing his mouth. "You happy now? Huh? What did you do here? What did you do?"

33

Whena they get back in the Jeep Karena is driving, because Charles is useless. He is screaming and sobbing, rocking back and forth with his hands over his face. Karena has never heard a man scream before. She hasn't known until now that whereas women scream from their throats and chests, men scream from their stomachs. This is not a lesson she has ever wanted to learn, and now that she has she can't unlearn it. Charles's screaming is a raw sound, ragged and wretched, as if it's being pulled from his gut inch by inch over something rough.

"Nooooo," he is screaming. "Oh God, oh fuck, oh my God, oh fuck fuck fuck fuck FUUUUCK—"

"Shut up!" Karena says, because she has to concentrate to get them out of there. The road is slurry with mud and melting hail, and her shaking is so bad it's as though an electric current is being passed through her body. She clenches her jaw to keep her teeth from clacking, presses down on her leg with one hand to force her foot steady on the accelerator.

Once she's made a three-point turn, though, and aimed them back in the direction they came from, she says, "Okay. Okay. It's all right, Charles. It's okay." Because now although Charles isn't screaming anymore, he's clawing his cheeks. He doesn't mean to, Karena thinks. He probably has no idea what he's doing. But he's digging his nails in and drawing blood and pulling down his lower lids to expose the vein-threaded bulge of eyeball. Like the Halloween scare faces they used to make at each other as kids.

"Charles," Karena says. "Charles, stop. Take your hands off your face. Put your hands down. It's going to be okay, Charles. You hear me? It's going to be all right."

"Howwwwww," Charles moans. "How can it be? I killed him, K! I killed him!"

"No," says Karena. "It's all right. Don't say that." She's driving as fast as she dares, which is only about ten miles an hour as the road is pocked with water-filled potholes two feet deep and she doesn't want to catch up with the hail core of the storm. "Don't think about it, okay? We'll get help. We'll go right now and get help."

"I want to die," Charles cries.

"No!" says Karena. "Shut up! Don't you ever ever say that!"

She grits her teeth and braces her arms and gives the Jeep a little more gas and slaloms through the potholes. Finally they reach the end of the cursed road. At the t-junction Karena looks in the rearview but can no longer see the motorcycle. I'm sorry, she thinks. Oh God, mister, I'm so sorry. She signals—ridiculously, on the empty road—and, making a guess, turns left. North.

"He might still be alive," she says, and her stomach lurches with the lie. The blood, all that blood spreading from the man's head. So much and so fast it was actually pumping, making a little rill over the washboard dirt like a stream over a rock. But still. The important thing is Charles.

"We'll go find somebody," Karena says. "Okay? We'll go to the first town we see and get help, okay, Charles? Just hold on. Do you hear me? Are you listening?"

"Okay," moans Charles. "Oh God, oh my Gooooood . . ."

"Okay," says Karena. "Okay." Please God, she thinks. Please help me find a town. Please just let me get us out of this.

About three miles farther they come to pavement, and then there is a farm, and Karena swings the Jeep into its driveway and jumps out, though something about the place doesn't look right. It's not very well kept; it's what Grandmother Hallingdahl would have called a dirty farm, with blue industrial plastic over the windows and the roof of the barn caved in. Still, this is no time to be picky. They need a phone. Karena is running toward the house when a striped dog with a head like a snake's rounds the corner, barking and growling, showing its teeth. Karena screams and races back to the car, slamming the door just as the dog thuds against it. It leaps up on the window, its nose leaving a smeary mark. Karena accelerates backward into the road. Charles is still crying.

The next farm they come to has a rusted trailer in the dooryard and huge coveralls flapping on the line next to it—a man's clothes only. Karena suddenly remembers a story about one of Frank's cases down here, involving a road nicknamed Dead Man's Curve not because it whipped back and forth at 120-degree angles but because the mummified body of a man was found in a shed at one of the hairpin turns. Apparently Iowa is an extremely dangerous place. Anyone could be out here, doing anything. Absolutely anything at all.

Karena is about to turn in anyway when she looks left and sees something so strange and frightening it numbs her instantly. The storm is still above them, a ragged purple-brown ceiling slowly turning. From the lowest part of its base a green funnel is emerging, crooking down like a finger. Haloed by a burst of brighter, phosphorescent green, it bends at a forty-five degree angle to point at the ground, perhaps at the spot where they just were. Karena sucks in a terrified breath and looks over at Charles. He's rubbing his eyes and hasn't noticed. Karena speeds up, passing the farm. She mashes her foot on the accelerator. But the tornado travels with the Jeep. No matter how fast Karena goes, it rides alongside them, bending, stretching, changing shape in a leisurely fashion. Karena can't stop cutting her eyes over at it. Every time she looks the green tornado is still there. Keeping them company. It's not until Karena reaches another t-junction and turns east that they leave it behind.

34

Half an hour later, by some miracle, they come to Highway 52. From there it's just a matter of running north to Decorah. Charles is quieter now, groaning like a tired kid. Karena doubts he knows he's doing it. He stares out his window, his head wobbling a little with the joins in the road. The storm has sped northeast ahead of them toward Minnesota and Wisconsin, and behind it the setting sun gleams on fresh-washed fields, the air clear and cool. It feels more like fall than July. If not for the puddles on the road and the droplets sparkling like diamonds on the irrigation rigs, Karena might not have known there had been a storm at all.

It's getting dark when they reach Decorah, which surprises Karena. She doesn't have a watch, and she forgot to check the dashboard clock. Now she sees it's almost eight thirty. Siri will be worried. How long have they been away? What time did they leave this afternoon? It's as though the events behind them, the purple-brown storm and green tornado and the dead man on the road, have all occurred out of time, have taken place outside the regular universe.

Karena follows College Road into Decorah, passing Luther College on the right, up on its hill—and that's another weird thing about Iowa, she thinks, how big the hills are here, just over the state line. College Road is quiet, since only summer school is in session, but in a month it will be packed with cars ejecting good Lutheran students and their families into the quads and dorms. Karena is grateful she won't be among them. Siri went to Luther in the days when students could be expelled for playing cards or dancing, and although it's no longer quite so strict, when Frank lobbied for Karena to go there, both Karena and Siri said no way. And then Karena won her scholarship to the U, which helped—but what is she thinking about? How can she be thinking about college when there's a dead man on the road back there? Forget the U. She's probably not going there at all, or anywhere else for that matter, except possibly prison. The juvenile detention facility in La Crosse—and then Karena remembers, and it's like cold water in her stomach. No. Not juvenile. She and Charles are eighteen today.

They cross the Upper Iowa River into town. The houses are pretty and neat on their squares of lawn, under the dark canopy of trees, most flying flags. Norwegian, American, flags with flowers, flags with trolls. Norwegian flags also hang from the streetlights, which are starting to come on. Karena pulls into the first gas station she sees, a Casey's, and even its canopy is decorated with rosemaling, the Norwegian style of flower painting. This is one town that's serious about its heritage.

Karena drives into the far corner of the lot, away from lights. Charles's face looks pretty bad, its gouges and scratches. He is staring out his window, his lips moving, and his head knocks against the glass when Karena parks. He'd better stay here, Karena thinks. She turns off the engine and starts to get out.

But Charles bolts upright.

"No!" he says. "Don't leave me, K. Please."

Then he opens his door and leans out. Karena can hear him retching and retching. A station wagon full of kids passes, and they honk. "Gross," a girl says, and a guy yells, "Dude, waste of beer!" More laughter as they pull away.

When Charles is done Karena hands him some wet-naps from the glove box.

"Here, Charles," she says. "You might want to clean yourself up a little," and she touches her face.

Charles pulls down the sun visor and winces when he sees himself in the mirror on the back. He starts applying the tissues, gingerly.

"Where're you going?" he asks.

"Bathroom."

"'K. I mean, okay. But come back soon, okay?"

Karena says she will. She crosses the service plaza past the pumps, which are bathed in shocking white lights. A country-western song issues from the canopy speakers, magnified and somehow terrifying. Inside the store too, it's too bright. It's not crowded, but the people in here—a couple of girls Karena's age, a large soft lady considering the Hostess cupcakes, a man in a trucker cap—they are all moving too fast, like film sped up and spliced badly together, their gestures sudden and threatening in the fluorescent light. Or is it Karena, is she moving strangely, dopey and slow? Her muscles ache from having been tensed for so long, especially the big ones in her thighs. Tonight she bets she won't be able to move them at all. Which reminds her: She probably won't be home tonight, either. Karena turns toward the counter to ask directions to the sheriff's office—but she really does have to use the ladies' room. She waits in the little hallway with the crates of soda pop, staring at the bulletin board with its flyers for puppies and outboard motors and houses, then uses the facilities. On the way to the counter she grabs a Diet Pepsi—she's parched—and a root beer for Charles too.

She stands in line behind the girls her age. They've obviously been swimming in the Iowa, their wet blond hair slicked back, towels around their necks. They're pooling their change to buy a pack of Virginia Slims—so they're over eighteen too, college girls maybe—and Karena realizes something: The counter lady probably can't tell them apart. These girls and Karena. In this town full of students, nobody would give Karena and Charles a second glance. Even his throwing up apparently isn't unusual. Their hecklers in the wagon likely assumed he was a freshman who couldn't handle his beer.

Karena's theory proves correct when the lady behind the register smiles as she rings up Karena's purchases. "Here you go, hon," she says. "You have a good night now."

"You too," says Karena and walks carefully out of the store, fearing she might still jerk spasmodically and run into something with sharp corners, like the hot dog machine or magazine rack. She crosses the lot to the Jeep beneath the bright canopy with its monstrous music and suicidal moths. It's true. That woman just wished her a good evening, not something you'd say to a killer. Karena can't believe it's not obvious, like a humpback or a limp, that these people can't take one look at her and know she and her brother left a dead man on the road a hour or two ago. How can they not tell?

But apparently this fact is invisible.

Karena opens the Jeep and gets in, then hands Charles his root beer. He grabs it and drains it in a series of long swallows while Karena unwraps her fresh pack of Marlboros and lights one. She sighs out smoke and cracks her Diet Pepsi.

"Better?" she asks Charles.

"Much," he says. "Thank you."

Karena nods. Leans her head back on the headrest, feeling a little dizzy. Then she remembers.

"Crap," she says. "I didn't ask directions."

"To where?" Charles asks.

"To the sheriff's office."

But as she's sliding out of the Jeep once more Charles grabs her wrist.

"Hold up, K," he says.

Karena looks down at his hand, the crescents of the nails dark with blood.

"What, Charles?"

Charles lets go and rakes his fingers through his hair several times. He blows out a long stream of air.

Then he says, "K, I don't think we should tell."

"What!" Karena says. She pulls her leg back in and slams the door. "Charles, you can't be serious."

She looks at him carefully. His face is strange because of the way the light is falling through the windshield, half illuminated by a streetlamp, half in shadow. And he is clearly scared and his scratches look terrible. But he also is himself—Charles. There is no trace of the djinn's malicious glee or dark, brooding expression or that weird super-charged energy.

But what he is saying is crazy, all right. "Charles," Karena says, "there's a man dead on the road back there. Dead!"

"I'm aware of that, K," Charles says.

"He's dead," Karena repeats, as if discovering this fact for the first time. "We killed him!" and she starts to shake convulsively, worse than before. Her teeth clack together.

"Stop," says Charles. "It's okay, K, stop. I'm right here," and as much as the gearbox will allow, he pulls her close. He rubs her arms, on which all the peach fuzz is standing up.

"Wuh-we have to t-t-tell sssomebody," Karena manages to say. "We have to—"

"I hear you, K," Charles says. "And under other circumstances I'd say you're right. Like if this had happened yesterday. Because we were seventeen then, remember? But today we can be charged as adults. They'll put us away, K, you know that, right? They'll lock us up for good."

Karena nods. She is starting to feel warmer, and she slumps against him.

"I was thinking the same thing earlier," she admits. "But maybe if we just tell the truth—"

"Which is what, K?"

That you were manic, Karena thinks.

"That it was an accident," she says, sitting up straighter. "That you didn't mean to—"

Charles scoffs. "Oh, and what, K, you think that's going to make it all right? You think I can walk into the sheriff's office and be like, Hey, officer, so sorry, but I was driving in this storm and I clipped a guy and killed him and now he's dead but I didn't mean to, so can you let me go, please? And oh, so sorry for the extra paperwork. You know it doesn't work that way, K. You know it."

"All right, maybe not," says Karena, "but Charles, what else can we do? We can't just leave him lying out there."

Charles looks around wildly, as if the sheriff and his deputies might be creeping up on the Jeep at that very moment.

"You're right," he says. "I'll bury him." He nods. "I don't know where it happened, exactly, but if it takes me the next year, I'll find him and bury him myself."

Karena huffs in disbelief.

"That is *not* what I'm talking about, Charles, and you know it. The point is, we killed a man! We did the worst thing you can do to another human being. We stole his *life*. We have to pay for that."

"Why?" says Charles, and then, as Karena rears up, "Wait, that came out wrong. Look, I totally agree we have to pay. Or rather, I have to pay. Because I did it. You didn't have anything to do with it. You tried to stop me—"

His voice climbs and cracks, as it did when it was changing, and he looks away and swallows several times.

"Which is exactly what I'd tell them," he says, rubbing his wrist over his eyes. "That I did it. So I'm the one who should pay. But it won't stop there, K. Even if they believed me that you didn't do anything, they still might consider you a—what is it, not an accomplice . . ."

"An accessory," Karena says.

"Yeah," says Charles. "An accessory. And think what would happen then. I'd go to jail, without question. And that would suck, although I could handle it. I think. Yeah, I'm pretty sure I could. But you, K!"

His chest starts to hitch. "You're just about to get out of here," he says, speaking faster and faster. "Out of New Hellishburg. You've got your scholarship. You've worked so hard for it. And when I think of you being stuck here because of me—that they might take away your funding—that they might not let you go to college at all—"

"Okay, Charles," says Karena. "Okay."

Charles subsides, wiping his mouth. Karena leans back against her headrest and looks out the side window. She's tired, so tired. She can't think. She watches a woman help her little girl climb out of the high passenger's seat of an RV pulled up to the pump. The girl is about three or four, towheaded as Karena and Charles used to be, with thick glasses. She takes her mother's hand and yawns as they trot across the lot, and Karena tries, and fails, to remember what it was like to be that small and have somebody else taking care of everything.

"Just think about it, K," Charles is saying. "That's all I'm asking. Let's sit on it for a couple of days. If you still think I should tell then, I'll do it. I'll go to Sheriff Cushing and tell him everything. But please, K. Let's not decide right now. Please."

Karena rolls her head to look forward. The sky glows pink and gold in the west, the trees black against it. Peppery shapes rise and fall above them—bats. Karena can hear the shouts from the river, some kids inner tubing down there, a bottle breaking, somebody's radio blasting "Sweet Home Alabama." It is such a normal night. Who would believe that not a hundred miles from here today there was a tornado, that a man died on the road? That he is still there? Such violence doesn't seem possible. The two worlds can't coexist. In fact it is starting to seem unreal that this afternoon's events happened at all.

And Charles. Karena doesn't look at him, but she can feel his stare on the side of her face, the same way he used to wake her up when he'd had a nightmare—not saying anything, not touching her, just standing by her bed and gazing pleadingly at her and in that way pulling her, like a tractor beam, from sleep. He will almost certainly go to jail, and there's no way he'll make it. It's bad enough what happens to guys in prison, especially first-timers—Karena's heard the stories, from Stace Rudiger's brother who did time for assault. Charles would be considered fresh meat, a tasty snack for some older inmate. That is, until he got manic and opened his mouth to the wrong person. Then he could get beaten to death. Or what about the times when he is curled on his side, moaning, insensible, helpless? Karena can't stand to think about what they might do to him, the other prisoners, the guards. It is unbearable.

So she says, "Okay."

"Really?" says Charles. "You mean it? You won't tell?"

"I *said* okay."

"Oh my God, K," says Charles, but then he grips her arm again. "Promise," he says urgently. "Promise you won't tell. We'll both promise. Promise!"

"I promise," Karena says.

"Oh, thank you, K," Charles says. "Thank you, K, thank you so much. You know you made the right decision, right? Now you can go to school and I can figure out some way to make it right, and I'm so sorry I got us into this mess, God, just so sorry—"

"Okay, Charles," Karena says, "enough already. I just want to go home now. All right?"

"Okay," says Charles humbly. "Okay. Sorry."

Karena starts the Jeep and checks the gas gauge. They have just under an eighth of a tank. She pulls over to the island and Charles leaps helpfully out to fill it. Checking her reflection in the rearview, Karena notices an object gleaming in the backseat. The wing mirror. She doesn't think Charles ever got more than a foot away from the Jeep back on that road, so Karena must have picked it up at some point. She must have put it in the back. She doesn't remember, but part of her must have made a certain decision already. On the way out of Decorah, she pulls over and Charles throws it into the river.

35

When they get home they have to go in through the front door like visitors, since Frank's one surviving car, the diesel Mercedes, is parked in the garage, blocking the inner entrance. "Oh, crap," Karena says. She has forgotten they made Frank swear to be home tonight—of course, for her and Charles's stupid birthday. Her stomach sinks. Of all the nights for Frank to keep a promise. It is going to make running this part of the gauntlet that much more difficult.

"You go in ahead of me," she tells Charles. "I'll cover for you."

Siri is where Karena has thought she would be, down in the sunporch, though when she hears them she comes running out into the living room.

"Oh thank God," she cries. "Where were you? I was so worried—"

Then she sees the scratches on Charles's face. Behind Charles, Karena bugs out her eyes and vehemently shakes her head.

"But!" says Siri. "You're both home now, and that's what's important. Are you hungry? Anyone want some supper? There're special birthday burgers just waiting to go on the grill."

Charles trudges through the living room to the dining area, where the steps of the cellar are. He starts to descend to his lair, head hanging.

Siri lights a cigarette. "Charles?" she says. "Honey? Would you like some cake?"

See, this is what Karena means about Siri. She can see Charles is hurting, that he's off-kilter. Yet she pesters him with questions. She can't leave well enough alone. Karena knows Siri tries, but really. Can't Siri exercise better judgment? Isn't she, as she always reminds them, the mother?

They don't have anything to fear from Charles tonight, though. Charles is done. He says, "No thanks, Ma. I'm really tired. I think I'll just go to bed."

"All right, honey," says Siri, "if you're sure."

"Yup," says Charles. "Night. Tell Pops good night too."

Siri and Karena stand holding their breath until they hear the plywood door to Charles's lair close. They wait a few seconds more to make sure he won't come up again. Then Siri says to Karena, "What *happened*?"

Karena shakes her head.

"Forget it," she says. "It's done. It was bad, but it's over. I really don't want to talk about it."

Siri frowns as she sucks on her cigarette, her upper lip working around the filter in a way that reminds Karena of a camel. The wrinkles there look deeper than usual, her clown furrows more pronounced. And are there more lines beneath her eyes that weren't there this morning? Is that even possible? Karena shivers. Charles is making their mom old.

"Are *you* all right?" Siri asks.

Karena shrugs and reaches for Siri's Marlboro but hastily drops her hand when the back screen door slaps shut and Frank comes in through the sunroom, on a waft of charcoal smoke.

"Why, Karena," he says in his soft voice, lifting his hands and clasping them. "If it isn't the birthday girl."

Karena has been prepared to be mad at Frank, in fact has been mad at him for ages. For returning to business as usual after the incident at the Starlite. For pretending everything has been taken care of. For not even knowing about all the terrifying Charles moments, big and small, that Karena and Siri have had to cope with. Justice waits for no man. But at the actual sight of Frank, Karena feels something trembling in her throat like a soap bubble, the secret of what she and Charles have done.

She would love to open her mouth and let it pop, to run to Frank and put her head on his shirt and tell him everything. She remembers when she was on her learner's permit and barreled backward out of the garage and ran over her mom's favorite planter, the ceramic one shaped like a pig. And her dad, her poor dad who has such bad luck with his kids and cars, just cleared his throat in the passenger's seat and said, *Well. I don't think your mother necessarily has to know about this, do you?* The next day, there was a new planter, Frank probably had his receptionist, Jill, pick it up at Menards, with the same ivy in it even. Nobody said anything more about the incident.

So Frank might be understanding. And if not, at least he would know what to do. But watching her dad come up the sunroom steps, Karena knows she can't tell him. He is a stern, quiet little guy nobody really knows, so fragile-looking and skinny. Frank's hair is totally gray now, his face lined. He looks startlingly like Lincoln. Three years ago he turned fifty. Frank may be tough in the courtroom, but if it got out what Karena and Charles have done, it would ruin him. For starters, having a son who's a killer would turn his practice into a joke.

So Karena just makes herself smile as Frank gives her a papery kiss on the cheek.

"Well now," he says. "Eighteen years old. All grown up."

"Hi, Dad," she says.

"Did you bring your evil twin home with you?"

"He's in bed, Frank," Siri calls. "He doesn't feel well." She has retreated to the kitchen with her Marlboro to avoid one of Frank's non-smoking filibusters.

Frank rubs his hands together and gives Karena one of his wry, infrequent smiles.

"Charles has already done a little too much celebrating tonight, is my guess."

"Something like that," says Karena.

"As long as he didn't do it in my cars," says Frank. "He's going to have to work all fall to pay me back for the Healey."

"No, we took Mom's Jeep," says Karena.

"Well," says Frank. He clears his throat again. "Good."

He laughs, a short bark. Nobody probably ever gets close enough to him to tell, Karena thinks, but behind his thick gold–rimmed glasses her dad has lovely eyes. They are a soft gray–blue, the color of Lake Superior as Karena remembers it from a long-ago trip to Duluth. They are Karena's eyes as well, though hers are more slate than blue.

"Are you ready for your birthday supper?" Frank asks. "The grill's all fired up. Your mom told me you made some great hamburgers."

He winks, making a joke on himself because he never eats red meat. Tonight Karena would like to skip the burgers too, given the similarity between the scraped-away face of the motorcycle man and the ground chuck into which this morning she mixed ketchup, Worcestershire sauce, and egg. Her stomach lurches and she gets that gagging, mucus-webbed feeling in her throat again. But if she and Charles are really going to cover up what they've done, somebody has to start acting normal around here, and it has to be Karena, and she might as well start now.

So she says, "Sure, Dad, hamburgers sound great." Tomorrow she will tell Siri about the missing wing mirror too. About the deer they clipped. The fight she had with Charles for control of the Jeep, during which she scratched his face.

Frank goes out into the backyard to finish grilling. The table has been set with Grandmother Hallingdahl's china and tablecloth and pewter horse candlesticks, the candles three-quarters burned down—Frank and Siri have been waiting a while. Siri brings out the salads Karena made that afternoon. She and Karena pour milk and, since this is a special occasion, Zinfandel. When Frank comes in with the burgers and the three of them sit down, Karena's parents toast her. They give her a watch for college—so she won't ever be late for class. Siri fixes Karena's burger, decorating the patty with pickle eyes and a ketchup grin to make a face. Karena laughs with her parents over this reminder of her childhood and claps when Siri produces a bakery cake—*Happy 18th, Karena and Charles!*—and Frank and Siri sing to her. Karena dutifully polishes off two slices, just as she finished her burger, potato salad, and pea salad. She will never eat any of these foods again.

36

Two nights later Karena awakens suddenly at four thirty A.M. She sits in bed for a minute, heart thudding, trying to figure out what startled her. Then she gets up, uses the bathroom, and wanders out to the living room. Although it's a warm, stuffy night her arms are covered with goose bumps, and she pulls them in against her ribs beneath her New Heidelburg Eagles T-shirt, leaving the sleeves empty. She curls up on the davenport and looks out the big window. The streetlamps fill the room with a baby-aspirin orange glow. The air pump at the B&M gas station across the street is still going *ticka-ticka-tick*. But nothing moves. In her parents' bedroom one of them—Frank, probably—is snoring in a deep, fluttery way. There's no sound from Charles's lair. The house is so deeply silent it makes Karena's ears ring.

She rubs her arms in her T-shirt. Normally she likes to sit in the living room if she wakes in the night, the little secret of being awake by herself, the solitude. But now all Karena can think about is how cheerful she has had to pretend to be, how smiley at her birthday supper. Is this how it's going to be from now on? Going up to the U, setting up her dorm room, meeting people, writing letters home—throughout all of it, Karena will have to watch her step, to weigh and measure her responses, to think, Is this normal? Am I acting right? The amount of all the pretending she'll have to do exhausts her. And she's suddenly unbearably lonely, as though somebody has taken her by the hand and led her away from everyone else on earth.

Behind her eyes a carousel of images advances in a loop, as it has ever since the incident, like the slideshow projector Tiff's dad loves to show off. *Tchk*: Tiff and her sister as toddlers in the wading pool. *Tchk*: Tiff's mom smilingly blocking the lens with one hand. Except in Karena's case, it's *tchk*: the clouds congealing in layers. *Tchk*: the hail. *Tchk*: the man on the road. *Tchk*: Charles digging at his face. The green tornado. The gas station canopy bright with lights. The bats in the dark trees . . .

Charles. Something is wrong with Charles.

Karena knows it, just suddenly knows it despite the silence, as surely as if Charles were standing there yelling in her ear.

She pushes her arms back through the sleeves of her T-shirt and heads toward the cellar. Pauses at the top of the stairs and tilts her head slightly. Listening. Then starts down, the metal no-slip strips on the steps cold on her bare feet.

"Charles," Karena whispers once she's in the main room of the cellar, the big room, where they used to play roller-rink in the winter. She stands still again, but she doesn't hear him crying, his telltale lowing. There's only the ringing in her ears, a high, atonal *eeeeeeeeee*—and the smell of old linoleum.

"Charles," Karena says again and walks toward the lair. There's a faint blue light beneath the door, flickering as if a TV is on.

"Hey, Charles," Karena whispers outside his door. She taps on it. "You okay? I just woke up suddenly, and I got scared . . ."

She tries the door. It's unlocked. She pushes it open. There's nobody in the lair. Only the papers on the walls, stirring in the breeze Karena has created. And the lightning in the lamps, the branches of electricity frantically crawling across the surfaces of the globes and discs as if seeking a way out.

Karena has been so convinced she would find Charles here that it takes her a second to realize he's not. So much for the twindar, she thinks. Still not working. Yet she bends over to look beneath the work-table, the cot—and then she hears it, a scrabbling on the other side of the wall like a rodent in the pipes. Of course. Charles's bathroom. She should have known.

She hurries from the lair and into what's essentially a cement closet, containing the creepy shower stall and lidless toilet the rest of the family used to use only during emergencies, when the one upstairs was blocked. Now this is Charles's bathroom, and Karena suspects that in the way of guys, the grosser it is, the more he likes it. And it is gross. Bare lightbulb. No curtain on the stall. Bugs in the corners. In the shower a bar of Irish Spring so old it has cracks in it yet is covered with soap mucus. And Charles, sitting in the middle of the floor in his boxers and T-shirt, taking handfuls of pills from the pile in front of him and popping them in his mouth. Swallowing with the aid of water from his Flintstones glass. Taking more pills. Swallowing.

"No, Charles," Karena says. "What are you doing? Stop, Charles! Stop it!"

Charles ignores her. He tosses more pills in his mouth. Sips from the glass. Swallows.

Karena runs over and kicks the pile of pills, scattering them like an anthill. Some are covered with lint, others half dissolved. Charles's lithium—and all the other medications Dr. H has tried him on, but it's the lithium that terrifies Karena. Although Dr. H has told them it's a salt that occurs in the body naturally, he has warned them that Charles's blood level will have to be carefully monitored while he's on it, because too much lithium is lethally toxic.

Karena sweeps her foot around, stomping on the pills, sending them into the corners. Charles crawls after them. "Fuck off," he cries. "Get out, K! Leave me alone."

"How many have you taken, Charles? How much have you taken, huh?" Karena spins in a circle, not knowing what to do. Then she drops beside her twin, wincing as some of the pills dig into her kneecaps.

"Throw up, Charles," she says. "Make yourself throw up. Right now. Or I'm going to make you do it."

Charles shakes his head.

"Fine," says Karena.

She grabs the back of Charles's neck and then, wincing, she shoves the second and third fingers of her left hand down his throat. His mouth is shockingly hot and wet and Karena grimaces wildly, praying he won't bite down. If he does, she'll lose her fingers. The strongest muscle in the human body is the jaw. But again Karena is banking on the fact that Charles won't hurt her, her of all people, and again she's right. Charles doesn't stop her, but he doesn't fight her, either. Karena slides her fingers farther down his throat and crooks them, tickling. She knows how to do this from Tiff, who's taught Karena how to make herself throw up when she's eaten or drunk too much. Karena, being naturally thin like Frank, doesn't take as much advantage of the skill as Tiff does, but occasionally it comes in handy.

Like now. After a minute Karena feels Charles's throat convulsing and the hot gush of vomit on her hand. She grimly keeps it there, letting the stuff slide down her wrist and patter on the floor. Only when Charles has thrown up three times and his spit is clear does Karena let him go. He falls back from her, gasping, and Karena collapses too, shaking her hand and wiping it on the cement.

"Ugh," she says. "Gah."

"Don't do that, K," Charles says hoarsely, coughing. "Don't do that, K. Use the shower."

Karena looks down at her hand. Its back is scraped and bleeding. She gets up and rinses it off under the stream, forgoing the slimy soap.

"Don't you ever fucking do that again, Charles," she says. "You hear me?"

Charles is sitting in the corner, his knees drawn up. He doesn't answer. Doesn't change expression. Doesn't blink. Karena can't tell if he hasn't heard her or is just pretending not to. She starts unspooling several yards of toilet paper, to clean up. As best she can, she scoops the mess on the floor into the toilet, flushing handfuls at a time so as not to block the pipes. Charles watches, his face dull with exhaustion.

Finally Karena stands, hands on hips, and looks around.

"I think that's as done as it'll get tonight," she says, more to herself than Charles. "I'll run the hose in in the morning."

Then she turns to her brother, who is staring at the wall.

"Get up," she says. "Come on. I'll help you."

She pulls Charles to his feet, and he stands there as if not knowing what to do.

Karena puts her arm around his waist. He's not smelling so fresh either and should probably go in the shower too. But she's had enough for one night. She's done.

"Come on, Charles," she says, and walks him toward his lair.

37

In the little room Charles settles onto his cot, wedging the pillow under his cheek. Karena shuts off the lightning lamps and fits herself in next to him, feet to head. Legend has it this is the way they always slept as babies too. Siri would put them right side up in their crib, and they'd suck each other's thumbs to get to sleep, but by morning Karena would always have migrated south, and they'd be fitted together like puzzle pieces, yin and yang.

It's not quite the same now, since Charles's shins have become bony and furry, but Karena makes herself as comfortable as she can, pillowing her head on one of his calves.

"You doing okay, Charles?" she asks. "I mean, can you sleep?"

Charles croaks and clears his throat. His voice is a low rasp from the vomiting. "I think so."

"Good," says Karena, though she feels as though she might never close her eyes again. She stares into the dark. She can tell Charles is equally alert, although he doesn't move and his breathing is calm enough.

Presently he says, "You shouldn't have come down, K."

Karena shifts uneasily.

"What are you talking about?"

"You know what I mean. You should have let me go."

Karena sinks her fingernails into the scant meat of Charles's ankle. He hisses in a breath.

"Ow!" he says. "What the fuck."

"Don't ever say that, Charles," Karena says. "Don't—ever—even—think it."

"Jesus, K, let go," Charles says, trying to pull his leg away.

"Never," she says. "I never will."

After a minute Karena feels his muscles relax, and she lies very still. She is terrified to move, to do anything, because Charles has broken the seal. None of the Hallingdahls has ever so much as breathed the S-word among themselves, not after Charles disappeared from the Starlite, not after he jumped twenty feet off the water tower ladder. Not during the days and nights he lies down here, lowing. They don't mention the uncle who disappeared in his boat on the Mississippi on a perfectly lovely summer day, the great-aunt who stepped quietly down the well. They don't talk about it because if they did they would invite it, and the only time Karena has ever mentioned the word suicide in connection with her brother was seventy-five miles from here, up at the Mayo, in Dr. H's office. A safe and sanctioned place where they were supposed to talk about it, where Karena was just doing part of her job to keep her brother safe by describing her observations and fears about his symptoms. *No, he's never said it directly, but—yes, I'm afraid sometimes he might—kill himself.* And even then, despite the doctor's kind gaze and encouraging nods, Karena had felt the superstitious free-fall terror of betrayal, of having concretized the possibility and made it real.

Now she is paralyzed with the responsibility of what to do or say next. If it's the right thing, Karena might plant the one seed in her brother's mind that will take hold, sprout, grow, prevent him from action whenever he considers the idea. But if she says the wrong thing?

It turns out to be a moot point, because Charles speaks first.

"I'm sorry, K," he says. "But I just don't know if I can do this. It's bad enough to go Into the Black, and now I have to deal with this guy all the time . . ."

"What's Into the Black?" Karena asks.

Charles sighs, then coughs.

"It's how I feel when I'm down here," he says. "When I'm down, I go really, really down, K. It starts out like that feeling we get sometimes, the Dreads. When you get scared for no reason. Then it gets worse. Everything is—tilted. All the surfaces are untrustworthy. All the familiar things seem hostile, and nothing is safe. The angles are all fucked up, the floors, the ceilings and walls and sky and trees. And they tip me off Into the Black. That's this tarry, oozy place that traps me and holds me while my brain is raked over and over with a comb made of knives."

Karena feels a shudder work through him.

"It hurts so much, K," Charles says. "It hurts the insides of my eyes. Everything hurts from the inside out. But I can't move. That's Into the Black. And time is different there. A minute could be a day or a month. It doesn't matter. It's like one of those melted clocks."

Karena tightens her grip on Charles's ankle.

"But you always come out of it," she reminds him. "Right?"

"So far," Charles agrees. "But every time I'm so worried I won't. That I'll stay there forever. Death is totally not scary in comparison. To make that needle thing stop combing, to never feel it again or know it's coming, that would be peace."

Karena doesn't know what to say to this. She considers and discards answers at light speed: No, that's not peace, that's death. Maybe there's a way to make this stop happening. Even the drugs have to be better—

"And as if that's not bad enough," Charles says, "now I have to deal with this guy."

"What guy?" Karena says.

"Motorcycle Guy. He comes at night now."

A chill washes through Karena. She sits up, but in the deep well of the lair she can't see her brother's face.

"Charles," she says, "the Motorcycle Guy—he's dead."

"No kidding, K," Charles says dreamily. "That's what he wants. For me to be dead too. For me to come with him."

Karena tries to respond to this but for a minute can only shake her head. Finally she says, "Charles. Motorcycle Guy? He's not real."

"He is, though," says Charles implacably. "He's as real as you are, K. I wake up and he's sitting on the cot watching me with his, like, half a face. And I can smell him. He smells like beer, you know how those guys get when they've been in the bar awhile. And Swisher Sweets. And meat, bloody meat, like when you take hamburger out of the freezer and the blood leaks into the plastic—"

"Okay, Charles," says Karena. "I get it. But Charles . . . Motorcycle Guy is a hallucination. Even if you can smell him, it's a fake out. It's stress, I'm sure, but, Charles, and don't get mad, it's also the chemicals in your brain."

"Maybe so," Charles says. His voice is still soft, pensive. "But that doesn't make him not real. If I see and hear him, isn't he real to me? Reality is subjective, don't you know that by now? It's how we experience the world that makes it real to us. Like the dish towels."

"What dish towels?"

"The embroidered vegetables on the kitchen dish towels," Charles says, "you know they sing to me. In those creepy children's-chorus voices. *Charles, we seeeee you. Charles, we know what you're doing.* And the anchor. The news guy on TV. When I was five. He really did talk right to me, K. Told me I was a filthy, disgusting little boy and I should go get my mommy so I'd be spanked. That really happened to me as surely as you're sitting here. It wasn't pleasant, my visions aren't always, but they're real."

"But Charles," Karena says. She struggles for a politic way to phrase what Dr. H has told them: *When Charles sees and hears things that aren't there, this is called a psychotic break.* "What about the fact that nobody around you can see or hear these things? Doesn't that mean that they're probably not really there?"

"Not for you," says Charles. "But they are for me, and did you ever think maybe I am just more advanced? I am a genius, you know. Plus, they're not all bad. The storms, for instance. They talk to me too. They each have a different—voice is putting it too simply, but essence. Personality. Some are screamers. Some mutterers. But I always know how to find them."

"Okay," says Karena. "But—well, isn't that a reason not to—you know. And your study, what about that. Your abstract. You'd never be able to chase again."

"I know," says Charles. "And I'd miss the flying dream. That's what it's like when I'm up, when I'm really really really really up, like that dream we both have? The one where I'm flying over the hills for like hours and turn a corner and there's a tornado there? I'm up so high I can see the pattern, and that's so beautiful, K. There's nothing like it in the world. I wish you could see it—I've wished that so many times. I'd really miss that if I were dead."

"Good," says Karena. She lies back down, tucking her spine against Charles's legs. "Think about that. Whenever you go Into the Black, think about it."

"I do," says Charles. "But I swear, K. Most days I doubt I'll see thirty."

"Shut up, Charles," Karena says fiercely. "Just shut up! If you—did that, don't you know it would kill me? Don't you know I'd die too?"

"That's primarily why I haven't done it—yet. But I think you should start preparing for life as a half, K. I'll be with you, I'll always be there, I just won't be here. I don't know if I can take it."

Karena seizes his ankle again.

"You have to," she says. "You just have to, that's all. Promise me, Charles."

"I can't, K," says Charles. "But I promise to try, how's that?"

"Not good enough," says Karena.

They lie silently for a while, pushing at each other with their minds. Karena thinks of the axiomatic struggle they learned about in physics class: an unstoppable force meeting an immovable object. And she thinks, there must be a way out. There is no way. I have to tell. I can't. He'll go to jail, and he'll never make it. There must be a way out. There is no way—

And then she starts to have an idea.

As if Charles feels her disengage to consider it, he sighs.

"I don't want to think about it anymore tonight," he says. "I'm so tired. I just want to go to sleep. Okay, K? Can we do that?"

Karena shrugs.

"Will you stay with me, K?"

"Of course," she says.

"And would you do me a favor?"

"Depends. What is it?"

"Sing," says Charles.

Karena can't help but smile. It has been so long since she heard this request from Charles, not since they shared the room upstairs. Then, often, when he couldn't sleep, his small voice would issue imperiously forth from the dark: *Sing!* And when Karena stopped: *More!*

"Any requests?" she asks.

"No, whatever you want's fine."

"Okay," Karena says. "Hold on."

She clears her mind, thinking about it, then sings:

> *Say say my playmate*
> *Come out and play with me*
> *And bring your dollies three*
> *Climb up my apple tree*
> *Slide down my rain barrel*
> *Into my cellar door*
> *And we'll be jolly friends*
> *Forevermore . . .*

"More, please," Charles says when she is done. His voice is drowsy now. So Karena repeats the verse, then again, over and over until she starts to wind down too, like a music box. By the time the arrow-slit window lightens with dawn, Karena, like Charles, is fast asleep.

38

The sheriff comes up the front walk with Frank at seven the next evening, and when Karena sees him from the living room window, she thinks she's going to throw up. She turns to Siri, who's been watching and waiting with her, and says, "What the fuck?"

"Karena Lien Hallingdahl!" Siri says.

"Sorry," Karena says. "But why is the sheriff coming? Is it for—"

She points to the floor, indicating Charles's lair beneath it.

"Of course," snaps Siri. "Why else?"

"It's just—" stammers Karena. "I didn't know— I didn't expect— Oh jeez."

She fans her face, her heart scrambling in her chest. This is not good. This was not in the program. What Karena came up with—just this morning, in the shower, it hit her—was that she should tell Frank about Charles taking the pills, and Charles would go back to the Mayo. Not ideal, but better than jail, and maybe Dr. H could find something, anything that could help Charles. But when Karena went to Frank's office this afternoon and stood in the doorway and said, *I'm worried about Charles, last night he tried to hurt himself—like, permanently,* she thought Frank would drive Charles to the clinic himself. Or maybe orderlies would arrive in an ambulance to take him there—but not this. Not the sheriff! This is a disaster. What if Sheriff Cushing knows about Motorcycle Guy? What if he looks at Karena and intuits her involvement? That's what he's trained to do, isn't he? Plus, even if the sheriff doesn't know—yet—the second Charles sees him he'll blurt it out, assuming Karena has tattled and the sheriff has come to take him away.

"What is wrong with you?" Siri says. "Stop fidgeting."

"You know, Ma, I've been thinking," Karena says, "maybe this isn't such a good idea after all. I might have been mistaken. About Charles—"

"What are you talking about?" Siri says.

"I mean maybe I just imagined—"

But it's too late. The screen door opens, and the front door with its louvered glass slats, and then Sheriff Cushing is in their living room like a bear in a house trailer. His whiffle cut nearly grazes the Hallingdahls' living room ceiling as he says his hellos, during which Karena's stare fastens on his giant black shoes. Normally she likes Sheriff Cushing— everyone does. He's the youngest sheriff ever elected in Foss County, and although Tiff, who prefers more sophisticated men, has declared him a typical no-neck New Heidelburg bullet-head, the sheriff has always been gentle with Charles, which Karena appreciates. But if she looks at him now he'll surely know what she and Charles have done. Right? How much does a Minnesota sheriff know about a hit-and-run down in Iowa? Would he even be aware of something like that?

"Karena, the sheriff's talking to you," Siri says.

Normal, Karena thinks, act normal. She gives Sheriff Cushing a huge grin.

The sheriff looks a little startled. "That's okay, Mrs. H," he says to Siri. "I know everyone's kind of distracted right now."

He smiles nicely at Karena.

"So, college girl now, eh?" he says. "You going up to the Cities then?"

"That's right," Karena says. "Next month." It's the first time she's realized it takes work to smile, that it requires actual muscles in the face.

"That's great," says the sheriff. "Good for you. That's real exciting."

Then, the niceties accomplished, the four of them just stand there. The silence thickens, punctuated only by Frank clearing his throat. The fact that they're all here, in this rarely used room with its fireplace and knickknacks and the prized desk with the relatives under glass, feels like they're participating in some awful, formal ceremony nobody quite knows the rules to. From outside they probably look like a diorama, Karena thinks, like the pioneer days scenes she saw once in the Great Platte River Road Archway Monument Museum on a field trip. Except in this case the exhibit would be called *Family In Trouble, 1988*. Maybe they should move into the kitchen.

As if he's having something of the same thoughts, the sheriff says, "Well, folks, should we get this show on the road?"

But nobody answers. They all remain where they are, rooted in dread. The atmosphere in the room continues to gather, tightening like a fist.

The sheriff's walkie-talkie squawks in a burst of static. He checks it, then asks, "So where is Chuck tonight? Is he here?"

"Downstairs, in his lai—his room," Karena says. "Do you want me to get him?"

At the same time Siri says, "Doug, I noticed you're on foot. Did you bring anyone to help? Just in case?"

"Sure," the sheriff says, "they're parked in back, over on Cedar Street. I figured we'd go out through the back, spare you folks any gawking."

He looks at Karena.

"You think it'd go easiest that way," he asks, "if you bring him up?"

Frank clears his throat.

"AHEM!" he says, "no, she's been involved enough," and Karena thinks of him praising her not an hour ago in his office, saying, *You're a good girl to have told me, Karena. A good sister.*

"I'll get him," Frank says.

"No way, Frank," Siri says, and Karena counters, "You can't, Dad, he'll know in a second something's up—"

But while they are all debating who should get Charles, he solves the problem for them by loping up the steps from the cellar. He stops at the top, wiping his mouth. He's been sleeping, deeply from the looks of it. His face is flushed, red pillow lines crisscrossing the fresh scratches on his cheek. His hair is flat on one side and sticking up in the back. And as they all turn to look at him Karena feels the pity she does when she sees cows being loaded into the perforated trucks for the slaughterhouse. Run, Charles, she wants to shout. Run!

But she just makes a noise in her throat.

Charles blinks at them, disoriented.

"Wow," he says, "quite a party, everyone's here, even Pops. What's going on?"

Then he sees the sheriff. His eyes widen, his nostrils flare. Karena feels in her stomach the cold bolt of shock that rises in his, and for a second she thinks he's going to make a break for it.

Then he looks at her and smiles.

"You bitch," he says. "You fucking bitch."

Karena shakes her head as Frank clears his throat and Siri says something and the sheriff says, "Now let's not have any of that."

Karena locks eyes with Charles.

"I didn't tell, Charles," she says. "I didn't tell them about anything except the pills, you hear me? Just about last night. Just about the pills. Only about that."

But Charles backs away from her, clutching his head.

"Oh my God," he says, laughing. "To think I trusted you. I can't believe I trusted you—"

Then suddenly, so fast she doesn't have time to move, he lunges at Karena.

"I trusted you," he yells in her face. He's got her by the upper arms, his fingers digging in. He shakes her back and forth. "I trusted you! You betrayed me! You totally fucking betrayed me!"

Then he goes flying backward, the sheriff yanking him off Karena from behind.

"That's enough, Chuck," he says. "Calm down now. Can you calm down? Your sister's just trying to help."

Charles bucks and thrashes in the sheriff's grip, his bare feet scrabbling on the carpet. His face is brick red.

"Oh yeah, she's really trying to help," he pants. "She's trying to help me right into a jail cell—"

"No!" says Karena and she steps forward. Her biceps throb where Charles grabbed her.

"Listen . . . to . . . me," she says into her brother's face. "I just told them about the pills. That's *all*. You are not going to jail. Just where somebody can help you. Where they can protect you from—things like you saw last night. Okay, Charles? Okay?"

She nods and maintains eye contact and thinks at him as hard as she can: I did not tell them about Motorcycle Guy, Charles. I would not do that. I will never do that.

Charles continues to struggle, but he looks uncertain. Slowly, he stops. He stands still. Then his face crumples.

"Oh, K," he says.

He begins to cry, those raw gut-sobs like he's retching, and lowers his head. The sheriff is still holding his arms and he can't do anything to wipe his face.

"It's all right, Charles," Karena says. "It's going to be all right. Trust me."

"She's right, buddy," says Sheriff Cushing, low and soothing. "Everything's going to be okay. Can you tell us what happened? Your sister told us you tried to hurt yourself last night. Is that true?"

Charles nods. Tears drop to the carpet.

"I guess," he says. "I guess so. Yeah, I did. I took a bunch of pills. I should have used a gun or something, but I was too much of a wuss to do it. She stopped me," he says. "K did. She made me throw up."

"Okay, good guy," the sheriff says softly. "Now we're just going to go somewhere to talk, get you some help. Can you do that, Chuck? Can you come with me calmly?"

Charles raises his head and looks at Karena.

"Don't make me go, K," he says. "Don't let them take me. Don't let them take me away. Please."

Karena can't hold it back anymore. She puts her hands over her face and cries very hard for a couple of seconds. Then she looks squarely at Charles.

"It'll be okay, Charles," she says. "It's *not* like jail, remember. It's a place where they can help you. I'll come as soon as I can."

"Promise," says Charles.

"I promise," says Karena.

"Okay, buddy," says the sheriff, "it's time to go now."

Gently he starts to turn Charles around.

"K?" Charles says, his voice breaking.

Karena nods.

"It's all right," Charles says to the sheriff. "I'm calm now. You can let go."

They walk through the dining area, Sheriff Cushing still holding Charles's elbow, and Karena wants to shout Wait! The word building up inside her as involuntary as a sneeze. No, wait, bring him back, please! I was wrong, I'll do better, I've changed my mind—

But she stands watching the sheriff and her brother move down to the sunporch, where he'll be escorted out through the back and spirited off across the back lawns so nobody will see, although of course they all will. The Clarences, the Zimmermans and Schmecks, they will all have noticed the prowler on Cedar Street, they will all be at their windows to watch that crazy Charles Hallingdahl get taken away. Again. At the screen door Charles stops, and Karena hears the sheriff murmur something like, *Just a couple more steps, buddy. Just a little farther. That's right.* Charles looks back at Karena, weeping, terrified. He tries to smile. Then they are through the door.

39

The Black Wing Asylum for inpatient care is a former elementary school perched on the bluffs of the Mississippi, halfway between New Heidelburg and Rochester. A few days after Charles has been taken away Karena makes her first visit there, stepping timidly through the corridor she's been directed to, clutching a slip of paper with Charles's room number on it in one hand. Her brother has been a good patient so far, the nurse at reception said. He hasn't given them any trouble, hasn't even had to go to lockdown once, so he's been assigned a Level 3 Room. Karena has no idea what this means. She's totally lost and incidental in this place that has sucked in her twin. She doesn't know how anything here works. She tiptoes along consulting the room numbers, trying not to see the other rooms' inhabitants: a man listing in a wheelchair, a woman making barking noises, a girl pulling her own hair. The walls are Depression green below the waist, the ceilings high, the very tall windows reinforced by bars and chicken wire. But at least they have windows in this unit.

Charles's room is 327, and at 325 Karena stops. She is alone because Siri is at the Back-to-School Bake Sale, and Frank, of course, is in court. They have all agreed it's especially important to put on a brave face at a time like this, to go about business as usual. At the moment, though, Karena dearly wishes Siri were with her, or even Frank. She takes a deep breath, knocks on her brother's door, and pushes it open.

But then she sees there's nothing to be afraid of, because it's Charles, after all. Just Charles. He isn't straitjacketed or bound in any way, not spread-eagled in restraints as Karena had feared. Just sitting Indian-style on one of two beds in a T-shirt and pajama bottoms, his elbows balanced on his knees, his hands dangling from his wrists. Looking out the wired and barred window at the lawn.

"Hey, brothah," Karena says, buoyant with relief. She walks to the other bed—empty, thank God—and sits. "Here I am, as promised, in the flesh. How're you doing?"

But Charles doesn't answer or turn, and Karena feels a little chill of fear. She ducks her head so she can look into his face, and then she sees the difference, all right. Her brother is a zombie. His mouth hangs open slightly, his eyes half closed. His hair looks oily and matted. One of his hands ticks, jumping over and over. He stares dully out the window at the pallid light of the overcast day.

"Oh, no," Karena whispers. Oh, Charles, she thinks. What have they done to you?

She moves over to the other bed and sits next to her brother. He doesn't move. He doesn't smell like himself, of Irish Spring and fast food, but of rubbing alcohol and urine. Karena's heart breaks—she can feel it, a literal pain in her chest, her throat. She moves closer still, her hip against Charles's, and pets his stiff hair.

"Hey," she says softly. "It's me, Charles. K. Can you hear me? I'm here."

Slowly, slowly, Charles turns his head. It seems to take him five minutes to look at her. His mouth twitches at one corner, and Karena realizes he is trying to smile.

"Hi, K," he says. "Iss . . . you?" His voice is low, slow, draggy, a 45-rpm record played on the 33 speed.

"It is," says Karena. "It's me, Charles. Here I am."

What have they got him on? she thinks. What the fuck have they put him on? Karena is used to seeing Charles on different medications, but she has never seen him like this. Charles is drooling a little, his chin wet.

In that infinitesimal slow motion, he lifts his arm, up, up. Wipes his mouth. Gazes at his hand.

"K," he says. "I guess . . . they got me. Pretty . . . drugged up."

"A little maybe," Karena says. "I guess they're trying you on something new. How are you feeling?"

Charles is still examining his hand, but at the question he raises his head, with enormous effort, and looks at Karena with his half shut eyes. His head wobbles back a bit on his neck. A runner of spit starts to come from his mouth, stretching and dangling, and Karena is reminded of Silly Putty, how she and Charles used to grab one end each of the stuff and pull in opposite directions until it spun out into airy nothingness.

She looks around for Kleenex, but seeing none, she is about to wipe Charles's mouth with her sleeve when he sucks the spit up himself, like a strand of spaghetti—*fsoop!*

"Sorry," he says. "'M . . . so gross."

"No," says Karena. Her throat aches and aches. "You're not, Charles. Never."

He lets his head tip back a little more so he can see her.

"C'n . . . I ask. A favor?"

"Sure. Of course, Charles. Anything."

"My . . . ledger," he says. "My . . . storm. Ledger. Could you . . ."

"Bring it?" Karena finishes for him. "Sure. Right away. Do you need anything else?"

But Charles's head swings sideways, and after a minute the rest of him follows. He turns toward the window again.

"Charles?"

Charles gazes out at the lawn, or maybe at something only he can see, or maybe at nothing. His chin droops toward his chest.

"Okay, Charles," says Karena.

She gets up and bends to kiss him. She is crying a little.

"I'll be right back," Karena says.

He is struggling to say something, and Karena leans closer.

"What? What's that, Charles?"

"Pruh," he says. "Pruh. Pruh. Promise."

"Oh," says Karena, straightening. "Of course. Yes. I will. I do, Charles. I promise."

She waits for a minute in case he says anything else, then kisses him and backs out of the room.

Once she's out in the hallway, Karena starts to run. She sprints through the corridor as if someone's chasing her, bursts through the unit's doors, explodes into the lobby.

"Hey," the nurse behind the desk calls, rising. "What's going on? Everything all right in there?"

But Karena doesn't answer. She doesn't have time to. She is on a mission. She has to get that ledger to her brother. She runs down the front steps, jumps into Siri's Jeep, guns it out of the lot. Then she is turning onto the River Road and speeding back up through the bluffs and Looney Valley to the plateau, the farmland on which New Heidelburg sits.

It should take a half hour to get home, maybe forty minutes; that's how long it took Karena to get to Black Wing, but she was going the speed limit then. Now she is driving seventy, then seventy-five, eighty. The speedometer really jumps up once she hits Highway 44. She blows past slower vehicles, sedans and pickups, giving the finger to a startled farmer on a Harvester who doesn't get onto the shoulder fast enough. She passes an Amish buggy with enough speed to rock it on its wheels. She chain-smokes and looks at herself in the rearview—face tight and patchy from crying, hair wild in the humidity—and presses her foot to the accelerator. "Get out of my way," she yells at the other vehicles. "Get out of my fucking WAY!"

She lights another cigarette. God, what have they *done* to him? If Karena didn't know better she'd think they gave him a lobotomy—or God, oh no, was it electroshock therapy? Was it? The thought makes her screech off onto the shoulder and throw the door open, to vomit. But when she just retches and retches, her head hanging over the gravel, she pulls back in and gets back on the road. No. It can't be. They wouldn't do that to Charles, would they? Karena would have known, wouldn't she? Wouldn't she have felt it, something so drastic, Charles's fear and terror and panic as they strapped him down, inserted the bit between his teeth like a horse, then threw the switch?

Although maybe they did, since Charles is so resistant to medication, refuses to take it—and no wonder. The lithium, what Dr. H had him on initially, nearly killed him with its side effects, the cure almost worse than the disease. First the blackheads, massing across his forehead like thick pepper. Then his stomach, attacks of diarrhea so bad Charles was afraid to leave the house, to venture more than a few feet from a bathroom. Then his inability to concentrate, to read, to think. *It's like my thoughts have to squeeze through a little door in my head, K,* he told her during the first week. *They're so slow. I just feel so stupid. I am not myself.*

And his hands. His poor hands. The second Sunday after Charles's diagnosis, the Hallingdahls were out again with the Budges, this time at the church supper up in Little Springs, where Frank and Mr. Budge had recently won a water rights case. They were celebrating. They were showing that everything was fine. They were sitting in the basement of the Little Springs Good Shepherd Lutheran Church, at a big round table with the Budges and a quartet of farmers and their wives, and everyone was discussing the case except Karena, who was watching in horror as her brother, his barbed-wire scratches from the Starlite incident still fading on his neck and face, tried to eat his sloppy joe. He bent over his paper plate, gripping the bun in his shaking hands. Meat scattered out of it, onto the table, his lap, the floor. Conversation slowed, then ceased. Carefully Charles set down the sloppy joe and attempted some potato salad. Potatoes pattered off the fork in gluey lumps. Frank cleared his throat and smiled around at everyone. *Excuse me,* he said. Then he tucked his napkin into his collar and moved over to feed Charles some hamburger.

It took about twenty-four hours for the story to spread through town, that Charles Hallingdahl had gotten hold of some weird drug, like bad coke maybe, that made his hands shake so he had to be fed by his own dad like a baby or a retard. Behind the scenes the medications were quickly adjusted. Yet for every change Dr. H made to the cocktail, there was some new and horrible trade-off. Charles's hands stabilized, but he developed a stutter. When he could speak clearly again, a rash appeared. There were night sweats, nightmares, hiccups, pustules, humiliations of such endless creativity and caliber that even Dr. H finally admitted, *It seems Charles is unusually sensitive to medication.* They returned him to the lowest possible dosage of lithium, but of course by then Charles didn't want to take it. Karena doesn't blame him. It is so unfair, she thinks, that her brother should have to pay this high a price for something that's not his fault to begin with. Yes, Charles is a genius, and he loves his manias. But Charles's disorder is the gift nobody wants to get given. There is no cure for it, no solution. Either Charles takes his medication and suffers, or he doesn't and everyone else does. It is colossally, sickeningly, definitively unfair.

When Karena reaches the house it is empty and quiet, the humidity trapping and amplifying the family's smells: the tuna hot dish Siri made last night that nobody wanted, her cigarette smoke, musty carpet. The light is sad and green, that patient watery light that precedes a rain. Karena runs down to Charles's lair. Where is it? Where is the storm ledger? She spies it on Charles's card table and grabs it. The lair is a bad place to be without Charles, a dead battery. Even the lightning lamps are quiet. Karena tucks the journal into her jeans jacket and thunders up the stairs.

She drives back to Black Wing just as quickly, but once she's in the lot she sits in the Jeep and smokes her last cigarette. The nicotine makes her a little nauseous, and Karena realizes she's had nothing to eat today, she was too nervous at breakfast. It is past three o'clock now, and the day has brightened a bit, the sun not strong enough to come out but making the sky a blinding white. Karena smokes and looks at the asylum, a tall old redbrick building on a vast green lawn. She tries to pick out her brother's window. She fails. She finishes the cigarette, butts it, gets out. Sticky condensation dots her hair and skin from the trees.

She takes Charles's storm ledger out of her inner pocket and grips it in both hands. Looks resolutely at the asylum. Time to go in.

But she can't.

She does try. She really does. She tells herself, Just do it now. She tells herself, You promised. Stop being a baby. She tells herself, You have to. It's Charles, Charles in there. Charles. Her brother. Waiting.

But Karena can't go in.

She doesn't know how long she stands in the parking lot, clutching the ledger, finally not even arguing with herself anymore but just staring at the asylum. Long enough for the ledger's cover to grow damp and imprint some of its marbled pattern on her hands. Then a crow caws, and a droplet falls on Karena's head from somewhere, and she gets moving.

She returns to the Jeep. Scrabbles in the glove compartment among the flashlights and napkins and packets of old orange crackers for a pen. She sets the ledger on the hood of the Jeep and tears a page from the back of it. Scribbles on it—her normally neat handwriting jumping all over the place—*Property of Charles Hallingdahl, Rm 327. Please make sure he gets this!!!!*

Using one of the bobby pins she also finds in the glove box, Karena secures this note to the front of the ledger. She darts up the asylum's stone steps and starts to push open the door, but she can't. She is such a fucking coward she can't even do that much. Instead she sets the ledger on the top step beneath the overhang, propping it against a sad-eyed stone lion. Halfway down the steps she pauses, rips off her jacket, and jogs back up to wrap the ledger in it. She doesn't want it to get wet. Hands shaking, throat dry, heart pounding in it, Karena again gives the ledger to the lion, tucking the bundle beneath the animal's stone mane. Says, "Take good care of it." Takes one last look at it. Then runs.

40

A month later, the day before she leaves for the U, Karena goes for one last drive with Tiff. Why not? She's got time. She's all packed, her room stripped of personal items, her suitcase and duffel sitting at the foot of her bed. And everyone's getting together on French Island for one last bash. Mike Schwartz and his crew will be there, Tiff says, and Benji R. and Weez and Jeff Wisneski, but Karena doesn't care. She's going only for Tiff. She can't believe she ever cared about these people, the guys her brother called the trogs, the troglodytes, that Karena thought what they did mattered, about a hundred years ago.

It is a gorgeous afternoon, as clear as a stained-glass window, all blues and greens and golds. Two nights ago a big wind came and blasted away all the humidity, leaving what feels like fall weather in its wake. The sun already has that September slant to it, a bright white glare like an unshaded bulb, although only a few leaves have started to turn. Karena and Tiff are in Tiff's dad's F-150, Tiff driving. They are on the Foss Line Road, which connects New Heidelburg to the Mississippi, corkscrewing down twenty-three hairpin turns through the bluffs. Usually Tiff—and Karena too—likes to whip around the bends as sharply as she can, so they can feel the drop in their stomachs and make themselves scream. But today, out of respect for this crossroads in their destinies, soberly conscious this is their last afternoon together, Tiff glides the big truck down the switchbacks as carefully as a grandma.

Tiff is nervous too, smoking and talking nonstop. She is flying out to Harvard the day after Karena leaves, and she has already repacked her trunk fourteen times. ". . . so I don't know," she is saying, "what do you think, the Keds or the Converse? The high-tops might be too, I don't know, funky, or like I'm trying too hard. But I don't want them to think I'm just some hick, you know?"

Karena gazes at a herd of cows standing in a muddy creek. They've reached Looney Valley, the bottomlands sandwiched between the Foss Line Road and the Mississippi bluffs to the east. Karena doesn't like this part. She feels hemmed in, and the farms down here look cramped to her. This is maybe what the land looks like in the part of the country Tiff is going to: western Massachusetts, Vermont. Frankly, Karena doesn't envy her. All those old folded mountains and sooty cities and snotty Eastern girls.

But she says, "Anh, don't worry. It's just Boston. It's not like you're going to New York City or anything."

"True!" Tiff says, brightening. "Very true." She flicks her Virginia Slim out the window—Karena wishes Tiff hadn't switched to those, everyone knows they make your lungs bleed—and immediately lights another, her rhinestone bangles jangling.

"Besides," says Karena, "you'll still be getting your allowance, right? Why don't you wait until you get there, then buy what everyone else is wearing?"

"Oh . . . my . . . God," says Tiff. "Why didn't I think of that? My brain is a total sieve. What'm I going to do without you, Kay? I don't know. I really don't."

Karena smiles. They turn north on the River Road and now she can breathe more easily. The big limestone cliffs still tower over the truck on their left, covered with brush and honeycombed with rattler dens. But the sky opens up over the Mississippi on their right. The river is a mile wide here, flowing around islands big enough to live on, until it laps up against Wisconsin on the other side.

Karena glances up the road toward Crescent City, then looks out at the water instead, at its barges and inlets. If they kept going north on the River Road, past Crescent City, they would reach Black Wing. But today she is not going that far.

Suddenly there's a hornetlike buzzing—*ffzzzzmmm, fzzzzzmmm!*—and a swarm of motorcycles passes them on both sides. Probably headed up to the ice cream parlor in Alma that for some reason is a popular hangout for bikers. Karena cuts her eyes at the motorcycles as they pass. She waits to be overtaken by the shakes, like the strange cold fit she had yesterday. She was at home then, no cycles in the vicinity—she wasn't even outside, just in the bathroom packing her extra shampoo and crimper in her bag. But then Siri slammed a cupboard in the kitchen or dropped a cookbook maybe. Either way there was a *bang!* and Karena had to sit down on the floor, right on the pink shag rug, she was shaking so badly.

Nothing like that happens now, though. Just a light ripple of goose bumps, as if Karena's skin had been touched by a breeze that is not gone. Karena can't say she's surprised. She has discovered something over the last month, since leaving her brother in Black Wing: Time will fold over the past if you let it. Sure, they are still there, the day of the storm, the man on the road and the green tornado, and part of Karena will always be stuck on that road, and in the Jeep and the lair and the boy bathroom. And in her brother's room in Black Wing and on the steps outside it too. But the images are embedded deeper in her now, and Karena senses she could let them go, sink, let everyday events close over them and hide them from view—even as the great muddy water to her right has been said to swallow fishing shacks, boats, even railway cars, pulling them down to its silty bottom where the muscular current carries them away.

"Holy shit, did you see that asshole?" Tiff is saying. "Like that last guy, he wasn't even wearing a helmet! Well, rock on, buddy. Thin the herd, I say. . . . Hey," she says to Karena. "Are you all right?"

Karena nods. "Sure," she says, "I'm fine."

She lights another Marlboro, feeling Tiff looking at her.

"It's okay, you know," says Tiff in a lower, more somber tone—Tiff's Therapy Voice is how Karena thinks of it. "It's healthy to talk about it—if you want. Him, I mean. Charles."

Karena resists rolling her eyes. Oh boy. The gossip situation must be really bad if Tiff is referring to Charles as Charles instead of Thing Number Two. "Nothing to talk about," Karena says. "There's nothing else I can do for him right now. So it's over."

"I'm sorry about what happened, though," Tiff says.

Karena sighs out a nasty-tasting stream of smoke and looks at her cigarette. The cherry is burning unevenly, only on one side. Somebody is thinking about her, this means. She takes a fierce drag to fix it and the paper crackles.

"Does everyone know?" she asks. "About Black Wing?"

"Well—yeah," Tiff says.

"So everyone's talking about it?"

Tiff checks herself out in the mirror—freshly maroon-streaked hair, navy eyeliner, feather earrings—for reassurance.

"Well—yeah," Tiff says again. "But only nice things," she adds hastily. "I mean, saying how much they support your family, stuff like that."

Karena smiles. It's not true, of course, but it's nice of Tiff to attempt the lie. Tiff is a terrible liar.

"Thanks, Tiff," she says.

"No sweat," says Tiff.

They drive for a few minutes in silence except for the radio, which Tiff has turned down low so they can talk.

Then Tiff says, "It's probably for the best, you know?"

"What's that?" Karena says.

"What happened with Charles," says Tiff. Her cheeks start to mottle and flush, but she forges gamely on. "At least he's got a diagnosis now, right? It explains a lot. Like, he's not just obnoxious—kidding, kidding. Seriously, now we know he's got an imbalance. A medical problem. And he's where they can help him, right, Kay? That's a total positive, that now they can really do something for him, get him on medication."

She shakes out her hair and glances sideways at Karena.

"That's got to be a relief at least," she says. "Right?"

"I guess," says Karena. She tries to take a last drag on her cigarette but it has kept burning only on the one side and extinguished itself. She feeds it to the slipstream. Maybe at the U she'll give up smoking.

"After all!" says Tiff in her psychologist voice, sticking her forefinger in the air. The bangles slide down her arm, jangling. "Have I not always said Charles needs clinical treatment?"

Then she says, "Hey . . . oh no . . . oh, I'm sorry, Kay, I didn't mean . . . hang on," and she puts her left blinker on and swerves into the lot of Leidel's Apple Stand, not open yet, though in a week it will be packed. She puts the truck in park and turns to Karena and holds out her arms.

"Oh, sweetie, c'mere," she says.

For Karena is crying now, really crying, whooping and sobbing and gasping for breath like a little kid. The tears pour from her in a rush, and she lets Tiff pull her in, lays her head against Tiff's shoulder and wails. The gearshift pokes Karena's hip and she smells the smoke in Tiff's coarse straight hair, and Tiff's apple shampoo that comes in pink bottles and her hairspray, and when Karena opens her streaming eyes she sees the River Road with the cars whizzing by and the railroad tracks beside it, the blue sky with its puffy white clouds, the steel bridge to Wisconsin and the islands with their brushy trees. The Mississippi flows slowly by and the sun shines clean over everything, and Karena knows Tiff thinks she is crying because of Charles, because her brother is stuck in a mental asylum instead of out and about on this beautiful day the way he should be, healthy and alert and comfortable in his own skin. And this is true; she is. But even more Karena is crying for herself. She cries because of her cowardice, because she told Charles she would come back and never did. She cries because of her selfishness, because she has turned him in not just so he could get help but so she would be free to go. She cries because of these things she has discovered in her own cold heart, and most of all she cries because there are so many things she will never be able to tell anyone, not even her best friend; because her whole life long, there will be so much nobody will ever know.

PART III

KARENA AND CHARLES,
AUGUST 2008

41

They drive into the Twin Cities on the early afternoon of July 22, Karena behind the wheel in her Laredo with Kevin, Charles following in his canary-yellow wagon. Karena starts to head home automatically, but Kevin points out it makes more sense for them to drop him at his place first, since he doesn't have his car. He lives on Grand Avenue in St. Paul, and he directs Karena along the wide old boulevards, through the leafy streets.

Karena is edgy, twitchy, looking all around—especially in her rearview, to make sure the bright wagon is still there. It is. Tailing her sedately, serenely, almost at walking pace, Charles perhaps steering it with one finger. Karena meanwhile is driving defensively, as if under attack at rush hour. She hunches forward, sitting too long at four-way stops, slamming on the brakes at intersections. Every time she does this, her brother gives her a *blip* on his horn, but she can't help it. She can't get over the amount of parked cars lining the streets, the houses and brown brick apartment buildings crowded so close together. There are so many *trees*. Karena thinks again of what she told Kevin in Austin, about feeling like a war correspondent, and Kevin replying that reentry can be rough. When Karena looks over at him now, she feels stranger than ever. She's used to seeing Kevin's profile against sky, clouds, grass. It's as though they're out for a drive in one of those old movies in which the car is stationary and the backdrop changes, except the scenery here is all wrong.

"Cognitive dissonance, Laredo," Kevin says, when Karena comments on this—and even her nickname gives her a pang, as though she's hearing an old song in a new place. "That's what my shrink buddy calls it. I get it every time I come back from chasing."

"You guys should put a warning label on the Whirlwind website," Karena says. "When does it go away?"

"The worst of it? A couple of days," says Kevin. "But it never really goes away completely. There are flashbacks. Like you'll be standing in a coffee shop or something and all of the sudden you'll be in Kansas, under a meso. You get used to it, though. It just gets integrated into who you are."

He laces his fingers through hers, and Charles beeps—although they are cruising down the middle of a one-way street with no stop sign in sight. Karena glances in the rearview. There's the real cognitive dissonance, following her in his yellow Volvo. She can't believe Charles is actually there. Every time she looks back it's like a gift.

They glide to a stop in front of Kevin's house, a duplex. He owns the upper floor. Karena leans forward and inspects it with curiosity. The house is dark brown and sits on a hill, very tall and narrow yet almost dwarfed by an even taller old black fir by its front steps. The roof is A-frame, steeply pitched, and Karena is bemused to see a border of impatiens straggling along the walk, as well as one of those mirrored orbs on a stand. The ball is hot pink.

"So, woman?" Kevin says, a little anxiously. "How do you like the man pad?"

"It's nice," says Karena. "Cute. Looks a little like a witch's hat."

"Witch hat!" Kevin roars. "Okay, now that I am totally emasculated!"

He makes a face.

"Although actually there is a witch living on the first floor," he admits. "Mrs. Axlerod. She's been there for at least a hundred years, cooking small children in her oven. I've been waiting patiently for her to go to that great broomyard in the sky so I can expand, but no such luck. Yet."

"That's nice, Mr. Wizard," says Karena, patting Kevin's thigh. "So I take it those are her flowers?"

"Naturally," says Kevin. "I am far too manly to grow flowers. My tomatoes are in back."

Karena smiles and they sit watching the breeze play in the leaves above the curb. A mourning dove coos from somewhere.

"So," Karena says, "I'll see you soon, like next weekend? Friday or Saturday?"

Kevin shrugs. "Your call, Laredo. I'm not the one who has a long-lost brother to catch up with. I'll just sit pathetically by the phone."

"Okay," says Karena. "I'll call you as soon as the dust clears a little. Let you know how it's going."

"Please do," says Kevin. He takes her hand.

"Seriously," he says, "not to be a downer or anything, because I know it's like the miracle of Lourdes you guys found each other and you must be so happy. As you should be. But if Chuck starts to exhibit even the slightest weird behavior, if he says or does anything that makes you feel even mildly uncomfortable, I want you to call me. Okay, Karena?"

Karena glances in the rearview. Charles's windshield is sheened with leaf shadow and reflected light, and she can't see her brother.

"I will," she says.

"Any time, day or night," says Kevin.

"Okay."

"I mean it, Karena. Or just come over. The door's always open."

"*Okay*, Kevin," Karena says. She pats Kevin's chest, which is puffed up. "Now, don't get all moosey. I'll be fine."

Kevin nods.

"All right," he says. "And I know you'll have an amazing time catching up. I can't wait to hear about it."

He slips on his aviators and reaches down for his laptop bag. He and Charles have already dismantled the stand and the ham radio back in Austin.

"Welp, happy trails, Laredo," he says. "I sure am glad I met you."

"Oh, I am too," Karena says. "I'll miss you," and she leans over so they can kiss.

Behind them, the horn blares.

"Sorry," Charles calls through his window. "My elbow slipped."

Kevin sighs.

"Why did we want to find him again?" he asks.

"Search me," Karena says.

Kevin kisses his fingers, touches Karena's cheek, and gets out. He goes around to the back for his duffel.

"See you soon, Laredo," he says, slamming the tailgate, and in her side mirror Karena watches him walk back to Charles's wagon with his laptop carrier slung across his torso, his bigger bag in hand. He leans down to say something to Charles, slaps the Volvo's roof and walks up the path to his pointy-hat house. Karena waits until he goes inside, then looks ahead at the street. The sun shines dreamily through the trees, two kids circle a lawn on dirt bikes. Behind her, Charles remains invisible, though when the breeze shifts the leaves Karena can see the object hanging from his rearview, a dream catcher.

She takes out her cell to call him—Charles's cell, Karena noticed when they exchanged numbers, is a pay-as-you-go model from a Walmart or gas station, which explains why she couldn't track him through a standard carrier. As she dials, her own phone buzzes in her hand.

"Jeez, you kids," says Charles when Karena answers. "Get a room."

"Ha ha, you're hilarious, Charles."

"Sorry about spoiling the tender moment," he says. "My elbow really did slip."

"Mmm hmm. Okay, Charles. So, you ready to go?"

"Of course," says Charles. "That's why I'm calling, to see if we're leaving or you're going to run into Wieb's for one more poke for the road. I mean, if you and Wieb want more alone time, I can go get an iced tea or something."

"Charles."

"Just checking . . . So can we go? I mean, I like the guy and everything, but I'd rather see where you live."

"We're mobile," Karena says. "Unless you really do want something to eat or drink—are you hungry? I probably don't have much at the house."

"No, I'm good," says Charles. "We'll do whatever you want to do, sistah. Lead on. I'm in your world now."

Karena smiles, although this last statement gives her pause as well as a thrill. She hangs up, waves so Charles can see her, then signals and pulls away from the curb. The yellow Volvo smoothly follows suit.

Because Karena has been away for a while and is distracted, and because she's not that familiar with St. Paul, she can't readily calculate the most efficient route home. She settles for the first way that comes to mind, taking Snelling to Lake Street and crossing the river. The Mississippi is wide here, and the sky opens up over the sluggish, powerful water, and Karena breathes a little more easily. She realizes one of the reasons she's been nervous since they entered the city is she can't see the whole sky. Now she notes the haze on the horizon, the Cu floating past—she will never look at clouds the same way again. Then they are on the other side, and the trees close back in.

Charles honks as they leave the bridge, and Karena holds up a hand in the rearview: *What?*

He points left, and Karena understand he means, Look, there's the River Road! which they used to take to Uncle Carroll's house. Actually, she thinks, and signals to turn. It's a better way to go, and for sentiment's sake Karena leads Charles past Carroll's house, a tiny bungalow almost completely hidden beneath grape ivy, then takes Minnehaha Parkway up through the city. She creeps along like a geriatric, which is surely driving Charles insane, but Karena doesn't want to risk even the slightest chance of losing him, getting separated by another driver cutting in or at a stoplight. She still can't believe it, that Charles is here, actually here, after so many years. She keeps expecting to look in the rearview and see nothing, or a strange car, to find that Charles has slipped away. Yet every time she checks, the yellow Volvo is still right there, behind her.

42

"C'mere, sistah," Charles says.

He pats his chest and spreads his arms. They are standing on the curb in front of Karena's house, where Charles has just parked his car. Karena hugs him willingly, happily, for a long time—a more peaceful embrace than the shrieking reunion back in Austin. Charles is so thin Karena can feel his ribs through his T-shirt, and he smells different, no longer like Irish Spring and fast food but salt and a whiff of patchouli. But he also just smells like Charles, a scent as familiar to Karena as her own breath. When they finally let go, Charles's eyes are damp and red.

"It is so fucking good to see you, K," he says.

"You too, Charles."

He begins dismantling his laptop and ham and scanner, and Karena starts unloading everything else. There's a lot. From the looks of it, as she suspected, Charles has been living at least part-time in his car. He has never been the most organized person, except when it comes to his data, so Karena collects armfuls of plaid flannel shirts and T-shirts, mismatched socks, a yoga mat—yoga?—and some bundles of what looks like brush.

"Charles," she says, holding it up, "what is this?"

"Sage. You burn it. To cleanse places of bad spiritual energy."

Oh boy, Karena thinks.

"Neat," she says.

"What're you doing, anyway?" Charles asks, backing out of the front seat.

"What's it look like? Taking your stuff in."

"You mean it's not safe to leave it out here?" Charles looks up and down the tree-lined street. "Seems like a nice enough neighborhood."

"It is," says Karena, "but—I thought—aren't you going to stay for a while?"

Charles shrugs.

"I don't want to intrude," he says. "I know you have your life."

"Don't be ridiculous, Charles," says Karena. "Of course I have a life. Now you're in it."

"Okay, but—"

"You just *got* here, Charles. Can we figure out later when you're going to leave? Like give it a couple of days at least?"

Charles nods, and his eyes grow red again. "Thank you, K."

"Forget it. Just help me move all your crap in."

They make several trips, carrying in bag after canvas bag, box after box. And a Mexican blanket. A Lakota drum as tall as Karena's waist. A case of green tea. Enough books to stock a small library: *Juicing for Life, The Naturopath's Guide to Herbal Medicine, Homeopathy for Dummies, Crystal Healing*. Uh oh, Karena thinks. The other books are meteorological: *Storm Chasing Handbook*. Flora's *Tornadoes of the United States*. Bluestein's *Tornado Alley*. *Weathering the Storm, The AMS Weather Book, National Audubon Society Field Guide to North American Weather*—when Karena picks this one up, several photographs of supercells scatter out of it. And there are stacks of the marbled black-and-white composition books Karena remembers from New Heidelburg. Charles's ledgers, his data. She looks at the topmost one for a moment—*mar-aug 2003* it says on the cover—and remembers the last time she saw one of these. Held it. Wrapped it in her jacket and set it against the stone lion. Karena chews her lips a moment, then hauls the ledgers up her front steps.

She has so often envisioned Charles in her house, what his reaction might be to this couch, that mirror, that the place has been practically decorated with him in mind. Yet now that Charles is actually here, Karena feels shy. She watches him wander around, exclaiming over her books and art, and she marvels at him, so the same and so changed. Time has been kind to her golden brother. It has erased the baby roundness from his cheeks, raised his hairline a little, shaded in his dark beard, etched lines in precisely the same places Karena has them: on the forehead, around the eyes. Other than this, he appears much the same—the main difference being, Karena thinks, that Charles is no longer prettier than she is. He is beautiful.

She gives him the tour, ending upstairs in the master suite. This is the part of the house Karena is proudest of. When she first bought it, from a German history professor and her aging but spookily beautiful mother, this second floor was a warren of rooms, full of light but cramped. Karena knocked out the walls, leaving the bathroom intact, and now there is nothing in it but space and her big white bed.

"This is freakin awesome, K," Charles says, boggling around. "It's like being in a big Cu!" and Karena has to laugh. She didn't intend this effect, but with the soft gray carpet and cream-colored walls, she can see how he'd think so.

"I'm glad you like it," she says, "since this is where you'll be staying."

"But isn't this your room?"

"Not right now."

Charles holds up his hands.

"Oh no," he says. "No way. I'm enough of an inconvenience as it is."

"It's no trouble, Charles. Half the time I fall asleep down in my study anyway," says Karena, and it's true. "This way we'll both have privacy. There's a bathroom up here, see?"

Charles goes to look. "It's amazing," he admits. "I'll agree, but only on one condition."

"What's that."

"We'll switch off. I'll take it for a few days, then you. Okay?"

"Fine," says Karena, to shut him up. "And guess what, you get to carry alllll the boxes up."

"Deal," says Charles, and hugs her again.

They troop back downstairs, defaulting to the kitchen like nervous guests at a house party. "I am actually kind of hungry," says Charles. And no wonder: The clock over the stove says seven fifteen.

"Wow," says Karena. "I had no idea it was so late. Where do you want to go, Mexican, Thai?"

But Charles holds up a hand and waves it, No no no no no, as he did on Marla's birthday video. "Forget that," he says, "I'm so done with road food, let's stay in. I'll cook."

Karena laughs and leans against the counter. "*You* will?"

"I find your lack of faith disturbing," says Charles serenely. "How'd you think I afford chasing, K? I have these things, they're called jobs. I like restaurant work because I can move around, take time off. I can do short order, fine dining, you name it."

He opens the refrigerator and peers in.

"Except I can't do this," he says. "Pickles, diet pop . . . and Jesus, what the freak," he says, slinging a dripping baggie toward the sink. "I think it tried to bite me!"

"Okay, Charles."

"No offense, K, but I'm scared. You eat like crap."

"I don't, actually," says Karena, "under normal circumstances. But I was out all week chasing after you, so it's not like I've had the chance to go to Lund's—"

Charles slams the fridge and turns.

"Wait," he says, "hold on."

He rakes his hands through his wavy hair in the distracted, semi-agitated way Karena remembers so well. "You were looking for *me*? That's what you were doing out there with Wieb? Not just chasing for the hell of it?"

"Charles, please. Why would *I* ever go chasing for the hell of it?" Karena snorts. "Of course that's why I was out there. After the call from the hospital—"

Charles grows very still.

"What hospital," he says.

"The hospital in Wichita. You gave them my name."

Charles props himself against the stove.

"They called you," he says. "And told you what?"

"Nothing. To begin with. But when I got there, that you'd had a panic attack and had been released. What?"

Charles is shaking his head.

"That distresses me," he says. "That distresses me deeply. I give them your name because they made me, they essentially bullied me into it. *We need a family member, sir. We need an outside contact.* And then when I do, very much against my wishes, they call you? They interrupt your work, your life, to drag you all the way down to Kansas? I am so sorry, K. I am so, so sorry."

"That's all right, Charles," Karena says. "It turned out fine. I got a story from it, for one thing. And more importantly, here you are."

"True," says Charles. He scrapes his hair back and blows out air. "Still. What'd they say that made *you* go chasing?"

They stare at each other, Karena's slate-blue eyes meeting Charles's brown.

"Nothing," she says again. "I . . . was just worried."

"Well," says Charles. "No need. It was just a stupid thing, I had a little freak-out. See, this is what I mean about the medical empire. They'd use a bomb to kill a mosquito. I knew I made a mistake going there. I never would have except . . . well, anyway. I am so done with the empire."

Uh oh, Karena thinks again.

"So *that* happened," says Charles. "Okay. Let's not let this spoil our time together. So you were out chasing, huh? That explains why my twindar kept going off all the time."

"Mine too," says Karena. "I kept missing you by inches. We drove right past you before that wedge."

Charles's grin, which has been starting to widen, fades.

"That was you?" he says. "That red Jeep out there was your red Jeep? Jesus, I'm going to skin Wieb for getting you so close. What was he *thinking*?"

"The question is," says Karena, "where the hell did you go?"

"Dropped back south," says Charles, "then over to Pine Ridge— the reservation. I've got a friend there, Eddie Black Cloud, who I hung with for a couple of days. Then decided to come visit you—but we can talk about that later. Jesus, K," he says, "that wedge was insane. Even I wouldn't chase that thing."

"Well, thank goodness," Karena says. "It was awful."

They look at their feet for a moment, positioned the same way on opposing tiles, then look up at the same time and say, "Let's get pizza." Then laugh.

"Jinx," says Charles. "Buy me a Coke. Actually, no, don't, I don't drink that crap anymore. Can we get veggie, please? And whole wheat crust?"

"Whatever you say," Karena says, "whoever you are."

She calls in the order, bemused, and she and Charles set the table in the dining room as if they've been housemates for years. Karena doesn't have to tell Charles where the silverware is, which plates to use, which napkins. He just knows. He dims the chandelier too, and says, "Candles?" while Karena is turning from the buffet with Grandmother Hallingdahl's candlesticks in her hands. She sets them on the table, smiling, and says, "I bet you forgot about these—" But Charles is regarding the little pewter horses with a tragic, fixed expression, and Karena winces. Of course. They remind him of Siri.

They pull out chairs and sit. Charles steers the horses around with a finger.

"How was it at the end?" he asks, not looking at Karena. "Did she ask for me?"

Karena sighs. By then, Siri wasn't capable of speech, just of raspy breath that went on and on, issuing from her skeletal throat, the skin around her mouth swollen and chapped from the tubes.

"She wasn't herself by then, Charles," she says.

Charles positions the horses at right angles, nose to nose as if they're kissing.

"And Dad," he says. "Jesus, K, you let him marry the Black Widow?" He makes the horses gallop away across the place mat, whinnying in terror.

Karena remembers standing beside Frank at the wedding, one side of the New Heidelburg Lutheran church choked with the Widow's multitudinous offspring, on the other just her. The strained smile for the photographer, Karena wanting to whisper in Frank's ear that he'd better get a food tester.

"It wasn't as though I had a choice," she says. "He's a grown man. . . . Waaaait a minute. How'd you know about the Widow?"

"I know everything," Charles says. "I know about Dad's stroke too. And how the Wid just stuck him in the Center when the going got tough. I visit him every once in a while."

Karena gapes at him. "You *do*?"

"Sure."

"You have got to be kidding me. God, Charles! Why the hell didn't you let anyone know you were there? I've been looking and looking for you."

"Oh," says Charles casually, "well, I didn't want to stir the pot. It looked like you were better off without me."

He canters the horses over to Karena's place mat and makes them look at her.

"I mean, this place"—he waves around the room—"and your job. I'm so proud of you. I read every article you ever wrote, you know that? Yup. Online. You did good, K."

"Thank you," says Karena. "But Charles—"

The doorbell chimes, and Karena sighs and gets up to go pay the pizza delivery guy. When she sets the pie on the table they both dig in, ravenous, dragging slices out of the box and trailing strands of cheese.

"I did try and see Dad once before the stroke too," Charles says, mouth full. "To make up. Right after they were married. I even brought a wedding present, one of those garden gnome things the Wid likes, with toadstools growing out of its head or some shit like that. But he must have been away on a case or something, and when she saw me she pretended not to be home."

"She did not," Karena says.

"She did."

"Maybe she really wasn't there."

"No, she was there all right," Charles says, picking vegetables off a slice still in the box and adding them to the one on his plate. "Her car was in the driveway and the TV was on, but when she looked out and saw who it was, what do you know, *boom!* TV goes off. Lights go out. End a story."

Karena laughs.

"That is so despicable," she says.

"I know," Charles agrees. "She's such a tool." He folds his slice in half and crams it into his mouth. "What do you think, K, did she do it?"

"Did who do what?"

"The Widow. Cause Dad's stroke."

"No!" says Karena, although the thought did initially occur to her, given the Widow's track record. "I think she just has really bad luck in husbands."

"I don't know," Charles says darkly. "I wouldn't rule out strychnine. Or arsenic maybe. Yeah, definitely arsenic. She's got that arsenic look."

"I really don't think so, Charles. Besides, if she did, she didn't do a very good job, did she?"

"Maybe she's slipping," Charles suggests.

"Clearly," Karena says.

Charles chews contemplatively. "Speaking of bad marriages," he says, "that British dope you married? What was up with *that*? I was so relieved when you kicked him to the curb."

Karena stops chewing and stares at him. The fact that Charles apparently has been keeping tabs on her as well as Frank is so huge and unbelievable Karena can't think about it right now. She files it away for later consideration.

"He wasn't so bad," Karena says.

"He totally was," says Charles. "He was an idiot. The Loaf is an upgrade, though not by much. I have to say, K, I don't think much of your taste in men."

"Nobody asked you," Karena says, then, "What's the Loaf?"

Charles tilts his chair back and grins.

"Wiebke," he says. "The Loaf. Doesn't his gut remind you of a loaf of bread? Like the loaves in the Richard Scarry books we liked, with steam coming from them?"

Karena can't help laughing. "I did think exactly the same thing," she admits, and Charles raises his brows and his palms in a there-you-go gesture, then reaches for another slice.

"So you and the Loaf," he says in a wheezy Godfather voice, wagging his forefinger back and forth. "How did this come to be?"

Karena explains, and Charles nods.

"Nooowwww it makes sense," he says. "I couldn't figure out how you got hooked up otherwise. It's not as though you're in the same league."

"What's that supposed to mean?"

"Come on, K. He's a loafy fortysomething bachelor science teacher. You're a star reporter. You do the math."

"I totally disagree," says Karena, thinking, Fortysomething? Kevin's over forty? She'll have to look him up. "Kevin's great, Charles. And I'm hardly a star."

"Don't sell yourself short, K," Charles says. "But I can understand how this happened. I used to see it all the time when I was working tours—did Loafy tell you I was a guide too, for a while? He didn't? Huh. Anyway, I'd see these chase romances go up all the time. You spend so many hours in an enclosed space together, then the drama and excitement of the storms—so intense, right? How could you *not* fall for each other? It's all so sexy, the meaningful glances across morning briefing, those stolen moments when nobody else is around. . . . If the Jeep's a-rockin', don't come knockin'—anh?" He winks at Karena. "Right?"

"You're a pig," Karena says, and Charles grins.

"Thought so," he says. "Don't worry, sistah, it's not just you. Happens to everyone. But then you get home," he adds, shaking his head sorrowfully, "and what happens? Suddenly—foop! You're just your normal boring selves again. A pumpkin. In this case, a loaf. And that's it, the end. Very sad."

"Okay," Karena says, "thank you, Charles."

"I didn't mean you, K. You're not boring. The Loaf's boring."

"Charles."

"Okay, okay," says Charles, letting his chair legs thump back down to the floor. "Sensitive subject, I can see. Sorry I said anything. I just don't want you to be disappointed."

He pinches some cheese off a slice in the box and regards Karena thoughtfully as he chews it.

"Actually," he says, "maybe I've been too hasty. Yes, I think I have. Because now I can see it. I can totally see it."

"Now what," says Karena, rolling her eyes.

"You and the Loaf," says Charles. "You two probably are really good for each other. Because come to think of it, you have a lot in common."

Karena starts to ask what, then realizes the most obvious similarity: She and Kevin have both betrayed Charles. They have both turned him in.

Flushing, she hits the volley back at him. "So what about you? How's your love life?"

"Oh, just hangin' with the ladies," Charles says, grinning and crossing his hands behind his head. "Makin' honey while the sun shines," and then, when he sees how Karena is looking at him, he says, "Okay, fine, I haven't found the right girl yet. I've got kind of a short attention span, you know? I did get engaged once, though."

"Did you now," Karena says. She gets up. "Want some wine?"

"No thanks," Charles says, "I'm not big into the booze. I'll take some of that green tea we brought in, though."

Karena brings in both from the kitchen, then sits back down. "So what happened?" she says, pouring herself a glass of Shiraz. "You don't have to tell if you don't want."

"No, I'll tell you," says Charles, uncapping his tea. He tips the chair back again. "Situ. Indian chick. Gorgeous girl. Met her on a chase in Kansas. She was working in her folks' motel, and I was looking for a room, and I walked into the lobby and there she was wearing this little pink cut-off T-shirt, and the motel had a hot tub, and I had a bag of very excellent weed, and I'll spare you the salient details."

"Thank you," says Karena, "I appreciate that. So you contaminated the hot tub, then what?"

"Then I left," says Charles, "went off to chase the next day, but the farther away I got, the more I thought, Huh, I think there might have really been something there. I felt kind of regretful, you know? So I finished up the chase I was on—dinky little cell that didn't produce anything—and then I turned around and went back. This time her dad was on the desk—Mr. Chowdhury. He really did not like me. Oh my goodness, no. But I was persistent. I got a room for the night and sat in the lobby until Situ came back and I took her out on an honest-to-God date—unfortunately at Pizza Hut. Small town, Pleasanton, whaddyagonnado. But it was kismet. I'm serious, K, I wanted to marry this girl and have ten kids with her."

"Really," says Karena, slit eyed. "So, why didn't you?"

"Three reasons," says Charles and lists them on his fingers. "One, Mr. Chowdhury. Two, Mr. Chowdhury. Three, Mr. Chowdhury. He did give me a job there, handyman stuff, working reception—they needed a white guy in there too. It was this tiny farm community like New Hellishburg, so can you imagine what the locals thought of the Chowdhury family? Oh my goodness, the crap I heard. That there were bugs in the rooms. That they ate bugs. That they sacrificed animals. Just the most ridiculous shit. Poor Mr. C, you really had to hand it to the guy, trying to make it work there. It wasn't his original game plan. He started out in Chicago when they came from Bombay, had a convenience store. But then some junkie shot Mr. C in the face, so when they heard about this motel for sale, they took it."

"They shot him in the face!" says Karena.

"Yeah, I know, nice American dream, right? So Mr. C wasn't too crazy about American guys trying to date his daughter, and oh, especially one who chased storms, that wasn't exactly in my favor either. He was convinced I was going to ruin Situ's life, derail her from going to med school, which they were saving up for. No matter what I did, I could not convince him otherwise. I'd hear them fighting about it in the office, like I'd be on front desk and Mr. C would be saying, *It is not enough you take up with an American boy, you have to find one who is crazy,* and Situ would be screaming, *He's not crazy, you are, and besides, I love him!* and I'd be like, *Welcome to Pleasanton Inn & Suites, we have continental breakfast from eight to ten.*"

Karena laughs, then presses her mouth on her wrist. "I'm sorry," she says. "It's not funny, you're just making it sound . . . So go on."

"So then what happened," Charles says, shoving his hands through his hair, "was I spent that fall and winter there, and we were really happy, K. That was 1999 to 2000, because I remember watching the Millennium in our room and having Jiffy Pop and champagne. But then in the spring of 2000 I started to feel a little antsy—I wasn't chasing, I forgot to say, because I wanted to convince Mr. C of my good intentions, and frankly Situ wasn't too happy with the chasing situation either. So I stopped. But you can imagine how well that went. I started to get wiggy, kind of irritable, and then I started to see things."

Karena is taking a sip of wine, and although her stomach jumps, she manages to ask calmly, "What kind of things?"

"Oh, you know, the usual," Charles says. "First the TV anchors started talking to me, blah blah, and then the gods in the Chowdhury shrine—that was a little creepy because it was Buddha and Vishnu telling me I'd better cut my tongue off, put my eyes out, stuff like that.

They were bad. I tried to avoid that shrine whenever possible, which was difficult because it was right in the lobby office. But there was a tornado siren out back too, which I thought was a great omen to begin with, so I'd hang out there for comfort. I'd go out there and stand next to it and be like, Hey, buddy, how are you, and once the siren said, Hello. But meanwhile I woke up one night and Situ was wildly upset. Apparently I'd hit her in my sleep because I'd seen Motorcycle Guy."

Karena's leg jerks involuntarily under the table.

"What did you tell her?" she asks.

"That he'd been there," Charles says absently, and then his eyes widen. He thrusts his palms out, waving them. "Oh, Jesus, no, K! I didn't tell her what really happened, nothing like that. Goodness, no. Just that ever since I was very little I'd had this—affliction, or gift, or whatever you want to call it; that I have visions. And that this is something I accept about myself as part of who I am, a scary part sometimes, but also the best part of me because it makes me who I am, you know? It helps me understand things. Enables me to find the storms. But without getting into all that, I tell her what's going on, honestly, which is hard for me because most of the time I keep it to myself, the world has such a misconception about it. And you know what she did?"

Karena can guess.

"She told her dad," Charles says. "Yup. She went straight to Mr. C and told him I'd been hallucinating. Nice show of support, right? But that's how crazy I was about this girl, K, I wasn't thinking straight. If I had been, I would've known that was going to happen, because what else could I expect from a woman who wanted to be a doctor, of all things? Can you imagine?"

"Well," Karena says cautiously, "yes, actually, and I don't know that it necessarily sounds like a conflict of interest. In some ways it could be ideal—"

"Yeah, if you accept I have an illness, and I don't," Charles says. He levels a finger at her. "I've done a lot of research on my condition, K, not just sources from our culture but others that are older and more advanced. And I've spent a lot of time with the Lakota, and you know what they call a man like me, K? A man who has visions?"

"No," says Karena.

"They call him a *wicasa wakan*," Charles says. "A divine man. A blessed man. Sure, somebody whose soul is eroded more quickly than other people's, especially if he uses his talents to help them. Because he can see things others can't, and that's a psychic burden. Still. It's not stigmatized like it is in our culture. It's viewed as it should be, with respect."

"Okay," says Karena, "I hear you, Charles. I understand—"

"You don't, though," Charles says. "You don't understand what it's like to have visions like me. Do you?"

Karena stares at her place mat. After a minute she shakes her head.

"I'm sorry, K," says Charles. "I didn't mean to raise my voice. It just frustrates me that otherwise we're like one person, but that's the one thing you don't get. And it's not just nature, it's nurture. You're a product of our culture. You've been brainwashed along with everyone else. Which brings me back to Situ. She was scared of me after that, asked me to see somebody—and again, I should have seen right then that she was not the woman for me, because if she were, she never would've forced me to go against my principles. But she did, so for that whole spring I went to a shrink in Lawrence. Sat in this office with posters that said INSPIRATION and TEAMWORK and changed them around in my mind so they said PERSPIRATION and ROADWORK, and this guy with a big mustache talked to me about bipolar this and rapid cycling that and had I ever been on lithium? He put me on four different drug cocktails, and I took it as long as I could, K. Which wasn't that long, because as you may remember I have an unusual sensitivity to medication. I stopped taking the whatever, and finally when the guy asked me had I considered ECT, it was making quite a comeback, I got up and walked out. I went back to the motel and packed my bags and said to the siren, I'm outta here, and I left. I haven't spoken to Situ since."

He stops, holds up a finger, and drinks his green tea in a single long swallow.

"I have looked her up online, though," he says. "She's a shrink now, in Denver. Ironic, isn't it?"

Karena nods and drinks some wine.

"I guess," she says, watching Charles, as she has been all along. Ever since he has started talking—no, since he stepped into her house, since he followed her here, since they met in Austin—Karena has been on high alert for signs of the djinn. She has been waiting for his monologue to swerve into incoherence, to become grandiose and insulting. For his expression to shift and change, to become that dark liquid scorn she remembers so well. But she hasn't seen the djinn, not today, not tonight, just her brother breathlessly telling a story. And Karena would know the difference, she's quite confident she would, even after all this time. The djinn is bred into her muscle memory.

"Well," says Charles, wiping his mouth with a napkin, "that's it. The tragic story of my broken engagement—Jesus, come to think of it, that's something *I* have in common with the Loaf. He told you about that, didn't he? Except from what I heard he was the dumpee, not the dumper."

"Yes, Charles," says Karena. "He told me."

Charles shakes his head. "Poor guy. You gotta feel for him. But I'm telling you, sistah. Your taste in men . . ."

"Charles."

"I'm just saying."

He stands up, yawning.

"I just hit a wall," he says. "Do you mind if I go to bed early?"

"Of course not. And you don't need to ask. This is your house too."

"Thanks, K," says Charles. He cricks his neck this way and that. "You wouldn't happen to know a good holistic chiropractor, would you?"

"Um, no," says Karena. "But I could find one."

"That's okay," Charles says. "I'll do it."

He comes around the table and kisses her head.

"Good night, sistah," he says. "It's so good to be here. We have so much to talk about . . . Love you."

"Love you too," Karena says. She watches him walk down the hall, turn and wave, then disappear up the steps to her room.

43

"Where'd you go, Laredo?" Kevin asks.

It is Sunday evening of that week and they are lying in Kevin's bedroom, the masculine quality of which, Karena has assured him, more than compensates for Mrs. Axlerod's scraggly impatiens and witch ball. The apartment is a railroad flat, long and dim, its windows screened by oaks and elms so it is like being in a tree house. The woodwork is brown, the davenport and armchair are black leather. But between the initial frenzied lovemaking on the sticky, squeaky couch and the second slower one in here, Karena has wandered the rooms naked, enchanted and exclaiming. There are rocks and fossils everywhere, ammonites as refrigerator magnets, geodes on the sills. The walls are covered with old survey maps—Minnesota, the grasslands, Texas, Cherry County—and with Kevin's photos of night lightning and supercells. In the bathroom Karena has discovered his childhood copy of *The Weather Wizard's Cloud Book*, with *Mr. Kevin Wiebke* written in painstaking bubble cursive on the flyleaf. And above his bed is a cloud mobile, a present made for him, Kevin explains, by his graduating eighth graders of 2003. The place is a combination of bachelor pad and natural science museum.

"Hello in there," Kevin says, tapping Karena's forehead. "Anybody home?"

"Maybe," says Karena. "Who wants to know?" She is lying with her head pillowed on Kevin's stomach, smoothing its curve with a hand. Loafy, she thinks, and makes a sound between a snicker and a sigh.

"Mr. Wizard wants to know where he took you today," says Kevin.

"First time or second?"

"Both."

"Greedy Mr. Wizard," Karena says. "Mmmmm . . . the first time, to the A & W."

"I took you to a root beer stand?"

"Hey," says Karena, pushing herself up on her elbow, "it's one of my very favorite places. You want to hear this or not?"

Kevin pats his stomach. "Just lay your pretty little head back down there, Laredo," he says, "that's right, smooth those ruffled feathers. I'm with you. Frosty mug, root beer float, the business. Then where?"

"Deer Creek State Park, north side of town. Did I tell you about that place? There's watercress in the creek, and you can actually eat it, the water's so clean."

"No, you didn't tell me about that," says Kevin, drawing Karena's hair over his chest. "Not until just now. But that's fine. I know you are a woman of many mysteries I must patiently reveal."

Karena sighs. Kevin doesn't know the half of it. He doesn't know, nor can she ever tell him, that she lied just now, that in fact both times they made love she went not to New Heidelburg but a location she hasn't visited for a long time: the road in Iowa. With the dead man on it. And the green tornado roving in the background.

"There's that bad sound again," says Kevin. "That sigh. Okay, what's up, Laredo? I know this is new for us and everything, but I can tell there's something else bugging you. Is it Chuck? Is he behaving himself all right?"

"He is," Karena says. "He's being an exemplary guest," and it's true. Charles has been very respectful. He makes his bed. Shops for organic local produce. Every night, he cooks.

"Wow," says Kevin. "Can we move him over here? My bathroom needs scrubbing."

"That's true, Mr. Wizard," says Karena, "I meant to mention that."

"Watch it, mouthy," says Kevin. "Seriously, what's it like, having him there?"

Karena thinks about how to explain it. On the one hand, waking up every day with Charles in her house brings a deep comfort and joy Karena hasn't known since childhood. It's like Christmas morning, only the present is her brother. On the other, having Charles around all the time is like hearing herself in stereo. As much of a blessing as it is to be with another person who knows her that well, it can also be tiring to have Charles finish her sentences, or to say things at the same time, or to look up and know from across the room what he's thinking. It can be claustrophobic. And Karena knows—of course—that Charles feels the same way, as indicated by his encouraging her to come over here tonight. *Are you sure you don't mind?* Karena asked, feeling guilty. *I feel like you just got here,* and Charles shooed her out, saying, *No, K, go get laid or something. You're starting to get uptight, and it's getting on my nerves.*

Karena tells Kevin all of this except the conversation, and he nods, looking at the cloud mobile, which spins gently in a warm draft from somewhere.

"That's really interesting, Laredo," he says. "I've always wondered— I guess most people do—what it's like to be a twin. Us non-twins fanta-size it's like having a best friend all the time, but I can see how you'd step on each other's toes too. So . . . what's it like when his mood swings? Can you feel that?"

"It's more like I'm more attuned to Charles's moods than anyone else," Karena explains, "but it's not what most people think, he cuts himself and I bleed, for instance. I don't get agitated when he's manic or down when he's depressed."

"Thank God for that," says Kevin.

He winnows his fingers through her hair, braiding it. He has five sisters, he has told Karena, and as the youngest he was sternly in-structed from a very early age in the art of hairdressing. Karena is being hypnotized by the gentle tug and pull, which she feels all through her body down to her fingertips and toes, when Kevin says, "So, Chuck's finally found some medication he can tolerate and he's on it? Taking it regularly?"

Karena's eyes pop open.

"Well," she says, "not exactly."

Kevin's fingers pause, then pick up again. "What does that mean," he says, his voice neutral.

"It means no, he's not on meds, but he seems to be doing really well," says Karena. "I haven't seen so much as a blink of the djinn since he got here."

"Huh," says Kevin. "And he told you this? That he's not on medication? Or is it just something you suspect?"

"No, I know he's not. He doesn't believe in it," Karena says. All her muscles are starting to tense, and she makes a conscious effort to relax them. "He has terrible reactions to medication, Kevin. He always has. Ever since we were kids."

Kevin doesn't say anything, and he continues to braid Karena's hair, but she can feel him taking deeper breaths, his stomach rising and falling under her cheek.

"What?" she says.

"I don't like it, Karena," says Kevin. "I don't like his being there with you and not being on medication."

Karena nods.

"I know. It's not what I would have wished for either. But you know," she says thoughtfully, "maybe he has learned to control the disorder. He knows a tremendous amount about alternative medicine. He meditates, he doesn't drink or smoke, he's so careful about what he eats, he takes supplements, he sticks to a regular schedule—"

"Karena, sit up, please," says Kevin. "So I can look at you."

He takes her hands and they sit Indian-style facing each other, the sheet pooled in their laps.

"What you're thinking," he says, "Karena, it's so dangerous. You can't fix bipolar disorder through herbal remedies and meditation. You can help it, sure. I'm sure everything Chuck's doing helps regulate his moods significantly. But it hasn't gone away, honey. It's still there, waiting to come out."

Karena shakes her head and the braid Kevin has finished whips her neck.

"I know that, Kevin," she says.

"I know you do," says Kevin, "in here," and he touches her temple. "But in here," and he puts a finger on her heart, "I fear it's a different story. You want it to be all okay now, just because you found him. But it's not."

Karena looks away, at a row of vertebrae lying on Kevin's dresser, next to a Mason jar of old wheat pennies.

"You don't know that," she says. "Not for sure. Did you know you *can* cure bipolar disorder? In some cases. When it's caught early enough. The medication corrects the brain's chemistry, stabilizes it. Permanently, I mean."

"I know that, Laredo," says Kevin. "I've read that too. But didn't you tell me Chuck's never stayed on meds? Even if you did catch it early, still, he would have had to get on it and stay on it faithfully, and—"

"Okay, Kevin," says Karena crossly. "I get it. It's just—there are more things in heaven and earth than are dreamed of in your philosophy, you know? It's not an exact science, psychology, any more than meteorology or any other –ology. How many times have I heard you Whirlwind guys say that even now, after all these years of research, nobody knows why one supercell spawns a tornado and another doesn't? Why wouldn't that be the case for people too? Every brain is different and responds differently to treatment, and what might not help one person, for instance holistic medicine, might help the next."

"That's an interesting hypothesis," says Kevin, "and I'll concede science is inexact. But if we're going to extend the analogy, I'd say your brother's disorder is an EF-4 or -5. It's really damaging. And the only way to test your theory is to wait and see if his moods can be controlled by holistic means. This isn't an experiment, it's a gamble, and frankly it's not a gamble I want to take."

"Well," says Karena. "Lucky for you, you're not the one taking it."

They stare at each other. Karena's chest has flushed in pink blotches, and she pulls the sheet up. Kevin looks away, his mouth compressed, his face flat and closed.

"Sorry," he says stiffly. "My bad. I didn't mean to overstep."

He gets up and walks naked from the room.

"Where are you going?" Karena says.

"Nature call, Laredo," says Kevin. "I'll be right back."

Karena waits, making a face at herself in the mirror over the dresser. She looks ridiculous, one side of her hair braided, the other not. When Kevin comes back, she has taken it all down and is sitting cross-legged in a square of sunlight.

Kevin stops in the doorway. "Um," he says. "What were we talking about again?"

"Come here," says Karena, and Kevin gets back in bed.

"I'm sorry," she says, rubbing his thigh. "I didn't mean to snap at you—"

"Just a sec," says Kevin. He captures her hand and sets it on top of the sheet. "There. You were saying?"

"Just that—no offense, but Charles is *my* brother. It's my business to handle him. And who'd know how to do that better than me?"

Kevin opens his mouth as if to argue, then shuts it and runs a hand over his hair.

"Karena," he says, "believe me when I say I'd rather eat my own arm than ask you this, but . . . do you want to take a break? From this—us? You haven't seen Chuck in such a long time, and there's a lot to negotiate. Not that I'd be going anywhere," he adds, "you could still call me if you needed to, and eventually we could figure out if . . ."

Karena holds up a hand—wait—and takes a gulp of air. This is where she should be a good person, should say, You know, you're right, maybe this isn't the best time. Should let Kevin go. Because there's Charles, and then there's Karena and Charles, and then there's Motorcycle Guy, and if Karena felt as if she'd fallen through a trapdoor just now when Kevin's face closed, how would she feel if it looked like that permanently? Because it surely would if he found out. He would be devastated.

But Karena doesn't want to let him go. She pictures the change in seasons, summer morphing into fall, visiting him at school. Watching through the little window in the door while he finished a class, standing in front of rows of boys with those Silly Putty faces in that stretchy phase of development—all of them, Kevin included, wearing blazers with crests on them. Swinging his hand in the hall, hearing him josh with the kids. Walking through leaves on a smoky afternoon, taking him to her favorite cabin in Duluth. She adores this man with his curious, nimble mind, his warm body, his watchful hazel eyes. How can she let him go?

"Is that what *you* want?" she says, looking down. "To break this off? I'd understand, I know it's a lot to ask, the twin thing and the crazy twin thing and—"

"And whatever," says Kevin. "Hell, no, I don't want to break it off. I don't even want to take a break. I'm just trying to be supportive here."

"Oh," says Karena and laughs a little shakily. "Thank goodness."

"Get on down here," Kevin says. He draws her back into the pillows and kisses her.

"That's more like it," he says. "But two things, Laredo, if we're going to make a go of this."

"Uh-oh," says Karena. "I should have known."

"One," says Kevin, "you have to let me know what's going on over there. I'll stay out of your business, but if you're my girl, you are my business, and I need you to be safe. The slightest thing out of whack, you tell me. Promise?"

"I do," says Karena. "What's the other thing?"

"We should get together, the three of us, sooner rather than later," says Kevin. "If I'm going to be in your life, Chuck needs to get used to it."

Karena nods and sighs. "You're probably right. I'll set it up."

"Woman," says Kevin, "I am always right. Now, I think that's enough Chuck talk for a while, don't you?" and Karena agrees, but as Kevin starts to kiss her more deeply her mind is elsewhere, and not in New Heidelburg this time but back in Austin. The moment when Charles first noticed Kevin sitting at the table in the Best Western breakfast room and looked from him to Karena and back again. *So you and Wieb, huh?* he'd said. *Nice, nice.* He'd grinned, but before that, just for a split second, his face had darkened. And now, even as Kevin rolls on top of her and does the Patented Kevin Wiebke Knee Sweep, Karena remembers that first glance and feels a cold foreboding.

44

The following Saturday they go to Lake Harriet, Karena and Charles and Kevin, for a picnic. Lake Harriet, three blocks from Karena's house, is her favorite of all the Minneapolis lakes. Unlike Calhoun, which is round as a platter, or the confusing, amoeba-shaped Lake of the Isles, Harriet has a fairy-tale air. It's because of the fanciful turreted bandstand on the north side, but it's also the shaded paths, the yellow willows trailing their fronds down into the water, the speckled rocks like hens' eggs Karena can see at its edge. The lake is a perfect mirror of the sky, alternately dark or gray or, like today, a bright blue. There are fish. There are boats. And there is the troll tree.

Charles stops a quarter of the way around, transported with delight. "It's still here?" he exclaims, turning to Karena. "I can't believe it!"

"Believe it," says Karena. "I pass it every day during my run."

Charles kneels next to the path. The troll tree is an oak with a little door in its trunk, complete with a tiny lion-headed gold knocker. There's a pebble path leading up to it, and twigs stuck on either side for bushes, and today the roots are also decorated with flowers. The door bulges open slightly with all the offerings the children of Minneapolis— and a good amount of adults too—have placed inside it for the troll. Bottle caps, Barbie shoes, notes folded into triangles, gumball-machine rings. If the troll is pleased with the treasure, the legend goes, he will grant the petitioner's wish.

"Oh my God," says Charles. "I used to love this thing. I still dream about it sometimes." He digs in his shorts pockets and gets up, knees pitted with dirt.

"Here you go, sistah," he says, handing a penny to Karena, "and here's one for you, Wieb," and he gives another to Kevin, who takes out his wallet and finds a coin for Charles in return.

"Ladies first," Charles says. "Go ahead, Wieb."

"Ho ho, Hallingdahl," says Kevin, but he stoops to put his penny in the tree. "Laredo? Your turn."

"Why don't we let these guys go first?" says Karena, smiling at two little girls who are standing shyly to one side, clutching their offerings.

"Yeah, Wieb, where're your manners?" says Charles. "Ladies, right this way," and he bows and rolls his hand out toward the tree. The older of the girls, maybe five or six, giggles, while the younger buries her face in her mother's thighs.

"And what do we have for the troll today?" Charles asks.

The elder girl unfurls her fingers to show a sparkly barrette on her palm.

Charles claps his hand to his forehead and staggers backward. "That . . . is . . . so . . . perfect," he says. "How did you know trolls love barrettes! It's their favorite lunch."

The girl giggles, whirls around to her mom, then turns back to Charles and shouts, "YUM!"

"Yum is right," says Charles, grinning up at the girls' mother—or au pair maybe, Karena thinks now, since she is about twenty and wears no ring. She tucks her long curly hair back behind her ears and blushes and smiles.

"Oh boy," says Karena. "Charles, we're going to keep walking toward the bandstand, all right? You can catch up with us."

"Okay," says Charles distractedly, "be right with you," and as Karena continues along the path with Kevin she hears Charles talking to the nanny, and the nanny talking back, and the little girls shrieking with laughter and calling, "Byeeee! Byeeee!"

"Namaste," Charles calls, "bye!" and he jogs up behind Karena, panting a little and flipping his hand open to flash the phone number inked there.

"Anh?" he says. "Who is the coolest? Who is the smoothest?" He nods and points to himself. "That's right, sistah. Me. Smoooooth as buttah."

"Oh please," says Karena.

Charles puts an arm around her. *"Thank heavens,"* he sings in his Inspector Clouseau voice, *"for little girls. . . ."*

Karena shoves him off. "Get away from me, you pervert," she says, laughing.

"What, K? You didn't think they were adorable? Wieb, help me out here."

"The nanny wasn't too bad either," says Kevin, impassive behind his aviators.

Charles grins. "Noticed that too, did you, Wieb? That's good. So you're not totally whipped yet."

"Hey!" says Karena.

Charles flaps a hand at her and unslings the canvas bag he's carrying over one shoulder.

"Woman," he says, handing it to her, "walk behind and carry the food. Let the men talk."

"Oh boy," Karena says again. "Whose bright idea was this? I'm going home."

But she lets Kevin take the bag and falls behind so the two men can stroll in front of her, conferring about something with their heads together, casually kicking stones. She can't stop smiling. Karena has envisioned a lot of outcomes for this outing, running the spectrum from lukewarm to atrocious, but she would not have believed what has actually happened, which is that from the moment Kevin showed up at the house—nervous, Karena deduced from the careful parting in his damp hair and the amount of Old Spice he'd doused himself in—the men looked at each other and lifted their chins, and Charles said, *Wieb,* and Kevin said, *Hallingdahl,* and instantly they were a boys' club of two. It makes sense, since after all Charles and Kevin have a friendship quite separate from Karena's relationships with either of them, close enough so that at one point, Charles has told her, they considered forming their own tour company: *Wiebke and Hallingdahl, Chasers-at-Large.* Karena can't remember the last time she was so happy to be excluded.

They reach the dock in front of the band shell and walk all the way to the end, then set out their picnic. Charles has made everything: curried tofu salad, tabouli, hummus, cherries, veggie sandwiches on whole wheat pita. There are also a couple of bottles of his special algae drink, which Karena passes up. She made the mistake earlier of trying one, and she won't do that again. Luckily, there is also beer.

"Think fast, Wieb," Charles says, tossing a bottle at Kevin. "Organic, brewed by Trappist monks. Better for the baby," and he slaps Kevin's stomach.

"Charles!" says Karena, but Kevin just uncorks the beer and drains half of it, then rubs his belly.

"Hoo-ah," he says, "baby's thirsty today. Thanks, Hallingdahl. You're a prince among men."

"Don't mention it, Wieb," says Charles, and they settle down to eat. Kevin picks suspiciously at his sandwich.

"Jesus, Hallingdahl," he says, "is this *eggplant?*"

"Just eat it, Wieb, you fucking puffball. When's the last time you ate a vegetable, in a past life?"

"Never," says Kevin, slinging the eggplant into the lake, where it promptly attracts a swarm of minnows. "How many times do I have to tell you, Hallingdahl? Vegetables are what food eats."

Karena leans her back against Kevin's and dangles her feet in the water, warmish and green-gold this close to the banks, laced with shimmering orbits of light. She devours her sandwich. And the salad. And the tabouli, and the hummus, and some cherries. They have a pit-spitting contest, trying to hit the nearest sailboat, and Karena wins easily, pinging its side. Even Charles pretends to be impressed. Then she reclines on her elbows on the sun-beaten boards and belches.

"Ugh," she says, "excuse me. I think I ate too much."

"That's what I love about you, sistah," says Charles. "You're so ladylike. Such a delicate flower."

"Fuck off, Charles."

"See," Charles says to Kevin, "how abusive she is? Man, I hope you know what you're getting into."

"Oh," says Kevin, stroking Karena's hair, "I think I have a pretty good idea."

"Jeez, you kids," says Charles, "do you never stop?" But he helps himself to another sandwich and chews thoughtfully, gazing out across the lake.

"I haven't been here in years," he says. "Remember how Uncle Carroll used to take us here every time we visited, K?"

"I remember," Karena says drowsily. Uncle Carroll, Siri's brother, has been dead for five years from a stupid accident, slipping in the shower and fracturing his skull, dead for three days before a neighbor found him. Every single person's nightmare. But before that he lived quite happily in his little bungalow, surrounded by fascinating samples, books of carpet and wallpaper swatches, rainbows of paint strips. Carroll was a decorator who'd worked in New York for several years, then returned to Minneapolis with a mustache and huge square smoked sunglasses. He had a laugh that soared into the upper registers when something was really funny. Karena remembers Carroll sitting on his couch, wrapped in a cowhide blanket, roaring until he squeaked at an episode of *All in the Family* on his rabbit-eared TV.

"God, I loved visiting Carroll," says Charles. "It was like the height of sophistication. Remember his glass coffee table we made forts under? And the rainbow painted across his bedroom wall? I thought that was so cool. And how he let us stay up as late as we wanted and made us those drinks?"

"I remember," says Karena. Carroll had favored old-fashioned ice cream and liqueur concoctions like Grasshoppers and Golden Cadillacs, and when Frank and Siri were out at a show or dinner he gave the twins each their own in a Dixie cup.

"One for you, Vanilla," she imitates him, "one for you, Rum Raisin, and one-two for me."

Charles laughs. "That's right, I forgot he used to call us that. Did I ever tell you about the nude male aerobics videos I found in his closet?"

Karena opens her eyes and looks over.

"You did not," she says.

"I did," says Charles. "After he died and Mom was going through the house. It was just like Richard Simmons except all the guys were stark nekkid. Oh, except they had sneakers. And those braided headbands."

"You are a total liar," says Karena.

"I'm not," Charles insists. He jumps up, overturning his plate into the water, and starts doing high kicks, batting the air with his palms. "One! Two! Come on, boys! Let me see you sweat! Sweat! Lunge! Lunge! Flex those pecs! Flex those buttocks! Ow."

He sits back down, breathing hard.

"I think I sprained something important," he says. "But you get the idea. Can you imagine what effect that had on a poor small-town boy of thirteen?"

"I think it explains a lot, actually," says Kevin.

"Oh, Wieb," says Charles, leaning over. "Give me a kiss."

Kevin pushes his face away. "Not on a full stomach, Hallingdahl."

"But that's what you love about me, Wieb. My spontaneity."

"Okay," says Karena, laughing, "why am I even here?"

She closes her eyes again. The sun is hot on her face, red through her lids. She listens to Charles and Kevin talk, now about sports, now about storms, now about chasers they know. Kevin breaks out the cigars he has brought and the smoke drifts out over the water. A jet ski buzzes past and waves slap the underside of the dock. Kevin toys with Karena's hair.

She wakes when the sun moves off her face. A breeze has come up, riffling the surface of the lake. The boats rock, their bells chiming. Kevin is watching her, his face hanging over hers like a moon, but upside down.

"Morning, Laredo," he says. "You got yourself a nice little sunburn here," and he rubs a thumb over the fat pads of Karena's cheeks.

Karena smiles up at him, closing first one eye, then the other. She's always amazed how much the perspective changes when she does this. "Where's Charles?"

"Went to get ice cream. Or seduce more jailbait. Not sure which."

"Oh, be nice," says Karena. "Are we jealous now, Mr. Wizard?"

"No reason to be," says Kevin. "No reason in the world," and he bends down to kiss her. It's an awkward angle, but his lips are cool and smoky and salty against Karena's sun-hot face.

"You have to admit," she says when they come up for air, "Charles is being really good. Isn't he? Isn't he being great?"

"Sure," says Kevin, smoothing Karena's hair back from her forehead. "I never said he wasn't. When Chuck's good, he's very very good. When he's bad . . ."

He lets the sentence trail off and raises his eyebrows. Karena turns her head, just in time to see Charles trip-trapping down the boards toward them.

"Hey, kids," he says. He's carrying a soft-serve twisty cone in each hand. "Whatcha talking about? Whatcha doing? Just loafing around?"

Karena sits up so quickly that she almost bangs her head on Kevin's chin. She slits her eyes fiercely at Charles: *Don't you dare.* Charles widens his at her: *What?* Karena darts a glance back at Kevin, behind her. Charles looks puzzled for a second, then understands: *Ahhhh, the Loaf.* He shakes his head—*no no no, K, didn't mean it, sorry*—and grins.

"Wieb," he says to Kevin, who has been collecting the picnic leftovers and stuffing them in the bag. He hands Kevin one of the twisty cones and Karena the other. "There you go, kids. Don't say I never did anything for you."

"Thanks, man," says Kevin. "Where's yours?"

Charles puts his hands to the small of his back and stretches, grimacing.

"Are you serious?" he says. "I don't eat that shit."

They clop back along the boards. Karena's face radiates. The evening is warm, and the ice cream melts fast, and she has to lick it off her wrist when it dribbles down. They turn onto the shady path toward her house, the men again ahead of her, the sun winking every so often as it descends into the tree line. Dogs run past with Frisbees, barking. People jog by with strollers, bicyclists dinging their bells and chanting, "On the left! On the left!" Charles asks Kevin if he's staying for supper, and Kevin says sure, and Charles says they could watch some of his chase DVDs from this year, and Kevin says sweet. They amble along, the one tall and slender and sandaled, the other short and stocky and powerful, reminding Karena of—not Laurel and Hardy, exactly, but the cartoon where two starving men on a desert island look at each other and one sees a hot dog, the other a hamburger. Maybe this picnic has been an anomaly, is something Karena will look back on when she's old as a day when she was happy. Maybe the three of them are just temporarily suspended in some shining bubble of time. But on the other hand, maybe things can always be this way, Karena thinks—people *are* happy sometimes, aren't they? Maybe everything will be all right. When they pass the troll tree, Karena slips her penny behind the door.

45

About a month later, at the beginning of the third week of August, the first of Karena's annual two-week vacation, she comes home from Saturday brunch with Tiff to find her house reeking of something foul. Tea. Charles's so-called tea. Every few days he makes another batch of it, despite Karena's begging him not to, using her good lobster pot to boil the mysterious contents of a package he receives each week in the mail. He left one of these unattended on the kitchen counter once, and Karena poked it cautiously, a supersize baggie bulging with twigs and knobs of wood and what look like slimy leaves. *It's a cleanser,* Charles said when Karena asked, *it balances my lymphatic system. And it's a colonic besides. You want some, sistah? No offense, but judging from your complexion you could use some—and the Loaf too, he needs a colonic like nobody's business.* Karena had demurred and hastily retreated, the way she did when Charles was sage smudging, waving the burning brush around her living room, and he said, *I'm ridding the house of bad spiritual energy, K, I'd think you'd appreciate that.*

Karena has tried hard to live and let live. After all, just because she and Charles are twins doesn't mean their habits have to be the same. But while Karena can handle the sage, and her house smelling on good days like a co-op, half incense and half medicine, and Charles's meditation mat on the front porch and the army of algae drinks in the fridge, and his wind chimes and his incense and his herbal remedies and his special lotion and his chanting to meet the dawn every morning while banging his Lakota drum—all this Karena can tolerate, barely. The tea she has a harder time with. It smells like the rot on the undersides of mushrooms combined with old sweat socks, and she has to mouth-breathe until she gets used to it.

"Hey, Charles," she says, walking into the kitchen.

Charles is standing over the stove, peering into the pot. He is wearing shorts and a madras shirt and numerous medallions on thongs around his neck, cowry shells and a rune symbol and a quartered circle he has explained to Karena illustrates the four quadrants of a man's life in the Lakota tradition, his spiritual path bisected by the sun. He is also wearing a very old, faded red apron of Siri's that says "Bitch Bitch Bitch" on the front.

"Sistah," he says and drops the lid on the pot with a *clang!* Mercifully the smell diminishes a fraction, although Karena eyes the spatter of what looks like gray juice on the wall behind her stove.

"How was brunch?" Charles asks. "How's Trog Number One?"

"Fine," says Karena.

"She didn't want to swing by and say hello?" Charles says, turning to open the fridge but not quickly enough to hide a grin, and Karena knows he is thinking of their get-together two weeks ago. Encouraged by the success of the Charles-Kevin experiment, Karena suggested she and Tiff and Charles take a walk around the lake—which made perfect sense in retrospect, like introducing two hostile dogs in neutral territory. But this time the setting did not work its magic, or it did until they were nearing the Rose Garden and Tiff—really, she started it—leaned past Karena to Charles on the other side and said, *So, this is all very nice and civil and everything, but since your sister's not gonna ask, I will: When are you going to start back on meds and get a real job?* and Charles had said, *That's a very good question, maybe about the same time you do. Weren't you supposed to be a doctor or something?* and Tiff said, *Yeah, so I married a doctor instead of becoming a doctor, you gotta problem with that?* and Charles said, *No, but apparently you do. Though I sympathize, it's got to be hard being a suckling pig for, what, five piglets now?* and Tiff said, *Get on meds, Charles,* and Charles said, *Get a life, Shamu,* and Tiff, who hasn't been overweight for years, who has a personal trainer and does Pilates and is actually so skinny her head looks too big for her body, had colored to her hairline and said, *You're a douche, Charles,* and Charles had said, *Ever the lady, Deep Throat,* and Tiff had turned and walked in the opposite direction. And that had been that.

So Karena says now, "No, astonishingly, she didn't want to come in, Charles. I wonder why that is."

A snicker comes from the refrigerator, which Charles is leaning into. He straightens up with an algae drink, chugs it, belches, and says, "Freaked if I know."

"Charles," says Karena. "You know, it'd be helpful if you could be a little nicer to her."

Charles's eyes widen in amazement.

"Me!" he says. "What'd I do? There I was just walking along, enjoying the nice day, trying so hard to let bygones be bygones, when she attacked me."

Karena sighs. This is true. But she is thinking about the unsaid part of her sentence: *If you're going to stay here . . .* She doesn't want to play the heavy, enforce house rules under her roof. But as much as she loves having Charles here, it has become something of a strain too. The other night Karena woke on her foldout in the den at four thirty and heard the thud of base, and she thought at first it was the neighbor kids down the block who liked to park their beater in front of the house and make out. She had gone to the front door to yell at them, then realized the music was coming from upstairs. She went to the door and listened. *Nn-tss-nn-tss-nn-tss,* a club mix, overlaid with the chants of Gregorian monks. Karena tapped. *Charles?* she said. *Nn-tss-nn-tss-nn-tss-whoomp-whoomp-whoomp-whoomp-whoomp.* Karena knocked again. *Charles,* she called, *could you turn that down a little, please?* No response. Karena had waited a while, weighing her options, uneasy, then gone back to bed.

Not that she wouldn't have been up at that hour anyway. And not that she wants Charles to move out of the city. God, no. Karena wants him as nearby as possible. She'll help him find a place, and she'll pay his rent, whatever he needs, until he gets acclimated. She could just use a little . . . space.

Charles turns back to his pot, stirring.

"So, sistah," he says, "I've been thinking, I probably won't be here much longer."

"What?" Karena cries. Of course, now that Charles has said what she's been thinking, she can't stand for him to leave. "You can't go! Where are you going? You're staying in Minneapolis, right?"

Charles sips from a wooden spoon and makes a face.

"Not exactly," he says.

"But where are you going?" Karena repeats. She feels as though some essential membrane in her chest is being ripped away. "And why? We could look for apartments in Uptown, starting today—"

Charles smiles sadly.

"That's lovely you want me to stay, K," he says. "And I wish I could. Believe me. But I've got something I have to do."

"What?" Karena argues. "What could be more important than this?" She gestures around her steamy little kitchen, encompassing the two of them.

"Not much," Charles admits. "But I have to do this, K."

He leans against the counter.

"I'm going to turn myself in," he says.

For a few seconds Karena doesn't think she's heard him correctly, that the switchboard in her brain has been scrambled. She stares at him, then laughs.

"Okay, Charles," she says, "very funny. Except it isn't. It's not funny at all."

"I agree," says Charles. "There's nothing remotely funny about a man's death. Or my being responsible for it. I killed him, and I'm tired of living with it, and it's time for me to pay."

Karena stares at him, then shoves off the counter and hurries across the kitchen, kicking over a stool in the process. She shuts the door and locks it, cranks closed the windows despite the steamy reek of the tea. This is not a conversation the neighbors need to know about. Then she returns to the counter. Careful, Karena is thinking. Kevin was right. Charles is manic. Or hypomanic at least, working up to it, because how could he make such an insane suggestion otherwise?

But when she faces Charles with a placating smile, he is watching her calmly, arms folded.

"I'm not crazy, K," he says.

Karena stretches her smile. "I wasn't thinking that, Charles."

Charles sighs. "Of course you were," he says, "but that's beside the point. The point is, I'm going to do this. I'm going to New Heidelburg maybe next week, as soon as I tie up some loose ends, and I'm going to tell the sheriff what happened."

"Okay," says Karena, scrambling to catch up and pull ahead. Meanwhile she evaluates Charles: his expression peaceful, even sorrowful. His posture relaxed. His speech a normal tempo. No sign of the djinn's staccato diatribes, the jeering, twitchy energy. At the moment, Charles appears perfectly sane, and that is the scariest thing of all. A cold needle slips into Karena's stomach.

"But I don't understand," she says. "Why now? Why are you doing this after all this time?"

"Because I'm tired, K," says Charles. "Because I'm so freaking tired of seeing the guy. Because I'm tired of waking up and finding him on the foot of my bed. He still comes every night, did I tell you that? Yes, he does. Every night at four thirty, on the dot. He never says anything, never does anything, just sits there and looks at me. Just like before, when we'd just done it, except he doesn't smell anymore, he's too desiccated. And his skin's bleached out—what's left of it—and the blood on his shirt's all brown because he's been dead such a long time—"

"I get the picture, Charles."

"Except you don't," says Charles earnestly. "That's just it, K. I can never say enough to make you understand how bad it is. I killed him, K, and he knows that, and the only way to make him go away is to turn myself in."

Karena pulls her hair back.

"Charles," she says, "you might not like what I'm about to say, but as your sister who loves you I have to say it. There is another way to make him go away, and you know it. You could take meds."

Charles shakes his head.

"No," he says. "I'm not going to do that. Don't ever ask me to do that, K. I mean, you can ask all you want, but I'm not going to. Never again."

"Okay, but," says Karena, "there have been so many advances since the last time you took them, Charles. Even since—when were you in Kansas with that woman? 2000, right? Eight years ago, and do you know how many new drugs they've invented since then? They come out with new drugs every day!"

"So what, you want me to be a guinea pig now?" says Charles. "To keep trying this one and that one like it's nothing, like they're vitamins or candy or something? They're not, K. Don't you get that? They fuck with my brain chemistry. They change my *brain*. So in essence, what you're saying I should do is compromise my very self, my understanding and feeling of who I am, to conform to what you want. Is that it?"

"No, Charles, not at all. Of course that's not what I meant. We were talking about Motorcycle Guy and how he terrifies you! Don't you want to make him go away?"

Charles scrapes his hands through his hair and looks at the slate floor.

"Not at that price," he says. "No. Never. And the thing is, actually, he may never go away, anyway, K. I've thought about this a lot. He may still keep coming even after I turn myself in. But at least when I look at him, I won't have to feel so *bad*. I can say, Hey, buddy, how you doing, sorry about what happened, but at least you can see I'm making amends here."

Amends! Karena pounces on this.

"Charles," she says, "I appreciate your trying to do the right thing. I do. But as you said to me once, what's it going to change if you turn yourself in? He's not coming back—Motorcycle Guy. You can't bring him back. Remember when you said that? So why don't you try to make

amends some other way, like—like working in a soup kitchen or something. Or working for FEMA. Sure, that'd be a good fit for you, helping people in communities destroyed by storms, like Oweeo—"

But Charles is shaking his head again.

"Stop, K," he says. "Believe me, I've run this all over in my mind at
least a million times. As of today, it's been twenty years, one month, and
six days since we killed him. How many days is that? That's how many
times I've gone over it. Anyway. It's a nice idea, but it won't work. The
karma is all out of whack. We took a man's life, and serving chicken
noodle to the homeless isn't going to fix that. The only way to do it is
to step up and admit what we've done. Because come on, K. As you said
to me that afternoon, we did the very worst thing we could do to another human being. We stole his life away. Are you trying to tell me you
don't ever think about that?"

Karena sighs and looks down, at her own bare feet with their
chipped-polish toenails, then at her brother's large, square brown ones.
Of course she does. Of course she thinks about Motorcycle Guy. Over
that twenty years, one month, and six days, she's had plenty of time to
wonder who he was—usually at four thirty in the morning. She's constructed a whole life for him, as if he's a Hell's Angel paper doll. She's
given him a double-wide trailer with a sink full of dirty dishes, a bu-
reau full of flannel shirts with cut-off arms, pot plants in the closet.
She's given him a La-Z-Boy recliner patched with duct tape and a
satellite dish so he can watch five hundred channels. She's given him a
drinking habit and mild pot addiction and the occasional sniff of coke,
because he had to be on something that day, didn't he? had to be coming back from the local watering hole where he was getting plastered
with his buddies, because why else would he ever have driven into that
storm? On a motorcycle? Who would *do* that? Karena has given Motorcycle Guy a cat, not a dog, because a cat wouldn't miss him when he
didn't come home, would just eat all the garbage beneath his counter
and then jump out the window and go feral. She has given him several
angry ex-wives who said good riddance when they heard he was dead

because he never paid alimony anyway, and she gave him one daughter who never received child-support checks and was better off without him. In fact, Motorcycle Guy has probably done some time himself, for B&E or assault or dealing, and although Karena knows everything she's imagined is a terrible cliché, every reporter's instinct in her screaming in protest, she can't stand to think otherwise. She can't stand to think Motorcycle Guy might have had a job, a family, a pet, a way to contribute, people out there who miss him.

But either way, it doesn't matter. Charles is right. Whether the guy was Gandhi on a Harley or a complete waste of space, what they have done is still wrong. They took his cat, his bike, his recliner, his breath. They have ended his life.

Then something occurs to Karena. She looks at her brother, who is watching her with grave compassion, and says, "Why do you keep saying we?"

"Because we did it," says Charles. "Or rather I did, but you were there, K. You had agency too. You could have done the right thing."

Karena cannot believe how unfair this is.

"But I didn't, Charles, because somebody begged me not to," she says. "Let's see, who could that somebody be? You, Charles! You!"

"Well, I know that, K," says Charles. "But I was wrong. I was scared, and I was just a kid. I didn't know any better."

"Oh, like I did?" says Karena. "In all my infinite eighteen-year-old wisdom? I was scared too! And if you recall, I was trying to protect you!"

"I know that, K," says Charles, "and I'll never forget that. You did protect me—at least, until you called the sheriff on me. But let's not get into that right now. The point is, this isn't like some high school prank you do and then forget about, like stealing somebody's car or whatever. I know it was twenty years ago, but still. We have to balance the scales."

"Okay," says Karena, "you do that, Charles. But leave me out of it."

"Oh, K," says Charles. "Are you sure? I'm giving you the chance to make things right. Are you sure you don't want to take it? It might do you some good."

Karena inclines her head.

"And what is *that* supposed to mean," she says.

Charles waves around at her kitchen, toward her living room, the light streaming in through the front windows, serene and sunny on a weekend afternoon.

"You've achieved an awful lot, K," he says. "I'm proud of you. You've got a great career, beautiful home, and you did it all by yourself. But that's just it—you're all by yourself. And that's just wrong. Come on, K. We both know you should have a husband, kids. You're a giving person. You're not cut out to spend the rest of your life alone."

For a few seconds Karena is so angry she can hardly see. Then she sees two of Charles, which makes it even worse. Is she having a stroke?

"Okay, Charles," she says, "thanks so much. You know who you sound like? Your favorite person—Tiff. Or Shamu or Trog Number One or Deep Throat or whatever you want to call her. She says exactly the same thing—that my life's useless because I don't have a husband and kids. Well, you know what? I like my useless life! So the two of you can both go fuck your judgmental selves!"

Charles is nodding sagely.

"Sure," he says, "I can see how it'd come off like that. But we're not trying to judge you. We love you. We're calling 'em as we see 'em. Shamu may be a raging bitch, but I never said she was stupid."

Karena gives a now-I've-heard-it-all scoff.

"Okay, as you wish," she says. "This conversation has devolved into utter stupidity. I'm leaving. I'm out."

"Fine," says Charles, "do whatever you want. I'm just saying, K, I know you've thought about this. I can *feel* you thinking about it, when you wake up in the night, and it's really painful. I just think, as long as you have this secret, you won't be able to get close to anybody. And that's a real shame."

Karena laughs, again.

"Oh my God, what are you, a talk show host now?" she says. "What is this, the Chuck Hallingdahl Show? Why do I have this secret, Charles? This absurd, hideous, festering secret? Because of you! You're the one who asked me to carry it in the first place!"

"And I regret that," says Charles. "I'm trying to make up for it. I know it sounds ridiculous, K, but just think about it. That's all I'm asking," and Karena hears this too, echoing back to her from that day in Decorah: *Just give me a little time, K, to figure it out.* Tiff and Kevin are right. Her brother will destroy her.

She goes out into the living room to look for her running shoes. The space is brilliant with light. And it is clean—at least it was before Charles got here—and boasts all the signs of a happy, well-lived life: the fireplace, Karena's books filling the shelves on either side, the shells she picked up on vacations lining the windowsills. The floorboards she sanded and painted herself. The couch and chairs she picked out, also by herself—and suddenly Karena remembers her former therapist, Dr. B, saying, *I just can't understand it. We've made such good progress, but I feel there's something you're holding back from me, that you hold back from everybody, that prevents you from getting close to people. Do you have any idea what it is?* and Karena had shrugged and held out her palms with a face that said search me. Then she had missed the next session, and the next, and after that, really, what was the point of going back?

Charles is watching her from the kitchen doorway.

"Plus, what about the Loaf?" he asks. "I won't tell, K. I swear. As far as the investigation goes, I was the only one in the Jeep that day, if that's the way you want it. But are you seriously going to try and keep this from him? As much crap as I give you about the guy, he's very smart and intuitive. The longer you wait to tell him, the harder it's going to be on both of you."

Karena straightens up and glares at Charles.

"Don't you dare," she says. "Don't you even talk about my relationship with Kevin. That's mine, that's my business. You leave it alone."

Charles retreats a few steps. "Okay, okay. All I'm saying is, I can see you're hopeful for a chance at something with him, and I wish you all the best. But how are you going to sustain the relationship if you don't have trust?"

"You know," says Karena, "I don't know, Charles. Maybe you can figure that out for me, since you're so wise now. And when you do, you let me know—when I come back. Because I'm going out now, and I'll be out for a while, and as far as I'm concerned, this insane conversation is over. As in o-ver. Okay, Charles?"

Charles shrugs.

"If you say so, sistah," he says, and although Karena knows this is not a real answer, that at any minute he could take off the apron and get in his car and drive to New Heidelburg and blow the whole stinking thing out of the water, she just can't stand to fight with him anymore. She pushes open the front door and goes out.

46

She spends that night at Kevin's, and with every passing hour the argument, which initially balloons in Karena's head to terrifying proportions, starts to lose power. In an odd way it helps that Karena can't tell Kevin about it, forces her not to think about it, her time with him a reassuring baseline normality. They see a movie, walk hand in hand along Grand Avenue and stop at a beer garden and sit outside, then return to Kevin's man cave. By the following afternoon, when Karena returns home, Charles's ridiculous plan seems like something she has dreamed, a nightmare that fades by midmorning. She decides to not even mention it to him. *Least said, soonest mended*, as Grandmother Hallingdahl would say.

But when Karena gets home, Charles's yellow Volvo is gone. And she knows the second she steps inside he's not in the house. It is muggy and close—Charles disdains the AC, says it contributes to global warming, so he shuts it off whenever he leaves. In his absence the rooms are so quiet Karena can hear the grind of the old clock over her stove, and the *thunk* of ice cascading into the ice maker makes her jump. She has to set the damned thing to Off. Ever since she got back from chasing it reminds her of hail.

She stands still, tapping her lips and thinking. It isn't unusual for Charles to be out. He has his errands during the day: food shopping, meditating by the lake—and sometimes, Karena suspects, seeing the au pair he met there. Karena hasn't asked, and Charles hasn't told. That's the way they've tacitly agreed to set it up. Charles has even been away overnight, when the forecast indicates the chance of a local chase. Karena has never worried that he's left again for good. Not without telling her. But that was before he threatened to turn himself in.

She goes to the foot of the master suite steps and hesitates. This is a total invasion of privacy. Ever since Karena has conceded her bedroom to Charles, she hasn't been up there. But there are certain things Charles would take with him if he'd gone to New Heidelburg. Not clothes, probably not even toiletries, but his herbal supplements and laptop, Karena guesses, although they would be confiscated, and definitely his ledger, which might not. Charles would never go anywhere without his ledger, the one item he asked for in Black Wing. Karena knocks, twice to be safe, then shakes her head at herself and goes up.

The carpeted stairwell smells a little scorched, like burnt sage. Karena will have to open a window in here, she is thinking. As long as she remembers to close it before Charles gets home so he won't know she's been up here—

Then she rounds the corner and comes up into the long open room beneath the eaves, and she stops. Stares. Her leg muscles tense for flight. She might as well have walked in to find a snake on the carpet.

Charles has turned the space into his new lair.

It is not an exact replica. There are no lightning lamps this time nor shelves of mysterious electronic equipment. And of course the bones of the room are still Karena's, the vaulted architecture, the airy space and sun filtering through the skylights. But the walls flutter with paper—if Charles dislikes the AC, he has no such objection to the old-fashioned oscillating fan he's dragged home from some curb or back alley. It sweeps right to left, left to right, ticking at the end of each journey and stirring the pages and pages and pages Charles has taped up. Lined notebook paper covered with his tiny handwriting, column upon column of numbers. What are these, map coordinates, barometric pressure readings, equations? There are photos tacked here and there, the ubiquitous tornadoes, lightning, the anvil-shaped supercells Karena now sometimes sees in her sleep. Drawings too of spirals, Sioux medicine wheels, cloud structures. Over the bed, next to a head-size dream catcher, is a list—

Kava Kava
Valerian
A, B, B6, B12, C, D, E, zinc
California poppy
St. John's wort
Green tea
Algae
Eddie's brew

Tiny checkmarks straggle to the margin of the paper. There is also a note scribbled in Bic pen—big writing, not Charles's—on a Casey's place mat:

> *The Legend Goes There Is A Brave With A Very Bad Temper. The Elders Of His Tribe Do Everything They Can To Cure Him With Medicines, But They Cant So They Lock Him In A Cell. The Brave Is Very Angry And Yells To Be Let Out. When Nobody Comes, He Paces. Round And Round For Many Nights, Faster And Faster, Until Finally He Explodes The Cell And Whirls Up Into The Sky. First He Destroys The Elders, Then The Village, Then The Tribe. Then He Whirls Away To Cause Destruction Elsewhere. The Great Spirit Catches Him And Holds Him Until Spring, But Every Year At That Time The Brave Returns To The Plains To Cause Destruction. It Is Part Of The Cycle Of Death And Prosperity. ~ Eddie Black Cloud.*

"Whoa," Karena says.

She sits heavily on the bed. How could she have overlooked what's been percolating under her own roof? How can she have been so stupid? Or has she? That's the tricky thing about Charles's disorder—Karena just never knows. Certain behaviors might mean something, or they could just be Charles being Charles. Karena begins toting up signs, starting with the basics—like any sick animal, when Charles is hypomanic, the disruptions begin in his sleeping, eating, and hygiene patterns. The music on all night up here—Charles may or may not be falling asleep listening to it. He might have been pacing, but because it's carpeted, Karena hasn't heard him. There's the accumulation of green tea bottles in the recycling bin—when Charles is winding up into mania he drinks and drinks and drinks. Then again it's August, everyone's thirsty. Hygiene: the madras shirt Charles was wearing yesterday, was he not wearing it the day before? Possibly the day before that? But he's a guy, and all his shirts look the same . . .

For every symptom Karena comes up with there's a convincing counterargument. Even Charles's wall collage, it's excessive, yes—but isn't it a messier variation of Karena's bulletin board at work, Post-its, printouts, pieces of an information puzzle she needs to keep before her? Even Charles's threat to turn himself in, could be a product of hypomania or just a Charles theory. Karena thinks of how calm he was while she was yelling at him, his dark and patient eyes. That's the thing, she would tell Kevin if he were here, it's true, the djinn is always there, but you never know when it's going to strike. All the conditions can be right and it remains dormant, then one day it appears out of the blue.

Kevin. Karena should call Kevin. She promised she would if she had the slightest suspicion—but how can she, when she doesn't even know where Charles is? He could indeed be in New Heidelburg confessing to the sheriff, at which point, Karena feels fairly sure, any involvement Kevin has in her life will become moot. Or Charles could be at the farmers' market, the Linden Hills co-op. He could be already full blown, reeling around Minneapolis deranged with mania, fending off visions from his own fevered mind. There's only one way to know for sure. She has to find the ledger.

Karena ravages the room looking for it, tossing aside armfuls of T-shirts and socks, towels, even checking the bathroom. Of course it is the last place she looks, the logical place, under the bed. Karena almost cries when she sees *aug 2009* on the cover and hugs the composition book to her chest. Charles hasn't gone to the sheriff. Not yet. Feeling physically sick, Karena opens the ledger. She would never do this except in an emergency, and she's no snoop. She doesn't read all the entries, only the last one, written this morning.

> *21 aug 2008 sunday, 10:53 AM. mostly sunny, se wind to 15, lo 62, hi 88, dews mid-70s. Poss severe forecast day 2, dakotas thru western and southern mn. shortwave troughs moving thru will likely cause siggy tor outbreak. not sure if i will chase bc might be in new hellishburg at the sheriff's, haven't decided yet. made the mistake of telling k yesterday & she basically pooh-poohed me. like patted me on the head & said that's nice charles but leave me out of it. cowardly bitch, like i'm the only one responsible for what happened that day on the road. tho that's not fair, she's not a bitch, she just doesn't get it. doesn't get what it's like to see the fucking guy every night. doesn't get how awful it is to be trapped in this skin knowing i did it, i killed him. just go work at a soup kitchen, she sez, looking at me w/ this great condescension. what a fucking dumbass thing to say & so easy for her to say it. it's all easy for her, she's got this nice setup here w/ job & house & car, except of course it's all a lie bc she's not telling the truth, & that's going to come back to bite her on the ass. i'm so tired of dealing with this all on my own, it's not fair, & i'm tired of K thinking i'm crazy—her & her little dog too. that's wieb, haha, tho really he isn't a bad guy i don't think, like not EVIL necessarily, it's just that like most weak people his vision is limited & he's jealous & it makes him do bad things. wieb knows he's nothing next to me, he's always envied my instincts & tried to push me out of the way. hence that day in ok when we were chasing that tor & he got me locked up, what the fuck was THAT? & how ironic is it that the two of them have ended up together? or maybe not, birds of*

a feather & all that, but the pt is K's over there right now plot-
ting w/ wieb & i can FEEL them talking about me, wieb's
trying to convince K i'm nuts, he totally wants me gone from the
picture except this time not to steal my data but to take my sister.
well he'd just better watch out the two of them had better watch
out because i know they want to put me someplace where they'll
give me more ECT & stick wires in my head—

"What the fuck are you doing?" says Charles from the top of the
stairs, and Karena turns. He is carrying a paper bag of produce and he
takes a couple of steps toward her, except it is not Charles, Karena sees,
looking at her with such open-mouthed suspicion, such dark and righ-
teous indignation. No, Kevin is right, and Karena has been wrong,
because Charles has been erased as efficiently as with a sponge. Her
brother is not here. But the djinn is.

47

Karena sits out on the front steps with her cell phone, calling and calling Kevin. She has to warn him, keep him from coming over if she possibly can. He's coaching soccer practice, which started last week, and Karena knows he turns off his cell and tosses it in the glove compartment while he does this, often forgetting to retrieve it until later that night. She can only pray this time he makes an exception, calls to see if he can pick up anything last minute, even goes home to shower so he'll hear the message Karena has left on his landline: *I'm okay, I'll explain later, but do not come here, Kevin. I repeat, do not.* Karena doubts she'll catch him, though. Kevin is already a half hour late for supper, which, Charles has reminded her, Charles is scheduled to cook for the three of them. *Why else do you think I went to buy all this fucking food, K,* he snarled, *to give you time to go through my shit?*

Karena is right: Kevin comes straight to the house. She jumps up as soon as she sees his Honda round the corner, but Charles is too fast for her. He barrels out of the house, almost knocking her over, freshly showered and holding a big brown bottle. He is wearing a pink button-down shirt and swim trunks with flames on them, and he trails the smell of his organic soap, patchouli with a hint of lime.

"Wieb," he says, bounding down the front walk, "Wieb, Wieb, Wieb, Wieb, Wieb! Good to see you, man."

He throws an arm around a somewhat startled Kevin as Kevin comes around the car and plants a smacking kiss on Kevin's cheek.

"Jesus, Hallingdahl, what the hell," Kevin says, shrugging Charles off. "I'm not that easy. You have to at least feed me first."

"Sorry, Wieb, sorry, sorry," says Charles and hands him the bottle. "Here, here's a beer, sustenance for the beer baby, he must be parched. It's so hot tonight, high dews too, I don't envy you out on that field. So how was it," he says, guiding Kevin up the walk, "how was school, how was practice, how are kids these days?"

"Brutal," says Kevin. "I knew I should have gone into hairdressing."

He looks at Karena and raises his brows: *What's going on with him?* She gives her head a tiny shake.

"Hold up a minute, Hallingdahl," Kevin says, "let me say hi to my girl here."

"Oh, forget her," says Charles, flapping a hand, "she's useless, this woman, does no work whatsoever. Would you believe I asked her to set the table an hour ago? An hour, a whole fucking hour, and has she done it yet? That's a rhetorical question, Wieb, you don't have to answer. I s'pose I'll just have to do it, the way I do everything else around here, no rest for the wicked as they say. Also we have to grill, I've already got the fire going, so come on, Wieb, let's go do manly things."

"Sounds good, Hallingdahl," says Kevin, "one sec," and he detours to Karena and hugs her.

"How long has he been like this?" he says in her ear.

"I'm really not sure," she says, smiling widely, and from on the porch Charles says, "Jesus, Wieb, could you be slower? Move your ass, the grill waits for no man."

"Coming, Hallingdahl," says Kevin. He looks at Karena over one shoulder—*Is this all right? Is this what we should do?*—and she nods and shrugs and follows.

Charles drags Kevin through the house and out onto the back patio, where Karena sets the table while the men grill Charles's vegetable shish kebabs. It is indeed a hot evening, the western sky orange-pink beyond the garage roofs, the bats cross-stitching it with eerie, stuttery

spccd. The neighbor kids splash in their pool across the alley: *Marco!*
Polo! The air fills with the smell of charcoal, and Karena brings out the
dishes Charles has prepared. Green salad, caprese salad, a selection of
farm cheeses, a baguette, and, Karena sees with a pinch, Siri's favorite,
sliced tomatoes piled high with sugar. Karena adds beer and ice water
and lights the citronella candle, and all the while Charles talks—and
talks and talks and talks and talks and talks. So what does Kevin think
about tomorrow? The forecast looks pretty healthy, huh? Is Kevin
going to chase? Oh, sorry, Wieb, forgot you had to coach, but if Kevin
wants to play hooky they could chase together, wouldn't that be sweet?
One last summer chase, Hallingdahl & Wiebke, a chase for auld lang
syne? Okay, dinner's ready! and they all sit down. Karena doesn't dare
look at Kevin, but she grips his hand under the table.

They eat. At least Karena and Kevin do, while Charles keeps talking. So what does Kevin think of this season anyway, would he say it was
slower than usual? More active? About the same? Good season, interesting, what makes him say so? And what does he attribute that to, El Niño?
Doesn't he think global warming has a lot to do with it? What does
Kevin predict will happen if the earth's temperature kccps rising a
couple of degrees a year? What will the effect be on severe weather,
particularly tornadoes, particularly significant tornadoes? Doesn't
Kevin think the parameters will totally change? "If this keeps up," says
Charles, "forget Tornado Alley, we'll all be chasing in New York City,
ha ha! That would suck." He pauses to drain a glass of ice water, pours
himself another, drinks that too, then wipes his mouth on his shoulder
and keeps going. "I'm telling you, man," he says to Kevin, "I'm this
close to submitting my abstract on rapid cycling, this close, thisclose!"
and he holds his thumb and forefinger an inch apart and shakes them in
Kevin's face. Kevin blinks and eats another forkful of mozzarella. "But
I might've been looking in the wrong direction. I should have been pay-
ing more attention to global warming and its effects on severe, that's the
future, Wieb, because that's where the study of meteorology is going."

"That's probably true, Hallingdahl," says Kevin, and under the table
he presses Karena's hand: *Still okay?* And she squeezes back: *Yes.*

"Really," says Charles, "really, you think so, Wieb? Then maybe, maybe, maybe we can look into piloting a study together," and he pours a third glass of water. The bowls and plates chatter lightly on the table from Charles's knee jackhammering beneath it and his eyes glitter and he rakes his hands through his hair, and although he sounds pleasant enough, in fact is being perfectly friendly, Karena knows what he's thinking. She told Kevin the truth when she said she can't usually intuit what's going through Charles's mind, but tonight the force of his dementia is so strong she feels herself getting sucked into it, can see how Charles is viewing them all. Karena is a sickly lamb, baaing, fearful, and sycophantic. Kevin is a neckless calf, unaware of imminent slaughter. And Charles, sitting between them, is neither animal nor human, exactly, but more a towering consciousness that mushrooms up and up and up over the table, above the yard, above the house and the block and city and countryside until he is miles above them, in the stratosphere, looking down and thinking, *Lord, what a bunch of fucking morons these mortals be.*

Suddenly he stands up.

"Well, I'm off," he says, "you kids can do the dishes, can't you? See you later."

"Where you going, man?" Kevin asks.

"Night lightning," says Charles. "I've been watching the southwest sky over your head, Wieb, and there's a pretty decent show going on over there. It'd be sweet to shoot a few CGs, maybe an anvil crawler or two. I'd invite you to come along but I know you kids want to be alone and speaking of which"—he winks—"be good now, use protection, and no wild parties or I'll call the cops, you hear?" and then he is gone, the screen door wheezing behind him.

Karena and Kevin stare at each other until they hear the front door shut too.

"Are you all right?" Kevin asks, and Karena nods.

"You?" she says.

"Drenched," says Kevin and lets go of her hand to reach for the water pitcher. He drinks a glass and pulls his T-shirt away from his skin. "He scared the bejesus out of me. That's the djinn, huh?"

"That was him," says Karena.

"He was bad in Oklahoma too," says Kevin, "but not that bad. I've never seen him this wound up. Has he been hearing or seeing things?

"Not yet," says Karena, "but probably soon. Kevin, I think I was wrong. I think he's been working himself up to this for a while and I didn't want to see it. I'm sorry, I've been such an idiot—"

"Don't, Laredo," says Kevin. "(A), you're not, and (B), that's counterproductive. The question is what we should do about him now."

"But what can we do?" Karena says. "Besides go after him. He shouldn't be in the car," and she starts to stand up. Kevin puts a hand on her wrist.

"I think we should call the cops," he says. "Let them handle it."

"And tell them what, Kevin? That he's manic? They can't arrest you for that."

"No, but couldn't we say he's driving under the influence?" Kevin argues. "What is that, reckless endangerment?"

"Maybe," says Karena. "But under the influence means alcohol or drugs, and he's—"

"Who're you kids talking about?"

Karena and Kevin freeze. Charles is back, standing at the side gate. He lifts the latch and strolls in, setting off the safety light over the door.

"Forgot my keys," he says, "must be early Alzheimer's setting in, I should start wearing them around my neck or something. There they are," and he snatches his carabiner key ring from the table next to the grill.

"So," he says, bouncing it in his palm as he walks over, "what's going on, what's up, what'd I miss? What's the hot topic of conversation at the dinner table?"

"Not much," says Karena, and Kevin says, "Yeah, just shooting the breeze."

"Oh, not much?" says Charles, sitting down and scraping his chair over. "My favorite topic. Deal me in. The light show can wait a little while. So, Wieb, who's this guy you're talking about?"

"What's that?" says Kevin. He takes another sip of water.

"That guy," says Charles, "that guy you were just discussing. Sorry, I couldn't help overhearing, it's not like I'm an eavesdropper or a snoop or anything. Unlike my sister here, I'm not into that kind of thing. But you're not exactly subtle, Wieb, in fact your voice carries like a fucking airhorn, so my question is, this guy you want to call the cops on, that wouldn't be . . . *me*, would it?"

"Actually, Chuck," says Kevin, "we were thinking you seem a little wound up."

"A little wound up," repeats Charles, rocking the chair on its back legs. He regards Kevin with his eyes half closed, a smile curling his mouth. "A little wound up, little wound up, that's how I seem to you, huh, Wieb?"

"Kevin, don't," Karena says softly.

But Kevin says, "That's right." He sounds calm enough, although blisters of sweat have formed at his hairline. "Maybe you should hang with us a while, just talk and relax. Play some cards—"

"No, let's talk," says Charles, his chair legs slamming down. He sweeps his plate aside and folds his hands on the table and smiles. "Talking's good. I like talk. Especially when it's among friends. And we're all friends here, wouldn't you say, Wieb?"

"Charles," says Karena, but Kevin says, "Sure, man. Absolutely."

"Did you hear that, sistah?" Charles asks. "Absolutely. Abso-fucking-lutely. See, K, Wieb agrees we're all friends. And friends should talk honestly among themselves, don't you think?"

"Sure," says Kevin. "Listen, Hallingdahl—"

"But you know," says Charles, "*somebody* here has a different definition of honesty. I'm with you, Wieb, I think trust is the basis for *any* relationship, friendship or otherwise. But *somebody* does not agree."

"That's enough, Charles," says Karena.

"And who could this *somebody* be?" Charles asks. He looks around dramatically, then clamps his hands to his forehead. "Oh my God! There she is!"

"There she is, right," says Kevin, but he is starting to look nervous. He licks his lips. "Come on, Hallingdahl, let's just go in and—

"Wieeeeb," says Charles. "Wieb, Wieb, Wieb, Wieb, Wieb. Wieb. I'm trying to do you a favor here! I know how important trust is to you— especially after that shit went down with your fiancée. Man, that had to hurt. I was so sorry to hear it. I'd hate to see you go through another heartache like that, Wieb, and K and I have talked about this, haven't we, K? And *I* think sooner is better than later to tell you, that the sooner you find out the truth, the better off you'll be."

"All right, Charles," says Karena, standing up. "You need to leave. Now."

But Kevin is looking back and forth from Charles to Karena.

"Tell me what," he says. "The truth about what."

"Motorcycle Guy!" says Charles, throwing out his hands. "The guy we killed."

There is a moment of perfect, awful silence. Then Kevin says, "What?"

"Yup," says Charles, "you heard me right. Although technically K didn't kill him, I did, she was just along for the ride. We were chasing, we were on this sweet storm, only Motorcycle Guy was out in it too, and the visibility in the core was really bad and I clipped him and killed him. It was a total accident, of course, but that's what happened. There. Doesn't everyone feel better now?"

Kevin is staring fixedly at the citronella candle, gripping the arms of his chair. Karena puts a hand on his.

"Kevin, no," she says in a low voice. "Don't listen to him. He's crazy, he's totally out of his mind—"

"What!" Charles shrieks, "I am not! Jesus, K, tell the poor guy the truth, why don't you stop lying for once in your fucking life."

But Kevin is not listening to either of them.

"He was on a motorcycle," he says, to nobody in particular.

Then, very slowly, he stands up. He doesn't push his chair back first, so his thighs collide with the table. A glass rolls off and smashes on the cement.

"Kevin, don't," says Karena. "Don't go. Kevin, wait. Please!"

Kevin walks across the patio and up the steps into the house.

"Wait," Karena calls, scrambling after him. "Kevin, wait!"

"I think he's gone," Charles says.

Karena spins and walks back.

"Fuck you, Charles," she says. She pushes his shoulder, hard. "I want you out of here, you hear me? I want you OUT OF MY HOUSE!"

She screams this last in his face, then runs into the kitchen. Through the dining and living rooms, out the front door. But she can hear Kevin's engine starting up when she is halfway through, and by the time she gets to the curb, calling his name, he is, as she has known he would be, already gone.

48

Because Karena is right behind Kevin and because she drives like a maniac across the river, she catches him as he is going up the front walk to his house. Karena springs from her car and runs after him. "Wait," she says. "Kevin! Please!"

But when Kevin turns from his stoop he gives her a look that stops Karena right where she is. His face is just as she feared it would be: flat, closed. His mouth and eyes narrow lines. It might as well be a plate that someone painted features on.

"What," he says.

Karena bends over, trying to catch her breath. She is panting as if she has sprinted across the city instead of driving.

"I'm sorry," she gasps. "I'm sorry, Kevin. I'm so sorry—"

"Great," says Kevin, "see ya," and puts his key in the lock.

"No!" Karena says. "Just one minute, just give me one minute to explain—"

Kevin crosses his arms like a hostile bouncer. He looks at his watch. "One minute," he says. "Go."

"Okay," Karena says. "Thank you, Kevin," and then she wastes precious seconds stammering.

"First of all," she says, "I am so sorry—"

"You already said that," says Kevin. "Forty seconds."

"But I am," Karena says. She steps forward to touch his arm. "You'll never know—"

Kevin looks down at her hand as if it were a slug. "Do NOT do that," he says, and Karena snatches it back. Kevin checks his watch.

"Fifteen seconds," he says.

"Oh!" Karena cries. "Kevin, Charles is crazy. You know that! You know how he gets when he's manic, he's evil, vindictive, he's cookin' with gas—"

"Time," says Kevin. "Good night."

"Please," Karena says. "Please just one more minute—"

"Why?" says Kevin. "Why, Karena? What difference does it make? We could stand here all night and I doubt you'd be able to explain this incredibly fucked-up situation. Let me ask you one thing. Is it true? About the Motorcycle Guy?"

Karena looks away, at the streetlight, concentrating on its cold glare to keep from crying. Even so, she feels her chin trembling and eyes swelling, her face blotching up. She knows her hair is in witchy disarray from rushing over here. She is ugly, so ugly she can't stand to have Kevin look at her, too ugly to belong to the human race.

"That's about all the answer I need," Kevin says. "Thanks."

He pushes open his front door, and Karena is galvanized.

"It was an accident," she yells. "It was just a stupid, awful accident! We were kids, Kevin. Eighteen. It was our eighteenth birthday, how's that for irony. Charles was totally manic, he was out of his mind, he was being physically abusive to our mom. I went chasing with him to try and stop him, and he drove us into that storm, and we thought . . . we thought it might be a deer . . . Oh, shit," she says, sniffling, "what a fucking soap opera."

"That's a very interesting and terrible story, Karena," Kevin says from his top step, and when Karena glances up she sees he is looking down at her as if she were a new species of bug. "I just wish you had told it to me before."

"I tried," Karena says. "I mean, honestly, no, I didn't, but I wanted to, Kevin! Oh my God, if you only knew how much I wanted to! I felt so bad about keeping it from you—"

"Did you?" says Kevin. "Boo hoo, poor you. Meanwhile, from the very beginning, what's the one thing I insisted on, Karena? That you tell me—the fucking—TRUTH!"

"I already said I wanted to!" Karena yells back. "But how could I? Put yourself in my position. It's not the kind of thing you can go around saying every day, like when I was eighteen my brother and I ran into somebody—"

A shadow moves in the downstairs front window, behind the branches of the fir, and the slats of the blinds are twitched apart. Mrs. Axlerod. Karena can see the woman's pin-headed silhouette.

"Kevin," she says in a much lower voice, "this isn't a conversation I can have on the street, all right? Can't we please go inside?"

Kevin shakes his head.

"I don't think so," he says, and at the thought that she may never see the man cave again, the black leather couch and the geodes and *The Weather Wizard's Cloud Book* on the toilet tank and the cloud mobile twirling gently over the bed, Karena starts to hyperventilate. She doubles over again and puts her head between her knees.

"Oh, fuck," she hears Kevin say.

After a minute, he comes down the steps. His Samba soccer shoes stop in the sidewalk square a foot from Karena's head. She focuses on them until she can breathe again, then straightens cautiously, blinking gnats of light from her peripheral vision.

She smiles tentatively, but Kevin's flat expression doesn't change.

"You know," he says, when it's apparent that Karena's not going to pass out on his lawn, "I have to say, it's not exactly ideal to have a girlfriend who's guilty of vehicular homicide. In fact it's pretty fucking far down on my wish list. But if you'd told me about it, Karena, we might have been able to figure something out. We could have put our heads together and decided on a way to deal with it."

Karena starts to tell him again why she couldn't, but Kevin holds up a finger. "Please do not interrupt," he says, "I am not finished speaking. What I was *going* to say is, boy, am I a jerk. I must be a real tool, right, Karena? Because the silly thing is, I was just starting to trust you. And I was starting to believe *you* trusted *me*. Oh, I always knew you were slippery. I knew you were always hiding something, that you'd been damaged in some way. Look how long it took for you to tell me the real reason you were on the tour. But once I put two and two together and found out you were Chuck's sister, I thought, Jesus, man, pay her out some rope. No wonder she's skittish. And meanwhile it's not like I find a woman every day who's beautiful and smart and funny and astrotravels in bed, so I figured, okay, if it's just Chuck, I can deal with it. He's a known quantity, and everybody's got something."

"Oh!" says Karena. She has been nodding throughout to show she's listening, but she can't help the exclamation when Kevin repeats what she was thinking on the road that day in Cherry County. "Yes," she says, "exactly, everybody's got something, and maybe now that we know what my something is we can cope with it—"

"BUT," says Kevin, "and again, I have to ask you not to interrupt, BUT, it doesn't work that way, Karena. This isn't exactly your garden-variety baggage. This isn't like oooh, you have a mean ex-husband or four kids or even intimacy issues. You and your brother killed a man. Let's not forget that, all right? Because I think it's kinda important. But what really kills me, Karena, what really fucking slays me is that after all this time, ignoring all evidence to the contrary, you still trust Chuck more than me. Your craaaaaaazy brother," and Kevin wiggles his fingers by his face. "You. Trust him. More than me. Do you have any idea how that makes me feel?"

Karena is still nodding, nodding, like a bobble head on a stick, maintaining eye contact in the way she's read you should in a hostage situation, to humanize yourself to your captor. Now she senses some other response is necessary, so she whispers, "No."

"Huh," says Kevin, "no, I didn't think so. Well, let me tell you. It makes me feel sick. It makes me feel contaminated, having watched the two of you. Having been your dupe. You know, Karena, I wasn't going to say this, but I always thought there was something grotesque about you and Chuck. Something not right. And at first I thought it might be a twin thing, you know? That I was just having a weird allergic reaction to it the way people sometimes do."

Karena nods yet again, this time because she knows what Kevin is talking about. Most people have been fascinated with her and Charles's twinship all their lives, approaching them with interest and curiosity. But there have been the handful of superstitious too, the ignorant and mistrustful. Their grandmother Hallingdahl, for instance, sometimes muttered about the bad luck of the double yolk. One client of Frank's wouldn't let them on his dairy farm because he said everyone knew twins curdled milk. In the pioneer days, identicals were sometimes carted around the countryside as a carnival sideshow. Karena thinks for a second of the two-headed calf in the display case at the Great Platte River Road Archway Monument. It's not the first time she has been called a freak.

"Then I told myself not to be ridiculous," Kevin continues, "that I was just jealous. I knew it'd be a challenge going in. I know the twin bond supersedes everything. And to top it off your twin just happens to be Chuck. Still, I kept telling myself it was a natural phenomenon— you guys are just eggs, right? Two eggs that got fertilized at the same time, totally organic process. I could not figure out why seeing you together made me so squeamish, and I doubted my own instincts, but now I know I was right all along. The murder, the guy you killed, that's bad enough. But then there's the grotesque way you and Chuck are. Laughing at everyone else. Thinking you're smarter. You think I don't know the two of you made fun of me behind my back, Karena? You think I don't know you probably have some stupid twin-code nickname for me?"

Karena flushes. "I—" she begins, but Kevin shakes his head.

"I don't want to know," he says. "I just wanted to tell you that tonight? When Chuck decided it'd be so funny to do the big reveal? I felt like I was watching a peepshow. And that's how I've felt all along, Karena. Like there's you and your brother doing your nasty little twin dance and I'm the necessary audience. Your idiot audience of one. Well, I'm done."

Karena waits, watching him. Kevin scrubs a hand over his hair.

"No, I mean, I'm done," he says. "I'm really done."

"Okay," says Karena. She takes a deep breath. "First of all, Kevin, it wasn't like that at all. It—"

"Did you not hear me?" says Kevin. "I'm done. With you. We're done. There's nothing left to see here."

Karena shakes her head.

"You can't mean that," she says. "Kevin, come on. After everything we've been through together—"

"Yeah," says Kevin, "well, I'm kind of done with that too."

He turns and starts back up the walk.

"Kevin, please," Karena says. "Turn around. Look at me! Isn't there anything I can do?"

"You can leave me alone," says Kevin. "Go home to your brother, Karena," and he closes his door.

49

S o Karena does. She goes home to her brother, because what other
choice does she have? Except as she speeds back across the Mississippi and through the neon pulse and throb that is Uptown on a
summer night, and swings around the lakes and toward her house in
Edina, Karena has but one goal in mind: to get Charles out of her
house. If he hasn't gone already.

Nope. When she drives past, his yellow Volvo is still at the curb.
Karena scowls at it and parks around back. She charges through the
patio, the destruction of dinner—chairs shoved askew, shattered glass,
candle burning fatly in its meltdown wax. The kitchen is a disaster
area, all spattered tomato seeds and vegetable peelings. The Rorschachs
of Charles's food preparation.

"Charles!"

No answer. Karena pounds up the stairs to the master suite, pokes
her head up over the railing. No Charles here, just the oscillating fan
turning its wire face back and forth. Karena runs back down.

"Charles!"

She looks in her den. Dining room. Living room. Out on the front
porch, onto the walk. Back inside.

"Charles! Where are you? I know you're here! Answer me!"

Down into the basement. Laundry room. Boiler room. Upstairs

again, out into the night. The garage? Karena stands with her hands on her hips, staring around the yard.

"Charles!"

In response she seems to hear the neighbor kids yell, *Marco! Polo!* although they have long since gone inside. There are only crickets and the faint laugh track of somebody's TV. Karena shakes her head. She is losing her mind.

Then she remembers Charles's other lair, in New Heidelburg. And its adjacent bathroom. Where Charles was the night he tried to . . .

Karena runs back upstairs to the master suite as fast as she can. The bathroom light is off, but when she flips it on she sees the blood. It is everywhere, bright red on the tiles and the walls. The closet door, once a mirrored slider, is now stalactites of reflective glass. More litters the floor, curving shards bigger than her arm, as thick as the icicles that hang from the eaves in winter. Charles is wedged against the far wall, between the tub and toilet.

"Charles!"

At the sound of her voice, Charles cinches up tighter, like a milli-pede that's been poked with a stick. His weeping ratchets up into that raw, rich, gut-shot sobbing Karena remembers from that day on the road. She crunches over the glass toward him, pinches a wicked sword of it out of the way, and kneels next to him.

"Let me see, Charles. Let me see your wrists."

But his veins are intact. Karena pats his face, his head, his arms, his torso, his legs.

"Where are you bleeding, Charles? Where are you hurt?"

It's his right ankle, the blood oozing from a gash there. Of course. He kicked the mirrored closet door in. The cut looks clean, though, no glass in it. And the flow is sluggish. Karena grabs a towel from the rack and applies it to the wound. Charles thrashes in protest and wails, but Karena says, "Stop!" and slaps him on the calf to make him calm down. Once he has, she presses hard on the towel.

"Owwwww," Charles sobs.

"Did you take anything, Charles?" Karena asks. "Drugs, lithium, anything?"

Charles moans something. Karena bends closer. "What?"

"Noooooooo," he says. "I'm sorry. Ah, God, I'm sorrrrrry-yyyy . . ."

Karena keeps her weight on the towel and considers whether he's telling the truth. Since Charles is Mr. Holistic now, he probably doesn't have anything stronger than herbs, and Karena herself keeps nothing heavier in the house than aspirin—

"What about over-the-counter stuff?" she asks, leaning in. Her hair, swinging, grazes Charles's face, and she flips it back with an impatient sound. "Did you take Tylenol, cold medicine?"

Charles shakes his head. His face is red, contorted, tears leaking out from beneath his tight lids.

"You hate me," he insists. "You hate me . . ."

Karena sighs. "No, I don't, Charles."

Charles whips his head from side to side.

"You dooooooo," he moans. "Ah, God. Please, just let me die . . ."

"Don't say that, Charles," Karena says, without her usual energy or conviction. She lifts the towel and peeks under the edge: The bleeding has slowed. Still, she keeps the terry cloth against the wound with one hand and smoothes her brother's hair back with the other. Some instinct tells her this is the right thing to do. At her touch Charles grips panicky fistfuls of her shorts and mashes his face against Karena's leg, and she stares down at his head, the fine honey-blond hair at his temples shading into coarser waves, and feels nothing. Not love nor pity, not even exhaustion. She knows the emotions must be there, but she can't access them. Kevin was right, Karena thinks, there is grotesquerie here, but it's not Karena and Charles. It's Charles's disorder, the way it reduces a grown man to sobbing panic on the floor. The way it renders Karena unable to feel. The way it takes you by the hand, nodding and smiling slyly, and leads you back to the same old place every time, so just when you think everything might be all right after all, you come home and open a door to a room full of blood.

Charles is lowing now, moaning, and as Karena strokes his hair she looks around the bathroom, her gaze and mind wandering. The ceiling has a crack in it, the light fixture holds dead flies. How much will it cost to replace the mirrored door, the rug? The tiles will have to be bleached too, the blood has seeped into the grout. And the walls.

Charles is saying something, words mixed in with the groans. Karena leans over. "What's that?" she says.

"I'm sorry," he gasps. His eyes are still pinched tightly closed, as if he can't bear the overhead light or maybe Karena looking at him. "I didn't mean to. I didn't mean to ruin your life. I'm sorry, I'm just so sorry."

"That's okay, Charles."

"Please," he says. "Please help me, K. Please."

Suddenly it's as though Karena's ears pop after a long flight, only it's her feelings. They come rushing back to fill her, her love for him and the pity.

"I will," she says. "I will, Charles."

"Please," Charles says again. He brings his hands up to cover his face. The Lakota ring looks sternly at Karena. "Please, K. Please don't hate me. I never meant to do those things—it's like there's a stranger in my head. Some guy I can't control—"

"Yes," Karena says. "I know that guy, Charles."

She pulls Charles's hand aside so she can speak directly into his ear.

"Listen," she says, voice low. "I will help you. I will help you, Charles, but you have to help me too, okay? The Stranger—he's terribly strong. But you're stronger. I know you are. You have to try. You have to help me beat him. You have to go back to the doctors with me, try different medications until you find ones that fit. It'll be tough, but I'll be with you. We'll do it together. You hear me?"

Charles nods vehemently. "Yes," he says. "Yes, yes, anything, K, I'll do anything you want. Just please don't leave me. Please don't leave me alone here in the black."

Karena leans back against the sink, and as she soothes him, yawning now, her eyes grainy, she thinks of a recurring dream she has. It's one she has never told Charles about, a dream she is quite sure he does not share. In it he and she are standing on an assembly line in some shadowy between-world, waiting to be born, looking down a long shimmering tube at the home they're about to join. There are the roofs of New Heidelburg, the spires of the churches, the blue lollipop water tower, the small rectangle that will be their house. Just before they jump, however, a cup is handed down the line toward them. Karena takes a sip to be polite, makes a face, starts to pass it on. But Charles, profligate even then, grabs it from her and drains the whole thing, then flings it aside and turns to her. *Ready, K?* he asks, smiling, and they join hands to begin their lifelong adventure.

She will never leave him. Because Karena merely sipped from the bitter cup while Charles drank it all, she will never abandon him, not for anything in the world. So as Charles weeps and begs Karena not to go, she reassures him she won't, she won't. And she means it. She'll wait until he falls asleep, then go only so far as the phone, to call Hennepin County Medical. Then she'll come back, she'll stay with him the entire time. But it's Karena who must sleep, she must be exhausted after all, because when she wakes the window is a bright square of sun, the blood drying dark and tacky. And she is alone. Charles is gone again.

50

Before Charles's arrival this summer Karena returned to New Heidelburg fairly often. But she realizes, as she speeds south on Highway 52 past the single spire of the Lone Oak Church, the Arch to Nowhere, that it's been a while since she has been there to visit Frank. How long? Early July? Late June? Over a month, which is shameful—and that's another thing about her brother's disorder, the way it sucks oxygen from other areas of her life, her friendships and obligations. Not that Frank will notice. He hasn't registered Karena's presence since before his stroke, which would have been—2002, at the Widow's Thanksgiving, when Karena sat among a flotilla of side dishes and tried to make conversation with her six stepsiblings, silent and thatch-haired as giants. Frank was at the head of the table and the Widow simpered at the other end, and when the meal was done Frank got up, patted Karena's shoulder, and disappeared into his new home office. Six years ago, and Karena can't remember for the life of her what her dad's last words to her might have been.

Now Frank spends his days either parked in his chair or as a thin ridge in a hospital bed, a husk smelling of urine and disinfectant, and the best Karena can hope for is that her dad isn't aware of anything within the prison of his body—and what is she thinking about Frank for, anyhow? Karena is in a bad way. Her thoughts are like water bugs, skittering all over the place. She keeps glancing at the note on the passenger's seat, anchored by her purse:

> *Sistah. I'm so sorry to take off like this after everything you've done for me, but I just can't stand to destroy your life anymore. I'm going back to where it all began, & you know why. Love you, sistah. Charles.*

The thing is, Karena doesn't know. But she can guess, and neither option is good. Charles is going back to New Heidelburg to turn himself in. Charles is going back to New Heidelburg to kill himself in some dramatic fashion, and Karena has no idea what to do. Should she call the sheriff? But she can't, because if the sheriff does find Charles, Charles will confess everything. Karena wants to weep. She exits in Pine Island for a pit stop and more caffeine and almost bursts into tears in the SuperAmerica over the convenience store smell of old coffee and hot dogs, the rack of corn nuts. She uses the bathroom and slaps cold water on her face.

Back on the highway, she checks the clock—almost noon—and pushes the Volvo to eighty-five. The tiny skyscrapers of Rochester wheel into view on the left. Tiff lives at Exit 49B, in the Little McMansion on the Prairie, as she calls it. If she knew Karena were nearby, she would invite Karena over for scones and a scolding. But Karena can't quite make herself pick up the phone. She hasn't talked much to Tiff since the disastrous lake walk, and she doubts Tiff will be very sympathetic to yet more bad news about Charles. *You know what to do,* Tiff would say. *Effing cut him off, Kay. Deal with your own life. Otherwise, I don't want to hear it. Talk to the hand.*

And Tiff doesn't know the whole story, so she wouldn't be much help. Only one person has all the pieces of the puzzle, would be able to advise Karena, give her counsel she trusts. And if she's going to call him, she'd better do it fast, since her cell phone loses service in Foss County. She is already through Rochester and on the two-lane road toward her hometown. Karena opens her phone and hits speed-dial 1. It's not that she thinks he will have forgiven her—not already, not yet. Maybe he never will. But Karena just can't believe Kevin wouldn't want to hear from her, if only to know where she's going, what she's doing. He has become her personal GPS, tethering her to the world. At first this seemed to Karena an amazing luxury, something to be marveled at and gloated over. Then it became habit, and now, apparently, it is a necessity.

Kevin picks up on the fourth ring, as Karena is entering the bluff-bracketed cornfields near Merrion, lush and steaming in the mid-day sun.

"Go," he says.

"Kevin? It's me."

"I know that, Karena," Kevin says flatly. "I have caller ID."

"Oh," says Karena. "Right." She waits, and when he doesn't say anything, she ventures, "How are you?"

"How the fuck do you think I am?"

"Um," says Karena. "Not very good?"

She tries a shaky laugh, but when that doesn't work, she says, "I'm sorry, Kevin. I really am. I'm going out of town for a bit, maybe a couple of days, but I was thinking when I get back, we could talk? Get coffee or something—"

"I asked you to leave me alone, Karena," says Kevin. "Remember?"

Karena nods. She clears her throat. "Yes," she says.

"Why do you disrespect that?" Kevin asks.

"I'm sorry," Karena says, gulping. "It's just that—I love you, Kevin. I should have told you that before. And I'm not just saying it now because I need you, although I do, I desperately do. But I love you more desperately than that, and more passionately, and more deeply. Happily, even."

She stops. Kevin doesn't respond, but Karena thinks she can feel his surprise. She can hear him breathing, anyway, and the creak of leather. She pictures him in his living room recliner, wearing slippery soccer shorts and a Whirlwind T-shirt, his hair sticking up on one side. Looking out the window at the bird feeder he has hung in the oak, the cardinals at play there, and her throat hurts until she can barely breathe.

"So," she says finally. "I have to go to New Heidelburg, I don't know how long exactly, but Charles is there. I think. Anyway, he's gone again, and I have to find him, but when I get back—"

"I'm sorry, Karena," Kevin interrupts. "I can't."

"What?" she says.

"I can't deal with this. With you or him or any of this. I need a break."

"Okay," Karena whispers. Then she says, "But a break is a good thing, right? Because it's finite, there's an end on the other side. So how long—"

"Karena," says Kevin. "Stop. Just stop."

Karena switches the phone to the other ear and waits.

"You're not hearing me," Kevin says. He sounds very tired. "I don't want this. Don't call me. Don't call me anymore or contact me in any way. All right?"

Karena doesn't say anything. She drives. Squints at the curving road.

"Good luck with your brother, though," says Kevin. "Sincerely."

He pauses.

"Bye," he says finally, and hangs up.

Karena keeps the phone wedged between her shoulder and her ear until the recorded lady says, *If you'd like to make a call . . .* Then she tosses it into her bag. Takes a sip of coffee. Her hand is shaking, so she sets the cup back in the holder. Carefully she steers the Volvo up and around a hill—she is deep in bluff country now, the road wending between blocks of corn so dense and green Karena can feel its humid breath through her window. She remembers playing in the Hallingdahl cornfield with Charles, how they would emerge from its secret, shady world soaking wet, covered in silk and cuts. At this time of year the crops produce moisture so intense it creates its own microclimate and helps form storms—evapotranspiration, Kevin has called it. And the sun is beating through rows of little clouds like lambs in heaven, AltoCu, altocumulus, sign of potential severe later in the day—

Suddenly Karena hears Kevin's voice not just in memory but in the car—coming from her bag. He must have called her back! Karena almost runs off the road scrabbling for her phone, but when she finds it there are no new messages. Yet Kevin's voice continues, and she understands: It's her recorder. When she threw the phone into the bag, it must have knocked the play button. Karena fishes the recorder out and props it upright in her lap.

. . . look at this . . . 45 percent probability is impressive, usually means significant, long-lived tornadoes. I wouldn't be surprised if we got upgraded to a high risk by morning.

That's good, right? I mean, depending who you ask.

Indeed, Laredo. It means we could have an outbreak on our hands. But remember Dennis's story, the one about the tire. That happened on a high-risk day. Things can get ugly fast. We'll have to watch our timing.

Wow. That's scary.

Not scary, Laredo. A learning experience. Remember what I said about fear too. You just need to know what you're doing . . . Like me. I'll learn ya.

Oh boy. Now you're just showing off.

True. But any more lip from you, young lady, and I'll make you stay after school. . . . Want to walk, Laredo?

Sure.

Karena listens to this conversation all the way through. When it finishes, she presses replay. She listens to it over and over, dazed with sorrow and wonder. Finally, when she gets to Norwegian Ridge, the town before New Heidelburg, she turns the recorder off. "God damn it," Karena says. "Oh, God damn it!" She hits the steering wheel with the fat side of her palm, wipes her face on an old Caribou napkin, and keeps driving.

O n the other side of Norwegian Ridge Karena starts to see the homecoming markers, which usually bring dread because they are harbingers of a difficult visit to Frank but today are welcome signs of familiarity—like little notes saying *You Belong Here*. The Lutheran cemetery where her mom and uncle and all four grandparents are buried. Siri's favorite contour-farmed field, the puffy parallelograms of corn between emerald-green grass. The New Heidelburg airstrip, its wind sock pointing northwest—which means, Karena calculates automatically, the winds are from the southeast, backed and bringing moisture from the Gulf. The New Heidelburg golf course. The Starlite Supper Club. The town limits sign—WELCOME TO NEW HEIDELBURG, WILD EAGLE CAPITAL OF SOUTHERN MINNESOTA!

And then all the businesses on the strip of highway bordering town: the Ford and Deere dealerships, the New Heidelburg Propane Co. with its belching orange flame. The IGA, the new American Inn & Suites, the dollar store and Dairy Queen. There is the water tower, visible over the trees—except there are two now, a second blue lollipop identical to the first, punctuating the north end of town. Karena doesn't normally notice any of this industry—it's just the backdrop of her birthplace, a topography she accepts has always been there and always will be. But now her perspective has changed, and when she assesses New Heidelburg through an adult lens—measures it against the ghost towns she saw this summer on the Plains—Karena finds her hometown doing well. And she does feel like a visitor here after all.

Out of habit she looks for Charles's yellow Volvo at the Elmwood Café and the Kwik Trip, where Karena and Tiff used to hang out in a booth and wait for boys. But Karena doesn't really expect to find Charles here. She knows where he is. She exits onto Main Street and drives into downtown, turning a block left and making the first right onto Lincoln. There is the B&M gas station, its fuel pumps still the kind whose numbers roll up, its air compressor emitting its eternal *ticka-ticka-tick*. The original water tower looms like a blue balloon at the end of the block. Karena parks and waves to the B&M brothers peeking curiously out of their garage, two sixtysomething bachelors with brushy hair and amiable faces. Charles's yellow Volvo is across from hers, at the curb in front of their old house. He is sitting on the lawn, Indian style, chewing a stem of grass.

"I wanted to go in," he says sadly when Karena walks up, "for one last visit, but nobody's home."

Karena thinks it shows remarkable restraint on Charles's part that he didn't just go into the house anyway, since like most in town it is probably unlocked. She sits beside him and Charles hands her a piece of what she sees now is not grass but parsley. It grows wild here, a runaway from Siri's garden. All Karena's adult life she has been ambushed by its sharp green smell, the bullet of childhood nostalgia it brings. She sticks the sprig between her teeth.

"Thanks," she says.

"Don't mention it."

They sit chewing and contemplating their childhood home. It too has changed, though subtly. Karena has driven past it a couple of times before and noted the new roof and driveway, the removal of the lilac hedge and the replacement of their old front door with its louvered slats with a more modern model, a slab of etched glass. The black pine in front of their bedroom window is still there, sheltering Siri's red maple, but altogether the house appears in much better shape. This is like a personal affront, and Karena wonders if it still smells like Siri's handbag inside, if the new owners finally chopped down the big bush in back and disposed of the boat swing. She sighs.

"I know," Charles says. "It's a mind-fuck, isn't it? It's like those place mat games: Find Twenty Things Wrong with This Picture."

He rips up a handful of grass, sieves it for another piece of parsley, and piles the remaining blades on the Ace bandage wrapped around his wounded ankle. Where did he get that? Karena wonders. It's already grubby.

"Charles," she says, "what are you doing?"

"You know what I'm doing," he says. "Having one last look around before the slammer."

Karena sags with relief that is woefully short-lived. Charles's plan to turn himself in is better than the alternative, but not much. In fact, Karena wonders if it isn't an oblique attempt at suicide. How does Charles imagine he'll survive in jail, without his holistic medicine, his exercise, his chasing? Does he really think he'll get through it?

"Charles," she says, "do you remember what we talked about last night? You promised to come see a doctor with me."

Charles leans back on his splayed hands, chewing. The sun highlights little cuts on his face Karena hasn't noticed before, from splinters of flying glass, and makes a bright dandelion of his hair.

"I know, K," he says, "and I'm sorry, but I can't. I just can't do it your way. I still don't believe in meds, for one thing. There's nothing in that black bag for me. And even if I did, I'd still have to pay for Motorcycle Guy. Without my fixing that, everything else is moot."

"With all due respect, Charles—" Karena starts, but Charles interrupts her.

"I know you don't agree," he says. "But I'm so tired, K. I'm tired of being a fuckup. I ruin everything, all the time. Your life. The Loaf's. Situ's. Mom's. Dad's—and don't tell me his stroke wasn't in some way my fault. I know it might have been some weird congenital defect, but the mental aggravation I brought him didn't help, that's for sure."

Karena would like to dispute this, but having had the same thought herself on occasion, she doesn't. Instead, she says, "But Charles—"

"But Charles nothing," Charles says. "Don't you get it, K? I can't control the guy in my head—The Stranger. Not without eliminating myself completely. My personality. And that I can't do. But Motorcycle Guy, I can make amends for. He's the one situation I can fix. And I'm so sick of it hanging over my head. Aren't you?"

Charles puts his hand on her arm. The stern face of the Lakota brave gleams in the sun.

"Don't answer quickly," he says softly. "Don't give me the knee-jerk reaction. Really think about it. Why don't you come with me? When I go to the sheriff. Because aren't you tired too, K? Goodness aren't you tired?"

Karena is about to retort with some wisecrack, to say of course she's tired, she was up all night with him. But she knows what Charles means. She is tired. Not ordinary tired, not even exhausted, but weary in mind, in spirit. Karena is tired of being on the outside looking in, feeling as though she can never join the normal human family. She is tired of editing her conversations, trying to remember who she told this information to, how much she gave away to that. She is tired of waking up at four thirty in the morning and feeling wretched over a man she never knew. She is tired of trying to control the damage and trying to repair it when she can't. She looks at her parents' old house, at the bay window she was sitting on the other side of when this persistent tiredness began, on the living room davenport in the night-light glow, and for the first time Karena considers giving it up. Handing the whole mess over to the people who are paid to take care of it, the authorities in charge. Officers of the law and courts who will parse the emotion out of it, reduce it to paperwork, sentencing, clarity.

But this is crazy. Has Karena lost her mind? This isn't some morality board game she and Charles are playing. This is real life. There *will* be sentencing. There will be charges and consequences. Karena will lose what little she has left—her job, her professional reputation, her house. And Charles. What will become of Charles?

If only she had more time. Just a little more time to convince him there are other options. To remind him why he should remain alive and free: The taste of iced tea on a hot day. Sun. The smell of wind. The chance to help people who aren't behind bars, a meal of his own choosing when he's hungry—

Karena will start with that.

"Come on," she says, standing and extending her hand.

Charles looks up, his expression divided between hope and suspicion. "You're coming to the sheriff with me, K?"

"No," says Karena, then amends it: "Not yet. Let's go have lunch, okay? Let's go somewhere and talk about it."

A sedan cruises down the center of Lincoln Street, slowing to a crawl so its occupants can get a good look at the grown man sitting on the lawn of the old Hallingdahl house. Karena recognizes the Rices, bridge partners of Siri's. She lifts a hand. The sedan zooms away.

"We'd better go somewhere nobody knows us," she adds, "if we're going to talk about this. La Crosse, maybe."

Charles squints at her, then turns back to the house, chewing his parsley. Karena makes an exasperated noise and walks out into the road, unhooking her keys from her belt.

"Seriously, Charles," she says, "I'm starving—" And then she sees it, burgeoning up over downtown like a nuclear cloud, although in reality it is probably fifty miles away or more. The familiar chef-hat shape. It still amazes Karena, how something so big can be so sneaky—or rather is surprising simply because it is so huge, the brain not calibrated to recognize something that size.

Karena has never been so happy to see a storm.

"Hey Charles," she calls.

"Hey what," Charles says.

"You want to chase this thing or what?"

52

Charles looks up.

"Excuse me?" he says.

"You heard me."

"Did you just ask me if I want to chase?" Charles laughs. "Who are you, and what have you done with my sister?"

"Stop screwing around, Charles. Do you want to chase or not?"

Charles gets up, scattering grass, and walks to the edge of the lawn. "Okay," he says, "I'll bite. Is there really a storm there?"

Karena points.

"Anvil," she says. "Ten o'clock."

Charles raises his eyebrows.

"I'll be damned," he says. "And listen to you, sistah. The Loaf taught you well."

Karena longs to hit him. She walks a few feet away so she won't be tempted, and the urge dissipates as quickly as it came, leaving her with the desire to do nothing more than sit right down in the middle of Lincoln Street, with its oil stains and sharp pebbles and bits of glass, and just stay there in deepest misery.

"Oh, shit," she hears Charles say.

He comes over to rub her back. "I'm sorry, K," he says. "He'll come around, though."

Karena looks at her brother's sandaled feet, the big square toenails, the grimy Ace bandage. "I don't think so," she says.

"He will, though," Charles insists. "I know him."

Oh, right, because you know Kevin so much better than I know Kevin, Karena wants to snap. Instead she walks out from beneath Charles's hand.

"Seriously," she says, "do you want to chase that or not?"

Charles slips his hands in his back pockets and inspects the anvil. "Do you?" he says.

"I asked you."

"Well . . . sure, I guess," he says, glancing at Karena. "One last chase before the slammer couldn't hurt."

"Charles."

"What?"

"Nothing."

When they're both buckled into Karena's car, Karena drives back through town and out the other side. Too late she realizes they could have, should have stopped to see Frank at the New Heidelburg Good Samaritan Center. It flashes past, a one-story cinderblock building beneath a cheery billboard: LET US ALL REMEMBER THE AGED. YES, EVEN *YOU* ARE GETTING OLD!!! But the storm is growing right in front of them, taking on its distinctive anvil shape. And others are popping up all around it, smaller ice-cream scoops exploding in the distance.

"Juicy setup today," Karena observes, as New Heidelburg's water towers dwindle behind them.

Charles, who has been gazing through the windshield, ducks his head in a way that suggests he's hiding a grin. "Sure is," he agrees.

"Make yourself useful," Karena says. "What's our best route?"

Charles opens the glove box. "Don't you have a GPS in here?"

"Uh," says Karena. They should have taken Charles's Volvo, since although it's a '98 like hers, it has been modified with radar and a ham radio and a laptop stand and an antenna for signal boosting and everything else they'd need, whereas Karena's has nothing and even her scanner, she remembers now, is uncharged, in the trunk.

"Chasin' old-school," Charles says, rummaging in the backseat and finding Karena's atlas. He flips to the state of Minnesota, checks the sky, glances at the map again, then tosses the atlas over his shoulder.

"Keep going up to I-90," he says, "then 90 West to Highway 13 North. Boom. Almost too easy."

"Copy that," says Karena. They're making good time, on the other side of Clinton already. The WELCOME TO IOWA sign winks past on the left, and Karena can't help glancing at it. Charles doesn't seem to notice. He sits with his arms folded, head tipped back, looking sleepy.

"I just hope you're not doing what I think you're trying to do, K," he says eventually, as they're passing through Plainfield. "Because you'll be disappointed."

"And what is it you think I'm trying to do?" Karena asks.

"Dissuade me," Charles says, with a jaw-cracking yawn. "Distract me from my mission. Tempt me away from turning myself in by reminding me what I love best in life—outside of you, of course. Chasing."

Karena scowls. As much of a blessing as it is to be known as well as Charles knows her—a need, Karena sometimes thinks, as primal as that for food or water or shelter—there are times when it's really inconvenient to be transparent.

"Could you be a little *more* egotistical?" she asks. "Did it ever occur to you that maybe I *like* chasing? That if it hadn't been for you grabbing all the storm genes in the womb, I might have turned out to be the chaser in the family? Did you ever think of that?"

"Um, no," says Charles.

"Well," says Karena. "There you go."

"Okay," says Charles. "I'm not debating you, K. I'm just saying."

Karena swings into the oncoming lane to pass a flatbed piled with hay, then back around it just in time to exit onto the Interstate. The highway darkens and brightens and darkens again as huge, fat-bellied Cu pass overhead. Trucks cough past them in the opposite lane, and their storm's anvil spreads toward them like pancake batter, starting to blot out the light. Karena sits forward to take stock, evaluating and reevaluating what she sees. She's surprised to find what she said to Charles is true, in a way: She has missed this, the skin-crawling alertness. *You have to kick it up a notch when you're chasing,* she remembers Kevin saying, *to be your best and sharpest self, that's part of the fun,* and Karena realizes too why she's scanning the shoulder even though Charles is right next to her: She's watching for Kevin. Even though he's probably at soccer practice, and although if he's not he could be chasing another of these storms—and just what does Karena think will happen if she does see him, anyway?—she can't help looking for him nonetheless.

"Hey Charles," she says.

"Yes, sistah."

"Are we going for the right cell?" Karena asks, for their storm is now one of several, a fleet of motherships silently ringing the horizon.

Charles shrugs. "Chaser's dilemma, K," he says, "you never know. And without radar it's impossible to tell."

"So?" Karena says. "What should I do?"

"Your call," says Charles, "it's your chase."

Karena frowns at him, annoyed. He is slumped listlessly against his door, watching the scenery with his chin propped on one hand, as if he's attending a rather dull movie.

"What would you do if you were by yourself, Charles?"

"Probably stick with the original."

"Fine," says Karena. "I will."

Charles points out Highway 13 when it comes up, and Karena takes the exit. Now they are on a two-lane road running straight north through the farmland. Instead of reaching the anvil, though, they start to encounter low clouds, formless and featureless. Drizzle condenses on the windshield, and the air in the Volvo grows so sticky Karena has to put the defrost on. The light dulls, everything around them gray and green. Karena squints up. "I can't see anything," she says. "I can't see the storm's structure."

"That's because we've hit a stratus deck," says Charles. "That's all right, though. The updraft looked pretty healthy, so as long as this crapvection doesn't choke off all the storm's juice, it should stay alive. Keep going—if you want."

Karena does want. As they pass through Otisco and Waseca she sits up straighter, monitoring the sky, which way the flags are blowing, what the light is doing. Soon the clouds thicken into their familiar layers, and near Waterville the storm's base comes into view. It is not a tidal wave like the Iowa storm, or purple-brown like the Ogallala supercell or black and gigantic like the parent storm of the wedge, but still, this one is big, gray, and ragged. Large triangular flaps of cloud hang from it like pointed teeth, and more clouds rise into it from the horizon, getting sucked up.

"Charles," Karena says.

"Huh!" says Charles, who has been dozing. He unsticks his cheek from his hand. "Uch," he mutters in disgust.

"What do you think of that?" Karena asks, pointing to the cycling clouds.

Charles looks. "That's just scud," he says. "It's not anything."

But the light disappears as they enter Waterville, the afternoon blackening to night except for that glowing white strip beneath the base to the north, like light coming from under a door. They pass a motel, two residential streets, a Sinclair gas station, and then they are on the other side of town. Karena has to pull over to let a state trooper go racing past, his light bar flashing, a string of pickups and muscle cars behind it. Yahoos, Kevin would call them, locals hoping to take pictures of the tornado with their cell phones. The chasers' nightmare, law enforcement too, because the yahoos don't know what they're doing around big weather and often get in the way, putting everyone at risk.

Then the Waterville siren goes off behind them, cranking up to a steady keen. "Whoa," Karena says, and then, "Look!" She pokes Charles, and they watch a solid gray curtain like a thick mushroom stem travel slowly across the horizon from west to east. Behind it tiny smoky funnels stretch down and pull back up, stretch down and pull back up, all at different times like carousel horses.

"Is that a tornado?" Karena asks of the stem.

"No, that's the core," says Charles. "Although . . ." He leans forward and peers. "There could be a rain-wrapped tornado in there somewhere."

"And those little—wispy things, are they tornadoes?"

"I can't tell if they're touching all the way down or not," Charles admits. "The trees're in the way, and I don't see any debris. But they're definitely funnels."

"So that's the area of interest?" Karena asks.

Charles cricks his neck back and forth. "This is all area of interest, K," he says. "We're in the bear's cage."

"Get out!" says Karena, then promptly does. She opens the door and steps onto the shoulder to look up. Right above the Volvo the black clouds are colliding, a bank moving west and another moving east, speeding toward each other as fast as cars—at least fifty, sixty miles an hour. They knit and swirl, directly overhead. It is like standing at the bottom of a sink drain.

Karena climbs back into the Volvo as the siren swings toward them. "I don't feel safe here," she says.

"What?" says Charles.

"I don't feel safe!" Karena yells.

Charles shrugs and says something.

"What?"

"I said okay," he shouts.

"I think we should go back to that gas station," Karena yells.

Charles says something else.

"What?" Karena shouts.

"Fine!" Charles says. "Let's go, K! Let it go."

Karena scans the highway in both directions, then turns around and drives the few miles back into Waterville. She has a terrible feeling, of being a chicken, of having been checkmated. There's nothing else she can do. It's all over. The Sinclair sign is a brilliant yellow-white against the black and swirling sky, and Karena pulls in beneath it, then points them north so they can still watch the storm. There's a small lake next to the gas station and a handful of trailer homes. Rain hits the windshield in fat spats.

"I'm sorry, Charles," she says.

Charles is picking at his unraveling Ace bandage. "What?" he says.

"I'm sorry!" Karena shouts, just as the siren winds down.

EEEEEEERRRRRRRRRrrrrrroooooooowwwwwwwwwrrrrrrrrr. She doesn't understand why they've shut it off, since the little taffy funnels are still pulling down, some just on the other side of the water. But nothing makes sense anymore.

"Forget it, K," says Charles. "I didn't want to chase anyway. It was your idea."

"I know," Karena says. "I'm sorry I made you do this. And I'm sorry about everything. I'm sorry about Motorcycle Guy, and I'm sorry I couldn't stop you that day, and I'm sorry I didn't protect you. I'm sorry I was so selfish and cowardly and just left you there in Black Wing—"

"You're not selfish and cowardly, K," Charles interrupts.

"Okay, but wait, just let me say this, all right? I'm sorry you got it. The disorder, or your condition or visions or whatever you want to call it, I'm so sorry you got it and I didn't. I've been sorry about that our entire life," Karena says. "More sorry than you know."

Charles lifts his head and looks out the windshield. "I do know, K," he says. "That's all right."

"No, it's not, Charles," says Karena.

Charles smiles a little.

"You're right," he says, "it's not. It's completely unfair, to be honest. But it's not your fault, K, and I appreciate your saying all that. I truly do. Thank you."

Karena sits back.

"Really?" she says.

"Really."

"Thank you, Charles."

"You're welcome, K."

They watch the carousel of funnels through the windshield. Behind them people have started to emerge from the gas station, to wander around staring upward as if waiting to get picked up by the mothership. Karena can hear them exclaiming, see camera flashes in her wing mirror.

"K," Charles says.

She looks over at him.

"You need to take me back now," he says.

Karena locks eyes with him: *Are you sure?*

Charles gazes steadily back: *Yes.*

They stare at each other: unstoppable force meeting immovable object.

Finally Karena sighs, puts the car in gear, and drives out of the Sinclair lot.

Heading south on 13, they encounter rain bands momentarily blinding, precipitation lifting off the fields. The edge of their storm's anvil runs into another one, so where there should be blue sky beyond, there is only a ribbon of it, then more solid cloud bumpy with mammatus. "Don't go back to the Interstate," Charles says, consulting the atlas. "We're surrounded. Take 14 East to 52, and don't go above fifty miles an hour or so. We should be okay that way."

Karena does as he says. They wend through the small towns, passing spotters on the shoulders, civilians standing on their porches with their faces turned to the sky. Charles waves, and most wave back. The going is slow, since they are boxed in by storms. There are towering Cu in every direction, lighting up like giant brains having bright ideas. Lightning skewers the horizon, pulses in tangles and snarls and flares. But Karena and Charles stay safe because of their steady pace, as if they are traveling in a little bubble, and by the time they intersect Highway 52 and turn south toward New Heidelburg, it is dark, the

fireflies coming out. There are masses of them, more than Karena or
Charles has ever seen before. Maybe they're responding to the lightning, Charles guesses, or the humidity of the purple-black night, Karena suggests. Either way they all come out at once, effervescing from
the fields on either side of the road. Thousands and thousands of fireflies, wave upon sparkling wave.

53

When they get back to New Heidelburg they check into the American Inn & Suites on Highway 44. It seems weird and counterintuitive to Karena to stay in a motel in her own town, but what choice do they have? "We could always go to the Widow's," Charles suggests, and Karena says, "That's a good idea, Charles. Call me and let me know how it turns out." The pretty girl on desk gives them rooms across the hall from each other, Charles in 106 with a front view, Karena in 105 facing the back. They consider and reject the idea of going to dinner, which at this hour, after ten, would mean driving out to the Starlite and having popcorn at the bar. Instead they hug quickly and say good night, and although Karena has the feeling of sundering she always gets when she's parted from Charles, no matter for how short a time, she is also relieved. He is too, she can tell. It has been a long day.

Her room is big and clean and cheerful, with the usual multicolored bedspread of abstract floral design, green flecked carpet, maroon curtains. As she sets down her bag and laptop and washes her face, Karena is gripped by a loneliness so profound it squeezes her chest. She thinks of Fern and Alicia, of Marla and Scout and Dennis and Dan. She thinks of the Sandhills Inn & Suites, the Stagecoach, Pierre. She thinks, of course, of Kevin. My summer of motels, she thinks, and pinches the coverlet off the bed nearest the window. Even in this new a place, it's probably still a petri dish of germs.

She opens the drapes and slides the window back. Instantly the room fills with damp air that smells like home to her: clover, sweetgrass, manure. The light over the back door shows Karena a view of a storage shed, a small electrical plant, and a tornado siren. Do all motels have their own sirens these days? This one is small and yellow and square, and Karena recalls Charles's story about the friendly siren in Kansas. She has to admit it does look like an entity with a throat.

It may well come in handy tonight. The storms are still visible to the northwest, persistent branches of horizontal lightning. Anvil crawlers, Charles would call them. The lightning is racing along the undersides of the anvils. The local news out of Rochester confirms that Foss County is still under a severe thunderstorm warning, the counties to the north—Fillmore, Olmsted, Sibley, Scott—under tornado watch. The segments at the top of the hour are all about the numerous tornado touchdowns in Minnesota today, including just outside Waterville, where a possible EF-3 killed an elderly man in a trailer home. Karena signs onto the Storm Prediction Center and confirms the EF-3 tornado crossed Highway 13. If she had kept going north, she and Charles would have driven straight into it. She wonders how the yahoos fared, whether they are all right.

She is checking Stormtrack, sighing at the irony, to see if K_WIEBKE has posted anything—he has not—when the room phone rings. Karena hooks it up with a hand, not looking away from her screen. So Charles is checking the reports too and wants to discuss them, or he's changed his mind about driving out to the Starlite—though Karena has not. "What, Charles?" she says. "I'm beat."

"Vehicular manslaughter," says Kevin.

Karena sits up straight and mutes the TV.

"Hello to you too," she says cautiously.

"That's what the charge might be," Kevin says. "Involuntary vehicular manslaughter. Not homicide. Because Chuck didn't mean to hit the guy, did he?"

"No, of course not," says Karena.

"Hence involuntary. And he was manic, you said, at the time of the incident? As in full blown? The way he was the other night?"

"That's right," says Karena.

"Good," says Kevin. "Or not good, but you know what I mean. If Chuck was manic at the time of the incident, it means he was operating under something called diminished capacity. He didn't know what he was doing, ergo there was no intent, ergo it wasn't homicide. Unless— crap, hold on. The mania was, um, organic, right? Not drug induced, like from pot or coke or meth?"

"Charles doesn't believe in drugs," Karena reminds him, deadpan.

"Right, right," says Kevin. "Then he was operating under diminished capacity, and he can't be charged with the big boys, the felony murders, like Murder One or Two. Not even vehicular homicide. He could get something light, like failure to report, or even leaving the scene."

"Okayyyyyyyy," says Karena, typing frantically. "Hold on, I'm taking this all down. . . . How are you, anyway?"

"So, you want to hear about sentencing?" Kevin asks.

Okay, Kevin, Karena thinks, if that's the way you want to play it.

"No," she says and laughs a little. "But I suppose I should. Information trumps fear, right?"

"Exactly," Kevin says briskly. "Stand by."

Karena waits, staring at her blinking cursor.

"Okay," says Kevin, "so there's good news and not-so-good news. The good news is for Chuck: Because he was suffering diminished capacity, his sentencing might be fairly lenient. He could do a couple of years, he could get probation. Depends on the judge. The not-so- good news is that since you, Karena, were not suffering diminished capacity at the time, you *can* be held accountable, even though you weren't driving. I know, I know," he adds, "there's no way you could have stopped him. But the law says you could, and since you knew right from wrong, you should have reported the crime."

"So what does that mean?" Karena says.

"So . . . the lightest charge for you would be leaving the scene. You could get probation. You could get fifteen years. It's up to the judge. On the other hand, you might be charged with involuntary vehicular manslaughter, and the sentencing for that . . . Um."

Karena's skin prickles. "Go on, please," she says.

"Well," says Kevin, "a couple of those cases have gotten life."

Karena has been transcribing everything, but at this last fact she stops. Her armpits are damp, her scalp feels too tight.

"Oh boy," she says.

"I know," says Kevin. "It's not pleasant."

"I'll say," says Karena. She sighs and hooks her hair behind her ears. "But better to know than not, I guess . . . Thank you, Kevin. Where did you get this information, anyway?"

"Lawyer buddy of mine," says Kevin. "I took him to Matt's and picked his brain over pitchers, and he was like, Sure, Wiebke, your *friend* hit somebody while he was stormchasing. Right, your *friend* clipped the guy. You sure there's nothing you want to tell me?"

Karena laughs.

"Well, thank you again," she says. "It was very kind of you."

"No problem," Kevin says. "I thought you'd want to know, just in case you . . . in case you decide to do something about it."

Karena stays quiet, trying to assess this remark. What does it mean? Does Kevin think she should? In fact, what does this whole conversation mean? Has he forgiven her? Is he starting to? Or is it just a favor for a hurting friend?

"Welp, that's all, folks," Kevin says. "SLM over and out."

"Okay," says Karena. "Good night—except, Kevin? How'd you find me?"

"A helpful little tool called information, Laredo," Kevin says. "You should try it some time, it'd probably be useful in your line of work. You said you were going to New Heidelburg, and there's only one motel there. It's not exactly a swingin' place."

"You'd be surprised," Karena tells him.

"Getting some weather down that way, are you?"

Karena looks out the window. "Some," she says. "Guess what I did today."

When they hang up a short time later, Karena is restless. She starts to look up Iowa criminal law, then shuts the laptop and sets it aside. She makes sure her room key is in her shorts pocket and goes out. Through the American Inn & Suites lobby. Out into the lot. The night is thick with humidity and insects, flitting and batting at the illuminated motel sign. There are haloes around the halogens. TV light flickers behind the curtain in Charles's room. Karena walks away from the motel, into the service road behind it. She's facing the same direction as her room, northwest, but without the safety light. A steady wind blows her hair back from her face. Outflow from the storms.

She can see them, or one of them, anyway, probably the last in the line sweeping the eastern part of the state. What the chasers call a tail-end Charlie. It is fist-sized at this distance, a tight ball of Cu, but it is going absolutely crazy with lightning, stuttering with it every other second. And Karena knows it's because she's seeing it through haze on the horizon, the same atmospheric trick that makes some sunsets look red, but this storm has colors. Its lightning is yellow and orange and purple and hot pink. Yet on the other side of the sky, the moon is rising above the highway. It is so clear and bright it outshines even the American Inn & Suites sign.

Karena can't stop looking at this, the storm on one side, moon on the other. She never would have believed such a thing was possible, chaos and calm sharing the same sky. Before this summer, she never would have seen it. She would have been asleep, she would have been working, she would have been on a blind date or out with Tiff. If there had been a storm, she would have viewed it on TV. If it had been a bad one, she would have been in the basement. She never would have known about this wild and violent beauty, would not have experienced it firsthand. She stands in the road, watching, for a long, long time.

54

All night the storms march past to the northwest, shaking the ground like distant artillery. When dawn comes Karena is awake to watch that too. She sits by the window on the side of the bed as the kaleidoscope of the sky turns from white to gold to blue. Then she showers, makes some coffee, makes herself as presentable as she can with the emergency makeup kit in her bag. Even the weak motel brew tastes good to her, and before she leaves her room she presses her face into her towel, inhaling the bleach, feeling the thin scratchy nap.

She goes across the hall to knock on the door, but it swings open before she can. Charles is already up too. The bruises under his eyes testify that he has spent a similarly sleepless night. But he appears calm, serene even. He seems to float over the motel's carpet in his sandals, a few inches off the floor.

They drive to the Elmwood Café, where they take a corner table among the regulars—mostly farmers and retirees throwing dice for breakfast. Conversation stops when the Hallingdahl twins walk in. Then Leslee Rotman of the realty company raises a hand from her stool at the counter, though she doesn't look up from her paper.

Karena orders an omelet, and Charles asks for Egg Beaters scrambled with vegetables, two orders of whole wheat toast, hash browns, a large orange juice. He polishes this off with great appetite while Karena drinks cup after cup of coffee from a vacuum-sealed urn, her food untouched. She wishes she still smoked. The sun clears the tree line across Highway 44 and bursts into the café, and the waitress goes around shutting the blinds. In the wake of the storms, it is going to be a beautiful day.

Charles leaves a 200 percent tip and once outside turns his face to the sky. He closes his eyes, breathing deeply. Then he says, without opening them, "Okay, K, let's roll."

"Charles . . . ," says Karena.

Charles puts an arm around her and pulls her close, kissing her hair.

"It's go-time, sistah," he says.

Karena drives into town as slowly as she can, holding up traffic like an old farm wife. If this weren't Minnesota, somebody might honk. Even so, the trip to the courthouse green takes all of five minutes. Karena pulls into a visitor's spot next to the sheriff's prowler and cuts the engine. They sit looking at the grass, the war memorial, the intersecting paths beneath the very old trees.

"Oh," Karena exclaims. "Charles, your car."

"Just leave it, K," says Charles, "like I'll need it anyway." He tries to smile, but Karena sees him swallowing, his Adam's apple hitching in his throat.

She looks away. She is so scared. She has never been so scared. She can feel the impending change bearing down on them, something irrevocable and heartless and powerful, like a train. She looks at the courthouse and remembers a ninth-grade class trip inside, the municipal warren of rooms smelling of funk and man sweat, the boxed caseloads rotting in the corners. The jail behind its old-fashioned bank vault door that Sheriff Cushing opened and closed by cranking a wheel. The *thud* of steel tumblers hitting home.

"Well, sistah," says Charles, "I guess this is it."

"Guess so," Karena says.

They get out. The double slam of the Volvo's doors—*chunk, chunk*—sounds very loud. They cross the sidewalk to the steps, passing a pair of birds taking a dirt bath, hearing a woman greet another on Main Street: *Well hello there, how are you?* The wind sifts through the trees.

"Oh no, that's okay, K," says Charles, when Karena follows him up the steps. "You don't have to go in with me. In fact it'll be easier on me if you don't."

"Well, that's too bad, Charles," says Karena. "Because I'm going with you."

Charles stops and looks at her.

"I'm going with you," Karena repeats.

She nods, trying to smile, until he understands. Charles's face works. He turns away for a minute, composing himself. Then he turns back.

"Thank you, K," he says.

"You're welcome, Charles."

They stand looking at each other in the morning light, the breeze playing in Charles's hair. Then Charles reaches for Karena's hand.

"You ready?" he says. "On three. One—two—"

He opens the door for her, and they walk through.

I t is almost a year to the day later when Charles comes to say good-bye. Karena is sleeping on the living room couch—or as close to sleeping as she can come these days. She is bobbing near the surface but still so tired that she doesn't let on she can hear them when Kevin lets Charles in and says, "Shhh, quiet, man, she was up most of the night, let's go out on the patio." She can feel them tiptoeing over to peer at her, though, and when Charles whispers, "Are you sure she has two more weeks? She's freaking ginormous," Karena mutters, "I heard that." But maybe she doesn't say it aloud after all, because their footsteps creak away, and the refrigerator opens with a clink of bottles, and then the back door, and then they are outside.

Their conversation comes to her in fragments, less what they're saying than the dueling tenor of their voices. It reminds Karena of lying in the backseat with Charles, coming home from the Starlite or the Hallingdahl farm and listening to Frank and Siri murmur in the front. Karena knows she should push herself up, join the men on the patio. There is so little time left with her brother. But her blood feels leaded, as though she is sinking into the cushions. She lifts a hand onto her stomach, seeking the baby's head—there. She drifts.

She is thinking about adaptability, its peculiarities and inconsistencies, the elasticity of time. Why, for instance, should it have taken her such a while to acclimate to being home after chasing, to shake the visceral aftershocks, when she has gotten used to other situations as instantly as flicking a switch? And moreover has come to take them for granted. Her pregnancy—Karena can't remember when her body wasn't distended, when she didn't have heartburn, when she was a skinny little runner who threaded through the world with grace and ease, without thinking about it. It seems like a story about somebody else. In this tale Karena was also a reporter, a woman who went to work in an office, wearing blazers and block-heeled shoes. Who was proud of her work. Who felt important because of it. Who drove there every day, singing behind the wheel.

Now Karena is accustomed to Kevin chauffeuring her around and pretending to complain mightily about it, to go to the market, to visit Frank, to run her outreach support groups. All the conditions of Karena's probation. *You, Miss Jorge,* the Winneshiek County district court judge had said in Iowa last December, peering at her over his bifocals—a tiny bald eagle of a man. *Since you are fortunate enough not to share your brother's affliction, you do and did know better. You should have come forward, for his benefit and the community's. You will work with bipolar support groups in the Minneapolis medical system for three years. For leaving the scene of an accident, your driver's license will be suspended for the same amount of time.*

And you, Mr. Hallingdahl, he had continued, *you must learn more about your disorder and how to better manage it. You also currently reside in Minneapolis, I see. There is an excellent outpatient program at the Hennepin County Medical Center. You will attend it for one year.* Charles, typically, had protested, had petitioned for a more extreme sentence—at least one as severe as Karena's. But the judge had told him to stop wasting the court's time and ordered the records sealed.

Perhaps the easiest thing for Karena to get used to, the condition that has felt most natural, has been having Charles nearby, across the city, in the student neighborhood known, aptly, as The Wedge. So close and yet far away enough. It will take her much, much longer to accept that he's going again, leaving for Arizona this time, a two-year program at the Southwestern College of Naturopathic Medicine and Health

Sciences. It won't be like before, Karena reminds herself. She'll know where Charles is. He'll have a cell phone, e-mail, a fixed address. They'll be in regular contact. He'll come for holidays. Yet in the most important respect it will be exactly like before, because Karena will have to go back to waiting for the call, for the phone to ring with the news that something bad has happened to Charles. That he has done something bad to himself. This dread might be familiar, she may have lived with it for the past twenty years, but she will never get used to it. Never.

As if protesting her mother's sorrow, the way Karena's heart constricts, the baby rolls—inasmuch as she can in such a cramped space. The movement always makes Karena think of young whales swimming alongside their mothers. She gasps. "Ooouf," she says, and struggles upright. "Okay, okay." She bundles her newly shoulder-length hair into an elastic—she is always roasting hot now—and rubs her face. She can't quite believe the baby will ever come, but she is more than ready to meet this child. She's had ample time to wonder at the Amazing Levitating Belly, and now she's done.

She is trying to heave herself off the couch when Kevin and Charles troop back in, and when they see her they come rushing over. "I'm all right," Karena says crossly as they each seize one arm. She can feel Charles shaking with laughter. But either they have both gone spontaneously deaf or they're totally ignoring her.

"You got a good grip there, Wieb?" Charles asks.

"Hope so, Hallingdahl. Let's git 'r done."

They haul Karena out of the cushions, making a big groaning and grunting production out of it, and set her on her feet. "Thanks a lot," she says. "I'm not *that* heavy."

"Yeah, you kinda are, K," says Charles, wincing. "I think I sprained my back."

"I'm sure you'll find some holistic poultice for it," Karena says as they go out through the front porch. Kevin rubs her tailbone.

"You doing okay, Mama?" he asks, and she rolls her eyes, then kisses him.

It is a quiet overcast day. Every so often raindrops patter from seemingly nowhere. The yellow Volvo is at the curb, a brand-new registration sticker displayed on the windshield. Who would have thought it, Karena marvels, Charles with proof of insurance. The wagon is crammed to the roof with his belongings, everything he's amassed over the past year in his studio. On its rack on the Volvo's rear, Charles's bike spins its tires sporadically in the wind.

"Can you see out the rearview, Hallingdahl?" Kevin asks doubtfully, circling the Volvo to inspect Charles's packing job.

"Rearview, what rearview," says Charles, tying his new longer hair back with a leather thong. "We don't need no stinkin' rearview, Wieb."

The two men embrace briefly and slap backs.

"Hallingdahl," says Kevin.

"Wieb," says Charles.

Farewells accomplished, Kevin comes up the walk and goes inside, blowing a kiss to Karena as he passes.

"Charles," says Karena, and Charles says, "Huh?" Then he says, "Oh, sorry, sorry, K," and leaps up the front steps to help her down.

"Thanks," Karena says, as they reach the curb.

"No, thank you, K," says Charles. "Thanks for the dishes. And the sheets and towels. And for not giving me a hard time. I know this isn't what you would have wanted for me. But I appreciate your respecting it's what I want."

Karena nods and tries to smile. They may yet come up with a drug Charles can tolerate. He may change his mind. She can always hope. They face each other by the passenger door, Karena planting her feet firmly in the grassy median.

"Well, sistah," says Charles. Then his eyes fill with tears.

"Oh no, you don't," says Karena, swatting him. "Don't you start. If you do, I will, the difference being I can't stop."

"I know," says Charles, sniffling. "I'm sorry."

"Let's look at it this way," says Karena, "it's only until Thanksgiving."

Charles blots his eyes on the sleeve of his Cuban shirt. "I just can't believe I won't be here when she's born," he says.

"You'll be the first person we tell," Karena says, inwardly shuddering at the thought of Charles and Kevin in the same delivery room. "I promise."

"Tell her I wanted to be there but her mean daddy wouldn't let me," says Charles. "Tell her Uncle Charles loves her." He bends over Karena's belly. "Yes," he croons, "Uncle Charles loves you, yes, he does. You know that, don't you, Loafette?"

The baby kicks enthusiastically.

"Ow," Karena says, gasping. "Do not call her that, Charles. How many times do I have to tell you? You know her name is—"

She repeats the name of the town in which, to the best of their knowledge, she and Kevin think the baby was conceived. Sometime during their New Year trip, anyway, the one they pretended was a reality show called Reconciliation Road.

"That's a silly name," says Charles. "She doesn't like that name, does she? Nooooo, she likes Loafette. Don't you, Loafette?" and the baby kicks again. "See," says Charles, nodding. "Uncle Charles knows."

"Uncle Charles better hit the road," says Karena, "before he sends me into premature labor."

Charles heaves an enormous sigh and looks off down the street.

"I guess you're right," he says. "C'mere, sistah."

He holds out his arms, and they hug as best they can over Karena's belly. This time, when they pull apart, Karena's eyes are wet while Charles's are dry.

"Here you go, K," he says, screwing his Lakota ring off his middle finger and handing it to her. "Early baby present. Good luck."

"Thank you, Charles," says Karena, taking the ring, warm from Charles's hand. She clutches it in her fist as he jogs down to the Volvo.

"Love you, sistah," he says as he's getting in.

"Love you, Charles," she says.

She waves as the yellow Volvo pulls away from the curb and glides to the end of the block. It pauses at the long light there. Its left blinker pulses patiently. Then the signal changes and it cruises away and is gone. Karena stays there anyway, looking at the empty street. She traces

Charles's route in her mind: Fiftieth Street to Lyndale Avenue to 62 East to 35 South to I-90 West—Beyond this, she can't bear to think. She realizes she is still holding Charles's ring and starts to slip it on her left thumb. Then she switches it to her right, away from the slim gold wedding band inscribed *KB1 SLM & Laredo, 2009*. Best to keep those two rings separate.

"Hey," Kevin says from behind the porch's screen door. "Woman, are you going to stand there all day? We have guests coming."

"They're your guests too," Karena says, and they are: Fern and her fiancé, Ben Hendrickson, a new Whirlwind guide Kevin introduced her to. *I know I look a bit of a hypocrite*, Fern wrote earlier this summer when she broke the news, *but he does adore me, and now I can move to the States, and enough's as good as a feast, isn't it?*

"In fact I believe you're the one who invited them," Karena says, although actually they both did. "You could do a little work around here too, you know."

"I swear, Laredo, you are the laziest pregnant woman on the whole block," says Kevin. "You're already barefoot and knocked up, why don't you get in here and cook something?"

"Oh, I'll cook something all right," says Karena. "Just you wait, mister. You're toast."

She takes a last look at the empty street, then starts trundling determinedly up the walk. This is her life now: this house and this man and their daughter. It will be a quiet life, maybe not what Karena dreamed of when she was a kid—but what did she imagine then, exactly? Now that she thinks about it, she never did have much of a plan for her future—not one that didn't involve Charles. And she was always too busy scrambling to catch up, to control the damage. But if she had dreamed something, it might have looked like this. Predictability. Acceptance. Peace. The knowledge that sometimes when you throw yourself upon the world, it will hold you up.

Kevin steps out onto the stoop, damp and spicy-smelling from the shower. "You need some help there, Laredo?" he asks.

"No thanks," says Karena, "we're fine," but she does take the hand

Kevin holds out to her and lets him haul her up. Her shoulder hits the bronze wind chimes Charles has given them as a wedding present, making them stir and bong, and as if in answer, the breeze gusts from the lake. But there is no severe in the forecast for the upcoming week, Karena knows. The season is almost over. This is just a little local front moving through, and that's another thing that is amazing, Karena thinks, as they go into the house: how warm the day can be when the wind is at your back.

ACKNOWLEDGMENTS

First, a word about storms and chasers: I've been really lucky to get to know many stormchasers while researching this novel, and they're a generous and exacting bunch. Any chaser reading *The Stormchasers* will recognize I took liberties with its storms, changing dates and locations. I'm grateful for their appreciation of poetic license.

I did, however, attempt accuracy with the meteorology. Everything I know about weather I owe to the guides of Tempest Tours, whom I've been privileged to chase with every summer since 2006: president Martin Lisius, Bill Reid, Brian Morganti, Keith Brown, Rob Petitt, Chris Gullickson, Dr. Bob Conzemius, and Jennifer Dunn. If you ever want to learn about big weather, go with Tempest (www.tempesttours. com); there's none better. I am especially reliant on the knowledge provided by *Weather Radios Across America* president Chad Cowan, whose expertise helped inspire many fresh scenes; my chase partner, Marcia Perez, the Ansel Adams of storms, whose exquisite photos bless this novel's cover; and my cherished mentor, Master Kinney Adams, whose wisdom about storms and life sustains me. These chasers have been endlessly patient with my questions, and everything that's right in these pages is because of their teaching. Everything that isn't is because of my persistent ignorance.

I would also like to thank my family: Franny Blum, Joey Blum, Judy Blum, and my dad, Bob Blum, in memoriam; Woodrow; and the Joergs, for their unremitting love and support. Chief meteorologists Pete Bouchard of Boston's WHDH Channel 7 News and Belinda Jensen of KARE 11 News in Minneapolis, who were kind enough to let me crash their studios and answer all my weather-geek questions. Christina from Doc's in Spring Grove, for everyday coffee and conversation. My O.G. editors Jean Charbonneau, Stephanie Ebbert Devin, and Sarah Schweitzer for seeing me through two novels now. Dr. Kathy Crowley and my Puppet Julie Hirsch, for their medical and psychological proofreading. Bram and Elizabeth deVeer, captive but willing stormchasers. Houston County, MN, Sheriff Doug Ely, for showing me around the Caledonia courthouse/jail and troubleshooting my scenarios. Hope and Mark Foley, my personal Red Cross, the most amazing neighbor-friends ever. Stormchaser-photographer Ericka Gray, for the read and the Flarp. Grub Street Writers, the very best writing community in the world, and especially my beloved Council. The Guymon girls: Elvia Hernandez, Melyn Johnson, and Rachel Sides; I'd ride fences with you ladies any day (and a tip of the hat to the Guymon, OK, fire chief for letting me kidnap Elvia). Sandy Hanson and the Monday Night Trash Gang for watching over me in Caledonia. Dennis Larson, Esq., of Decorah, Iowa, for helping me with legal logistics. Sonya Larson, for vetting the twins. The Patel family, owners of the Caledonia, MN, AmericInn, who were such gracious hosts during my two-month stay there to write the first draft. The Perez family in Oklahoma City, who provide my stormchase home away from home. The Tempest Repeat Offenders: Leisa Luis-Grill and Rob Grill, foxy Kirstie Johnson, Stacy Williams, and David Yamada. Brian Tart and the wonderful crew at Dutton, especially Erika Imranyi, who has two tools no editor should be without: eagle eyes and a delicate touch. The Writer Girls, Cecile Corona, Kirsten Marcum, and Erin Almond, for listening to my ideas about this book through so many incarnations over the years.

To my wonderful readers: Not a single day went by that I didn't open my e-mail and receive kind comments from you on my first novel, *Those Who Save Us*, and questions about *The Stormchasers*. "When is the second novel coming out?" was your persistent refrain. Here it is, with my deepest thanks for the daily inspiration you provided—there is none better. I am so obliged to you for hosting me in your homes and communities, inviting me to speak about my writing, making my dreams a reality and keeping my characters alive in your hearts and minds.

Finally, my greatest gratitude to three extraordinary people: Dr. Lydia Baumrind, who led me out of the woods. The incomparable, fierce, and dedicated Stephanie Abou, who demanded a scene a day and gave so much more. And Andrew Brewster Ballantine, my trusted navigator in all matters. This book would not exist without them.